SINS OF THE SON

ROWDY CLOUD

ISBN: 978-1-957619-10-1

carrioller.com/oller-publishing-co-llc

CONTENTS

CHAPTER 1

The cool early morning air bit at the neck of Detective Luke Burrows as he walked down the sidewalk. He threw up the collar of his coat. It was his father's coat. Since the elder Burrows' passing last winter, he always wore his father's coat. The wool-lined coat was old and had a few holes in the worn navy fabric, but Luke didn't care. He was glad of the reminder of his father. Henry Burrows had been a strict man, but not without compassion. He was noble but not without his vices. Luke could still smell the faintness of bourbon oozing from the woven fibers of the thick fleece. A constant reminder of what his father did, keeping himself accountable against the same folly.

Luke looked at his watch-- 4:36 A.M. He was walking quickly. As soon as he received the phone call, he rushed out of the station and headed east. That was twelve minutes ago. The streetlights illuminated the dark street, casting individual pools of white. Luke's partner, Mason, had their work car, and there were no cabs in sight, so Luke decided to walk.

He rounded a corner and could see that crowds had started to gather. Not good, he thought. Picking up his pace to a slight jog, Luke hurried down the sidewalk. With the lateness of the hour, he had hoped that most people would still be in bed. But, of course, everyone loves a spectacle. A cold gust jumped at him, clawing at his ears and nose. Luke huffed in a breath.

He was a block away now. There were far too many police cars here for his liking, six in total. Their lights flashed, adding to the spectacle of the dismal affair, and drawing people to them like moths to a porch light. He shook his head, wishing he had remembered to grab his hat off of his desk. His brown hair was a mess in the wind. The officers had already blocked off the area with police tape. Three of them were attempting to keep the growing crowd back and away from the scene.

As Luke approached the barrier of tape, he reached into his left pants pocket and pulled out his detective badge. He flipped it open to show the blue-uniformed officer standing guard over the scene. The officer glanced at it and nodded him through. Then, ducking under the yellow tape, he walked toward another officer standing in the center of the ring.

"Are you the one who called it in?" Luke asked. The officer looked at him and shook his head.

"No, sir. That would be Officer Beatty. He's inside talking to the night manager."

Luke looked to his right. The fourteen-story brick building rose from the ground like a Redwood in the forests of California.

The building was old. Built in 1962 by Marco Sorelli, The Cicero was a beast of a hotel. With over 100 rooms, it housed a more immaculate lobby than anything else in St. Louis. White marble washed over the floors and broke upon golden walls, inset with deep purple accents that stretched upwards of eighty feet and dissolved into the ceiling.

The hotel has had many upgrades throughout the passing decades, including shiny incandescent lighting–a welcome change from the harsh fluorescent lights of the past. All were new, except for the crystal chandelier that hung in the center of the room and descended over the front desk.

The Cicero also boasted one of the best kitchens in the area, along with an infamous pool hall home to thirty regulation-size tables. In addition, monthly tournaments of nine-ball, eight-ball, and Snooker, were hosted in this room. Some of which paid out seventy-five thousand dollars to the winners.

Luke had been after the Sorelli family for three years. So, his hopes were up that this incident would be the one to bring them down. But, he dared not say anything to Mason or Chief Reilly.

"It's circumstantial." "It'll never hold." He could hear them saying it already, but Luke was determined.

Granted, they were probably right. Just because this happened to be in front of Sorelli's hotel didn't necessarily mean they were involved. Luke frowned to himself. Hopefully, he could find a real connection to the Sorelli family and take them down himself.

He heard the mumbling of the crowd and the constant gasps of newcomers. A faint smell of lavender entered his nostrils, and he wondered where it came from. He glanced to his left. All kinds of people were here. An elderly woman–who couldn't be younger than 75–stood behind the yellow barrier in her baby blue nightgown, mouth agape, not believing her eyes. A man, who looked to be about Luke's age, stood gazing also. The young man's blonde hair was disheveled. He was wearing black shorts and a rumpled gray t-shirt. He could've been going out for a run or was renting a room from the motel across the street and had pulled on the easiest things he had. His brown eyes were wide, and his body rigid.

Luke turned back to the officer guarding the scene, but he had left. Luke noticed the Crime Scene Unit van had pulled up and spotted the officer speaking with the lead CSU Investigator. From where he stood, Luke thought he recognized the shorter man with dark skin and short black hair.

Will Johnson, Luke surmised, has to be him.

The man ducked under the tape and came walking towards Luke. Crime scene gloves already shielded his hands, and his inspection kit was in his left.

"Detective Burrows," the man said as he approached.

"Will," Burrows responded in greeting.

"What a depressing site," Will stated to no one in particular. "I'm not sure where to begin."

"I suggest you start taking photos. I can help measure. Once Mason arrives, he can continue the photos, and you can start sketching."

"Have you an idea how long it will take Mason to arrive?" Will asked, frowning. His voice was skeptical, and Burrows couldn't blame him.

Luke looked at his watch. 5:05 A.M.

"He should be here any minute. I called him as soon as I was on my way." Luke said with an optimistic tone.

"Your new partner is not the poster boy for punctuality," Will stated.

Luke looked down at the pavement. No, he was not, Luke thought to himself.

Detective Brandon Mason had recently moved to St. Louis from Kansas City seven months ago. He was a good detective and was not much younger than Luke. Mason had eyes that could see through anyone's B.S. and a sixth sense about women. It baffled Luke how many times Mason had been able to pick up any waitress anywhere at any time. Yet, shockingly, none of them harbored any ill will toward him the next time they would wait on the detectives, even though he never called on them again after sleeping with them. It was crazy.

Mason sure could run his mouth when interrogating suspects, though. Hell, Reilly had nearly suspended him for antagonizing a suspect so much that the man broke Mason's nose.

"I know you need to push their buttons," Reilly had said, "but you can't be that wreckless, or they could bottle up just to piss you off. And then we won't get anywhere."

A wind gust hit Luke on his left side. He shivered. Will had started taking photos of the scene. The snap of the camera lens filled Luke's ears with each whiny CLACK. Then, finally, an officer came out of the glass front doors of the Cicero. Finally, Luke thought. He strained to read the officer's name tag as he got closer.

"Officer Beatty," Luke ventured.

"Yes, sir?" Beatty responded.

"Did you see anything out of the ordinary when you arrived on the scene?"

Officer Beatty's eyes narrowed, and he looked toward Will, who was still snapping his photos.

"Aside from the obvious," Luke clarified for the man, a hint of agitation in his voice.

"No, sir." Officer Beatty said.

"And you made sure to guard the scene until backup arrived?"

Now Beatty looked annoyed. He was not the least pleased that Luke thought he needed to ask such a question.

"I'm no rookie, sir," Beatty stated with pride and irritation seeping into his voice, "I've been on the beat for four years now. I know how to secure a crime scene."

Luke grimaced, remembering how it felt being berated by detectives. He wasn't trying to be hard on the kid, but he couldn't risk anything that could compromise this chance to potentially take down Victor Sorelli.

Victor Sorelli. The name hung in Luke's mind, bringing bile into Luke's mouth. How he despised that man. All he did was bring debauchery into this city. Gambling, prostitution, drugs, murder, all of it. All while living well beyond his means.

Luke had tried to take him down several times over the years through informants, who would suddenly die of an accident or disappear. On a few occasions, he had tried to catch Sorelli and his goons red-handed, only to have their lawyers get them off on some technicality. Once, Luke even tried going after Sorelli through taxes, the same way the FBI managed to take down Al Capone. Unfortunately, Sorelli's hotel, gentlemen's club, restaurant/bar, and medicinal marijuana dispensary proved to be better laundries than Luke had imagined. Not one dollar was found out of place. It was infuriating.

"I have to ask," Luke said, "Nothin' personal."

Beatty relaxed and took out his notepad from his jacket pocket. "Yes sir," Beatty replied.

"Now, tell me what happened."

"I was driving my normal route. It was about 3:50 in the morning, nothin' unusual. I was pulling up near the hotel when I saw something on the sidewalk. It looked like a body. I got out of my car and called to what I assumed was a person. Nothing happened. I withdrew my weapon, turned on the flashlight, extended it in front of myself, and walked slowly toward the object. I called again, but still no answer and no movement. As I moved in closer, I finally saw what it was. I radioed it in immediately and proceeded to wait. Within three minutes, another cruiser pulled up. Officer Cruz and I were setting up the barrier when another two cruisers showed up."

Luke turned away from Beatty. Will had finished his photographs and was now measuring. A slight twinge of guilt began to rise in Luke's stomach. His offer to help Will had been genuine, but then Officer Beatty emerged from the belly of the beast, and Luke needed to hear his statement.

The roar of an engine caught Luke's attention. Turning to his right, he saw a black Charger speeding toward the crime scene. The headlight's beams glowed white in the night. Luke glanced at his watch again. 5:19 A.M.

The Charger came to a halt behind the crowd of onlookers. The engine died, and a tall man with thick black hair leapt from the driver's seat. He had on an oversized dark coat and navy slacks. Detective Brandon Mason had finally arrived.

"Will, your assistant, has arrived," Luke said loud enough for Mason to hear above the murmurs of the onlookers. Will looked up and shook his head.

"Well, what do we got?" Mason asked. His voice was full of curiosity.

He either didn't hear the jab from Luke or decided to ignore it.

"You better have brought breakfast," Will quipped and began to sketch the crime scene. Mason turned and gave him a smirk.

"None for you, William," he said. Will kept sketching.

Mason turned back to Luke for the answer to his question.

"Exactly what you see here," Luke said. "That's what we have."

Mason rounded and began his examination of the scene. The scent of lavender crept into Luke's nostrils again.

"Not much to go on at first glance," Mason stated. Luke nodded his head in agreement.

"Any witnesses?" Luke asked Beatty.

"None that I am aware of. I interviewed the night manager of the hotel, and he didn't remember hearing or seeing anything."

The sound of a car horn interrupted their conversation. Everyone turned to identify the cause of this intrusion. It was hard to see through the crowd, but Luke thought he saw a pickup truck nearly on top of a sedan. The sedan had probably slowed to try and see what all the commotion was about. Unfortunately, the pickup truck driver wasn't paying attention and nearly ran into him. Luke watched as the sedan drove down the street. Traffic was starting to pick up. Not good, thought Luke.

"When's Dr. Wright supposed to arrive?" Mason asked. He was staring at what was before them.

"I thought she was going to beat you here," Luke jabbed. Mason grunted a laugh in response.

Luke looked down again. He couldn't make heads or tails of it. There on the sidewalk, just past the glass front doors of Victor Sorelli's Cicero

Hotel, lay something that puzzled them all: The naked body of a young woman.

CHAPTER 2

The man ushered his gray sedan slowly down the street. He could see the flashing reds and blues from here. Coming here was not a wise idea, but this whole thing had taken so long to implement…he would not miss this chance to see the chaos. He glanced at the faintly glowing speedometer—23 mph. Barely under the 25-speed limit. Still blocks away but speeding around could cause unnecessary attention.

He gazed at the odometer. It read 136,568 miles. He'd gone well past the 130,202-mile mark. Having the oil changed in this thing needed to be made a priority. He breathed deeply. The scent of pine stimulated his senses. How he loved that smell. Always had. Easing to a halt at a stop sign, he gently pressed the brake pedal. The sedan rolled to a stop. He glanced in the rearview mirror. There was only darkness behind him, other than the evenly spaced circles of light cast on the concrete from above. He sat in silence. The clock on the radio read 5:15 A.M.

He stared out the windshield. Listening. The hum of the car's engine was a never-ending purr. He had turned off the heat earlier. The lights on the tops of the St. Louis Police Department patrol cars danced. Red and Blue. Back and forth. No sirens, though. There was no need. The emergency was over.

She could not be saved.

He smiled.

His thoughts drifted to when this plan was first conceived. It was so long ago, years, in fact. Some might not understand why it would take so long. They were lesser beings, prone to impulsiveness and buyer's remorse. These were the fools that bought into daytime television commercials. Instant gratification was their drug of choice. They disgusted him. Patience. Intelligence. Knowledge. Commitment is the most important of all. These were what one needed to succeed. He had used all of these to plan and execute the scene before him outside the Cicero.

The Lessers could, at time's exhibit one or two of these qualities but never all four. Sometimes they would even trade them out, exchanging knowledge for patience or intelligence for commitment. They'd start with one, and with a sudden, fleeting revelation, they knew they would need one of the other traits to succeed. However, instead of being able to hold on to the one already in their possession, they would cast it aside because it had not attained their goal. They could never grasp why they failed so constantly.

He pressed down on the accelerator. The sedan resumed its forward momentum. As he drew closer to the scene, he could make out the yellow tape blocking the front of the brick building. Looking upwards towards the heavens, he could make out the many square carve-outs, inset with glass. Portals for those inside to look out into a world they were soon to enter. The neon sign on the roof glowed yellow against the star-studded sky. He turned his attention back to street level. The black awning sprang from the brick out front, a tongue outstretched to welcome its victims.

She did not make it under the awning. She fell just shy of its embrace. He had watched her from afar, binoculars in hand. He wasn't sure how far She would be able to go. Hopefully, she would make it inside the red-bricked beast, he thought. Her physical body had given up on itself sooner than he had imagined. However, she did make it far enough for his plan to still be in motion. He was pleased.

He was in front of the hotel now. The crowd that had gathered made it nearly impossible to see her. At times when people would leave, he could make out a man standing over her.

The detective.

He grinned.

Periodically, he saw small flashes of light peppered in among the larger, brighter flashes coming from inside the scene. The smaller flashes must have been the enamored crowd taking photos with their cellular phones, no doubt. The larger flashes had to be Mr. Johnson, the SLMPD's best forensic investigator. You have your work cut out for you this time, Mr.

Johnson, he thought.

An engine roared from down the street, heading this way. Its white headlights pierced the darkness before them. The clock on the radio read 5:19 A.M. A dark Charger sped toward the hotel. It pulled up beside the CSU van. The crowd had spread to block the van from the view of those inside his grisly scene. The headlights died, as did the car. A man in a dark overcoat emerged from the driver's seat.

The partner.

The new arrival pushed his way through the crowd, presumably flashed his badge at one of the officers posted at the yellow barricade, ducked under it, and went to gather information. The partner had been an unexpected hiccup to his plans. The man was insufferable. He was a loudmouth; worst of all, he could see through almost any façade.

Almost any.

The partner would be dealt with in due time.

A horn blasted behind him. He snapped out of his focus on the scene before him and looked in the rearview mirror. A pickup truck had nearly rear-ended him. He silently cursed at himself. Then, pressing the accelerator, he started forward. He wasn't overly worried. It was still dark enough for his vehicle to blend in and hide any distinguishing features. He was merely a curious onlooker. No harm done. He would, however, have to be more careful if he ever decided to pay a visit to any of his victims in the future.

CHAPTER 3

"Is there anything you can tell us that would be of importance?" Luke asked Will as the man sketched the scene.

"When I measured the body, I could smell lavender on her," Will said. So that's where the smell was coming from. But why? What purpose would there be in making her smell of lavender? These questions plagued Luke's mind. It didn't make sense.

"Maybe she wanted to smell nice as she went out of this world," Mason suggested. Mason raised his right hand and coughed into it.

Luke looked down at the young woman lying dead in front of him. She was on her stomach. Her pale back screaming at the sky above. Her left arm was stretched out in front of her as if she had tried to use it to catch herself. Her right arm lay at her side. Her auburn hair seemed to glow against her ivory skin. Her head was turned, eyes wide, blue as the sea. Freckles decorated her face, shoulders, and arms. Her lips were pink and slightly parted. She seemed to be staring at the hotel. From what Luke could see, there was no obvious bruising or any sign that she was restrained. The wind bit at him again.

"Why would she come here naked?" Luke asked. "It's thirty-three degrees with a strong northern wind." He glanced at Officer Beatty. "You and some other officers canvassed the surrounding area, correct?"

"Yes, sir, detective. We canvassed a five-block radius of the hotel."

"And you didn't find any sign of where she undressed herself?"

"No, sir."

Luke stepped under the black awning of the hotel and peered through the glass doors. Gold letters glittered across the panes: THE CICERO . Guests from the hotel were beginning to amass inside the lobby and were creeping toward the doors.

"Officer Beatty," Luke started, "grab another officer and have them guard the front doors. I don't want anyone trying to sneak out here for a closer look."

Beatty nodded and went to grab the young officer Luke had spoken with when he had first approached the corpse sprawled before them. The young officer went to guard the doors, and Beatty took up the man's former post.

"Maybe she's a meth addict," Mason was saying.

"I don't see any signs of that," Luke replied.

"It's the only thing that makes sense to me," Mason retorted. "You know as well as I do that when people overdose on meth, their body temperature gets too high, right? So they subconsciously start to compensate. Stripping to their birthday suit, going outside in frigid temperatures, trying to climb into freezers, all sorts of things."

Luke clenched his jaw. Mason was right, but he couldn't shake this feeling she was connected to the Sorelli's. She has to be, he thought. Sorelli has to fall. Mason and Reilly would say he's not being open-minded. 'You need to let facts guide your theory instead of your theory guiding the facts.'

They were right, of course. He had a tendency to put blinders on whenever the Sorelli name was brought into a case. He even admitted as much to both of them. Keeping the blinders off was easier said than done.

"Let's see what the Doc has to say," Luke said. Mason glanced around at the crowd of onlookers.

"Where is she?" He asked.

"I'm not sure," Luke confessed. "She should be here by now."
As if they had summoned her with their words, Luke saw a dark

ambulance-looking vehicle approaching in the distance.

"Speak of the devil," Luke said.

Mason spun around to see the large motorized monster heading towards them. White letters seemed to jump off the side of the vehicle. ST. LOUIS METROPOLITAN POLICE DEPARTMENT MEDICAL EXAMINER.

Luke looked down at his watch. 5:33 A.M.

A tall woman hopped down from the driver's seat. Her hair was tied up in a ponytail. She walked to the back of the van and opened the doors. A few minutes later, she was pushing her way through the crowd and entered the crime scene. She toted her examination kit in her gloved hand.

"Gentlemen," The doctor greeted them drily as she approached. Her voice was a lower pitch than usual for a woman. She was in her mid-fifties, with streaks of gray weaving in and out of her dark hair. Round glasses sat atop her nose, perched like a cardinal on a tree branch. She stared down at the lifeless body on the sidewalk. A sigh escaped her lips.

"We've got to stop meeting like this, sweetheart," Mason said, smirking.

She glared at him with a look that would've chilled the Sahara. Mason just kept smirking.

She walked over to the woman and bent down, examining her face. Then she moved on to the arms and down the sides of the torso, working her way to the dead woman's legs and feet.

"No obvious signs of trauma," Dr. Wright said. "Her hands have been meticulously manicured, though."

Luke cocked his head to the side. "Really?" He asked.

"Come and take a look," She invited as she lifted the woman's left hand so that Luke could see.

Luke crouched down and noticed that the doctor was right. The woman's nails looked perfect. No sharp edges, no cracks. No signs of dirt or grime underneath the nails either. Strange, he thought.

"Cleanliness must be important to him," Luke said without thinking.

"Him?" Mason questioned, "What do you mean 'him'?"

Luke closed his eyes and braced himself. He knew what was coming next.

"Sorelli, right?" Mason paused, letting the question hang in the air for a few seconds. "We don't even know the cause of death, or who she is for that matter, and you're already chompin' at the bit to go bust down Sorelli's front door?" Mason let out a half chuckle. "Reilly will eat you alive if he finds out."

Luke straightened, not bothering to look at his partner. Dr. Wright peered up at Luke with knowing eyes. How he wished he would have kept his mouth shut. But Mason was right. He did want to go bust down Sorelli's front door. He wanted to drag him out kicking and screaming, to hear him admit it. Admit this was his fault. Admit that because of him, there is one less beauty in the world. How it tore at Luke's mind. The constant war between what he wanted, what he was sure was right, versus what was in front of him.

"Brandon," Dr. Wright said, "would you do me a favor?"

"Anything for you, darling," Mason replied sweetly.

"Grab a pair of gloves out of my case, and help me turn her over."

Mason walked over to Doc's examination kit and took out a pair of latex gloves. He inserted his hands into them, making sure to stretch the gloves to the tips of his fingers. Then, letting each one go at the wrist with an obnoxious Smack!, Mason proceeded to walk over to the feet of the dead woman. He bent down and wrapped his hands around her ankles. Dr. Wright counted to three, and they picked her up and laid her on her back.

Luke looked her over. She was stunning. Her face was round with full cheeks. She had a soft nose and jawline. The freckles that danced across her face seemed to only accent her beautiful features. She was slender, the envied hourglass figure. Her breasts sat on her chest like two symmetrical hills in the countryside. Why would someone kill this beautiful creature? Thought Luke.

From what seemed a lifetime ago, his mind flashed to Emily, his past girlfriend. The woman lying before him wasn't much younger than her. He closed his eyes and tried to remember her touch, the smell of her hair. Oh God, how I miss her! He screamed to himself.

He opened his eyes and brought himself back to the present. This young woman needed him now. She needed him to find whoever did this to her. Now that they had rotated her, he noticed what looked to be minor red rashes on her knees, stomach, left forearm, and left palm. A large dark spot covered her abdomen, parts of her thighs, and left forearm.

"Road rash," Doc stated. "From the fall." She pointed to the red marks Luke had noticed.

"The dark pools are where the blood settled. Also, since there weren't any signs of blood pooling on her backside, that tells me she wasn't moved." Dr. Wright stepped to her bag and pulled out what looked like a long metal T. The liver probe. She inserted the pointed end into the dead girl's abdomen. They waited. After a moment, a small beep erupted from the probe. Pulling it out of the woman's flesh, Dr. Wright read the temperature to herself. She then looked at her watch on her left wrist.

"Time of death was between three and three-twenty this morning." The smell of lavender hit Luke again. His ears told him that traffic was now humming along the street at a more steady pace. He glanced at his own watch—5:49 A.M.

"Will," Luke called out.

"Yes, detective?"

"Do you have everything you need?"

"I do."

"Alright then. Doc, let's load her up and get her ready for her autopsy. Mason, tell the officers that once Doc and Will have vacated the area, we will need their help to interview the guests of the Cicero." Luke ordered. Mason nodded and waited for Dr. Wright to return with the gurney. Once she did, they hoisted the dead girl and sat her on top, covering her with a sheet. Then, the officers escorted them to the back of the Medical Examiner's van and assisted loading the gurney and its unfortunate occupant. By the time they were finished, Will was already gone, headed back to his lab. Luke silently hoped that between Dr. Wright, Will, Mason, and himself, they had found all the evidence needed to bring in Victor Sorelli.

Luke looked over to Mason.

"Let's see if we can get a look at the surveillance footage from early this morning."

He and Mason stepped under the awning, letting the monstrous hotel swallow them whole.

CHAPTER 4

Victor Guiseppe Sorelli sat alone at the dark, oak wood table in his dining room. Empty chairs marched down both sides of the twenty-foot wooden slab, coming to a halt at the opposite end where another empty chair sat facing him. He stared down to the far end of the table, imagining what he must look like. Perhaps a vampire staring into a mirror as he drank the blood of one of his victims. Vampire? He thought. How poetic. Vampires drain the life from their quarry, much the same as Victor drains the life from this city with his crooked ways. Vampires were also known as the seducers of the monster world. Another fitting description. Perhaps not for Victor himself, but for the pleasures he promised to provide willing patrons. He procured vices for everyone.

Victor's pitch-black hair was slicked back. In the past several days, he'd begun to notice a few stray, gray weeds trying to take root in his scalp and wasted no time yanking them out one by one. He knew age would catch up to him, but he still chased the uncatchable dream of immortality. Victor frowned to himself. He wished he could take the deep plunge into retirement and let time catch up to him, but Anthony refused to step up. Anthony…his son. Where had he gone wrong with him? Isabella, his wife, had died when Anthony was only ten years old. Grief had swallowed Victor for nearly two years before he managed to crawl out of its jaws. The butler, maid, and nanny tended more to Anthony in those two years than Victor had. Even when he emerged from the throes of despair, his son was distant. Raising Anthony alone had been one of the hardest tasks he had ever faced. Maybe he had been too harsh on him every now and again, but the boy needed to grow up. Anthony needed to be ready to take over the business after all.

Victor had done his part; he had trained Anthony in everything the family had its hands in. He had taught him the family's history: how Anthony's great-grandfather, Marco Sorelli, started their empire during the era of Prohibition. Victor reminisced on the day he passed their origin story on to his only son.

Marco was ruthless. An Italian immigrant in a foreign land, he made a name for himself by procuring illegal goods. Many of Marco's competitors took advantage of the hatred towards immigrants that oozed from the bowels of America. One night while working the bar at his tiny, four-hundred-square-foot speakeasy, police officers burst in and arrested Marco. The cops were chatty S.O.Bs. They gloated over Marco, unintentionally revealing the names of the men who had turned Marco in. Marco served three months in jail for the illegal sale of alcohol. After being released, Marco and his two brothers, Roberto and Lorenzo, hunted down those who had betrayed him, taking over their profitable businesses. With control of almost ninety percent of all alcohol sales in St. Louis, the building blocks of the family empire began to take shape.

Of course, alcohol wasn't enough. So Victor had told Anthony; Marco also began collecting women desperate for food or cash. Within a year, he owned the St. Louis prostitution hub. Any whore in need of cash worked for him. It wasn't all easy pickings, though. Many police raids on his speakeasies and brothels spread throughout the city. Your great-grandfather needed to get the heat off him, Victor had said. So he sent out his muscle and spies to gather information about high-ranking government officials in the city. When it was all said and done, he had thirty-seven officers, eight detectives, three judges, and the district attorney either on his payroll or under his thumb.

Once Prohibition was repealed, Marco turned his speakeasies into legitimate watering holes, gave them names, obtained his liquor license, and paid his taxes, the whole nine. He even ensured his lower-end girls stayed out of the up-and-coming neighborhoods. His high-end call girls worked the bar on the inside. Eventually, he commissioned your grandfather, Anthony, your namesake, to build the Cicero, somehow convincing the older man that gambling was the obvious next move to obtain unadulterated wealth since the legalization of the sale of alcohol. The Cicero would house a secret room large enough to host three round tables that sat eight plus the dealer. In addition, they would build a legitimate pool hall and host tournaments sponsored by local businesses to help hide the money coming in from the high-stakes gambling room.

Eventually, your grandfather took over, and Marco played golf throughout the week. He knew the empire he had built was in good hands. Cautiously, your grandfather began to delve into the drug market– another unexplored avenue with high-income potential. Starting off, he primarily dealt with dope, but as the years progressed, he began making inroads with crack cocaine and methamphetamine. Of course, you know this already, but the drug trade was and still is our smallest venture. Most of the time, the sluts we own buy our drugs– unbeknownst to them, of course. Oh, the irony of it all. We pay them to spread their legs, and they pay us for the drugs they use to forget how much of a shit-show their life is; it's like we never paid them.

There are always roadblocks to success. He had told Anthony. Governors and mayors vow to 'clean up the streets in time for the next election. So, our number of girls started to drop. Well, by this time, your old man had come of age to begin contributing to the family business. I had the idea of opening Crystal's. I laid it all out for your grandfather. I told him we could put in the seedy part of town and have the girls rotate shifts working the club. It was golden. The strippers start the patrons' juices flowing, and the hookers step in to seal the deal. We make money off the dancers and our normal profits from the hoes we own.

You know the rest, of course. You were around when we opened the restaurant downtown and the medical marijuana shop. I hope to retire within the next fifteen years, son. To do that, I need you to step up and really learn the ins and outs of this thing. To learn who we own that is on the side of law and order. Victor had clasped his son's shoulders and squeezed ever so slightly. This will all be yours soon enough.

It's been ten years since Victor explained everything to Anthony, and the boy still refused to heed his words. Anthony was enthusiastic for the first year or two. He had learned how everything in the business was compartmentalized, had given orders to the trusted seconds in command, and even showed his commitment to the business in the family way: Murder. It was afterward Anthony began to grow distant again. He became depressed and– even more unfortunate–addicted to painkillers. Victor shook his head. What was it about the murder that relentlessly tore into his son? Victor had no idea but was determined to bring his son back to him.

Last summer, Anthony had even been arrested for possession of prescription drugs. That had worried Victor. With the state his son was in, he wasn't sure what Anthony might say or do while they held him in custody. Luckily, Victor had been notified by one of the officers on his payroll. Victor immediately rang up their lawyer, who swiftly freed Anthony from jail. The boy ended up with three months of community service, but that was an easier pill to swallow than prison.

From a corner of the room, the grandfather clock sang out the time with deep notes that echoed in Victor's ears, undulating down the mansion's hallways.

CHIME! CHIME! CHIME! CHIME! CHIME! CHIME! CHIME!

Seven o'clock meant breakfast would be served shortly. Anthony had not come to the table yet, and Victor was growing impatient. Where was that boy? The click-clack of shoes on hardwood stirred Victor from his thoughts. Glancing toward the sound, he saw Jonathon walking towards him with the breakfast tray.

Jonathan was dressed in his customary uniform. A white button-up shirt jumped out of the abyss of the butler's black suit jacket. His blood-red tie cut a river through the ivory sea beneath it. Covering his lower half was a pair of black slacks ironed so finely that Victor could see the creases from his seat at the far end of the table. His dark shoes rapped on the charcoal floor, announcing his arrival long before he actually appeared.

Jonathan approached his employer and sat the silver tray in front of him. As he raised the lid, the sweet smell of fried bacon filled Victor's nostrils. It was intoxicating. His lips curled into a smile.

"Thank you, Jonathon. Give my compliments to Clarice as well."

Victor said as he grabbed a piece from the tray.

"I will, sir." Jonathan bowed and turned to go.

Victor's teeth slammed into the piece of swine and tore it in two. The saltiness made his taste buds sing with glee. Slowly, he chewed at the piece of meat, savoring it, the bones in his mouth grinding it down into smaller and smaller pieces. Finally, swallowing, he gave a refreshed sigh and dropped the second half of the bacon onto the plate in front of him.

"Also, please wake up, Anthony. He cannot miss breakfast again." Jonathan nodded and exited the dining hall as Victor reached for more pieces of bacon. Victor grabbed the fork beside the ebony plate, took three more slices of bacon, and piled them on top of the piece. Next, he carefully lifted another small plate holding four white, orb-like morsels. He tipped the plate and gently herded two of the orbs onto his plate next to the pieces of pork. Next, Victor reached for the salt and pepper shakers on the tray's center. He grabbed them both by their tops and brought them near. Choosing the salt first, he turned the glass cylinder upside down and lightly shook it over the whitish spheres before him. Two short shakes of the wrist were all that was needed. Next, he lifted the black pepper. Victor was a bit less frugal with these grains. Six shakes would suffice.

Jonathon entered the dining hall again and walked briskly towards Victor. Anthony was not behind him. Victor's brow furrowed. Perhaps Anthony was taking his time to punish his father.

Victor took his silver fork and sliced it into one of the white orbs. Orangish-yellow liquid seeped from the center and painted the ceramic beneath it. Lifting the egg to his mouth, he opened and closed slowly over the end of the fork, letting the solid bits of white and the yellowish liquid fall from its tines and onto his tongue. He savored the bite.

"Sir," Jonathon began with a hesitant voice. "Anthony was not in his room."

Victor paused in the middle of his next bite. He picked up the napkin from his lap and wiped his lips.

"We have also checked all the bathrooms and the library. He's not in the mansion, sir."

"Thank you, Jonathon. I will find him. You may go."

Jonathan strode away to attend to his other duties, leaving Victor staring for a moment at the chair opposite him.

Empty.

Anthony had been out yesterday. Victor had assumed he came home sometime in the night, as was his routine of late. Where could he be? Chewing vigorously, he cut off some more eggs and shoved them into his mouth. He was agitated that he did not know the whereabouts of his son. The glass of orange juice sitting to his right still needed to be touched. Victor grabbed it and took a swig. The sweet and tangy liquid washed the food down his throat. Sam would soon arrive for his shift. Unlike usual, today, Sam would not accompany Victor on his errands. Instead, he would search the city for Anthony.

Five pieces of toast lay on the tray before him. Lifting his left arm, Victor plucked one from the tray. He raised the butter knife in his right hand and scooped the smooth butter onto the end of the blade. He then proceeded to scoop a large mound of purple jelly on the knife and smothered the butter with it. Finally, his hand brought the decorated toast to his lips, and he sank his teeth into it.

Victor continued with his breakfast, stewing in irritation that Anthony had absconded. Some may berate him for not showing enough concern, but if there was one thing Victor was sure of, it was that his boy was not dead. Anthony was being defiant. At thirty years of age, this had gone on far enough. It was time for Anthony to grow up.

The sound of more shoes on the hardwood floors caught Victor's attention. He looked up from his plate to see a young man with brown hair and a chiseled jaw walking towards him. His eyes flicked to the clock in the corner. 7:43 A.M. Sam still needed to arrive on time. The young man strode toward Victor at a steady pace. He was wearing a dark gray button-down shirt with the collar open. A black suit jacket draped his broad shoulders, and he wore slacks tailored so well he could have been walking a runway. Coming to a halt on Victor's right, Sam let his arms hang loose in front of him as we clasped his right wrist over his left.

"Good morning, Mr. Sorelli," Sam said in a welcome tone.

"Good morning Sam. Have a seat." He gestured to the chair beside him. Sam did as he was told.

"You won't accompany me today, Sam." Victor started.

Sam's face showed no hint of how he felt about this change of plan.

"I need you to track down Anthony."

Sam nodded as Victor continued.

"I'm not sure what kind of trouble he has gotten himself into. But I need him back here before midday."

He gestured toward the tray of food. When Sam declined the offer, Victor went on.

"We have much to discuss about his future and my own. Make sure he understands this is not a request."

"I will, sir. Is there somewhere specific you believe I should begin my search?"

"No. I'll leave it to you. You know him better than I, being that you are one of his oldest friends and close to him in age."

Sam winced at being called Anthony's friend. But, not surprisingly, things changed between the two of them when Victor hired Sam to be his personal muscle. Yet another reason Anthony resented his father.

"I will find him and bring him here no later than noon," Sam touted. Rising to his feet, he stepped from the front of the chair, pushed it in, and left the room.

Victor leaned back against his chair and sighed. He had a notion of where Anthony might be, but with no physical location, the information wouldn't aid Sam in his search. Anthony had recently been seen with a young woman around the city. She was poisonous to him. Victor could sense it the night he surprised the two of them at the restaurant. She had dug her claws in and begun twisting Anthony against his family with talks of running away. She was convincing him that his father was a tyrant who had no idea how to love. Victor's hands curled into fists. Rage boiled inside of him. He, his father, and his grandfather did not build this empire just for it to come crashing down at the whims of some ginger WHORE!

His fists crashed against the oak table with a loud THUD! The silver tray of food shook as the tiny vibrations ran from the point of impact across the wooden surface. His son had the same debilitating weakness of all young men: that sweet prize between a woman's legs. Victor shook his head. Anthony would come to his senses, one way or another.

CHAPTER 5

A blast of sirens jolted Anthony Sorelli awake. His eyes were still filled with sleep. The sirens kept blaring. He rubbed at his eyes, desperate to remove the gunk that clouded them so that he could turn off his alarm. As his vision slowly returned, he reached out with his hands toward the sound, only managing to push its source further across the glass top of the coffee table. He hit a hard object with his right wrist, causing it to clatter off the table and roll onto the carpeted floor below. He leaned over, searching for his phone. His fingers grazed the familiar rectangular shape and lifted it to his face. He stabbed at it blindly with his index finger, hoping to hit the off button. The phone finally fell silent.

Anthony crashed back onto the cloth couch beneath him. He flung his right arm over his eyes, carefully keeping a tight grip on his cell phone. He lay there for another minute, not moving. Then, reluctantly, he removed his arm from his face and looked at his phone. The screen was dark. He gave it a tap. 7:47 A.M blinked back at him. Had Wendy decided not to wake him up when she came home? She always woke him up if he was asleep.

Glancing around, he noticed he had knocked over Wendy's flower vase. Its contents vomited across the table, drenching the forgotten gray coat on the floor. Huffing out a breath, he rose to his feet and walked to the kitchen, shoving his phone in his right pants pocket as he did. The paper towels were on a rack beside the sink. An assortment of dirty dishes sat untouched in the stainless-steel basin.

Not wanting to return for more towels, he grabbed the roll in its entirety and returned to the living room. He bent down, lifted the vase from the floor, and sat it back on the table. He proceeded to pick up the flowers and return them to their watery home. While holding the paper towels firmly in his left hand, he grabbed the end with his right and began to spin the roll until a thick layer encompassed his hand. The smell of cinnamon suddenly stimulated his senses. Wendy's wall-plug air fresheners. She always did love the scent of cinnamon. He often referred to her as his dash of cinnamon. A smile teased at his lips.

Reaching down, he began to wipe up the water from the table. The liquid ran from the thirsty, white cloth and soaked into the thick fibers of the floor. Once the table was dry, he started stamping the towels into the wet carpet. He went to the kitchen and threw the now sopping wet ball of mush into the garbage. He peered down the hallway to his right. The lights were off. He walked down the hall toward Wendy's bedroom, planning to sneak in and crawl into bed next to her.

BEEP! BEEP! BEEP!

Anthony started. Damn phone! He thought to himself. He reached into his pants pocket and pulled out the blaring brick. Looking at the screen, he hit the off button. Stupid Anthony, he chided himself. I must have hit snooze by mistake earlier. Glancing at her door, he waited to hear if she moved around. Nothing. No sound of sheets rustling, springs creaking, nothing. Anthony's brow furrowed. There's no way she didn't hear that. Could she be faking? Seeing if he'll still try and climb in next to her?

Softly, he tiptoed to her door. The white wooden barricade was firmly shut. He lifted his hand and turned the knob. Then, being as quiet as possible, he pushed the door inwards. It made no creaks, silent as the grave. Her room was dark. Sunlight tried and failed to fight past the heavy, pink curtains covering her window. He glanced over the bed and saw it was unkempt as always, but there was no mound under the blankets.

Wendy was not here. Anthony's heart skipped a beat. Why was she not here? Where could she be? He switched on the light. A faint yellow glow illuminated the room from the weak lamp above. Wendy's room was a mess. It always baffled him. The living room, kitchen, and dining room were all practically spotless. He always wondered why she didn't hold her bedroom to the same standard.

Gazing around the room, he took stock of everything around him. The small tv on the wooden dresser was blank, dead to the world. A small lamp sat on her nightstand. The shade was missing. Clothes lay strewn across the floor in all directions. Jeans, sweatpants, socks, and underwear were littered everywhere. Four different colored bras hung from the handle of the open closet door. He noticed a crimson sweater with the letters OU in white vinyl across the chest. The University of Oklahoma. Wendy was originally from Oklahoma, Anthony remembered. She had only moved to St. Louis a couple of years ago for work.

Anthony moved to her bathroom. Switching on the light, he noticed it was no better off than the bedroom. The white tile floor was covered with pink and red towels. A pair of purple panties lay beside the porcelain toilet. The vanity was littered with various tubes and vials of make-up, soaps, moisturizers, and other personal hygiene products. Wendy's curling iron and blow drier were left out as well, lying haphazardly beside the sink. Anthony looked up, staring at his own reflection in the mirror. His jet-black hair was still slicked back from the day before, and his jeans and blue t-shirt had obviously been slept in. His hazel eyes bore into his soul like a stranger's in the dirty mirror. Turning back to the bedroom, Anthony started to feel dizzy. He stumbled to the bed and sat down.

This can't be happening, he thought. She must still be at work. Why else would she not come home? Anthony raised his fingers to his temples and began to massage them deeply. Something wasn't right. He didn't tell her he was coming over last night, but that had never bothered her before. That's why she had given him a spare key so he could come and go at his leisure.

He had a rough day yesterday. His father had gone on and on about how he needed Anthony at the mansion to learn to take over the business. Anthony wanted to get away, wanted to get high. He had left his family's property and drove to meet his dealer in a rush. When he arrived at the alley behind the usual drug store yesterday afternoon, he just sat outside in his car. He had reached for the door handle three times but couldn't go through with it. With hot tears filling his eyes, he drove to Wendy's, angry at himself. She was at work, but she'd be home by eleven tonight–or so he had thought. He had let himself in and sat down on the couch to wait for her. He must have fallen asleep at some point, though he couldn't remember.

Anthony had always assumed he would take over the family business when he was a kid. After his mom was diagnosed, however, things weren't so simple. He never understood it when he was younger. To him, his family could do anything they wanted. They merely had to pay enough money, which always worked out, but money couldn't save his mother. She suffered for months on end. His father took her to the best doctors in the nation for treatment. Everything was paid for upfront. None of it worked. Near the end, when things became really bad, Anthony did something he had never tried before and hadn't tried since. He prayed. For an entire week, he spent hours on his knees begging, pleading with this supposedly all-powerful God. He promised never to tell another lie, to go to church every week for the rest of his life, and even to make his father go. Still, no miracle came. Little Anthony was willing to give God anything He wanted if his mother could be healed. Finally, Anthony swore that he would make his father shut it all down as a last-ditch effort. The whole business. Everything. Little Anthony wasn't aware of everything his father was into, but he knew people feared him. That had to be worth something. When his mother eventually passed, Anthony silently cursed himself for believing in something foolish.

He had never told anyone any of this. Not even Wendy knew. She only knew that his mother had died when he was ten and that he had been angry about it for a long time. He had told her about his father's two-year bout with depression, but only he knew about his intimate journey with the so-called God. Though if he were to tell anyone, it would be Wendy. She's the only person who has shown compassion toward him. Even when he became angry with her, she was always ready to forgive him for the ugly things he said and did. He had never hit her, but there were times when he didn't recognize himself. Kind of like now. He thought about his own strange eyes reflected at him in the mirror. It could be a side-effect of quitting the drugs.

The drugs…

His hands began to shake. How long has it been? Four days. He'd been clean for four days now.
You know they'll help, he heard himself say. *You know he still has some. Come on! Let's go, you worthless wimp! You won't survive without them!*

Trying to fight away the thoughts of getting high, he slammed his eyelids shut and squeezed them tight. He needed to find Wendy. She could help him. He had to find her before he did something stupid. Rising to his feet, he strode down the hall and out the front door.

CHAPTER 6

Detective Luke Burrows sat at his desk, head in his hands. So far, they had found no new information about their Jane Doe. He leaned back against his chair and stared at the monitor on his desk. The scene had not altered. Instead, a pixelated black-and-white image of a body lying on the ground outside the Cicero hotel filled the screen. The night manager had given him and Mason the tapes from that night without hesitation, pulling Mason further away from the theory that the Sorellis were involved.

Cigarette smoke filled his nose. Turning to his left, he saw Detective Bill Watts standing close behind him. The man was a damn chimney. Luke returned his attention to his desk. Papers covered it like leaves on the forest floor. A stack of case files he had yet to turn in watched him from their corner of the unstable ecosystem. The desk lamp rose up and bent over, its silver husk waiting to spotlight the coffee stains that branded the many papers scattered about.

Luke began to pick them up, examining each one so that he could organize them properly. One page had the title: WITNESS STATEMENT, CASE NO. 4351. That file was in the stack on the corner of his desk. Standing to his feet, Luke grabbed the heavy stack of folders and searched for the corresponding file. Once he located it, he opened its manilla mouth, slid the white paper into its gullet, and clamped the jaws shut. He continued to clean up his workstation, even managing to turn in two of the case files that were in the stack. The paperwork was already done; he had just forgotten to submit them for review.

He relished this small, personal victory when he returned to his desk. His chair wore his father's coat. Lifting his right hand to meet his left, he began to unbutton the crimson sleeve. He repeated the act on the right side. Rolling back the red snakes to the elbow, Luke sat down and once again peered deep into the screen before him. The computer mouse sat frozen to his right. Luke seized it and rewound the video until it was at the beginning. He and Mason had started the tape at midnight and watched at 2x normal speed. Every once in a while, the shadow of a passing car crossed the side of the building. This camera angle only focused on the north part of the hotel entrance. They had taken the footage from all three cameras perched on the Cicero's nose, peering to see who decided to walk into its open mouth. The other two camera angles didn't have anything on them. No one was spotted by those eyes during the relevant time frame. This one, however, did catch at least one person: the victim.

Luke's head was propped against his left hand as he watched the tape again. Nothing but darkness and white splashes from the street lights. Luke checked the time stamp on the video. 3:14 am Then, at the edge of the blackness, movement. Here she comes, thought Luke. A figure began to take shape before his eyes. The recording was in black and white, with grainy resolution. It would be hard to tell anyone apart if multiple people appeared in the camera's line of sight. The figure was walking slowly and appeared to be drunk. Walking in a straight line seemed impossible for the poor girl. She staggered onward, one step at a time. Then it happens. She falls forward, her knees hit the concrete, her left arm flying out to try and prevent her face from meeting the sidewalk. Her flailing attempt buffered her fall just enough that her head didn't bounce off the hard surface. There she lay, not moving. There was no movement until 3:51 am when Officer Beatty arrived on the scene.

"Are you watching that thing again?" Mason's voice startled Luke from his trance. Raising his eyes from his computer, Luke saw Mason standing in front of him, holding a steaming cup of joe in his left hand.

"You're not going to find the answers there," Mason stated, pulling the chair from under his desk and flopping down.

"What would you suggest?" Luke volleyed, leaning back.

"We have officers canvassing the neighborhood with her photo, Will and Doc are still working with the physical evidence. You and I should review recent missing person reports to see if they match Jane Doe's description."

Luke's eyes shifted to the clock above the door to the station. 10:22 am He looked back to Mason, stared at him for another five seconds, then nodded.

"You're right." Luke resigned. This tape only confirms Doc's time of death and Officer Beatty's story, Luke told himself.

"Great." said Mason, "Maggie is compiling the reports for us as we speak."

Lifting the cup to his lips, Mason took a satisfying sip of his coffee. Luke folded his arms across his chest and let out a small sigh. Mason put the cup down and leaned forward, speaking softly to Luke.

"You didn't go home last night, did you?"

Luke looked away, not wanting to have this conversation again.

"I had paperwork to catch up on," Luke replied casually.

"From the looks of things, most of it is still stacked on the corner of your desk."

"Even if I had gone home, it wouldn't matter. I can never sleep for more than four hours at a stretch," Luke admitted, eyes downcast. After a moment, he looked up to see Mason staring intently at him. Sympathy filled the man's emerald eyes.

"I'm not going to pretend to know what you're going through," Mason started, "but you need to get some sleep. You're no good to anyone functioning fifty percent." Mason's voice was full of compassion. Luke knew Mason meant well. He'd even agreed to help Luke track down the person responsible for the incident. Luke was confident he knew who it was. Mason didn't throw out the possibility, but he never seemed to commit to the notion either.

"I promise; I will go to the drug store this evening, buy some melatonin, and go home and crash," Luke said with his right hand raised. Mason cracked a smile.

"I appreciate it, boss." Mason leaned back against his chair, "This is as much for me as it is for you." Luke cocked his head.

"How so?"

"I don't want a sleep-deprived partner watching my back. So I'll have Reilly put you with Watts."

"What'd you say, Mason?" Watts' scratchy voice echoed from across the room. Luke and Mason chuckled.

"Nothin' you ole smoke stack!" Mason called out. At that moment, Maggie arrived with a stack of papers.

"Here are all the missing person reports filed this month," Maggie said. Her voice was very matter-of-fact. The young woman had joined the force three months ago and had already seemed fed up with the Detectives' antics.

"Thanks, doll," Mason joked, giving her a wink. Maggie's brown eyes rolled deep in their sockets as she turned and walked away.

"I think she likes me."

Luke shook his head as he split the stack of papers in half, giving one half to Mason and keeping the other half for himself.

When Maggie returned, Luke was about one-third of the way through his stack of missing persons. Her face remained expressionless. She looked at the two of them for a few seconds before speaking.

"Chief Reilly would like the two of you to meet him in his office." She turned to leave just as Mason spoke up.

"Hey Mags…"

She paused, glaring in Mason's direction.

"We're going to be at this for a while. So be a dear and grab us some lunch in a little bit."

Turning back to face Mason, Maggie locked eyes with him. His face wore a wry smile as he held her gaze. For five heartbeats, nobody spoke.

"I'd prefer to watch you starve." Maggie sneered, her comment cutting the silence like a knife. She whirled around and stormed off. Mason was still smiling. Luke shook his head and rose to his feet.

"Shall we go see what Reilly wants?" Mason conceded and gestured for Luke to lead the way.

*   *   *   *

St. Louis Metropolitan Police Chief, Gregory Reilly, stood behind his desk, staring at the wall, an unlit cigar in his mouth. His thick white hair was parted on the left side of his scalp. His snowy white mustache and goatee were perfectly trimmed and groomed on his round face. Not a hair lies out of place. Framed photos and accolades lined the walls of the office. His high school diploma, a plaque bearing his bachelor's degree from the University of Missouri, and a Peace Officer Standards and Training (P.O.S.T.) Certificate jutted from behind Reilly's large maple desk. Snapshots of Reilly, his wife, and two daughters decorated the desk and added a touch of warmth to the otherwise cold, impersonal room. Photos of Reilly with three St. Louis mayors and Missouri Governor Richard Tyson gleaned from a place of pride right in front. An American flag rose from the corner of the office behind his desk like a sentinel on guard.

Reilly protected and served the city of St. Louis for over forty years. In all that time, he did what he could to rid his city of the scourge known as Sorelli. Sure, he had busted several girls for prostitution, and many lowlifes for dealing drugs, both of which he was sure Sorelli was responsible for. None of what he did seemed to make a difference. Either the perps were bailed out within days or left to rot with someone else replacing them on the streets. Some mayors, judges, and even his fellow officers, had asked him on multiple occasions why it mattered. To them, crime would happen with or without Sorelli. On a fundamental level, they were correct; crime would not vanish from St. Louis just because the Sorelli Empire crumbled. However, it was a simple fact that organized crime seemed to be allowed to flourish, which gave criminals boldness they would not otherwise possess.

Reilly removed the cigar from his lips by raising his right hand to his mouth. He was curious to know if anyone else would come along with the guts to stand up to the Sorelli family, though he would soon find that his doubts were unfounded. Four years ago, a young officer was promoted to detective. Within a year, the rookie had developed an insatiable hunger to take on Sorelli. Reilly had taken Burrows under his wing, giving him all sorts of knowledge, he had acquired over the decades. Unfortunately, Reilly had underestimated the young man's zeal. It was ravenous, unquenchable. Within four months, the kid had led raids on Sorelli's hotel, gentlemen's club, and restaurant. One of those raids was performed without a warrant. The kid had requested one but was too impatient to wait for its release. Burrows had planned to surprise the gentlemen's club with the raid, thinking that once it was all over— and the evidence had been collected— the warrant would have been approved. Needless to say, it did not end well. The manager of the club was not caught off guard, and no evidence of any illicit activity was found. After that, Reilly was pressured by the mayor to fire Burrows. Reilly went to war for the kid, laying his own reputation on the line. Soon after, he took Burrows aside and advised him to take a more undercover approach if he wanted to make any headway.

Chief Reilly hung his head. It had started well. They had been able to get multiple informants into Sorelli's circle. But one by one the informants began to disappear, never to be heard from again. A month after his disappearance, one man had been found in the Missouri countryside, eaten away by the elements and wildlife. Not long after that, Burrows had the idea of going through Sorelli's taxes—never the way a law officer wants to bring in a criminal, but if it got the job done…It didn't. Sorelli's books were amazingly well documented. Not a figure out of place. It was infuriating. Reilly stuck the cigar back in his mouth and shoved his hands in his pants pockets. Soon after that, tragedy struck. Just over two years ago, Burrows had lost his girlfriend in a terrible accident. While walking to a southside bus stop across the street from her job at the rehab center and run over by a drunk driver. She died on impact, and they found the driver less than a mile down the road crashed into a telephone pole. Burrows had been confident the Sorellis were involved somehow. Reilly couldn't blame the kid for hoping; Burrows had been a thorn in Victor Sorelli's side. Unfortunately, the fact that they found the car with the driver, and no evidence to even point to Sorelli, meant that there wasn't much they could do. Reilly ordered Burrows to keep his distance.

After three months' leave for grieving his loss, Burrows returned to work. Reilly assigned Charles Wallace to be Burrows' partner when he came back. Charlie was an older detective, and Reilly needed someone whom he could be certain would watch after the boy. The two worked well together, solving three high-profile cases in the eleven months they were together until one day when Charles didn't arrive at the station. After that, Burrows and Reilly both called him multiple times. Mrs. Wallace, Charles' wife, finally called Reilly back. Charles had suffered a stroke in the night and passed away. Charlie was one of Reilly's closest friends. They'd gone through the academy together, worked the same beat on the streets, and were even partners when they were young detectives. That had been a tough loss for Reilly to comprehend.

A smile tugged at the corner of his mouth, remembering the day they had asked Charlie to be chief. He had turned it down, saying, "I'm not made to ride a desk and play kiss ass to a bunch of politicians who can't tell their armpit from their crotch." So, Reilly had gotten the job. He'd always wanted it. A single tear rolled down Reilly's left cheek. He wiped it away and scratched the side of his head. As he did, he caught a glimpse of himself reflected in one of the glass frames. The lines in his face were deep, canyons that only time and stress could carve. His mustache and goatee seemed proud on his upper lip and chin. Grayish eyes peered at him from the distorted reflection. An itch tickled the back of his throat. Bringing his hand up to his mouth, he began to cough. The itch was not going away. After removing the cigar from his lips, he descended into a coughing fit, coughing harder and harder as he tried to chase the irritation from his esophagus.

A knock sounded at his door at that moment. The door handle turned, and a small crack appeared.

"Chief?" came Burrows' voice from behind the heavy door. Reilly turned toward the door and gestured the two men inside.

"Come in gentleme…" his greeting was cut short by another burst of coughs.

"You alright, Chief?" Detective Mason asked.

"I'm fine, just fine," Reilly answered, "please sit down." His voice was deep and raspy from all the coughing. The two took their seats in front of Reilly's maple desk. Reilly remained standing.

"Tell me about this new case."

The men shifted in their seats and looked at each other.

"Well, sir, the body of a young woman was found around four o'clock this morning by an officer on patrol. She was completely nude. No idea who she was or what she was doing. Will and Dr. Wright are combing through all the physical evidence as we speak," Luke reported.

Chief Reilly's held his cigar between his middle and index finger on his right hand. He glared at them. Something was off.

"Where was she found?" Reilly questioned. No answer. "Burrows, where was she found?" Luke glanced at the floor before answering.

"Outside The Cicero."

Reilly leaned forward and placed his large, calloused hands on the back of his chair. "The Cicero," he whispered. The words seem to hang in the air above their heads. Reilly knew the implications of this, especially with Burrows involved.

"We're keeping all avenues open, Chief," Mason said, breaking the silence.

"You're damn right you are," Reilly spits out. "We cannot give Victor Sorelli one more reason to try and cut off our heads." Lifting his hand, he inserted the cigar back into his mouth, turned towards the wall behind him, and drew in a deep breath. The scent of the tobacco filled his nasal cavity. Calmness seeped back into his mind. "What's being done to identify the girl?" Reilly asked through cigar-filled lips.

"Officers are canvassing the area around the hotel, showing her picture, trying to see if anyone recognizes her. Will should have her fingerprints. Hopefully, that will answer the question." Luke said.

"And Burrows and I are going through missing person reports to see if any of them match Jane Doe's description," Mason added proudly.

"Good," Reilly responded. "I will repeat myself so that I will not be misinterpreted." Then, turning to the men, he removed the cigar from his mouth and leaned forward. "Do NOT go anywhere near Victor or Anthony Sorelli without iron-clad evidence."

"Yes, sir," the detectives replied in unison.

"Now go find out who this girl is, who killed her, and why they thought they needed to do such a thing." The two younger men rose to their feet and left Chief Reilly's office.

Gripping the back of his chair, he pulled it from under his desk and sat down hard. I don't know how much longer I can do this job, Reilly thought. He looked at the cigar in his hand. Quitting seemed like a wise idea two weeks ago. He longed for a deep drag on the tobacco-filled stog in his hand. He had purposely taken all his lighters home and kept his cigars in the top drawer of his desk in his office. He would be the first to admit his willpower could use some help. He worked over the case in his own mind—the dead girl in front of The Cicero. The whole thing was a conundrum. Reilly's gut had rarely failed him, and this time it told him Sorelli was involved. He just hoped the boys could prove it. He tapped his fingers on the wooden slab in front of him.

A rap on his office door brought him out of his thoughts. "Come in," he said. His secretary, Jessica, opened the door, poking her head in, her face grim.

"What is it, Jess? Spit it out?"

"Um, there's a phone call for you, sir."

"Who is it?" asked Reilly, annoyed.

"The mayor, sir." Jessica left the opening and closed the door.

Reilly glanced at the black phone sitting on his desk. Next to the number two, a red light blinked at him. Reilly reached for the phone and muttered to himself, "I've got a bad feeling about this."

CHAPTER 7

Rays of sunlight pierced through the windshield of Anthony Sorelli's Honda Civic, warming his face. It was a cold day outside. The gauge on his rearview mirror read thirty-five degrees Fahrenheit. Hot air leapt from the vents on the dashboard. A voice was singing, "I did it my way." Sinatra's voice. Anthony leaned forward and muted Frank's baritone crooning. He let his head fall back against the headrest.

Wendy was still missing. He searched her work, the gym she always went to, the library, the park, the local grocery store, and nothing. Nobody had seen her since last night. Finally, reaching into his pocket, he pulled out his phone. After unlocking it, he clicked the phone app icon. Anthony's call list appeared on the screen. The name at the top said 'Wendy (14),' in red lettering. He pressed the name again and lifted the phone to his ear. It rang once, and then he heard her sweet, soft voice come over the line: "Hey there. Sorry, I'm unable to come to the phone, but if you leave me your name and number, I will call you back." A small beep entered his ears, signaling the caller to begin their message. Anthony ended the call.

Where could she be? He asked himself.

He was parked in the library parking lot. A tremor returned to his hands. Shutting his eyelids, he tried to recite the Serenity prayer in his head. The prayer was said at every AA, meaning that he went to. He never gave it much credence, though, and he told his sponsor as much.

"I'm not a believer either," his sponsor had said, "but the larger meaning behind the prayer is what matters. Whether or not you think there's some big, bearded being in the sky, you have to accept responsibility for your life and try to do better."

Anthony hadn't been to a meeting in months. He had no idea where his sponsor was or what the man thought of him. Anthony also didn't care. The only person he cared about was Wendy, and she was missing.

Anthony's own voice boomed in his skull. He lifted his hands to his head and covered his ears.

You only care about yourself! Isn't that why you want to find Wendy? Cause Daddy's being mean to you, you want to lose your mind in Oxy and Morphine!

"SHUT UP!" Anthony screamed aloud. Tears leaked from beneath his eyelids, the warm drops running down his face.

Oh, boo hoo! Grow up. When did you ever go to Wendy when she needed you? Never! Where were you last month when she thought her ex was stalking her? Huh? Where were you when she called because her sister had been diagnosed with cancer? Where! Were! YOU?!?!

Anthony let out a loud scream so long it caused his throat to ache. Then, lurching forward, his head smacked the steering wheel.

"Shut up," he whispered. "Shut up."

The voice stopped and left Anthony to sulk in the driver's seat of his car. Sweat soaked his underarms and back. He lifted his right hand and shut off the heater. A twinge of defiance grew in Anthony's spirit. *I will find her,* he thought. *I will help her.*

A knock came from his left. He turned his head and saw Sam standing outside the car. His father had sent him. Anthony scowled at the man. Then, slowly, he moved his hand to the control panel on the door and clicked a button. The driver-side window lowered barely two inches.

"Your father sent me to find you," Sam said. He cocked his head to the right. "You ok, Tony?"

Anthony just glared at him.

"Look, your father's worried about you. Come with me back to the estate." Sam's voice was caring, and he hadn't asked to be pitted between father and son. So why did he accept his father's job offer? Anthony never understood.

"Tell my father I'm busy." Anthony began to roll up the window when Sam jerked the driver's door open. The cold air snapped at his face. "What the hell are you doing?" Anthony demanded.

"I'm taking you to the estate," Sam said, determination in his tone. He reached in and grabbed Anthony by his shirt. Then, he tore the taller man from the car with a heave. Anthony swung at Sam's head with his right fist. Sam noticed the ball of flesh and bone aimed at his head and blocked the jab with his left arm. Anthony responded with a left jab to Sam's ribs. Sam sucked in a gulp of air; his left hand still tight on Anthony's shirt.

He shoved his friend against the vehicle with a THUD. Sam let him go suddenly, and Anthony dropped to the asphalt. With the withdrawal side effects eating away at his physical strength and the battle between him and himself in his inner critic going strong, Anthony resigned himself to Sam's will. Leaning forward into the car, Sam turned off the ignition, took the keys, and slammed the driver's door shut.

"Tony," Sam began, "fighting is futile. Now let's go. It's a thirty-five-minute drive home." Bending at the knees, Sam grabbed Anthony under his arms and brought him to his feet. He quickly threw Tony's arm over his shoulder and crossed the parking lot with Tony staggering beside him. Once they arrived at the vehicle, Sam ushered him into the back seat of the black town car. Sam stared at his friend in the rearview mirror. The man needed help. Hopefully, his father could give it to him. Pulling his phone from his pocket, Sam checked the time. 11:21 A.M.

CHAPTER 8

The anonymous call he had made to the mayor had been a success. The mayor was clearly surprised by the news of a dead woman outside the Cicero. Mayor Robert Tyler was a fool. Content to sit in his office, sign papers, and let his master pull his strings, Tyler was like many other mayors before him. He was a righteous man to the public, pledging to ward off crime and wash away the debaucheries that plagued the city he was elected to govern. Privately, however, Tyler was a notorious gambler drowning in debt. The fat fool couldn't control himself. There was always a seat reserved for him in the secret back room of the Cicero. Some nights he was allowed to win, keeping him on the hook. Most nights, though, went something like this: Tyler would win two hands, lose four, win three, lose two, win one, lose six, and so on until he would eventually either resign or run out of money.

The man shook his head. Fools, he thought to himself as he drove to the city's outskirts. The sound of the car's motor filled the air. He looked at the radio, 11:36 A.M.

Mayor Tyler had indeed called Chief Reilly by now, demanding answers and receiving none. So naturally, Reilly would expect the anonymous caller's phone number. Tyler would give it to him, but no matter. It would lead them nowhere. Putting the mayor on edge was vital for his plan to stay in constant motion. Any prolonged stagnation at this point could jeopardize everything. With Mayor Tyler worried about how long the Cicero would be under surveillance, he would constantly pressure Reilly, who would pressure the detectives. They needed to stay focused.

The partner, Mason, could still be a problem. However, he would stay informed through the several officers and few detectives they owned. Mason would be taken off the board if anything were to happen that could derail his plan.

The black car bounced slightly as it dived and sprang back out of a pothole. Gritting his teeth, he swore at himself. He needed to pay better attention to the road. Sunlight attacked the tinted window to his left.

Lifting his hand to the dashboard, he unmuted the radio. The guitar solo from AC/DC's "Highway to Hell" blared from the speakers. If all went accordingly, it would be over in about three days.

CHAPTER 9

A large, black wolf was mounted to the wall behind Victor's desk. Standing erect and foreboding, the dark canine stretched over six feet– a terrifying sight to anyone who entered. Its obsidian glass eyes surveyed the interior landscape around it. The walls, a deep crimson, provided solitude from the world outside. Other wildlife forms brought more of nature into the space. A massive, tan bull elk was anchored to the south wall, directly across from the wolf. From the east came a silver fox suspended in the air, pouncing on unseen prey. A pronghorn antelope stared at the leaping critter from the west, its horns rising over four feet from its skull. Charcoal gray carpet covered the floor. The burning of incense filled the room with a woody aroma. A coat rack stood solemnly in the southwest corner; its branches bare. In the center of the room, a tall, leather chair sat behind a great oak desk, its occupant a terror to behold. Facing the oak workstation were two small seats, one occupied by a man the same age as Victor's son.

The two men faced each other, the silence between them filled with nothing but respect. Then, finally, Victor cleared his throat and pushed the chair away from his oaken post. Opposite of Victor sat the family's lawyer, David Quentin. Victor had asked to meet him today to finalize his last will and testament; a task Victor had put off long enough. Quentin had been on the Sorelli legal team for nearly a decade. He had taken over as the family's head counsel two and a half years ago, at the behest of Victor himself, after his predecessor, Isaac Goldmann, passed away from a heart attack.

Quentin wore a navy suit with gray socks inset black threaded diamonds. Victor sported a black blazer over the top of a white shirt with black pants. Quentin's blonde hair was combed to the right and had begun to darken over the past year or so. Hazel eyes stared out of his square-shaped head. Occasionally, during their meetings, Victor sensed that he'd seen Quentin before the man began working at the law firm. Impossible, of course, but deja vu was still a mystery to mankind.

"Have you brought the documents?" Victor asked, his voice deep and authoritative.

"I have," Quentin replied, bending at the waist to grab the brown leather briefcase beside the chair he occupied. He unlocked the attaché, and removed the papers. "Everything is as you requested." He said as he handed the documents to Victor. Quentin's eyes darted to the wolf above Victor's head.

"Do you like my pet?" asked Victor.

"He is magnificent," Quentin ventured. "You've never told me where you acquired him."

"There's not much to tell," Victor replied, "I bought it from a Russian long ago." Victor's gaze began bouncing across the sheets in his hands. The lawyer remained silent as Victor read the lines of legal jargon that handed everything he owned over to his son at the time of his death. Quentin crossed his right leg over his left while glancing about the red-walled office. "Everything looks to be in order," Victor stated, breaking the silence. Lifting a golden pen from his desk, he turned it slightly, forcing the point to emerge from its burrow. Gently, he pressed the pen onto the indicated lines, signing and initialing his agreement with the designations in the documents. Handing the papers back to Quentin, Victor felt relief wash over him. Now that the legal future of the family's estate and its assets were taken care of, it was time to get Anthony in line.

"How's your son, Mr. Sorelli?" Quentin inquired as he placed the completed documents back into his briefcase.

"He's doing better," Victor answered, his face blank. The blonde-haired man had been the one to get Anthony off on the last possession charge.

"I appreciate you keeping an ear to the ground regarding his…previous issues."

"Of course, sir," Quentin said, rising to his feet. "He is my future employer, after all."

Victor also stood, smiling at Quentin's comment. He will be, even if it's the last thing I ever do, thought Victor. Gesturing to the door behind Quentin, Victor gave a curt nod. The lawyer took the hint, reaching for the door handle and pulling it open.

"I'll file these with the court as soon as I return to the office," Quentin said as he exited the room.

"Thank you, Quentin," Victor replied. He let out a small sigh as he returned to his seat behind the great desk. Victor glanced at the gold watch on his left wrist, 12:13 P.M. Sam should be back by now with Anthony. There was no doubt in Victor's mind that Sam wouldn't dare return empty-handed. Heat began to radiate from Victor's face. He began to inhale long, deep breaths attempting to calm himself. His son would probably be an emotional case today; Victor would stay controlled. Opening the top right drawer of his desk, he removed an old flip phone, held down the number 2, and placed the phone to his ear. It rang twice before Sam's voice answered.

"Bring him in."

*   *   *   *

Anthony had arrived at his family's estate fifteen minutes earlier. Forcibly brought here by his former friend, Sam Hunter. The shaking in his hands had subsided on the ride over, thankfully. Facing his father with signs of withdrawal was a death sentence. Sam had decided to turn on the radio while they drove. Anthony was grateful for that. The lilting melodies and soft harmonies from the car speakers took over his mind, and he gladly let himself drown in them. Once they arrived, the guard opened the gate, and the black town car made its way to the six-car garage on the side of the house. Sam killed the ignition and turned to Anthony.

"Am I going to have to drag you inside?" he asked.

Anthony responded by opening the passenger side back door and stepping onto the gravel. The tiny rocks crunched underneath his weight as he walked toward the mansion. Sam jumped out of the driver's seat and, with three long strides, caught up to Anthony. Once inside the large dwelling, Sam ushered Anthony to wait for his father in the library. Apparently, the elder Sorelli was meeting with their lawyer and didn't want to be disturbed. Sam had always shown loyalty. At first, it was to Anthony when they were in private school. Now his fealty resided with Victor. Mentally, Anthony shook his head. When they were kids, he had told Sam about how cruel and manipulative his father could be. This was obviously some misguided attempt by his father to restore Anthony's faith in the family. Poor Sam was just an unwitting tool, soon to be discarded if Anthony shaped up and returned to the fold.

The fireplace was ablaze and spewing heat into the Sorelli Atheneum. Anthony took a seat in a grandiose armchair. Lifting his legs, he placed them on the matching ottoman. Shelves of books lined the walls of the library. Ivory cases rose halfway up the walls before receding inwards to make space for the encased literature. His grandfather had amassed an impressive collection over the years. The vast library housed many jewels, including first editions of Great Expectations, War and Peace, The Lord of the Rings Trilogy, 20,000 Leagues Under the Sea, and The Adventures of Huckleberry Finn. The library also hosts many reference books, biographies, histories, and even some poetry. Anthony had spent many days and nights in this room. At first, it was at the behest of his father. After his mother had passed, Jonathan, the family's butler, had encouraged him to read as a means of escape. The worlds between the bindings had swept him away on journeys he had never thought possible. A grin formed on his lips as he remembered fighting orcs with Aragorn and Legolas and floating down the river with Huck and Jim. A phone buzzed, and Sam pulled it out of his pocket.

"Your father is ready for you."

CHAPTER 10

Anthony sat across from his father, with his back straight, tall, and proud. The office hadn't changed in decades, not since Victor had bought the taxidermied wildlife and hung them on the walls. Victor's regal gemstone ring on his left middle finger stared at Anthony as Victor drummed his fingers on the arm of his chair. His father's left ankle rested upon his right knee. There was a time when sitting here would have terrified Anthony. Not today, he thought.

Anthony's father seemed to tower over him. The wrinkles in his face demanded respect. Victor Sorelli was not a man one wanted to cross. Anthony knew how his father dealt with people. The memory of a woman walking across a street flashed in his mind's eye for a mere half second. Anthony blinked the image away. Staring at his father, Anthony refused to initiate the conversation.

You wanted me here, so speak. So, I can find Wendy…

Victor held Anthony's gaze for another ten seconds.

"Where have you been?" he eventually asked. But, again, there was no concern in his voice, just aggravated curiosity.

"Out," replied Anthony flippantly. Knowing how his father felt about Wendy, he didn't want to bring her name into this.

"Out," Victor repeated, "Getting high or screwing your whore?"

Anthony felt his face go red. His jaw tightened.

"Don't. Call her that." He said through clenched teeth. "You don't know anything about her."

Victor looked to the side and huffed out a breath.

"No, I don't. But from what you've told me, she wants nothing to do with your future." Victor leaned forward in his seat and set his arms on his desk; hands clasped together. "You must get this through your head, son. You are destined to rule this city one day. It's damn well past time you started acting like it!" His father's voice was resolute. He would not let Anthony leave here without accepting his destiny.

"I don't want to rule," Anthony said, his voice wavering.

"What was that?" challenged Victor.

"I don't want to rule," Anthony repeated, more sternly this time.

"You seem to be under the impression that you have a choice in the matter." Victor leaned back in his chair; his hazel eyes boring into his son's. "Let me make myself perfectly clear…"

He raised his hand and pointed a stern index finger at his son.

"You will take over this empire, rule in a manner that honors those that preceded you, and in due time you will marry and sire an heir of your own."

"Why?" Anthony snapped, "To make more money? To rid the city of your enemies? What exactly does this kingdom of crime provide for us? We have plenty of legitimate businesses."

"The legitimate businesses are merely fronts; you know this. They make very little money compared to what our other endeavors bring in," Victor retorted. "This is about control, power, the Sorelli name bringing fear and respect through the ages." His father's voice was deep and powerful.

"Why not expand?" Anthony pressed, "Why have we cowered in this city for nearly a century?"

"Two reasons: One, to prevent any notice from the federal government. Two, to prevent the empire from fracturing and mutiny from within." Victor said. Anthony's head began to spin. Withdrawal attacked him again. Anthony reached into his pants pocket and removed his phone. Wendy had yet to return any of his calls or texts. With hands on his lap, Anthony leaned his head against the back of the chair. A slight rattle came from the ceiling, followed by a low hum. The HVAC unit had kicked on, pouring warm air into the chilled office.

"I'm sorry. Do you have somewhere else to be?" Victor asked incredulously.

"Wendy's missing," Anthony admitted, looking Victor dead in the eyes. His father's face was expressionless. Not a hint of glee or concern crossed his aged face.

"I need to find her," Anthony continued. "I need to know she's safe."

"What you need to do is forget about her. From this moment on, act as though you never met her and start educating yourself on how this operation functions." His father's voice was not cruel but firm.

Anthony's hands were clasped together on his lap. He bounced his right leg lightly. Heat rose from the pit in his stomach to the top of his scalp. A drop of sweat rolled down his left temple. Victor's eyes narrowed. Anthony's heart pounded in his ears. The silhouette of the woman filled his vision. Anthony squeezed his eyes shut and began muttering to himself.

"Shouldn't have done that. Shouldn't have done that. Shouldn't have done that." Victor had heard this same phrase multiple times from his son's lips.

"Move past this," came Victor's voice, "you did what needed to be done for the benefit of the family."

The woman's shape drew closer and closer to him. He had to warn her. She didn't deserve this! The lights before him finally reached her figure, and she froze, wide-eyed and mouth ajar. A scream came from her throat and pierced Anthony's ears…

SMACK!

Pain shot up Anthony's right cheek. Opening his eyelids, he saw his father standing over him. Anthony's eyes widened and filled with tears. Victor's face remained expressionless.

"The blood of the innocent is on all our hands, boy." Contempt crept into Victor's voice. "It's time you accept what you did and embrace it. So many more will die merely by the words uttered from your lips."

Anthony sat motionlessly. Giving no sign, he heard his father. Victor returned to the leather throne behind his desk.

"Now, I have tried to let you deal with this addiction on your own, but I can see it's time for me to intervene," Victor said. Anthony's left hand twitched slightly. "I will have Sam sequester you in your room for the next month. After that, we will return to this subject with new enthusiasm." Victor reached for his phone. "And do not concern yourself with your… redheaded friend anymore."

A few moments later, Sam entered the office and grabbed Anthony roughly by the arm. The two men exited the crimson room and walked down the hall to Anthony's room. Sam followed Anthony, making sure he would not try anything. The walls on either side of them were lined with photographs of the Sorelli family throughout the decades. Black and white stills of Anthony's great-grandfather and great-grandmother hung next to a color photo of Marco and Anthony S. Sorelli–Anthony's grandfather– in front of the newly constructed Cicero Hotel.

Further down the timeline was a framed picture of Anthony's eighty-year-old grandfather inside Crystal's Gentlemen's Club, a blonde on his right and a brunette on his left, both women topless. Finally, near the end was Anthony's favorite photo. It was of himself at eight years old, and arms wrapped lovingly around his mother's neck. She was gorgeous. Thick, black hair flowed down her head, reaching way past her shoulders. She had blue eyes that sparkled in the sunlight and a smile that could melt the coldest of hearts.

I miss you, mom, thought Anthony as he passed the framed memory. All at once, Anthony knew he couldn't stay here. He would not give in to his father so quickly. Not this time. Wendy was out there somewhere, and he was going to find her.

What about the drugs?!? His voice screamed in his skull. *We need the drugs now!*

They reached Anthony's room. Lifting his right arm as if to open the door, Anthony put his elbow into Sam's jaw. Sam's teeth came together with an audible Clack! Having no time to waste, Anthony spun, bringing his left elbow to bear against Sam's temple. Solid contact. Sam fell to the floor, stunned, his consciousness fleeting. Hastily, Anthony tore down the hall, through the living room, past the library, into the entrance atrium, and out the front door.

CHAPTER 11

Steadily, the ebony Charger cruised down the street, the afternoon sun warming its carbon fiber exterior. Det. Luke Burrows sat quietly in the passenger seat, staring out the tinted window, seatbelt sitting snugly across his torso. Traffic hummed along at a leisurely pace. Sharp, high-pitched squeaks randomly danced on his eardrums– vehicles needing brake replacements. A musky aroma filled the cab of the vehicle. Luke noticed the new, black-scented tree hanging from the car's rearview mirror. Outside, a woman about Luke's age was walking quickly down the sidewalk. Her blonde hair was tied up atop her head, and she wore jeans and a red overcoat. Clutching her right hand was a little girl, all bundled up to keep the cold air off her. They were on their way somewhere, and Luke wondered where to go. As he watched them, he imagined Emily holding the hand of what should have been their child, going to the pharmacy or the grocer, fulfilling the errands that the day demanded.

Motion in Luke's peripheral startled him from his trance. Swiveling his head slightly, he saw Mason had picked up his foam cup from the holder and sipped the contents through a straw. Fizzy brown liquid filled the plastic tube as Mason drank; tiny bubbles sporadically accompanied the caffeinated syrup. Mason sure does love his pop, Luke thought to himself. Straightening himself in the seat, Luke gazed out the windshield. A show of brake lights filled his view. Colors of blue, red, and beige blinked festively from the trunks and fenders of the cars and trucks lined up along the avenue as it stretched out before them. Mason sat his drink back into the cupholder. The clock on the radio read 4:54 P.M. Luke started to reflect on the past few hours of his day.

He and Mason had sifted through every missing person's report and come up empty-handed. Not one report matched Jane Doe's description. That had taken a good chunk out of the clock, and to Mason's chagrin, Maggie had not brought them anything for lunch. With their stomachs empty and having found no new leads, the two detectives had decided it was time to refuel themselves. Mason offered to drive them to one of his favorite local diners. The savory scent of cooked meat and frying oil saturated the air of the eatery. Seating themselves at a small table in the back of the mom & pop establishment, they waited to be served. A vivacious, older waitress called out her greeting from behind the busy counter, snaking her way around to bring them a pair of menus and let them know that Sarah would be with them in a jiffy. Sarah was one of Mason's current conquests. A cute girl in her upper twenties, she had curly brown hair and dimples on her cheeks, giving her a youthful charm. Mason smiled at her as she approached to take their orders.

Luke ordered his usual— a hamburger with no pickles, ketchup only for the sauce, and lemonade to drink. The meal came with a side of freshly made french fries. Mason had a bacon cheeseburger with everything on it, fries, and a small chocolate malt. While they ate, Mason insisted on shooting the bull.

"We can talk shop in a bit," Mason had said, "Let's talk about football, music, movies, anything but work."

Luke conceded, and they engaged in a lively debate over whether the Kansas City Chiefs had a chance at this season's Super Bowl. Having come from Kansas City, Mason was dead, certain they were going all the way. Luke was a Dallas Cowboys fan through and through, and, knowing his team had no shot at the title, prodded Mason about the Chiefs' poor defensive line and the fact that their first and second-string receivers were still out for injuries. Eventually, they moved on to movies. It had been over a year since anyone had been to see a film in a theater. The most recent film Luke remembered seeing that he had enjoyed was Netflix's The Highwaymen, which had come out over two years prior.

Simpler times…Luke's voice whispered to himself.

After the movie talk fizzled out, Luke decided it was time to discuss the murder case. The two men sat and discussed possible causes of death, motives, and suspects. Neither one could come up with a real probable theory without more information, namely the woman's identity. Officers had finished canvassing the neighborhood an hour earlier, and no one seemed to recognize their Jane Doe. Currently, the only real clue was the Cicero, which pointed to the Sorellis. Chief Reilly had expressly ordered them to steer clear of Victor and his son unless solid evidence presented itself. Luke leaned back against his seat, deep in thought.

"Let's go drop in on Doc," Luke began. "I'm sure she's still working on the body, but she's gotta have found something by now." Mason nodded and waved Sarah over to bring their check. He ordered a Coke to go and paid the bill with his card. Luke left a five-dollar bill on the table. As they were leaving, Mason gave Sarah a wink and a flirtatious smile; the girl's cheeks flushed red. She raised her hand, gave him a short smile, and waved in return.

Once back in the car, the sound of Mason's voice humming an undefinable tune brought Luke out of his reverie. Luke looked down at the radio clock, 4:57 P.M. Traffic was again moving, and Luke felt a slight lurch as Mason pressed down on the accelerator.

"You good?" Mason asked while tapping his fingers against the steering wheel to a rhythm only he could hear. "You were staring into space for a minute there."

"I'm fine." Luke responded, "Just thinking about the case." Then, somewhere up ahead, a driver honked his horn at somebody. "We're almost to the morgue. I'm sure Doc will have some insight for us," Mason assured.

Luke nodded in agreement. They drove for another six minutes before reaching the St. Louis Morgue. Mason pulled the charger into a parking spot at the end of a middle row beside an old Ford pickup. The two detectives hopped out of the car and walked to the entrance.

Luke and Mason found Dr. Melinda Wright in the examination room, sewing up the Y-shaped incision she had cut into Jane Doe's chest. Melinda's glasses were firmly secured to her face by rubber straps that reached around the back of her head. Her hair was tucked under a tight surgical cap to prevent strays from contaminating the evidence. An apron smeared with blood and bodily fluids graced Dr. Wright's torso over her green scrubs.

The room smelled of bleach and rubbing alcohol. Initially, both detectives stood silently, watching her work. There were three other stainless steel examining tables in the room; all three were empty. Huge fluorescent lights hung above each table, spotlighting anything that could be amiss. Body coolers lined the east wall, with thirty-eight lockers in total.

When she finished sewing the girl up, she wiped her forehead with the back of a gloved hand. Then, lifting her head toward the door, she finally saw the two men stoically watching her from afar.

"Gentlemen," she said as she removed the stained gloves from her hands. "What a surprise. What might you two be doing here?"

Luke and Mason strode toward her, their shoes covered with disposable shoe covers.

"I was coming to see if you were free for dinner tonight when Burrows asked to tag along," Mason said, smiling. Melinda gave him an amused look that said, 'you're gonna have to do better than that.'

"Brandon, I've been playing this game longer than you, and I can say with complete confidence you need to rethink your playbook," Dr. Wright countered.

"I'll be sure to do that," he conceded, with a playful smile still on his face.

"We're hoping you can tell us something that could help us out with this case," Luke interjected into their banter. They had reached the table, and the young woman lay between them, exposed under the harsh light.

"I haven't had a chance to dig through everything," Dr. Wright said, "but I'll tell you what I have figured out." She went to a set of drawers on the north wall and grabbed a white square. Returning to the examination table, she opened the square, revealing it as a sheet. Carefully, Dr. Wright covered Jane Doe's body and asked Mason to help move her into the cooler labeled 32, in large print on the shelf. Dr. Wright returned to the silver table and gave Luke a clipboard that listed her initial findings. Luke scanned the pages as Melinda spoke.

"I found no physical indications that she was held against her will," Melinda began. "The only bruising and signs of trauma were from her fall to the concrete. I took samples of blood, hair, skin, nail clippings, and stomach contents. I swabbed her nasal cavity, her mouth, and her ear canals. It has all been sent to William for analysis." Melinda's hands were resting on the sides of the table.

"Any indication of sexual assault?" Mason asked, trying to read over Luke's shoulder.

"None," Dr. Wright answered. "In addition to her manicured nails, her feet were meticulously groomed. She was strangely clean too, her body, I mean." Both men glanced at her waiting for elaboration. "The only trace of dirt or grime I found anywhere on her was where she made contact with the sidewalk."

"So, you still have yet to determine a cause of death?" Luke asked.

"Sadly, I have not. There are no tumors or aneurysms and no signs of massive internal bleeding. Nothing to indicate a broken neck, crushed windpipe, or cardiac arrest. If not for her demise's strange circumstances, I'd call it a natural-looking death."

Luke released a frustrated sigh and handed the clipboard back to Dr. Wright. "Still in square one," he muttered.

"I would only discount something once William finishes all of his tests. There could be something I can't detect just from looking."

"Thanks, Doc," Luke said, his mind already racing. "We'll get out of your hair." He turned to leave.

"See you later, Sweetheart. When this is over I'm taking you out for a drink." Mason threw out as he turned to follow suit. Melinda gave him a wry smile and shooed them out the door.

CHAPTER 12

Anthony sped away from his family's estate as fast as he could. Gravel flew into the air as the rubber tires clawed at the earth, trying to grab hold of something solid. The guard at the front gate was just barely quick enough to open the iron barrier before Anthony zoomed past him in the black town car. Needing to put as much space between himself and his father's search dogs, he took the first turn hard. The rear of the vehicle swung wide and skidded through the loose rock. Anthony straightened the wheels and tore down the pavement. His thoughts were a jumbled mess. On what mattered more at this moment, the war inside him raged.

Wendy! We must find Wendy! He urged himself.

NO!! We need the Oxy. If we don't get the drugs, we will fall into an irreversible state of delirium! The addiction countered.

That's crazy! We've been sober before!

You will be the death of us all!

Wendy is missing! She needs our help!

Eventually, his conscience beat out his selfish desires, but surely that clarity would not last forever. With the need to find Wendy and to avoid being found by his father's minions, he settled on a thin plan of action and pushed on toward the city. He slowed to the speed limit as he reached the city limits, not wanting to attract attention. Looking out, he could see the silhouette of the Gateway Arch looming above the metropolitan area. That's where he would go first.

Once he arrived at the Arch, Anthony parked the town car on the street and walked a few blocks away. He ordered an Uber to pick him up and take him to the library. His family's cars had GPS trackers that were only ever activated if the vehicle was used without authorization— which was his most significant reason for buying his Civic several years ago. The Uber dropped Anthony off at the library's entrance. He hopped out and walked over to the side parking lot, feigning casual so as not to draw attention. There was his Civic, parked just where he had left it. He reached under the fender near the driver-side rear tire and pulled out the small magnetic box holding his spare keys.

Anthony drove around town, stopping by some of his and Wendy's favorite haunts: restaurants they frequented, the movie theater they always went to when wanting to see the newest film, even the local mall, and still no sign Wendy had been to any of these places since the last time he saw her. As a final hail Mary, he returned to the hospital where she worked.

Nothing.

So, he ended up here, across the river, at an abandoned train yard. Wendy had brought him here for the first time seven months ago. They had walked the empty tracks for hours. Sometimes talking about their futures, the meaning of life, and Anthony's struggle with narcotics and other times, no word was said. Just the sound of their feet landing on gravel or wooden planks squealing beneath their weight. A faded green rail car stood open on one of the iron tracks. Anthony climbed inside and sat, legs hanging off the edge, remembering.

Anthony took a deep breath and held it for several seconds before exhaling. The old storage car smelled of aged wood and must. A thick layer of dirt and dust covered the floor of the vehicle. The light was fading, and the sun was almost gone, disappearing slowly beneath the horizon. His cell phone had died shortly after returning to his car at the library, so he had no idea of the time. This time of year, though, the sunset was around five-thirty in the evening. Goosebumps covered Anthony's arms; he had forgotten to grab his jacket when he left Wendy's this morning. He shivered as a gust of wind bit at his bare skin. Scooting backward onto his haunches, he retreated deeper into the train car. The worn, wooden walls blocked the breeze.

Where could she be? He asked himself. *She wouldn't leave without telling me.*

Darkness enveloped the train yard, the last rays of sunlight gone until morning. Anthony sat in the blackness, silent. Then, he heard an owl hoot outside.

Her disappearing can only mean something terrible has happened. Do you know who thrives off bad things happening? Dad. Dad does evil things and makes a living from it. But why would he do something to Wendy? To keep me here, to keep a hold on me. With Wendy gone, he is all I have… No, Dad knows I care for her. He wouldn't do that to me. Not to me… The many possibilities of what had caused Wendy's absence gripped his mind. For hours he went back and forth on positive and negative outcomes, who had been involved, and the why behind it all. Eventually, exhaustion took hold of him, and he slipped off into a deep slumber.

Hours later, he jolted awake, unsure of where he was. He looked around himself frantically. He was still in the train car. The night air had grown colder with the passage of time. Rubbing his eyes, Anthony picked back up on his internal deliberation on what he should do. Finally, with nothing to go on besides that she was missing, and his father didn't particularly like her, Anthony decided he needed help. A cold chill ran up his back. Only one man could help him find answers…

CHAPTER 13

Silently, the man stood in the shadows outside the parking lot of the Gateway Arch. The town car Anthony had taken when he made his brash escape was parked along the curb outside the lot. Anthony's departure from the estate was expected, but Anthony's brute force came as a surprise. He'd presumed the man would wait until dark and sneak out when everyone had gone to bed. But, instead, Anthony was as distraught and in the wind as he needed him to be.

A northerly gust of wind smashed against him, trying desperately to penetrate his dark overcoat. To his left, a stray cat waltzed out of an alley. Suddenly he was assaulted by the smell of rotting meat, cooked grease, and fermenting fruits. The wind had called in reinforcements from the surrounding dumpsters. He looked to the heavens. Light pollution made it barely possible to make out the tiny dots in the black sky. Finally, he decided to surrender to the wind and its putrid companion. Turning to his left, he began to walk back toward his car. Anthony would not be found tonight, and that was for the best. Rest was what he needed now. The return of daylight held many possibilities. His black shoes fell softly on the concrete with each step.

Once he reached his car, he opened the driver's door. The interior light above the dashboard remained off. He had removed the bulb earlier, not wanting to attract unwanted attention. Putting the key into the ignition, he turned it to the right, and the machine came to life. The head and taillights remained dormant until he was a few blocks away from the arch. He drove slowly, guided in the dark by the streetlamps above. Ahead, a stoplight changed from green to yellow to red. As he approached the scarlet light, he gently tapped the brake pedal. He sat at the light for an inappropriately long amount of time, seeing as there were no other cars on these two intersecting streets. Glancing at the radio, the clock read 1:12 A.M. Outside the passenger window, a homeless person lay asleep on a bus stop bench, wrapped in a dirty jacket and a nasty-looking hat.

Finally, the light switched from crimson to emerald. He lightly fed the motor gasoline, and the vehicle responded, as usual, with forward momentum. The ball was now in Tony's hands. Whatever he decided to do would need to be responded to appropriately for the plan to continue with as few hiccups as possible.

CHAPTER 14

Turning the key to unlock the door to his apartment, Luke was apathetic about coming home. There was a case to solve; a young woman appeared to be murdered. But he'd promised Mason that he would go home and get some rest. Reaching for the handle, he turned it and pushed open the door. Luke crossed the threshold, shut the door, and locked it behind him. He flipped the switch on the wall that signaled the bulb in the open dining area to ignite. Warm light filled the space, leaving shadows cowering in the living room and the back of the kitchen. It was a modest dwelling: one bedroom, one bath. The kitchen had plenty of storage space for food and cookware; his dining area was home to a brown wooden table with three matching chairs. The table was covered with unopened mail, coupon books for fast-food chains, and bills.

The living room held a small, black wooden coffee table. A forty-six-inch Vizio sat atop an entertainment center that matched the coffee table, and a tall silver lamp rested beside it. Luke had learned in college that most apartments do not include lights in their living room set-ups, so he had to scavenge a few mismatched ones of his own. Absolutely ridiculous; Luke had always thought about the inconvenience. Several different take-out containers from various local eateries lined the coffee table, each one with varying amounts of food still in them. The entire apartment had hardwood floors except for the bathroom; its floor was covered in white tiles held together with dark, brown lines of grout.

Luke tried to keep his home clean, but with no one to entertain anymore, it hardly seemed worth it on most days. Sure, there were dirty dishes in the sink and half-eaten meals in cardboard containers on the coffee table, but his counters were clean of grime, and he swept and mopped his floors once a week. Habits he had acquired when Emily was still alive and would come over multiple times a week.

Slowly, Luke made his way down the short hall to his bedroom. Flipping on the light, he walked over to his nightstand and placed the bottle he'd been holding on top of it. Mason had stopped by Walgreens and bought Luke the melatonin. The nightmares weren't every day anymore, but the sleep aid would help him fall into deep sleep faster than if he'd tried to naturally.

Luke unholstered his 9mm from his waist and sat it on the nightstand beside the bottle of melatonin. He needed a shower. He began to undress, carefully setting his father's coat over the footboard of his bed and letting the rest of his clothing fall to the hardwood floor. Exiting his room, he walked to the bathroom and turned on the water for the shower. Fifteen minutes later, Luke returned to his room, fresh and slightly more relaxed. He stepped to his dresser, opened the top drawer, and put on a pair of navy boxer briefs. Swiveling his eyes back and forth, Luke examined his room. White walls separated the space from the rest of the dwelling. His queen-sized bed extended from the center of the west wall, gray sheets lying unkempt on its mattress. Beside it, his dark nightstand sat rigidly. Across from his bed stood the black dresser housed his clothes within its four drawers. The closet door was open wide, and silhouettes of shirts and pants peered at him from the darkness. A white hamper stood next to the dresser, its mouth agape, articles of clothing hanging out of it and falling onto the ground below.

Luke walked to the end of his bed, bent down, and took his phone out of his pants pocket. Stepping back to the door, he cut off the circuit to the bulb illuminating his bedroom. Other than the thin lines of light from the streetlight outside his window, the darkness engulfed him. Carefully he walked to the nightstand and fumbled on the floor for the charging cable. Once it was in his hand, he placed the metallic end into the port on the bottom of his phone. The lock screen came to life, indicating the device was charging. Luke looked at the time, 11:55 P.M. He placed the phone on the nightstand. Reaching out, he felt for the plastic bottle. When he found it, he unscrewed the lid and dumped two pills into his hand. Popping them into his mouth, he choked them down and sat the bottle down. Crawling into the spring-filled mattress, Luke lay on his stomach, pulled one of the sheets over him, and let his head fall to the pillow below. He was unsure how long he remained conscious, but eventually, the supplements did their job, and Luke entered the throes of sleep.

Luke was frying an egg when the knock came at his front door. He went over and opened it. There she stood. Brown hair in curls, a denim jacket over a yellow top, wearing denim jeans. Her white teeth sparkled as she smiled up at him. Her emerald eyes were full of joy and hope. Emily.

"Are you going to invite me in or just leave me standing out here?" Her voice was soft and beautiful.

"Of course," Luke said clumsily. "Come in. I was making breakfast." She walked past him, her hips swaying from side to side. Luke's eyes followed their rhythm. The faint smell of strawberries wafted into his nose as she passed, her shampoo no doubt.

"What're you makin' me?" Emily asked, turning to face him. Luke shut the door and smiled at her as he returned to the kitchen.

"Eggs, bacon, and toast." He replied.

"Over medium?"

"Over easy."

She walked to the kitchen and breathed deeply.

"Who taught you how to cook?" Emily asked, eyeing him curiously.

"My mother," Luke said, focused on the eggs in the skillet.

Emily walked over to him and wrapped her arms around his waist. She pressed her face against his strong back and breathed deeply. She squeezed him gently.

Luke turned around, Emily's arms still around him. Emily's green eyes bored into his blue, yearning for him. Gently Luke caressed her chin with his left hand. He leaned down and kissed her softly on the lips. Emily reached up, placed her hand against his head, and pulled him in, returning his affection. Luke's left hand pressed against the small of her back and brought her close. He kissed her longer and deeper, the taste of mint transferring from Emily's mouth to his own. Breathing deeply, Luke began guiding her onto her back. The two of them began to fall, still embracing.

They landed softly onto Luke's bed, bouncing ever so slightly. They continued to kiss each other passionately. Emily ran her hands through Luke's short brown hair, gripping it gently. Luke ran his hands down her sides and burrowed them under her shirt, his calloused hands gliding over her smooth abdomen up to her breasts. Luke kissed Emily on the neck as she wrapped her legs around his waist. Her breath was warm against his left ear.

"I love you, Em," Luke whispered to her.

"I love you t.." She began, but her voice cut off. Her hands loosened their grip on his hair, and her legs seemed limp.

"Em?" Luke prompted. He looked at her face, it was pale, and the life in her eyes had gone out.

"Em..." Luke's voice was quivering, looking at her in the eyes, begging her to answer him.

"Emily!!" He screamed.

BOOM!!!

The sky roared from above, and white lightning flashed before his eyes.

The cold wind hit Luke in the face. He was holding her lifeless body in the middle of a dark street. He brushed a strand of hair from her face, and tears streamed down his cheeks. The heavens rumbled above and shot more blue-white bolts to the earth. Rain began to fall on him. Emily's beautiful face was red and scraped from hitting the pavement. The dark clouds opened wide, pouring rain onto the abandoned street.

"Em," Luke muttered through his sobs.

The sky answered with more monstrous drums of thunder. Luke was now soaked through his clothes from head to toe. His sobs were uncontrollable, his body shaking. Burying his head into Emily's neck, he let out a cry of anguish. The lightning illuminated the area around them.

The wind was harsh, pelting the rain against his skin. Above, the heavens bellowed deep, menacing notes as they sent more shards of electricity crackling through the dark. Turning his face to the sky, Luke let out an anguished scream.

"AAAAAHHH…"

Luke bolted upright, still screaming. Glancing around, he realized he was back home in his bed. He breathed in short deep breaths of air, his eyes wide. A cold chill ran up his back, and he shivered. Sweat soaked his body and drenched his sheets. Anger briefly flashed hot in his mind. Sorelli will pay for this, he thought.

Luke reached over and tapped the screen of his phone. 3:50 A.M. The anger gave way to grief and sorrow. Rolling onto his left side, Luke lay in bed and wept.

CHAPTER 15

     Victor was seated at the large dining table with a cup of black coffee in his hand. Smoothly, he brought the white ceramic mug to his lips and gulped the hot liquid. On the table in front of him sat a newspaper, opened to the crossword puzzle. He enjoyed these word games. He usually only ever got up to two words wrong. The current word he was stuck on was a nine-letter word for 'concoct .'Glancing at the spaces, he also noted the answer needed to start with the letter 'F .'Victor tapped the eraser end of his pencil against the newspaper. Suddenly it came to him. He took the pencil and wrote in the squares: A-B-R-I-C-A-T-E.

FABRICATE.

     Smiling to himself, Victor looked up at the grandfather clock. Its hands told him it was 6:38 A.M. Breakfast would be served in about forty-five minutes. Anthony had escaped Sam's custody yesterday afternoon and had taken off back towards the city. Sam apologized for his failure and promised to bring Anthony back. Victor presumed they came in sometime after he retired for the night. Victor would instruct Jonathon to take a tray to Anthony's room later.

     Why can't he understand, Victor thought. This is all for him. The boy had at one time worshiped Victor. Anthony would go on and on about how he wanted to take over the family businesses. But, after Isabella's death, Anthony seemed to have changed his mind. Victor had brought him back and reinvigorated his enthusiasm. Though now, ever since Victor ordered him to kill that woman, Anthony was lost again.

     Victor turned back to his crossword. An eleven-letter word for 'disgust' was the next clue. The spaces crossed the 'B' in fabricate and the 'I' in ancillary. Victor forced the lead in his hand to create the letters A, B, O, M, I, N, A, T, O, N.

ABOMINATION.

How could Anthony not see that if he didn't take charge and run this operation correctly, he could end up in prison, and all the family's wealth would go to the State? Victor asked himself. Everything his forefathers had built would be gone in a matter of moments.

The grandfather clock began to chime, signaling it was seven o'clock. Just then, the doors at the end of the dining hall swung open, and Jonathon came striding towards Victor. No tray was in his hand. Setting his pencil down on the newspaper, Victor gave Jonathon his full attention.

"I'm sorry to bother you, sir," Jonathan said.

"Not a problem Jonathon. Is everything alright?" Victor asked, curious.

"Mr. Hunter telephoned and requested I inform you that he could not locate Anthony last night and is resuming his search this morning," answered Jonathon. Victor gave a slight nod, and Jonathon retreated from the room.

CHAPTER 16

The station was pretty empty this early in the morning. The shift change wasn't for another hour. Three uniformed officers stood near the coffee maker, making small talk. Luke passed them when he arrived. He listened to the middle of their conversation about how Japanese cars would drown out Ford, GM, and Dodge within ten years. The other two officers shook their heads and pressed the first on his claims. Luke went to his desk and let the officers' conversation fade into background noise. Then, unbuttoning his overcoat, he surveyed his desk. Nothing had changed since he left last night. The stack of case files was still piled in the corner of the desk. His lamp remained dormant; the accumulation of missing person reports sat on the left side of the workstation.

He wrapped his coat over the back of his chair and reached down to turn on his computer. The program start-up notes sang to him, as the fans and gears inside the device came to life. On his monitor, the DELL logo appeared, and a small ring of dots began taking turns illuminating below it. Laughter erupted from the officers across the room and continued for another two minutes. The noise would die down and, all of a sudden, come roaring up again; they were unable to compose themselves. It had been a long time since Luke had laughed like that. Finding joy in life had been difficult since Emily had been taken from him.

He didn't know how, but Luke was certain Victor Sorelli was involved in her death. He'd spoken to Chief Reilly about it on several occasions. Reilly understood Luke's frustrations, anger, and reasons, but there was no physical evidence nor any witnesses to tie Sorelli to it. Luke had even tried interviewing the drunk driver. But, unfortunately, the man had been so wasted that he barely remembered entering his car. So even after Reilly assigned Charlie Wallace to be his partner, Luke secretly kept working on the Sorellis.

It hadn't been easy, and nothing much had come of it. Reilly had him and Charlie on so many back-to-back high-priority cases there seemed to be no time for any extracurricular inquiries. To all outside appearances, Luke had backed off the Sorellis, but Luke had been the one who called in the anonymous tip on Anthony Sorelli's drug possession. That also went bust. The young man had gotten off with a few months of community service.

Charlie had tried to counsel Luke through his grief and loss. He was a wise man, and Luke appreciated his mentorship. Then Charlie died of a heart attack in his sleep– a sad day for everyone in the SLMPD. Charlie had been there so long everyone thought he'd outlive them all. Luke cracked a smile, remembering Charlie telling the story of how he and Chief Reilly once went chasing after a suspect. The man had run into a car wash, and Reilly barreled in after him. "I went around the car wash to cut him off. I got the S.O.B., and Greg came a-tearing out of there, all drenched and covered in soap. 'You've never smelled better,' I told him." Charlie had recounted while laughing fitfully.

More officers had arrived at the station, either coming in to file their reports or showing up early for their shifts. The scent of brewing coffee filled the stale air. Glancing at his monitor, Luke noticed the login screen was waiting for him. Quickly, he moved in front of his chair and sat down. Placing his fingers on the keyboard, he typed in his password and hit 'ENTER .'A small circle appeared and began to spin. Luke leaned back and waited for the home display to fill the pixels before his eyes. Once it appeared, Luke checked to see if he'd received any new emails. There were seventeen unread messages. Most of them were of little importance at the moment, except for one. This message was from Crime Scene Investigator William Johnson. It was sent to both Luke and Mason. In it, Will detailed his initial findings. It read as follows:

To: Luke Burrows; Brandon Mason
From: William Johnson
Subject: Case No. 5123 Initial Findings

Case No. 5123

Jane Doe, approximately 30 years of age, was found with a road rash on her left arm, forehead, and knees. Dirt and particles found inside the wounds match samples taken at the scene. Her blood alcohol level was zero percent. The contents of the victim's stomach contained traces of a protein bar. Most likely consumed hours before her death. The chemical makeup of the lavender scent found on the deceased suggests it is from a homemade perfume. The victim's fingerprints are not in the federal or Missouri criminal or firearm registry databases. There were no fingerprints or foreign fibers found on the victim. The chemical analysis of the hair samples taken from the victim indicates her hair had been recently washed. The remaining blood tests and tox screens show the cause of death was a morphine overdose.

Luke stared at his screen, reading and re-reading every word of the email. There was still no clear motive or suspect pool, but they did have a cause of death. Morphine overdose. Opiates like that are high-end and hard to come by without a prescription.

It makes sense with how groggy and unsteady she appeared on the security footage, Luke thought to himself.

"Heads up, Burrows!" A voice echoed from behind Luke.

Spinning in his seat, Luke was just barely able to throw up his hands and catch the round form flying at his head. It was a food wrapper with food still inside it. The wrapping paper had the restaurant logo stamped all over it.

"Thought you could use some breakfast," Mason said as he walked past Luke. He placed a cup of fresh coffee on Luke's desk and sat at his desk across from him.

Luke unwrapped the package to find that it was a sausage biscuit. The aroma filled his nostrils and ignited his hunger. Mason whistled at him. Luke glanced up just as his partner threw him a packet of grape jelly.

"Thanks," Luke said, grateful for the fuel for his body.

"No problem. I figured you were already here. You always beat me to the station," Mason mused before taking a bite of his biscuit, stacked with sausage, egg, cheese, and bacon.

"I always beat you no matter where we're supposed to meet."

"Touché," Mason conceded.

Luke set the biscuit on his desk and removed the top. Then, carefully, he ripped open a corner of the jelly packet and squeezed its innards onto the sausage patty. Replacing the top of the biscuit, Luke picked up the sandwich and took a bite. The sweetness of the jelly complimented the sausage and the bread perfectly. After swallowing his first bite, he informed Mason about the email they had received from Will.

"Morphine?" Mason questioned through a mouthful of protein and carbs.

"That's what Will's tests have concluded." Luke took another bite of his breakfast.

"So, she's a junkie."

"I don't think so. Why was she naked? Why does no one around that area know who she is?" Luke queried.

Mason shrugged. Reaching down, he picked up a foam cup and took a sip of the dark, hot coffee. "I don't know. Maybe she was broke and desperate for a high, so she slept with her dealer. Then, after taking too much, she's out of it, walks outside, and eventually ends up outside the Cicero."

Luke's eyes narrowed as he took the last bite of his biscuit. He crumbled up the wrapping and tossed it into the trash can beside his desk. Swallowing the food, he picked up the cup of coffee and took a swig.

"That's pretty thin," Luke said.

"Unless we figure out who she is, this is all we have."

"True enough," Luke agreed, letting out a small sigh. He wanted her, no, needed her, to be connected to the Sorellis. They had gotten away with murdering Emily, and Luke refused to let them stay free any longer than absolutely necessary. Leaning forward, he brought up the security recording of Jane Doe's final moments and began watching intently.

Mason finished his breakfast and brushed his hands together, knocking away any crumbs that clung to his fingers. Next, he bent down and turned on his computer. Then, rising to his feet, he looked at Luke.

"I'm gonna hit the head. Don't solve the case without me." With that, he turned and walked away.

Luke gave no sign he heard the man. He was focused. Sure, he had watched the tape at least ten times yesterday, but he was determined to find anything he could use. Here she comes, he narrated, stumbling and groping the air. There she goes, falling to the ground. No shadows pass over her, no glints of light behind her.

Again. He rewound the tape.

Stumbling, groping, falling, dead.

Again.

Stumbling, groping, falling, dead.

AGAIN.

STUMBLING. GROPING. FALLING. DEAD.

Luke leaned back against his chair and rubbed his eyes. Nothing here, just like yesterday. Shame crept into Luke's soul. He knew there was nothing to find, but he so desperately wanted there to be something.

Removing his hands from his eyes, he saw Mason had returned and was staring at him. Mason didn't say anything, just gazed solemnly at him. Luke looked away towards the clock hanging on the wall. 7:54 A.M.

The noise in the station seemed to grow considerably as officers paraded out of their briefing with Chief Reilly. Mason had begun logging into his computer when Luke saw Reilly heading straight for them. His expression was grim. The snowy white mustache and goatee on his face even looked downcast. The light blue button-down shirt he wore was nice and starched. The khaki pants covering him from the waist down were likewise impeccable. The chief's large hands were shoved deep into his pants pockets.

"Mason. Burrows." Reilly greeted them, his gruff voice echoing around the small space. "Any update on our Jane Doe?"

"William says his tests conclude that she died of a morphine overdose," Mason answered, swiveling in his seat to face Reilly.

"Interesting." Chief Reilly murmured to himself while shifting his eyes around the room. "Mayor Tyler called me yesterday after you two had left my office," Reilly began, "He is insistent on closing this case within the next seventy-two hours." Reilly coughed slightly as he finished the sentence.

Luke and Mason glanced at each other with surprise. Unless they got a break in the investigation, they weren't sure it could be done.

"The mayor needs to understand that we can't make deadlines like that," Luke said.

"Yeah, this is police work, not car manufacturing," Mason added.

Shaking his head slightly, Chief Reilly looked at the two men before him. "I know, and I will do my best to keep him at bay. Mayor Tyler is nervous because the girl was found outside the Cicero, and Victor Sorelli most likely funded his campaign."

Luke rolled his eyes and scoffed.

"Just keep me updated on any new developments," Reilly said before he turned and walked back to his office.

Mason shook his head and turned his attention to his monitor. Luke closed down the surveillance video, opened the tab to his email account, and began to go through it again. Nothing was heard but voices in the various conversations throughout the rest of the office. The smell of the coffee from his cup called to him. Luke picked it up and drank deeply. Soon, an older female officer approached them.

"Detective Burrows?" She asked.

"Yes, ma'am," Luke answered, curious about what she needed. She shifted on her feet before responding. "There's someone here who insists on speaking with you."

Luke narrowed his eyes, trying to think of who it could be. "Who is it?" he finally asked.

She paused slightly before giving her answer.

"Anthony Sorelli."

CHAPTER 17

The police station foyer was bustling with officers leaving for patrol, officers bringing in culprits, and civilians milling about, waiting to fill out reports for all sorts of offenses. Anthony sat in a chair against the wall, across from the reception desk. The female officer he had spoken with had left and asked him to wait here for her return. Presumably, she was going to see if Detective Burrows was here and if he had time to speak with him. Anthony didn't like waiting. He needed to find Wendy. The air smelled of body odor and dirt. It wasn't a faint smell either; it constantly assaulted his senses. Reaching up, he grabbed his blue shirt, lifted it to his nose, and sniffed. Instantly he recoiled– the awful smell was him. He'd been in such a state; he had left the train yard and came straight here. Anthony couldn't remember the last time he had taken a shower. It had to have been at least two days ago. A thin layer of dirt and dust covered his clothes, skin, and hair from his night in the train car.

An officer entered the station with a young man in handcuffs. The perpetrator was begging the cop to let him go. "I won't do it again," he was saying. The lawman ignored him and sat the kid in a chair while he went to the desk to grab some forms. Anthony looked at the kid. Caucasian, he noted. He couldn't be more than nineteen years old. The kid was wearing a gray hoodie with black jeans with a hole in one knee. His ears were pierced and held small stud earrings in the lobes. Anthony didn't know if this was the kid's first offense, but how the cop treated him didn't matter. The young hooligan sat with his head hung low, staring into the tile floor. So why was this kid here? Anthony thought. Does he work for my father in some way, down at the bottom of the food chain? Anthony couldn't be sure, but if he did, it wasn't likely Victor would shell out the family's legal team for this pup.

Voices hummed around the waiting area; phones rang, the sound of shoes walking on the floor, and distorted mumblings came from radios on police officers' shoulders. Anthony wasn't sure how long he'd been sitting here, but it felt like an eternity. He was keenly aware that some of the people employed here also worked for his father and would report that he was here if they hadn't already. But, unfortunately, time was not on his side. Then, like an answer to an unspoken prayer, the female officer he had spoken with returned. Rising to his feet, Anthony walked to the desk.

"Detective Burrows will speak with you," she said.

*   *   *   *

Anthony Sorelli was in a disheveled state. The man was covered in grit and grime, and he stank. He was about as rank as any dumpster Luke had ever walked past before. Anthony was near Luke's age, and it amazed him at their differences. Luke is on the side of law and order— clean and respectable. Anthony, on the side of lawlessness— dirty, feared. Both were products of their upbringings. Looking at Anthony now, though, sitting in that chair, fear lacing his hazel eyes, Luke pitied the man. He hadn't ever thought of Anthony as a victim, but maybe he was.

A vision of his father, Henry Burrows, screaming at him and his mother, with a bottle of bourbon, gripped tightly in his left hand, flashed in Luke's mind. We don't get to choose our fathers, Luke thought. Mason had plopped himself down on the corner of Luke's desk, one foot swinging slightly above the floor. Anthony's eyes darted about the room; his hands were clasped on his lap.

"You've got to help me, detective," Anthony pleaded, his voice barely above a whisper.

This piqued Luke's curiosity even more than it already was. He leaned forward in his seat.

"Help you with what?" Luke asked genuinely. Anthony bowed his head and was silent for a moment. Then, raising his head, he looked Luke square in the eyes.

"My girlfriend has gone missing," Anthony began. Luke shot a quick look at Mason behind him. Mason's left eyebrow had raised a bit at that. "She didn't come home the other night, and she's not answering my calls or texts. No one around town has seen her in a couple of days." Anthony's voice was beginning to quiver.

"Do you have a photo of her?" Mason asked. Inserting his right hand into his pants pocket, Anthony brought out a cell phone.

"I do, but my phone died, and I haven't thought about charging it," Anthony stated.

"I have a charger here at my desk," Luke said. "You can plug it in here if you like." Opening his hand, Luke extended it toward Anthony. Reluctantly, Anthony placed the device in the detective's hand. Luke turned and plugged in the phone. Then, tapping his keyboard to wake up his computer, Luke spoke. "Can you give us her name and description?" Small clicks erupted from the keyboard as Luke pulled up the database.

"Um, yea," Anthony started, his voice calming somewhat. "Her name is Wendy Grayson. She's a nurse at Memorial Hospital. She has red hair and freckles. She's twenty-nine, probably about five-six or five-seven. Um, maybe a hundred and thirty pounds."

Luke tried his best to hide his facial expression from Anthony. His description matched their Jane Doe to a tee. As Luke typed in her name, watching as profiles appeared before him, he found one with a picture that resembled the woman he was looking for. It was a Facebook profile, and the photo was several years old, but it could be her. Moving out of Anthony's view, he motioned to the screen.

"Could this be her?" Luke asked. Mason remained silent as a grave. Anthony came close to the monitor and stared intently at the image illuminated on the screen.

"It's possible," Anthony said before returning to the chair they had offered him.

For a full minute, no one said anything. Luke wasn't sure how to proceed. On the one hand, this could be a significant breakthrough for the case, proving that the Sorelli family was involved. On the other, this could all be a coincidence, and the woman they had found dead yesterday wasn't Anthony's girl after all—and Luke couldn't let anyone perceive he was influencing Anthony's identification of the body. The fastest way to move this thing was to have Anthony taken to the morgue to I.D. Jane Doe.

"I'm going to be straight with you, Mr. Sorelli," Luke said with sympathy. " The body of a young woman was found early yesterday morning..."

Anthony's eyes widened, and tears began to form in them.

"What do you mean 'the body'?" Anthony interrupted. "Was she dead?"

"Her description matches that of Wendy Grayson," Luke finished.

Anthony was distraught. Tears sprung from his eye sockets, and his face crumpled before hardening into a tense mask. Luke was sure the man had considered the possibility before coming here, but most people always hold onto hope for as long as their souls will allow them.

"No, that can't be her." The dark-haired man was saying, his voice defiant. "That has to be somebody else. Wendy is missing, an..an..and I came here so that you could help me find her. Alive," he added, pointing his left index finger stiffly at Luke.

Luke looked at Mason; the man's face was solemn. Of course, Anthony could be right, this could not be her, but they had to be sure. Standing to his feet, Luke stepped to Mason.

"You need to take him to the morgue to identify the body," directed Mason, who nodded his agreement.

"What are you going to do?" Mason asked.

"I'm going to call Doc and ask her to try and find Wendy Grayson's dental records and see if we can match those to the x-rays she took to cover our bases. Then I'm going to dive deeply into Miss Grayson to see what I can find out."

"And if it's not her?" Mason asked skeptically.

"Then Wendy Grayson will still be missing, and whatever I learn will hopefully aid in finding her," Luke replied. Mason looked over Luke's shoulder at the mess of man beyond. Anthony leaned over, his head in his hands, muttering to himself.

"Alright," Mason began, "but if it is her, we're going to have an even bigger predicament on our hands."

"How so?" Luke asked, frowning.

"Because I can only think of one person that would dare kill anyone involved with the Sorelli family."

Luke's eyebrows arched with understanding as he began to put the pieces together.

"Another member of the Sorelli family, and there's only one more of them."

CHAPTER 18

Anthony was lost in his mind as he sat in the passenger seat of the black Dodge Charger. Det. Brandon Mason was taking him to the city morgue to identify Wendy's body possibly. Neither man spoke as they drove through the bustling streets. Even the slightest possibility that the woman they found could be Wendy made his stomach turn. He didn't want it to be her, and who would? Nobody would like to see themselves where Anthony is right now.

Staring out the tinted window to his right, Anthony didn't recognize anything outside. Shapes resembling human beings journeyed up and down the sidewalk, some carrying things, others looking into the computer bricks they seemed to carry with them at all times. The buildings, made of wood, metal, brick, and mortar, were nothing more than backdrops for the scene beyond the glass. A high-pitched screech pierced his ears as Detective Mason engaged the brake pads as they approached a red light.

Frigid air stormed into the vehicle from the cracked windows. The detective had rolled down all four windows about half an inch before they ever left the police station. Anthony didn't blame the man. The stench radiating from Anthony's pores was foul and pungent. Being so focused on finding Wendy and his internal battle over opiates, personal hygiene hadn't even made a cameo in his thoughts. The car began to progress again, with each rubber rotation on the pavement bringing Anthony closer and closer to an answer. All the possibilities played in his mind repeatedly. Shards of fear stabbed into his soul, sometimes blocked by shields of hope, mostly ripping those shields to shreds. Wendy couldn't be dead. Why would she be dead? Everybody loves her. Dad doesn't. Dad wouldn't do this to me. Maybe she went home to Oklahoma. Why didn't she tell me? What if she's been kidnapped? Why are there no ransom demands?

Perhaps this is revenge for what you did, and a small voice cut into his rambling thoughts. A flash of the woman's silhouette filled his mind briefly. Anthony shook his head and leaned back against the leather seat. He needed to get to the morgue and find out once and for all if this dead woman was Wendy.

* * * *

While researching Wendy Grayson, Luke found a payment to a local dentist's office in her credit card statements. After calling Dr. Wright to give her the new information, he resumed digging. Wendy Grayson had no criminal record and had recently moved to St. Louis from Oklahoma. Anthony Sorelli had told Luke she was a nurse. Luke also found this to be true. Wendy's social media presence was sparse– strange for anyone today, but Luke's social media accounts were bare. She had a Facebook account that looked to not have been updated in at least four years, no Twitter, and an Instagram account with few more recent posts than Facebook. Luke could find nothing pointing to why anyone would want her dead. Outside of the fact that she was apparently in a relationship with the son of a crime lord, she seemed to be an ordinary, law-abiding citizen. On a hunch, Luke retrieved Wendy's phone records. Her text messages held nothing to indicate anything mischievous, and there were no calls or texts to any burner phones that he could see. However, her phone's GPS went offline at 11:38 P.M. two nights ago, just outside the hospital where she worked. Bill Watts walked past Luke's desk, emitting a thick smell of cigarettes from every fiber of his clothing. Luke never understood how anyone could immerse themselves into something so rotten. Returning his attention to his screen, Luke decided to investigate the specifics of Anthony Sorelli's drug charges. Even though he was the one who had turned Anthony in, he never knew what exactly the man's drug of choice was.

According to the initial report, Anthony was arrested for illegally possessing one-hundred milligrams of Oxycodone and one hundred and thirty milligrams of morphine. That caught Luke's eye. Perhaps after his initial bust, Anthony had needed to change suppliers and, at some point, started a relationship with this nurse so that she could steal pharmaceuticals for him. What if Victor kidnapped and killed her with the same drugs she was supplying his son? The question planted itself in Luke's mind, digging its roots deep. Even with all the vices the Sorelli family peddled to anyone that could afford them; Luke had never heard of the Sorellis themselves participating in this dirty underworld. He was confident they did, though surely it was behind closed doors guarded by a hydra of lawyers.

A belt of laughter erupted from across the room. Glancing up from his computer, Luke turned his head toward the sound. Detective Watts was cackling hysterically next to the water cooler. Standing beside Watts was Detective Brian Adams, a smile on his face. Luke was unsure what would cause the man to bellow like that, but whatever it was, Watts loved it. Setting his arm on his desk, Luke began tapping his index finger against the treated wood. Mason could be right; Victor Sorelli could very well have ordered the murder of their Jane Doe if she was the missing Wendy Grayson.

"Detective Burrows."

Luke immediately recognized the voice coming from behind him. Closing his eyes briefly, Luke prepared himself for the man he was about to face. Slowly rising to his feet, Detective Burrows turned around to find his suspicions were correct. Before him stood David Quentin, attorney for the Sorelli family. The older man stood eye to eye with Luke with a stone-faced expression. Quentin stood straight and tall, determined to have what he came for.

"How can I help you, Mr. Quentin," Luke said, apathy weaved into his tone.

"Where's my client?" Quentin asked.

"Which one?" Luke prodded. "You've been here many times, representing so many different people; I was beginning to think you were a public defender," Quentin smirked at the jab.

"You know which one."

Luke put his hands in his pockets and shrugged his shoulders. But, of course, he knew why Quentin was here. One of his rats informed him that Anthony was at the station, and not only at the station but conversing with Detective Luke Burrows. The very detective who relentlessly went after the Sorelli family. After about ten seconds of silence, Quentin finally spoke again.

"Anthony Sorelli, where is he?" Irritation had crept into Quention's vocal cords.

"He's not here," Luke admitted, giving no more information. Quentin pointed to the hallway behind Luke.

"Are you holding him in one of your interrogation rooms? Did you even inform him of his right to an attorney?" The lawyer began moving past Burrows toward the hall. Grabbing Quentin by the arm, Luke stopped him in his tracks.

"He's not there, Mr. Quentin. He's not anywhere in this station." The detective and the attorney locked eyes for a solid five seconds. Luke released the man's arm and turned to face each other again. Mason had the brilliant idea of taking Anthony through that hallway, towards interrogation, and out the back, hoping to confirm their suspicions. The scheme had worked. Whoever the informant was, they didn't know Anthony was gone; otherwise, Quentin wouldn't be here demanding to see his client. He would have come in and quietly waited for Mason to return with Anthony. The attorney let out a slight sigh.

"If he's not here, then where is he?" Quentin asked impatiently.

"I haven't the slightest notion," Luke lied. But, of course, he convinced himself it wasn't all a lie. He knew Anthony had left with his partner, and he knew where they were going, but he had no idea where Anthony was at this very moment. Quentin narrowed his eyes and glanced about the room.

"Do you mind if I go and have a look for myself?"

"Not at all." Luke escorted the well-dressed man through the station, opening every door demanded of him and making sure to let him search the men's and women's bathrooms and locker rooms. After finding no evidence that Anthony Sorelli was in the building, Quentin resigned.

"If you happen to see him again," he began, even though Luke never admitted to seeing Anthony, "tell him to call me."

With that, David and Quentin exited the station. Luke let out a breath and sat in his chair behind his desk. Turning around, Luke noticed Anthony's cell phone charging on the worktable. Silently, he let out a curse. He wasn't sure the lawyer had seen it, but this could turn ugly sooner than expected if he had.

*   *   *   *

Stainless steel tables stretched across the medical examiner's room, seeming never to end. Anthony had never been here before, and, standing here now, he never wanted to return. The room felt dark, even under the fluorescent lights. The ascetic scent of alcohol filled the air, sterilizing his nose hairs. Anthony stood next to Detective Mason while waiting for the medical examiner to appear.

Brandon Mason was about two to three inches shorter than Anthony. Anthony was above average height, six foot three inches the last time he measured. The detective was dressed in a maroon button-down shirt and black pants. The collar button on his shirt was undone. They stood before a wall of stainless-steel doors, each bearing a number and a silver handle. Anthony's heart thudded in his ears. Since they had entered this room, each pump of blood seemed to grow louder and louder. Unconsciously, Anthony began tapping his foot on the hard floor. His patience was beginning to wear down. Surely they called and informed the medical examiner before we left, Anthony thought.

As if he had said it out loud, shoes echoed down the hallway in response. Looking toward the sound, he saw an older woman, mid-forties at least, walking in their direction. She was tall for a woman and had gray streaks in her brown hair. She was wearing a white coat over her blue blazer and black pants; the name on the coat read: Dr. Wright. Detective Mason gave her a curt nod, and she returned the gesture.

"Are we ready?" She asked, her voice calm. She turned her eyes to Anthony, and he noticed the detective was also staring at him. He looked at her and nodded twice. Anthony's heart began racing, drumming so loudly in his chest that he thought the two standing near him surely could hear it. His breathing became short, and anxiety rose in his chest, threatening to burst from beneath his skin. Dr. Wright raised her hand and gripped the shiny handle of the door labeled thirty-two. She opened the stainless-steel sarcophagus with a crack and pulled the sliding table drawer out.

There below him on the cold surface lay the shape of a human being covered from head to toe with a crisp, white sheet. Anthony's cardiac system seemed to go into overdrive, which he had thought was already happening. Gently, the doctor lifted the sheet with both hands and uncovered the person's face, revealing the young woman just below the throat. Anthony's breath caught in his chest.

It was her. It was Wendy.

A cry soared from his throat, and he lunged forward; the detective was on him before he reached her.

"I'm sorry, Mr. Sorelli, but you can't touch her." The detective was saying to him. Anthony fell to his knees, sobs wracking his body. Streams of saltwater tore down both of Anthony's cheeks.

"WENDY!" Anthony cried, his wails echoing through the room. He could barely see through the tears.

"I'm so sorry, sir," came the doctor's sweet voice. She covered Wendy's face and returned her to her tomb. Dr. Wright politely walked away, retreating into the other room to her other duties. Detective Mason bent down and embraced the rank, dirty, hurting man. Anthony buried his face into Mason's shoulder and sobbed.

CHAPTER 19

Victor Sorelli ended the phone call he was having with Sam Hunter. Sam had been out yesterday afternoon and, presumably, all last night looking for Anthony. With no luck, he'd resumed his search this morning. Victor had eaten today's breakfast–which consisted of two sausage patties, a buttermilk biscuit, two over-medium chicken eggs, and a cup of black Colombian coffee–while waiting for Sam's report. After breakfast, he'd retreated to his office to begin dealing with the issues of today.

Before sitting at his desk, Victor stepped to the table against the east wall and lit a stick of incense, filling the room with its woody aroma. In the midst of all the family drama that had transpired, Victor still had an empire to run. A couple of his drug dealers had been pinched by the cops. One man was a loyal hound that Victor relied on, so he ordered Quentin to send someone down to get him off. The other man, really a boy, no more than twenty years old, was of little consequence and could not be directly linked to Victor's operations.

Nevertheless, the poor sap would serve his time, and if he sniffed around Victor's business again, he would serve time for eternity. There was also some trouble with one of the girls at the club– a john had taken things too far, and she needed medical attention. Victor had no problem paying for the girl's medical bills. However, the man that beat her would compensate Victor for the money spent. If he refused, he'd end up eating through a tube in the hospital.

Sam's phone call had come just after Victor had finished giving orders to the man running the gentlemen's club. Plucking the phone off his desk, he answered it hoping for good news. He was disappointed. Sam had found his son's car two blocks from the police station. Victor couldn't fathom the idea of Anthony willingly going to the cops. Surely, they had found him in his car, high as a kite, and had taken him into custody again. Sam told Victor that he had waited outside the station to see if Anthony had emerged from the building. While he waited, he saw David Quentin pull up to the station and exit his car. Quentin entered the building and exited fifteen minutes later with no Anthony.

Jumping out of his car, Sam said he went to talk to the lawyer. Quentin told Sam that he had received a call from one of his informants that Anthony was seen speaking with Detectives Burrows and Mason this morning inside the station. The attorney had promptly made his way to the police station to try and figure out what was going on and to get Anthony out of there. However, unbeknownst to him, Anthony had left. Quentin's informant never saw him leave the building. Strangely enough. Quentin told Sam that he would stick around this part of town if Anthony returned to the cop house. Sam returned to his car and made the call to Victor. Victor told him to return to the mansion and let the attorney handle the law enforcement officers.

Victor's head was reeling from this information. Anthony had been spotted conversing with detectives and had somehow disappeared from the police station without a trace. If he'd been picked up on another possession charge, Quentin would've found him being interrogated for information about Victor—especially with Detective Burrows on the case. But instead, the man was unyielding in his pursuit to destroy Victor and his empire. Leaning back in his leather chair, Victor stretched his right arm out and tapped his desk with his fingers.

Victor had received a phone call yesterday from the night manager of the Cicero. A body had been discovered just outside the front doors of the hotel. Victor pressed the man for details, but he hadn't had many. All he had known was that it was a young woman. If Detective Burrows was trying to link him to this dead girl with the sheer fact that she was outside his hotel, Burrows was more desperate than Victor had imagined. Anthony's concern for his missing woman would surely bring him to the detective's attention, but the girl had no friends or family in the area, so Anthony was the only one who could report her missing.

Victor shook his head. It was all preposterous. Even if Anthony reported her as missing, and even if the woman they found was identified as Anthony's girl... His thoughts trailed off as he came to the realization that this could incur more damage than he originally conceived. Hopefully, all of this was just a coincidence. Hopefully, the woman found outside his hotel was just some runaway or prostitute. But, if it happened to be Miss Grayson, Victor would have words with Mr. Hunter.

CHAPTER 20

As he entered the coffee shop, he couldn't help but be in awe of Anthony's audacity. He'd anticipated Anthony going to the police, but this wasn't even close to the top five moves he thought Tony would make. The beverage shop was packed with people here to grab a cup of caffeine, maybe a breakfast croissant, before heading off to their different occupations.

Some patrons remained inside the establishment on laptops, either operating remotely or working on a college assignment. Several tables remained empty since most left after receiving their beverage.

Under his right arm, he carried a newspaper. Three people were in front of him in line: two women, one young and the other approaching middle age, and between them, a young man with red hair and glasses. The younger woman was at the counter ordering some ridiculous half espresso and half macchiato concoction. That included; three pumps of vanilla, one teaspoon of creamer, soy milk - NOT regular milk- (she was adamant about that), shaken, not stirred, and a partridge in a pear tree. The man behind the register nodded, pressing buttons, and typing away in a muddled attempt to keep up with this patron's requests. The others before him in line were glued to their cell phones. It baffled him, always had. People missed out on real human interaction for what? He hadn't the foggiest idea. It could be because social media made people feel like their lives meant something. The constant likes and retweets, follow, and shares boost their self-esteem more than reality ever could. They can become famous in their little virtual bubbles, where everyone is the center of their worlds. So, what has society come to? Self-indulgence on a whole new level, not of the flesh, but of the mind. It made him sick.

The older woman was ordering now, and another man had joined the line behind him. Behind the counter, the employees were scrambling, making drinks as fast as possible and hopefully making them correctly. None of them wanted to deal with some middle-aged woman with short hair screaming at them for making it wrong and demanding a new drink. It always seemed to be middle-aged women that made scenes like that. Finally, he'd made it to the register. His order was a simple black coffee with milk. He could see the relief on the young cashier's face as he asked for his name. Giving the cashier an alias, he stepped to the side to wait on his hot drink. He inhaled deeply. The smell of coffee beans was intoxicating. The number of inhabitants has dwindled since many have left for work. About ten people were seated at the various tables, all on some electronic device, except for two older gentlemen playing chess against the far wall. Finally, his alias name was called out from the bar. Stepping over to the counter, he grabbed the cup and walked to an empty table in one of the far corners of the room. Sitting down, he took a sip of his coffee and opened the newspaper he'd been carrying. The front-page headline read:

Woman Found Dead Outside Cicero Hotel

The memory of that night flooded back to him, how he'd waited for her outside the hospital. He'd taken her at gunpoint and forced her into her car. He made her drive to the outskirts of town, where a hunting cabin stood solo in the woods. Aiming the gun at her, he told her to enter the structure. Once inside, he made her ingest a small dose of morphine to keep her dazed. After she succumbed to the meds' effects, he began manicuring her hands and feet. Once he finished that, he undressed her and led her to a small bathtub, where he washed her. He gave her another small dose of the drug and dried her off. Then, gently, he began putting drops of a homemade lavender perfume on her. Examining her, he understood why Anthony liked her so much. She was an exquisite creature. Smart, too, a registered nurse. He had no idea what she saw in a pathetic chump like Tony Sorelli. Carefully he picked her up and carried her to the car, where he laid her in the back seat. He drove back to town and stopped on the dark street several blocks away from the Cicero. Guiding her to her feet outside the car, he brushed her off, making sure there were no foreign fibers or other particles that could be traced back to himself or the cabin, and forced the remaining morphine down her throat. He told her to walk straight; once she reached the hotel, she could only ask for help. He'd returned to the car's driver's seat, reversed several more blocks, and parked in the shadows.

He smiled and turned the page to see what else was newsworthy. Nothing else really caught his interest, some story about Mayor Tyler's new public park project, another about a local high school football coach signing a deal with the university. The comic strip was a Garfield short. He'd always enjoyed Garfield. He knew that he should be getting back, but after the past couple of days he had, he deserved a little rest before he went back to work. A loud shattering of glass filled the coffee shop, and a young woman muttered a curse. Everyone looked to see what had caused the disturbance. An employee had dropped some cylinder she was trying to use for some reason.

His thoughts returned to Anthony. Even though he'd pitched a curveball going to the cops as he did, the man had prepared himself and planned to hit this one out of the park like any other. He took another sip of his coffee and continued with his morning paper.

CHAPTER 21

Detective Luke Burrows and Detective Brandon Mason stood staring at each other outside the men's locker room of the St. Louis Police Station. The muffled sound of men's voices, running water, and metal doors swinging open and shut came from beyond the doorway between them. Off-white walls stretched out on either side of the two detectives, creating a six-foot-wide hallway. The putrid odor of Anthony Sorelli was now glued to Mason. Luke tried not to imagine how badly their car now smelled. Mason had recently returned to the station with Anthony Sorelli after the man had identified the female corpse as Wendy Grayson. The two men reentered the building through the same back door they had left, and a distraught Anthony was escorted to the locker room and instructed to shower. Mason offered him some of the spare clothes he kept in his locker. Luke didn't have a chance to see Anthony before he'd been exiled to the washroom. Looking deep into Mason's eyes, Luke could tell he felt sympathy for Anthony. A shadow seemed to cast itself over Mason. His lips frowned slightly, and an aura of sorrow seeped from deep in the man's soul.

Mason believed Anthony to be innocent of this crime. Luke didn't blame the man; seeing anyone lose a loved one is heart-wrenching. Having lost the love of his life, Luke should be able to sympathize with Anthony Sorelli better than most. However, the thought of a member of the Sorelli family as a victim brought bile to his mouth. A vision of Emily's sweet face flashed before Luke's mind. Rage began to broil within him. Luke balled his right hand into a fist. Against all physical evidence, Luke still believed the Sorellis were involved in Emily's death. Regardless of what Anthony was experiencing, his family, the Sorelli family, would pay for what they did to her.

Luke began conjuring theories on why Anthony might kill his girlfriend. Maybe they got high together, and she didn't realize how much she had taken. No, that wouldn't happen; she's a registered nurse. Maybe he threatened her and forced her to take too much? Again, no. None of his conjectures seemed even the slightest bit plausible, but even if they just questioned the man, it might break him just enough that he might reveal something about his family's business.

Mason would be against the interrogation. It was written all over his face. Luke let out a sigh and stared at the floor. Chief Reilly would also be opposed, but Anthony had come to them. They didn't conjure up some excuse to bring him here. He willingly stepped into the station and asked for Luke by name. Mason and Reilly wouldn't like it, but Luke knew he had what he needed to green-light the questioning. The biggest problem would be the lawyer, David Quentin. If one of Quentin's spies got word to him that Luke and Mason were interrogating Anthony, it'd be over sooner than it began. There had to be a way to keep the attorney unawares.

"So, what's next?" Mason's voice brought Luke out of his thoughts. He was staring intently at Luke, already guessing what Luke wanted to do.

"We need to question him," Luke responded, calm yet filled with a weight of finality. Mason shook his head.

"The man just found out his girlfriend is dead. He's an emotional wreck right now."

"All the better. He'll be less able to try and hide things with his emotions all out of whack," Luke retorted.

Just then, the door to the locker room swung open, and an off-duty officer stepped out, passed between the two detectives, and walked down the hall. Luke and Mason waited until the man was out of earshot.

"What would he have to try and hide? Do you think he had anything to do with this? 'Cause I don't. I saw how he reacted to seeing her. He broke down and couldn't compose himself for well over forty-five minutes. So, there's no way he was involved," Mason hissed back in a loud whisper.

Luke let out a sigh.

"Look, even if that's the case, you said it yourself, the only person stupid enough to cross a Sorelli is another Sorelli, and there's only one of them. So, let's go with that theory. Anthony would know why and how his father would have put out a hit on Ms. Grayson."

"And what of Quentin?" Mason asked while shaking his head. "He's bound to find out we have him here again. Once he shows up, then what?"

"All we have to do is make it clear to Mr. Quentin that Anthony is not under arrest and is willingly assisting us in our investigation. Then, he can't make Anthony leave if he doesn't want to," Luke explained.

"Then we need to be careful on how we approach him." Mason allowed. "Because if we come across as though we're accusing him, or if it seems like we're trying to manipulate him, it could turn him against us, and he may leave before the lawyer even shows his slimy head."

"So, you agree we need to question him?"

"I never said we didn't. All I was getting at was we should give him time, maybe the rest of the day, before we asked him back."

"And you think we'll ever get him out of that mansion outside the city once he leaves here? No. They'll have him locked down tight, with enough legal tape wrapped around him that we won't even get past the front gate," Luke said brusquely. "This is our only chance."

* * * *

Streams of hot water rained down on Anthony's face, ejected from the perforations in the shower head like consistent lasers. Anthony stood drenched, staring into the blue-gray tiles that lined the walls and floor of the hot room. Steam rose from the shower into the open air above him. Everything seemed out of focus. Whether that was him or if it was caused by the water running down his head in front of his eyes, Anthony didn't know. The only thing Anthony knew was that Wendy was dead. His Wendy was dead. Slowly, his bottom lip began to quiver. Anthony shut his eyes tight, trying to block out the image of her lifeless body lying before him on the cold stainless-steel slab.

Trying with everything he had, he brought an image of Wendy to his mind, bringing more tears to his eyes. She was wearing a yellow sundress, her red curls blowing in the breeze. She smiled that beautiful smile that made her look like she was lit from the inside out. Sobs began to escape from Anthony's throat. Lifting his arms, he put his head in his hands and let the dam inside him break again, not caring if anyone else heard him. His weeping filled the cavernous room. Anthony dropped to his knees, the hot water attacking his back. Some drops hit and ricocheted off; others stayed and formed little rivers running down onto the tile floor. The woman's silhouette filled his mind as she walked across the street. Anthony's head jerked up, and his eyelids sprang open, dispersing the vision.

He needed to figure out how long he'd been in the shower. He lifted his hands and looked at his fingers; they'd begun to raisin. Detective Mason told him to take as long as he needed. Detective Mason was a kind man. He didn't look or act like it, but he was. Pushing himself up, Anthony rose to his feet. He wiped away any remaining tears and took several deep breaths in through his nose and out through his mouth. The detectives were still his best bet at finding out who killed Wendy. A white bar of soap lay on a beveled-out shelf, jutting from one of the tile walls. Reaching out, Anthony picked up the soap, stepped back from the waterfall, and began lathering himself with it. At the very least, this shower would make him feel refreshed. Hopefully, it will also help clear his mind. Once covered in suds, he stepped back underneath the hot water and began washing. A small bottle of shampoo also rested on the small shelf. Anthony grabbed it, squeezed some liquid into his left hand, sat the bottle down, and began scrubbing it into his greasy black hair. Standing under the water, Anthony closed his eyes and began rinsing the shampoo. A picture of Wendy formed in his mind, but it was not a good one this time. Her cold, dead body splayed across the sidewalk. Her eyes were wide open, no longer windows to her soul, just empty balls of white with small black circles encased by rings of sapphire at their centers. Anthony's hands began furiously scrubbing at his hair, wanting desperately to open his eyelids and scour the image from his mind. His breathing began to quicken, another fifteen seconds of scrubbing, and Anthony wiped his eyes and opened them. The blue-gray tiles and gray grout filled his view once more. Standing under the hot water, Anthony remained still, trying to regain control of his breathing. Eventually, he was back to normal. Anthony turned off the water. The streams retreated into their pores, leaving behind those who weren't quick enough to make it back, with each abandoned droplet smashing into the tile with a tiny tap.

Sticking his head out of the shower, he saw where he had placed the navy towel on the bench against the outside shower wall. Anthony picked up the woven fibers and began drying himself off. Detective Mason had generously lent Anthony some clean clothes, including a pair of boxers, gray sweatpants, and a black t-shirt. At the time, Anthony didn't think much of it, but now he was skeptical of whether the clothes would even fit. The boxers fit well, and even the shirt (surprisingly enough) wasn't too small. The pants, however, were another story. They do Anthony's waist well enough but need to be longer. The gray chinos barely reached past his shins. Mason had also left a bottle of spray deodorant. Once he was clothed and had applied the antiperspirant, he headed to find the exit. When he was escorted in, he needed to pay more attention. His mind had been lost to grief. To his right sat a row of gray lockers. He decided to try that way. Walking past several more showers, he reached the lockers and saw he was at a "T" intersection. Lockers spread to his right and his left. A few men were undressing to his left. He walked over to them, carrying his nasty clothes under his arm.

"Excuse me," Anthony started. A large man with broad shoulders and huge biceps turned toward him. The large man was in the process of unbuttoning his shirt. "How do I get out of here?"

"Walk straight that way." The man indicated the direction with his head. "When you get to the end, turn right, walk a little way, and the door will be on your left."

"Thanks," Anthony replied and began walking in the direction pointed. His feet squelched uncomfortably in his shoes with each step he took. He was curious if Mason had a spare pair of socks he could borrow, but he'd ask when he found him. He arrived at the end of the walkway and turned to his right. As he proceeded to look for the door, his chest began to feel heavy, and he could feel tears starting to form in his eyes once again. He never knew someone could produce so many tears in this short time. Finding the exit door, Anthony stood before it and took three deep breaths, doing his best to keep himself composed. Reaching his face, he wiped away the stray tears that had escaped their ducts. He reached for the door and pushed it open. It's time to find some answers, he told himself.

CHAPTER 22

The interrogation room was dimly lit by a single light that hung from the ceiling in the center of the room. A metal table sat in the middle of the room, directly below the light. On one wall was a one-way glass window. Two chairs sat at the table, back to the glass, and another sat on the opposite side facing the glass. Shadows covered the walls as they tried to escape the illumination from the bulb hanging from the ceiling. A video camera sat perched in the far corner of the room, facing the table, and focusing on the single chair.

The door to the interrogation room swung open, and Anthony Sorelli was led inside by Detective Luke Burrows. Detective Brandon Mason stepped into the empty observation room to turn on the video camera and start recording. Luke motioned for Anthony to take the chair facing the one-way glass. The freshly cleaned man was still carrying his two-day-old clothes under his arm. Bending at the waist, Anthony laid the heap of cloth onto the ground next to the chair. Anthony had been reluctant to talk to the detectives in an interrogation room. However, Luke and Mason persuaded him that it was their best course of action to keep this meeting out of Anthony's father's reach for as long as possible. Even though they risked him being identified in the locker room, that was all the gambling they wanted to do.

Luke eyed the camera in the corner until a small red light illuminated, indicating it was recording. Looking back at Anthony, he saw that the man was doing his best to stay composed. Yet, sympathy dug at Luke's heart. He knew better than most what the man in front of him was experiencing. Anger, rage, grief, sorrow, confusion, all swirling inside, colliding with one another as they try to boil over and out into the world. Yet, all the while, the person housing those emotions tries to hold down the lid for as long as possible, wanting to present nothing but stoicism. Luke didn't know how many of these questions Anthony could take at the moment, but he did know that he would not have another shot to ask them with Anthony alone.

Glancing at his wrist, Luke read his watch. 11:00 A.M. It had been quite a busy morning. First, Luke reached into his back pants pocket and removed a small notebook. Then, reaching into his shirt pocket, he produced a black pen and placed both objects in front of himself on the table. Anthony's eyes were dancing about the room. It had been a while since the last time Anthony had been in one of these rooms. Luke wondered if the man even remembered or if he'd been too high at the time. Mason entered the room, closed the door behind him, and sat next to Luke. Both men faced Anthony. Ten seconds passed before anyone spoke.

"So," Luke began, opening his notebook and clicking his pen to reveal the point. "Anthony, can you tell us how you and Wendy met?"

Anthony let out a breath and shifted his feet under the table.

"Yeah. We met a couple of years ago. Um..it was at Marco's. She was having dinner by herself." Anthony gave a little half chuckle, "She had ordered the fettuccine alfredo, and she did not care for it." Anthony chuckled again at the memory. "Anyways, she was sitting at the table trying to eat enough of the food not to offend anyone politely, and I couldn't help but go over and talk to her. 'Not enjoying your meal?' I said. She blushed and looked away, not wanting to answer. 'It's alright,' I told her. 'May I join you?' She said yes, and so I took a seat. We introduced ourselves, and I had the waiter bring us a bottle of red wine. We talked for two hours before she had to go."

Luke stared hard at Anthony. The man was far off, reliving that moment and not wanting to let it go. Then, glancing to his right, he saw Mason eyeing him. Marco's was an Italian-style restaurant owned by the Sorellis. It was named after Anthony's great-grandfather.

"Did she know your father owned Marco's?" Mason asked.

"I eventually told her," Anthony replied, "She didn't seem too surprised. I'm sure she had guessed it that first night we met."

Luke restrained himself from investigating exactly how much Anthony had told Wendy about the Sorelli family business. It was too soon to try and pull those details from him. Besides, first and foremost was making sure Anthony wasn't involved in her murder. Setting his hand on the metal table, Luke let out a slight cough.

"Did Wendy know about your drug history?" Luke queried, staring intently at Anthony. Anthony ran his fingers through his black hair. Then, after a beat, he spoke.

"Yes." answered Anthony, "She knew. She was even trying to help me get sober." Anthony paused, his mouth slightly ajar and a single tear racing down his left cheek. "I tried, ya know. And I did well for a while, but I failed her again and again." Anthony's voice was beginning to get shaky. "And do you know what she did?" He paused to see if the detectives would respond. But instead, they just sat silent and waited. "She helped me dry each time, and when I was on edge, she was there to talk me back." More tears escaped from Anthony's ducts; lifting his right hand, he wiped his face. "She deserved better than me. So much better…but I couldn't let her go. I needed her. She was the only one who saw me as a person, not just some spoiled rich kid."

"So, she never got high with you?" Luke asked as he made more notes in his notepad. Anthony's face scrunched up; he closed his eyes and shook his head.

"No, she never did. She…was…a nurse and knew more about how all that stuff works than the three of us combined," Anthony responded, his tone becoming defensive.

Luke and Mason exchanged a glance. They hadn't told Anthony what Wendy's cause of death was yet. Luke wasn't sure how the man would handle that news, but they'd have to tell him sooner or later.

"And you're one hundred percent sure about that?" Mason asked. "You never saw her take anything that wasn't for medicinal use?"

Again, Anthony shook his head, confusion building on his face. "Why are you pressing this?" he asked.

Luke let out a breath and hung his head for a second. When he lifted it, he looked Anthony square in the eyes.

"Wendy died from a morphine overdose." Luke let the sentence hang in the air, watching for Anthony's reaction. Instead, the man's eyes went wide with surprise, and his mouth dropped open.

"I'm sorry, what?" Anthony began, "Morphine? No. There's no way. You've made a mistake." Anthony started shaking his head vigorously. "She would never take Morphine unless she was hospitalized. She barely took aspirin."

"There's no mistake Mr. Sorelli," Mason was saying. "She did die of a morphine overdose. I'm sorry."

Lifting his right hand to his face, Anthony cupped his mouth with his right hand and crossed his left arm over his abdomen. His eyes were wide and filled with tears. Luke and Mason sat patiently and gave him a minute to process what they had just told him. Luke's patience was wearing thin. He wanted to start sinking his claws into this thing and ripping out the answers. However, he needed to. Mason was usually the impatient one of the two of them. However, this time was different, and Luke couldn't figure out why. Maybe it was because Mason had seen how Anthony reacted to identifying Wendy's body. He might have been letting it affect him more than it should. A full two minutes passed, and Luke deemed it enough time.

"Mr. Sorelli," Luke started.

Anthony looked up at him, "Where were you Tuesday morning between two and four A.M.?" Anthony's eyes darted from Luke to Mason and back again. Slowly he took his hand away from his mouth and continued staring hard at Luke. A fire seemed to spark behind Anthony's hazel eyes.

"What are you insinuating?" Anthony asked defensively, "Do you think I killed my girlfriend?" Anthony's voice began to increase in volume, and his tone began to harden. "How dare you. How dare both of you. I came to you," Anthony pointed a finger in Luke's direction, "for help. And you sit there and accuse me…" he broke off.

"We have to ask," Mason said. "It's protocol. We can't rule someone out just because they came to us or because the victim is the person's lover."

Anthony leaned back against the chair and looked up at the ceiling. Then, after a minute, he replied, "I was at Wendy's house, asleep. I went there late Tuesday evening to wait for her to get off work and fell asleep."

"Can anyone corroborate that?" Luke asked.

Anthony shot him a look of disdain. "No."

Luke sat his notepad down on the table, placed his pen on top of it, and slid it to Anthony. "Could you write down her address for us?"

Mason threw a look at Luke and arched an eyebrow. Anthony picked up the pen and wrote down the address. Sliding the pen and notepad back to the detective, Anthony's expression was stern. Luke could tell he didn't like being blamed for Wendy's death. Who would? Anthony also had to be aware that Luke has been after his father for years and is undoubtedly thinking that Luke's trying to pin this on him to get to Victor. Anthony was wrong; of course, Luke was beginning to think the man was innocent of this crime, and he would not frame an innocent man to take down Victor Sorelli. It was mighty tempting, though. Even if he wanted to, Mason and Chief Reilly would not let him get away with it, nor would the Sorelli's lawyer. No, Anthony was safe from any false accusations, at least in these circumstances.

"Did Wendy have any enemies?" Mason's voice cut into the silence.

"Of course not," Anthony said. "Everybody loved her. She's a nurse, for crying out loud."

"I've had some pretty shitty nurses before," Luke said. "They do nothin' but come into your room, check your fluids, etc., and when you ask, 'em a question or request something, they roll their eyes and either never do it or take forever to do it."

Anthony said nothing; he just sat and stared at the window behind the detectives. The tears were no longer in his eyes. Instead, anger had replaced grief, and if the detectives weren't careful, rage would follow.

"Of course, I never wanted to kill any of them," Luke said. "What about your father, Anthony?"

Anthony's eyes darted to Luke. Still, he remained silent.

"Did your father and Wendy ever meet?"

Silence.

"Yes? No?" Luke prodded. Anthony's face showed no emotion.

"They met once. Wendy and I went to Marco's to celebrate our one-year anniversary as a couple. Dad was there. He stopped by the table and talked with us for a bit."

Mason was getting nervous. A bead of sweat trickled down the left side of his head. Luke could tell he'd pushed Anthony to a limit, and Mason didn't want to lose what ground they'd gained.

"Did your father approve of your relationship?" Luke pressed. Anthony clenched his teeth.

"I don't see what that has to do with anything," Anthony replied. Luke leaned back against his seat.

"It's not that complicated, Mr. Sorelli." Luke began, "you say you didn't kill Wendy. Okay. I believe you, I do, but you have no alibi." Luke raised empty hands, shrugging his shoulders. "You say Wendy never partook in illegal opiates. Fair enough, no reason to believe otherwise. However, Miss Grayson died of an opiate overdose. Again, I believe you. Her being a nurse, even if she did have a drug habit, would know how much she could take before ODing. Therefore, she was murdered. But by whom? Who would murder that beautiful young woman? Hence, why I ask about how your father felt about your relationship with Miss Grayson."

The room fell silent. Anthony held Luke's gaze for a whole minute.

"He did not approve of it." Anthony finally said. "But there's no way he's involved. I've thought about it repeatedly. He didn't have anything to do with this."

"Because he would never be involved with any murder?" Luke asked.

Anthony didn't answer.

CHAPTER 23

The sun warmed Victor's skin as he sat in the sunroom of his mansion. Rays of light, the essence of life, pierced the glass walls, heating the room's interior. Victor was seated in one of the many chairs and sofas spread throughout the space. The sunroom looked out onto Victor's many acres at the back of the mansion. This was Victor's favorite place on his whole property. He loved coming here to clear his mind or to sit and think through any complicated issues. It always seemed to bring clarity.

During this time of the year, there wasn't much to look at. The trees had yet to begin to bud; empty branches sprawled forth from many different size trunks, reaching for the sky above. Empty bird nests sat lonely in the arms of many trees, no longer sheltered by the seasonal foliage. The grass was brown and dormant. In the spring and summer, however, this scene was magnificent. A sea of Bermuda, with patches of darker fescue, laid a lush carpet of green under the trees that dotted the open lawn. The trees were full of leaves, helping to shade the vulnerable fescue. Sycamore, Oak, and one Maple–Victor's grandfather had planted these trees when he bought this property all those years ago.

If only he could see them now, Victor thought.

Victor sighed and looked at the clock on one of the end tables beside the chair he was sitting in. 11:43 A.M. He received a phone call from Sam more than two hours ago. The man had yet to arrive back at the mansion. That wasn't like him at all. Sam always followed his orders with haste. Either he'd gotten hung up in some unforeseen traffic jam, or he was aware that Victor had figured out that he'd taken care of Wendy Grayson and broken Victor's number one rule. If you leave the body, make sure it's not traceable to the family. Maybe Sam was scared and decided to leave town. Not the worst idea. Victor wouldn't have killed him, but he might have cut out his tongue. Victor shook his head. Yesterday, his plan to hold Anthony here until he came to his senses went awry, and today the police had Anthony, and Sam was conspicuously absent.

Pulling his cell phone from his pocket, Victor dialed Sam's number. He raised the device to his right ear and listened. The phone rang multiple times before Sam's voicemail cut in. Victor ended the call and tossed his phone on the glass table in front of him. The phone hit the top of the table with a loud Whack! that echoed slightly around the sunroom. Letting out a sigh, Victor raised his right hand and placed his thumb and forefinger against the corners of his eyes. He shut his eyelids, applied slight pressure to the spot, and took a deep breath. Victor racked his brain, trying to make sense of it all. He'd told Sam that Miss Grayson would need to be taken care of, but he didn't mean so soon and not so public.

On top of everything, he still had a business to run. Victor leaned forward, grabbed his phone, and shoved it back into his pocket from whence it came. Then, standing to his feet, he exited the sunroom and headed back toward his office.

The memory of finding Anthony dining with the ginger-haired woman at the restaurant flooded back to him as he walked down the dimly lit hallway. It was the only time she and Victor had spoken to one another.

Anthony had not appreciated being blindsided, but Victor knew it was the only way he would get to see them together without either of them putting on an act for his benefit. Both Anthony and Wendy had been super uncomfortable and on edge. Victor had held nothing back. He'd pressured Miss Grayson on every issue known to man, from the legalization of marijuana to abortion to gun rights and sex work. She held her own for the most part, but Victor knew she was not the woman for Anthony. She was too self-righteous; that she was a nurse and aided in the saving of lives only added to her arrogance. Anthony and his drug problem were nothing more than an extracurricular activity to her. She didn't care if Anthony got clean or not. She wanted him to keep failing so that he could return to her, validating her pathetic hero complex. Victor was certain.

It was too late for his son; however, he'd already fallen prey to her seduction. After that night, it only got worse. Anthony mentioned running away with her. She'd whispered her poisonous words in his ears and had turned Victor's son against him. No matter what Victor told the boy, it went in one ear and out the other. From what he'd gathered, though, Anthony had still not informed Miss Grayson about the woman he'd killed. She wouldn't stick with him if she knew Anthony was a murderer. He wasn't sure what his son told her about why he started using drugs, but he was sure it wasn't true.

Victor reached his office. Lifting his left hand, he turned the door handle and pushed the door open. His pets remained in their places, hanging on the blood-red walls. He stepped behind his large desk and sat in his leather chair. The smell of incense in the air eased his tension slightly. Victor picked up the stack of papers on his desk and read them mindlessly. Most of them were expense reports from his various businesses. In addition, there was a letter from the mayor requesting his attendance at an event next month, detailing several purchase orders he needed to approve– all the day-to-day tasks required to keep this place afloat. Most of it was not glamorous but necessary. Anthony needed to be here. He needed to learn what he was responsible for.

Victor sat the pages back on the wooden surface, putting his elbows on the desk. He leaned forward and put his head in his hands. If he didn't get Anthony here, out from whatever the police were investigating, and teach him how to run this place, it would all fall when he died. Everything his grandfather and father built would be for not. In all his years, he never imagined it would ever come close to this. He'd hoped the family empire would endure for at least another three or four generations.

A knock came from the door, drawing Victor out of his head. He cleared his throat before answering.

"Come in," he said, leaning back in his seat, not wanting to show weakness.

The door opened, and Jonathon stood in its frame. His blonde hair was combed, and his white shirt and black slacks were ironed and creased perfectly—a blue bowtie decorated the collar of his shirt.

"Would you like anything for lunch, sir?" Jonathan asked.

"Not today, Jonathan. Thank you," Victor replied.

Jonathan gave a slight bow and shut the door. Victor was not the least bit hungry. He had too many things plaguing him to think about food. He'd have something small for dinner. He still had to keep his strength up, especially if he had to keep running the business by himself soon.

Reaching under his desk, Victor clasped the lone key hung from a small metal hook. Only those who knew it existed knew where to find it. Taking the key off the hook, he bent over at the waist and unlocked the very bottom drawer on the right side of his workstation. Slowly he pulled the drawer open and stared at the object housed there. Gently he picked up the object and held it in his hand, resting his arm on the edge of his desk. He felt the eyes of his pets on him, analyzing his every move. In his hand resided a Smith & Wesson .45 revolver.

The dark-stained wood hand grip is attached to a gray steel revolving chamber, trigger, hammer, and barrel. Victor opened the chamber and counted one, two, three, four, five, and six bullets. Fully loaded. Closing the chamber, the steel felt cold against his fingers. He could count on one hand how many times he'd fired this weapon. Each time was difficult. Victor only used it for those closest to him that decided to betray him. He looked past the gun and stared at the two empty seats before his desk. The sound of a gunshot echoed in his mind. A silhouette of a man slumped over, his body slack, filled his vision. Victor blinked away the tear that threatened to escape. Slowly he turned the gun over in his hands, admiring the craftsmanship of the weapon. After about ten seconds, he returned the gun to its home and locked it away.

Placing the silver key back on its secret hook, Victor swiveled to his computer and tapped the keyboard. Tiny lights illuminated the screen before him. Victor pulled his cell phone out of his pocket. The time was now 12:03 P.M. Victor redialed Sam. Voicemail. Shaking his head, Victor ended the call and set the phone on his desk. Turning back toward his computer, he typed in his password and waited for the home screen to appear. Sam was going to be as much to blame for the recent chaos as Anthony, but Sam didn't have the same saving grace as Anthony. Sam wasn't blood.

*　*　*　*

Consciousness slowly returned to Sam's mind. He had no idea where he was. A throbbing pain pierced the back of his head. He'd been hit from behind. Ambushed. Sam had no idea who would dare attack a member of Victor Sorelli's entourage–either someone was very ballsy or very stupid. Perhaps both. Sam opened his eyes and saw that his face was covered with a black cloth bag. His mouth felt dry and sore. He'd been gagged with a rag of some sort. He also realized his hands were tied behind his back and that he was scrunched up in some small space. His right leg began to cramp. He tried with all his might to stretch it as much as possible, but it was no use.

Sam concluded he was most likely in a car trunk, although there was no sure way to test that theory. He could see nothing but darkness. Sam remained calm and kept his breathing regulated. This would not be the end for him if he could help it. Mentally, Sam berated himself. How could he have let himself be so careless? Too focused on Anthony. Suddenly, the sound of an engine filled his ears, and the smell of exhaust attacked his nostrils. There was no disputing it now. He was in the trunk of a vehicle. Sam had to devise a plan for when they opened the lid to deal with him. He had to fight his way out of this.

CHAPTER 24

Chief Reilly stood in the observation room, hands in his pockets, watching Burrows and Mason question Anthony Sorelli. Burrows had discreetly informed Reilly that they'd be questioning Mr. Sorelli and that Mr. Sorelli had voluntarily come to them. Reilly was skeptical, of course. Such a thing had never happened in all his years on the force. It also turned out that Anthony knew the Jane Doe that had been discovered yesterday morning. Reilly couldn't believe it. Perhaps the universe was finally ready to punish the Sorelli family.

"My father has nothing to do with this." Anthony's muffled voice came from beyond the glass.

"Okay, let's say that's true," Burrows said. "Do you have any other ideas on who would want her dead?"

Anthony shook his head. They were going in circles, Reilly thought. They needed him to give them probable cause to search the Sorelli family estate and to bring Victor in for questioning. Anthony was not budging, though. Unless they could provide him solid evidence that his father was involved, he would never testify against him. Still, without Anthony incriminating his father, they could not collect the evidence to prove Victor was engaged in Wendy Grayson's death. Reilly hung his head. They'd reached an impasse. He was still determining how long the two detectives planned to continue this line of questioning. It can't be for much longer. They press too much more, and Anthony is liable to walk, Reilly thought.

"What about your drug dealer?" came Mason's voice. "Did they take offense to Wendy wanting you to get clean?"

"No," Anthony responded, "They didn't know she existed."

"Are you certain about that?" Mason pressed.

"Yes," Anthony said with a sigh. "Besides, they would never use their product if they wanted to get rid of somebody. They hated losing money. They'd use a knife or bullet or something."

Reilly gently stroked his white goatee. He admired Mason's ability in this situation. Usually, he'd be the 'bad cop,' interrogating suspects with a no-mercy approach, but today he played 'good cop' and seemed to have compassion for the boy. However, burrows' patience was wearing thin. Reilly could see that from here. The man was restless, couldn't sit still, rubbing his temples, crossing his arms over his chest. This whole interrogation was like walking on eggshells. Burrows loathed the Sorelli family, and after all his years chasing them, this was his best shot at putting a nail in their coffin. But he couldn't go the whole hog after Anthony as he wanted; Anthony was a victim in this situation and had to be treated as such until proven otherwise. This meant Mason had to be the voice of reason.

Motion caught Reilly's attention out of the corner of his eye. Mason had reached into his pants pocket and pulled out his cell phone.

"Excuse me," he said as he rose and exited the interrogation room. Reilly went to the gray door of the observation room and opened it. He stood in the doorway, watching Mason pace back and forth in front of the off-white walls of the hallway.

"Got it. Thanks, Sweetheart," Mason said, his back to Reilly. Turning around, he noticed Reilly staring at him. Mason held up his forefinger, signaling to give him a minute. Mason emerged seconds later, stepping back into the interrogation room with Burrows in tow. Both men walked to Reilly and stopped in front of him. Reilly's nose was assaulted by the slightest of odors. It was rank, body odor. Scrunching his nose in response, he took a half step back from the detectives.

"I just received a call from Dr. Wright." Mason began. "She has compared the dental records of Jane Doe with those of Wendy Grayson. They're a perfect match."

"Was there ever any doubt?" Burrows asked incredulously. Mason shot him a look that said he needed to cool it.

"You know, as well as I, we needed to have more than an in-person identification," Mason retorted. "Okay, I think we need to check out Miss Grayson's house, interview her coworkers, etc."

"You do that, and I'll keep working on Mr. Sorelli," Burrows said.

"No, you won't," Reilly cut in, his voice gruff and authoritative. Burrows let out a short breath through his nostrils.

"Sir, if I may.." Burrows started.

"No," Reilly interrupted. "Without Mason in there, you'd bulldoze over him, and he'd storm out of here, and we'll never get anywhere near him again. And if it got out, I'd lose my job, and I'd be shocked if you didn't as well."

Burrows looked sheepishly at the floor. His cheeks were turning red, either from embarrassment or anger, Reilly didn't know which.

"Do you think the Mayor will care whether Anthony Sorelli submitted to this interrogation willingly? No. You'll go and dig into Wendy Grayson's life to try and find some more answers." Reilly stated with finality in his tone.

"What about Mr. Sorelli?" Mason asked. "We can't force him to stay here while we investigate."

The three of them pondered this for a long moment. It was quite a dilemma. If they left the man here while the two of them were out, he could go or be spotted by a mole. The lawyer would then show up and coerce him to leave. But, on the other hand, putting him in a holding cell would imply that they considered him a suspect, and if the attorney got wind of that, it would also be game over.

"What if we take him with us?" Burrows said.
Both Reilly and Mason looked at him with wide eyes. The mere idea of taking a potential suspect along while you investigated the death of his lover was beyond crazy.

"How would you make that work?" Reilly asked, doubtful.

"Well, we could have him stay in the car's back seat," Burrows replied. Reilly scoffed. It was ridiculous. There's no way it would work.

"And what's to keep him in the car?" Mason asked, "We're not in a squad car. The back doors can't remain locked. He can reach forward and unlock them anytime he wants."

Reilly nodded his agreement. Burrows couldn't expect Anthony Sorelli to sit contently while they tear into his girlfriend's home.

"Curiosity," Burrows began, "curiosity will keep him in the car. He's going to want..no, need to know what we've found. He wants answers even more than we do. So, if we give him a choice to either wait here or tag along with us but lay out the ground rules, he'll come along. And he won't leave." Burrows leaned against the wall, satisfied with his argument. Reilly had to admit. It did make some sense. Mere curiosity might be enough to keep him along for the duration. Reilly shook his head. It was still crazy.

"If you lose him, it's your ass," Reilly conceded.

A gleam sparkled in Burrows' eyes, and a smile tugged at his lips. "Understood, sir. Thank you," Burrows said, trying to hide how pleased he was.

Reilly shook his head and walked back to the squad room and his office. As he walked along the eggshell-white walls, he heard Burrows say to Mason, "You better go air out the car. Because if he smells like he did when he arrived, he might not stay with us for long."

*   *   *   *

Anthony rose to his feet. He was tired of sitting in the same spot. He had no idea how long he'd been here, getting questioned by the detectives. It felt good to stretch his legs and his back. The stench from the pile of disgusting clothing on the ground crept into the air. Pacing back and forth past the gray wall behind him, he thought about Wendy. How badly he missed her. Her smile, her laugh, her voice. Anthony did his best to remember what she sounded like. Losing that would be devastating, though he knew it would eventually happen. Anthony had no idea what his mother's voice sounded like. At one point, he did, but with the passage of time and how busy life became, it was only natural. His memory banks needed to make space for other things.

Anthony was about ready to leave. He wasn't sure if these detectives were interested in helping him or just arresting his father. The younger man, Detective Mason, was trying to find answers. He seemed to care for Anthony and was trying to find other angles to pursue. Detective Burrows, however, would not ease up on blaming Anthony's father. Burrows kept baiting Anthony, waiting for him to say anything that would incriminate Victor. Of course, Anthony knew his father could and had ordered people killed before, but his dad needed him to run the business. That's all he cared about. He wouldn't do anything to jeopardize that. Anthony was positive. Sure, he couldn't blame the detectives; to them, it made sense that Victor was involved. There's no good way for Anthony to explain anything without incriminating his father.

Raising his right hand, he placed it on his forehead. Maybe this whole thing was a mistake, thought Anthony. But they did help you find Wendy. Anthony ran his hands through his unkempt hair. Then, turning to his left, Anthony began walking around the table and chairs, making numerous circles around the room— his own Jericho. Keeping silent, he thought through his predicament.

The picture of Wendy's corpse filled his mind's eye. Anthony stopped walking and closed his eyes, willing the image to change. Lifting his hands to his face, he began rubbing his eyes. The image shifted to Wendy standing in her kitchen wearing only one of Anthony's t-shirts. The shirt was so oversized she could've worn it as a dress. It rode from her shoulders down to her mid-thighs.

Just then, the door to the room he was in opened, and in stepped Detective Burrows. Detective Mason did not follow. Anthony crossed his arms, and the two men stared at each other. Burrow's brown hair was parted and combed to the right. He had broad shoulders, and his black button-down shirt was wrinkled. Anthony had no right to judge the man's appearance with how he had shown up at the station.

"We have a proposition for you, Mr. Sorelli." the detective said. There was no harshness or patronizing in his tone. Anthony didn't respond right away. Instead, he wanted to test the man's patience a little more.

Anthony put his hands in the pockets of the high-water sweatpants he was borrowing.

"Which is?" Anthony responded.

"We need to investigate Wendy's home, her work, interview her coworkers, etc." Detective Burrows put his left hand on his hip. "And we don't know what to do with you while we investigate." The sentence hung in the air for a few seconds. "We decided to let you make the decision. You have two choices. First, you can wait here. We don't know how long this will take, but you're more than welcome to wait in the squad room." Anthony wasn't sure what other option could be, but he waited for the detective to inform him.

"The problem with that is you'd be identified, and your attorney, Mr. Quentin, would surely show up and drag you out of here tooth and nail. Then we'd never get to share our findings with you. All communication would be through Mr. Quentin or one of his associates. So, your second option would be to come with us while we investigate."

Anthony's eyebrows raised at this. He was still determining what he'd expected. But this was not it.

"If you choose to join us, sadly, you will not be allowed to leave the car. Instead, you would have to wait for us to return, but when we finished at each location, we would share with you what we found," Burrows finished. Anthony remained silent. He tried his best to keep his expression neutral. Of course, his gut instinct was to go with the detectives, but what if this was another one of their traps to try and get him to turn on his dad? On the other hand, Burrows was right: If Quentin found him here, he'd never let him stay, and once he was taken home, there was no way he'd get away a second time. Anthony looked Burrows up and down before giving his answer.

"When do we leave?"

CHAPTER 25

Outside his window, a bird was chirping a song. The sun was high in the blue sky, and a few puffy, white clouds sailed lazily through the air. It was a lovely day, even though it was forty degrees Fahrenheit, according to the weather app on his phone. Sitting in the driver's seat of his car, binoculars in hand, he kept an eye on the police station. He has parked a reasonable distance away, of course. With the end of his game so close, he couldn't risk getting caught– especially with Mr. Hunter in the trunk. The acquisition of Mr. Hunter was key to keeping everyone off balance, mostly Victor, but that was what was important at this moment. His car's engine wasn't running, which would run the risk of Mr. Hunter dying of carbon monoxide. Mr. Hunter would die. There was no denying that, but this was not the time. The man was as strong as an ox and heavy as one to boot.

Mr. Hunter had awakened a little while ago and tried to kick down the back seat. A useless exercise, as he had installed several pieces of rebar between the truck and the back of the seats. There was no gap big enough for Mr. Hunter to fit his feet. Reaching down, he picked up the plastic bottle in the cup holder. He unscrewed the lid and took a sip of the water inside the plastic container. The liquid wet his parched lips and tongue.

He screwed the lid and placed the water bottle back in the holder. There had still been no sign of Anthony since he'd arrived at the cop shop earlier this morning. It was a curious thing. He figured Anthony would have left by now. Raising the binoculars to his eyes, he looked far down the street. There sat Anthony's car in the same spot against the curb. He lowered the binoculars to his lap. His cell phone rested on his console. He tapped the screen, and it came to life, displaying the lock screen. He read the time, 12:37 P.M.

Glancing up, he saw something moving from the back of the police station. He raised the dual spy glasses and focused on the object. A dark-colored vehicle; if he had to take a guess, it would be a Dodge Charger. Two silhouettes filled the front seats. If he were right, that would be his harrowing detectives. He continued to watch them as they drove farther and farther away. It was hard to tell, but he didn't see anything that resembled a third person. So, they'd left Anthony alone in the station. He won't be happy with that, especially because they most likely put him in a holding cell, treating him like a suspect. A smile formed at the corners of his mouth. He needed to find out where the crime solvers were off to, but it didn't matter. He reclined his seat slightly and continued to watch the street before him.

*   *   *   *

Sam's body was getting stiff. Having been stuffed into the car's trunk like one might squeeze a bicycle into the same small space–enough room to fit, but not comfortably–he'd been sweating from every pore his skin had. The cold air penetrated the car's exterior, making him shiver when it hit his sweat-drenched body. Tiny, thin slivers of light slithered their way into the darkness that encompassed him.

When I got out of there, he thought I would need one hell of a chiropractor. He figured the trunk lid had to be rigged to where it wasn't closed to let in the fresh air so he wouldn't run out of oxygen. This meant even his captor didn't know how long he'd be here. Sam had tried to shove his shoulders against the lid and bust it open, but he didn't have enough room to use the proper force. All he managed to do was give himself some nice bruises.

After a little while, he tried to kick down the back seats, but his feet kicked into something hard and immovable. Sam was baffled. His captor had planned to hold someone back here for an extended period of time and had prepared accordingly. Sam didn't know if he was the intended target, but he couldn't imagine anyone around here taking him by accident. Surely his captor's intent wasn't to kill him. If it were, he'd be dead already. So, who would want me taken alive? Sam asked himself. He racked his brain but could think of no one. Any enemies he had were from enforcing orders from Victor Sorelli, and those people knew better than to cross Sorelli. Sam was more embarrassed than anything. He'd gotten overconfident, and this was the price. The faint smell of pine entered Sam's nasal cavity. It might be coming from outside, or it could be an air freshener. Sam didn't know who would put air fresheners in their trunks, but maybe this whack job did. Pain shot up Sam's neck when he tried to readjust himself with what little room he had. Gritting his teeth, Sam pushed through the sharp pain and managed to wriggle himself around to an ever so slightly more comfortable position.

A memory of Sam and Anthony going on a double date in high school flooded Sam's mind. He had to smile. It was a good time. The four of them had gone to a movie and an arcade and then grabbed some ice cream afterward. The two young men had reeked from an overdose of body spray. They'd laughed and had a grand time. Sam had also managed to make it to third base that night. Anthony had said he'd reached second before being called 'out .' Sam would give anything to go back to those days. He missed his friend more than anything. One reason he'd accepted Victor's offer was to remain close to his best friend. Unfortunately, that didn't work out how he'd pictured it. Anthony had become frustrated at Sam and grew distant. Sam told himself that Anthony and I would have a long talk when I got out of this.

*　　*　　*　　*

Anthony sat upright in the back seat of the detective's car. They had instructed him to lie down to avoid prying eyes on the streets around the police station. He'd complied. Now that they were far enough away, they told him he could sit up if he wanted. Anthony had rolled his eyes; of course, he tried to sit up. Detective Burrows complained about the smell of the car when he got in the passenger seat. Detective Mason just shrugged and said he did the best he could with his short time frame. Burrows had rolled down his window to try and air out the rotten odor. The air flying through the car was chilly. Goosebumps ran up and down Anthony's skin. He shivered. Detective Burrows had given him an extra pair of socks to wear. Anthony had put them on and put his shoes on over them. His old clothes were in a bag inside an empty locker in the men's locker room at the station.

Anthony stared out the back passenger's side window; buildings, cars, and people came and went from his view. They were headed to Wendy's house first. Anthony wasn't sure how he felt about staying in the car, but he knew it was for the best. He wasn't sure they'd find anything, but who knew? The two men sitting in front of him were trained and experienced detectives. They knew where to look for clues and what they needed to be looking for. Surely they'll find something, Anthony said to himself.

A memory of Wendy and himself entered his mind. They were at Mitchell Park having a picnic. Anthony hated picnics. He always felt they were cliche and didn't enjoy fighting bugs for his food. Wendy just giggled at him. She insisted it would be a good time. They'd taken a blanket and a wicker basket filled to the brim. They'd found the perfect spot under a shade tree. After setting up, Anthony began making the sandwiches. It could have gone better; they'd unknowingly set up their picnic near an ant hill. Within minutes ants were crawling over the two of them and had infiltrated their basket.

Anthony turned red and became very upset over the whole ordeal. Wendy tried to laugh it off and attempted to get him to see it as a funny mishap. When he didn't, they'd gotten into a heated argument. Looking back now, Anthony smiled and chuckled at the whole thing. A pit began to form deep in Anthony's gut. Instead of enjoying Wendy's company, even in the face of things falling apart, he'd blown up at her and, as he had put it, "her stupid, lousy date idea ."Regret began to fill the pit in his stomach. How many times had they argued over the stupidest things? And how many of those arguments had he started? These questions began to plague Anthony's mind as he rode in the backseat of the black Charger. It wasn't until this moment that he realized he hadn't eaten anything all day. Nausea began to sink its claws into Anthony's body. Anthony's head began to throb viciously. He didn't remember the last time he'd felt nauseous. His withdrawal from the opiates had diminished until now. He needed to eat something but feared nausea wouldn't let him keep it down—quite the paradox.

"Can we pull over?" Anthony asked. Detective Burrows turned his head towards Anthony and raised an eyebrow.

"Why?" Detective Burrows asked, confusion written across his face.

"I'm gonna be sick. Unless you want me to vomit all over the floor back here, I suggest you pull over the first chance you get," replied Anthony as he closed his eyes and tried to hold on to the contents of his stomach. Burrows let out a sigh. Detective Mason had pulled over to a curb within a few minutes, and Anthony swung open the passenger-side back door. He managed to get his head out of the car before bile and water launched from his mouth. Anthony heaved three more times, emptying his already barren stomach. The liquid burned his esophagus with each lurch. Then, reaching his left arm forward, he wiped his mouth, sat in the car, and closed the door.

"I didn't realize you got motion sick," Detective Mason said from behind the steering wheel.

"I don't," Anthony replied. "I don't know what this was."

"Well, I appreciate the heads up," Mason said with gratitude.

Anthony gave him a slight nod and leaned back against the seat. Now all he could smell was the bile he'd exhumed from his gut on his breath. The voice of his addiction, loud in his head, began berating him again.

You weak fool! Why are you bothering these pigs? They can't help us. We need morphine. Now!

The pounding in Anthony's head intensified. Raising his hands to his head, Anthony began to put pressure against his temples and rub his fingers in circles across them.

Wendy is dead. She can't help you anymore. Only drugs can. Come on, jump outta the car. We can walk the rest of the way.

"Shut up," Anthony whispered through gritted teeth.

You may not have killed Wendy, but you're still a murderer. Want to forget about that? Want to erase everything that's happened today? Go get the morphine.

Anthony slammed his head hard against the back of the seat. He couldn't give in to himself. He knew it was all lies. The voice would go away until the drugs wore off again. Then it would all be back with a vengeance.

Who cares? A little relief is better than none at all. Anthony pressed his fingers harder into his temples, trying to push away the pain.

CHAPTER 26

Luke inserted the spare key Anthony had provided them into the deadbolt slot. Mason had entered the backyard through the side gate. After he cleared the backyard, he would find the key– which, again, Anthony had informed them of– that Wendy hid under one of the potted plants on the patio and enter the house from the rear. Luke didn't expect to find any trouble, but they had to be prepared. Holding his firearm in his right hand, Luke slowly turned the key with his left. The sound of the deadbolt sliding into its burrow signaled the key had done its job.

Taking the key from the deadbolt slot, he slid it into the slit on the doorknob and turned again. Luke placed his left hand on the doorknob and slowly turned it, pushing the front door open. He stepped inside Wendy Grayson's house, raising his 9mm out in front of himself. The sound of a lock turning caught his attention, and he moved quickly to find and aim at the back door. The white wooden door spun inward with a loud creak, and standing beyond it on the patio, gun raised, was Mason.

Giving Mason a quick nod, the two detectives went room by room, clearing every possible hiding spot. There was not a soul to be found.

With that taken care of, Mason returned to the car to retrieve their evidence-collecting gear. Luke remained inside. A faint scent of cinnamon tickled Luke's sense of smell. When Mason returned, he opened the case and pulled out two pairs of latex gloves. Shoving his right hand into the stretchy material, Luke pulled it over each of his fingers, letting the glove go at his wrist with a POP! Mason grinned slightly at Luke's over-dramatized action.

"Where would you like to start?" Mason asked. Luke looked around the house. They were standing at the dining room table; from here, he could see the kitchen, across the hallway, and into the living room.

"I'll check the front and back doors for any sign of damage. Then, you can start in here and work your way into the kitchen," answered Luke.

Mason gave him a nod.

"Do you really think Sorelli will stay in the car the whole time?" Mason asked as he examined the table and the four chairs surrounding it.

Luke responded, as he turned the corner and walked to the front door, "I hope so. He was starting to act a little funny there for a bit. Mumbling to himself and whatnot."

Luke examined the locking mechanisms and the door's frame when he reached the front door. Finding no sign of forced entry, he rounded the corner again, walked through the dining room to the laundry area, turned right, and examined the back door—no signs of tampering or forced entry there either.

"Yeah," came Mason's voice from the kitchen. "I think the shock may finally be wearing off."

Luke's footsteps were heavy along the wooden floor as he walked back toward the washing and drying machines. The laundry room was dark. A string dangled from the ceiling in front of Luke's face. Reaching up, he pulled on it, and a light bulb came to life, shining yellow light on the bulky, white machines.

"Well, if anyone entered this house, they didn't break through the doors," Luke said as he opened the lid to the washing machine. Empty. Putting his hand inside, Luke spun the internal drum. He watched as the shiny, porous cylinder went round and round. He noticed a small curtain above the cleaning units when he shut the door. The curtains were short and black, hung on a wooden dowel rod. Luke pulled back the curtains to reveal a small shelf that was home to the supplies needed for the cleaning machines: an orange bottle of detergent, half full, a blue bottle of fabric softener, also half full, and an empty orange box of what looked to be dryer sheets. Pulling each down, Luke examined them and found nothing out of sorts. Moving to the dryer, the only thing of note he observed was that Miss Grayson didn't know how to empty the lint filter. It was packed. Full of gray and blue lint and dust. Luke was surprised she hadn't burned her house down. Stepping back into the dining area, he saw Mason was still in the kitchen.

"Anything interesting?" Luke asked. Mason shook his head.

"Half a carton of eggs, about one cup left of a half-gallon of milk, and some frozen foods in the freezer," Mason said as he opened a cabinet door. Luke walked through the hallway and into the living room. Before, he sat on a fabric couch with a glass-topped coffee table in front of it. On top of the coffee table was a vase with some flowers, which Luke assumed were lilies. The vase barely had any water in it. The living room floor was covered with a gray carpet. Opposite the couch sat a small entertainment center with a flat-screen television. To the right of the tv sat a black bookshelf that housed a dozen or so DVDs and some books. Luke stepped to the bookshelf, bent down at his knees, and looked through the contents. Most DVDs were cheesy romantic comedies–The Notebook, A Walk to Remember, and Sabrina, to name a few. The books were pretty much all self-help. A couple of them dealt with finances, some with weight loss, and others with time management. The layer of dust on the shelf told Luke that no one had ever used anything on it. Letting out a sigh, Luke rose to his feet. A single recliner sat in the corner of the room with nothing beside it but a tall, black lamp. Moving to the sofa, Luke began pulling off the cushions and checking the innards of the long multi-seater. This is going to be a long day, Luke said to himself.

* * * *

Go! Come on! They're distracted. This is our shot! Screamed the voice in Anthony's head– a constant siren, blasting its alarm louder and louder since arriving at Wendy's quaint tiny home. His mind was trying to tell him to run and buy more drugs. Instead, Anthony's right leg bounced vigorously against the floor of the car, so much so that the car itself began to shake slightly with the rhythm he created. He hated being alone with his thoughts. They always pushed him down the wrong path.

Anthony needed to find some distraction. Quickly he patted the pocket areas of the gray sweatpants. They were empty. His cell phone was still plugged in on Detective Burrows' desk. He cursed silently. Puffing out his chest, Anthony arched his back as if somebody had put ice cubes down his shirt, trying to stretch his stiff muscles. The fact that he was taller than average and sitting in the backseat of a car also didn't help. He felt cramped. Lying down on his back, he closed his eyes and tried to focus his mind on something else. Anything else? All that came to mind was Wendy, which only exacerbated his empty feeling of loneliness. It also encouraged his internal voice to become louder.

Come on! This time we can see if he'll give us some shrooms. Huh? What do you think about that? Then we can be with Wendy again, even for a little while. Does that sound good? You know it does. We can get high and take all this heartache away.

With brute force, Anthony began slamming his right fist into the back seats. He would not give in to this. The image of a woman's silhouette, illuminated with yellow headlights and a pinched scream from her throat, entered Anthony's mind. Anthony's eyes snapped wide, and he took in a deep breath.

Do you want that memory to go away? You know what you have to do. He was right. It was the only way he knew how to silence the guilt, shame, and sorrow that continually plagued him. Sitting up, he looked out the window to the front porch. No movement. With speed like a tiger attacking its prey, he pounced at the door, took hold of the handle, and opened the passenger-side back door. He flung the door wide, and the brisk air hit him in the face, sending chills down his body. The hinged barrier was open. His freedom lay beyond its frame. Anthony remained frozen. Not a muscle in his body moved. This isn't right, he told himself. His mind fought back, screaming at him to run, abandon the detectives, buy some drugs and escape into bliss. Anthony's body refused to cooperate. He dared not even place any part of his body outside the vehicle. Staring down the row of yards and concrete driveways, he resolved to remain where he was. For Anthony, any other choice was as good as death.

*　　*　　*　　*

Once Luke had finished going through the living room, he started down the hallway. Mason had moved from the kitchen to the guest bathroom. Walking past him, Luke continued down the tan corridor and stepped into the master bedroom. Luke had noticed earlier that it looked like a tornado had been through this room. He would have to ask Anthony–if he was still there when they finished–if her room always looked like that or if he'd been the one to clutter it up.

Flipping the light switch, a yellow glow filled the room. Pink curtains covered a pair of windows above the bed on the far wall. Clothes were everywhere, all over the floor, though some had made it to the hamper. A wooden dresser sat against the wall across from the foot of the bed. On top of it was an even smaller tv than the one in the living room. Pulling open the top drawer, Luke began going through Wendy's clothes, removing them from the drawers and shaking them out. He worked his way down the dresser. Not a thing in any of those drawers could help their investigation. Then, stepping across the room, Luke opened the closet door. Different colored blouses, pants, and dresses hung from the rack on metal hangers. Below the clothing were dozens of pairs of shoes. Removing each one, Luke made sure there was nothing hidden inside any of them. Once he'd finished with the footwear, he noticed three decent-sized boxes sitting on a shelf above the clothing rack.

Lifting his arms, he took down each one and brought them to the queen-sized bed. The bed was adorned with a turquoise comforter and black sheets. Luke opened the first cardboard box. It was full of high school and college memorabilia. Replacing the lid, he moved on to the second box. It contained a bunch of birthday and Christmas cards. In the third was a bunch of manilla folders, each one home to a different set of important documents. Many were tax filings and returns from previous years. One folder contained the mortgage agreement for the house she had bought when she moved to St. Louis. Luke figured it wouldn't hurt to go through her finances, so he set the third box aside. Returning to the closet, he ran his hand along the shelf. Finding nothing, he returned the other two boxes to their former position in the cabinet.

"Find anything?" Mason's voice rang from the doorway.

Luke turned around and began walking toward the master bathroom.

"Just some financial documents. Not sure if they'll be of any use, but you'll let me know once you've examined them."

"Ha!" Mason cackled sarcastically. "I am the last person you want around numbers."

"Find anything in the bathroom?" Luke continued.

"Some standard Tylenol and over-the-counter meds," Mason said.

"You bag it?"

"Of course."

"Good. Will should be able to confirm that it is what it claims to be." Luke said.

Luke entered the large washroom. It was just as much of a mess as the bedroom. Finding only a small bottle of allergy medicine, he bagged it and went to see how Mason was coming along in the guest bedroom.

"This the last room?" Luke asked as he looked at his watch. 2:12 P.M.

"Yup. This is it," Mason responded. Luke took a deep breath.

"Alright," Luke began, "I'll start dusting for fingerprints."

CHAPTER 27

Mayor Robert Tyler's irritating voice came through the receiver of Victor Sorelli's landline, slightly distorted but unmistakably aggravated and paranoid. Victor had paid for the man's campaign and was (almost) single-handedly responsible for the overweight gambling buffoon winning the election. Now he was paying the dues, listening to the man's incessant whining about the investigation of the dead woman in front of The Cicero. Victor gripped the receiver in his left hand, barely holding it to his ear, as he paced the length of the room. With his free hand, he scratched at his chin and right cheek.

Most everyone questioned why Victor kept the landline. Typically, he told them because they were harder to trace. When telephones were first invented and became affordable, everyone needed one. Nowadays, though, it doesn't matter. The technology had far surpassed the relic in his hand. If he were honest with himself, he would admit he kept the old phone because it reminded him of the past. 'The Glory Days' as many people referred to them. Were those days so glorious? The thought plagued Victor's mind. The days when accomplishing a simple drug drop was tedious, and the threat of discovery loomed more significant—the days when people's morality wasn't as flexible. The days were filled to the brim with dirt, sweat, grime, and blood. So much blood.

Victor blinked away memories that had given way to myths and legends. It was much easier to live as a criminal in the world that he, his father, and his father's father had built. However, Victor wanted to make sure Anthony knew what it was to be genuinely committed to this life, to this family. Anthony had carried out the assassination with precision and tenacity, but the act had cracked something inside his son. A part of the boy couldn't handle what he had done.

It was as if Anthony was on a raft in the ocean, and the raft had fractured, allowing water to slowly seep in, sinking the boat and taking Anthony along with it. Try though he may, his son knew he was sinking, but he'd grown complacent with the bit of water that had entered. First, he failed to recognize the deluge that threatened to engulf him. Then, it was too late when he began trying to remove the water. To make matters worse, the boy had three life rafts to choose from: the one that Victor tossed him, wanting him to grab hold and come aboard the family's boat; the second inflated for a period of time before deflating, only to repeat its queasy ebb and flow again and again as time passed and the effects of the drugs wore off; the final life raft was thrown to him by the redheaded whore, with her promises to bring him onto her boat, but it was all lies. Instead, she would drag him along while he clung to the small and insignificant life she provided him. Victor let out a small sigh.

"...and Chief Reilly is stonewalling me at every turn." Mayor Tyler's high-pitched, distorted voice roused him from his thoughts. The man was a chatterbox.

Victor turned slightly and took in his surroundings. It had been a long time since he'd last been in the parlor. The mansion's receiving room boasted gleaming white walls, each with spiraling columns of Venetian red marble reaching from floor to ceiling. Spread throughout the room were several baroque-style sofas, chairs, and ottomans, each covered with sumptuous leather. Darkened oak end tables, topped with gilded glass ashtrays, bookended the sitting area. Inset at the base of the east wall was an ornately sculpted alabastrine fireplace, with hand-carved golden cherubs gracing the white stone. At the room's center sat an enormous custom pool table. Wooden legs rose to hold a large marble slab crowned with smooth, blood-red velvet. Victor, his father Anthony, and his grandfather Marco brought the high-ranking city and state officials to the mansion. They entertained them in the parlor with authentic Cuban cigars, smooth Italian Grappa, and some friendly games at the pool table. Sometimes his wife, Isabella, would drop in and pay a visit to their esteemed guests. Isabella.

How he missed her. She had been an exquisite creature. Her slender face and impeccable figure danced in his mind's eye. Tender lips sat beneath her sharp nose, and blazing green eyes sparkled with mischief, beckoning him to join her in the dream scene. Her thick, black hair was so long it flowed like a river from the top of her head to the middle of her back. She'd been the one woman able to handle him, the best companion Victor could've ever wanted. Even with her independent spirit, she understood her place and the role she was to play for the future of the family. Taking his seed and producing him a son, helping raise the boy to be the man he needed to be to take over someday. She was unable to fulfill those requirements by no fault of her own. She'd been taken from Victor too soon, and he and Anthony had both suffered at the loss of such an incredible woman.

Victor had never tried to replace her, though that isn't to say he no longer had any carnal needs. His sexual appetite had dwindled with Isabella's passing, but it had not been removed from him. He took extreme precautions to keep Anthony in the dark when having one of his concubines over to the mansion. He took great care in safeguarding these trysts. Any woman he intended to have relations with was to be sterilized. This, of course, was a consensual gesture. Victor never forced any of them to go through with the procedure. He did, however, offer them a sizable compensation if they did. Victor could not have any bastards running around trying to claim the empire for their own or try and carve out a section of it for themselves. It belonged to his only heir: his true-born son, Anthony.

Decades ago, he had nearly ruined everything. First, Isabella had been unable to conceive, and Victor had pushed her away for a time. Then, he began to have an intimate relationship with their maid, and the woman became pregnant. Weeks later, so had Isabella. He'd realized his horrid mistake in time to convince the poor woman to terminate the child growing inside her and never to contact them again. Thankfully, Isabella had never found out.

"Are you planning to do anything about this?" the mayor's nagging voice asked.

Victor snapped out of his reminiscence and put the phone near his lips.

"Don't worry about anything, Robert," Victor's voice was deep and authoritative. "I will handle it. All of it."

Victor could hear the mayor's heavy breathing as he pondered Victor's words. Patiently, Victor waited for the man to respond. Initially, Victor had backed Tyler because his platform wasn't too conservative or progressive–and the man had an itch that he knew how to scratch. With the gambling illness that plagued Tyler, it was no difficult task to make sure he understood who he ultimately worked for. Of course, it didn't hurt that in addition to being malleable and a good orator, the man was an imbecile.

Victor sat down in the small leather chair next to the telephone.

"You're sure, Victor?" Mayor Tyler begged for reassurance. Victor winced; he hated it when people other than his family used his first name. Then, keeping his cool, he let out a breath and answered.

"One hundred percent, Mayor. You need not worry more about any of it for a minute."

"I hope you're right," Tyler acquiesced, "because I heard something through the grapevine..."

Victor shut his eyes and inhaled deeply. He knew where this was going. "It regards your son. He seems to have been spotted conversing with detectives down at the station. Now I don't know about you, Victor, but I don't like it. Whatever could your son be talking to detectives about if not me gambling at the hotel?"

Removing the receiver from his ear, Victor shook his head. The nerve of this fool. To be so narcissistic as to think that Anthony would go out of his way to turn in the mayor for something so inconsequential was astonishing.

Victor released an incredulous sigh and returned the receiver to his ear. "Trust me, Rob, even if it is true that he was there, he wouldn't be discussing your affairs. Now, I'm going to lay this out for you as best I can: I will handle Everything. I will handle the cops, the hotel, Anthony, Everything. Okay? You hang tight, sign your paper, and play blackjack on your phone for the time being." Victor's tone held a twinge of aggression, but he was able to get his point across to the doltish man.

"Okay, Victor. I will let you handle things. You will notify me when the poker games resume, won't you?" Mayor Tyler asked with haste.

"Of course, sir. Good day to you."

With that, Victor roughly sat the black receiver back on its base and reclined against the back of the chair. I'm getting too old for this, Victor said to himself. He needed Anthony to come to his senses and return home, to let Victor help him get over what he's going through and learn to do his part for the family. Victor rose to his feet. As he did, his hip gave a loud POP! He let out a small groan and ambled slowly toward the pool table in the middle of the parlor. He reached down to pull the release lever, and the sound of the hard pool balls stampeding from their cage rang in his eardrums. The spheres of pure ivory rolled across the soft velvet, corralling together in the pit at the end of the table.

Victor stepped to the north side of the fireplace, where the pool sticks, and ball rack were kept. The rack was hanging on the wall, just below Victor's line of sight. He grabbed it and went back to the red-topped game table. Setting it gently on the table, he bent down and began haphazardly moving the solid and striped balls to the tabletop. Once they were all there, he began organizing them in the triangular rack. At the top was the solid, yellow ball with the number 1 at its center. From there, he started the sequence down the size, alternating types, from striped to solid to stripe to solid, all the way around on all three sides. Once done, only three balls remained the solid brown ball, number 7; the brown striped ball, number 15; and the solid black 8-ball. Victor grabbed the 7-ball with his left hand and the 15-ball with his right, placing them accordingly in the rack. Last, he sat the 8-ball at its rightful place in the center of the triangle. Pushing the rack full of pool balls back and forth over the velvet, he finally felt comfortable with how they rolled. With a SNAP, he slammed the balls tight to the front of the triangle, shoving his old, bony fingers behind them to hold them tight as he slowly removed the wooden rack.

Having finished that, Victor returned the rack to the wall and picked up his favorite pool cue. It was long, handcrafted, dark maple wood, protected with a polyurethane coating and a leather tip on the end. Reaching down, Victor grabbed a small cube of blue chalk and began rubbing it onto the tip of his pool cue. As he did so, he looked at the clock on the mantle. 3:24 P.M. He still hadn't heard anything from or about Sam. Shaking his head, he walked back to the table. He couldn't believe it; the man better hope Victor never saw him again, or there'll be hell to pay. Victor made it to the end of the table, opposite the pool balls, sat the cube of chalk on the edge of the table, reached down, and picked up the white cue ball. Placing it before him, he leaned over, lined up his stick with the cue, and hit the white ball with perfect force. The ivory balls collided together with a loud Clack! Before rolling away towards their splayed destinations.

*   *   *   *

Chief Reilly sat behind his desk, reading through final case reports. The overhead light in his office was off. Only the small desk lamp and the two-floor lamps in the far corners of the room brought forth illumination. His white hair was somewhat frazzled. He'd been running a hand through it for the past couple of hours, hoping he'd made the right decision letting Burrows and Mason take Anthony Sorelli on an impromptu ride-along. The possibility of the man running off, never to be seen or heard from again, ate at the aged detective's mind. So far, Anthony Sorelli was their only link to the murdered woman—who, with Anthony's identification and Dr. Wright's later confirmation, was now known to be twenty-nine-year-old Wendy Grayson.

The words on the white sheet in his hands began to blur together. Sitting the papers down, Chief Reilly rubbed his eyes with his hands. First, he needed to figure out which report he was currently reviewing. This had been happening all afternoon. He'd managed to get through two reports so far, but four more waited patiently on his desk. Silently, he'd been praying all day that his decision had been purely objective and not influenced by his deep-seated desire to see the end of the Sorelli family criminal empire. Sitting on his desk, beside the mouse for his desktop computer, lay his cigar. The end of the tobacco-filled wrapping was soggy from resting in Reilly's moist mouth. Reilly picked up the cigar and studied it for a moment before bringing it to his nose and deeply inhaling its intoxicating scent. Frowning, he tossed the thing into the trash can beside his desk. Reaching to his collar, Reilly unfastened the top button of his shirt. Perspiration beaded at his neck and throat. He'd received no news from Burrows or Mason since they had departed. Hopefully, that was good news. God only knows; He could use some of that.

Reilly was certain the mayor would call him again—which would be the second time today—to get an update. So far, there hasn't been a call. Maybe the man finally understood that you couldn't rush these things. Leaning back in his seat, Reilly folded his arms across his chest. He needed to find a way to take his mind off this particular case. Being the big boss meant that he could not show special treatment to particular cases. But when cases involve the Sorellis... Reilly's thoughts drifted off. There wasn't a single case he could recall that had directly involved a member of the Sorelli family. Not until this one. He knew Burrows would do his best to link one of the two Sorelli men to the murder. All Reilly could hope was that the man would do it right and not try to fudge anything.

Standing to his feet, Reilly stretched his arms, back, and legs the best he could. The man had been sitting for hours, and it felt like every muscle he had was cramped. Then, like a tortoise, Reilly began slowly pacing the width of his office. With each step, he attempted anew to clear his mind. He began by thinking about his family, his wife, and daughters and what they might be doing at this very moment. How were his daughters doing with their respective boyfriends? What would his wife be making for dinner? Maybe pasta? Eventually, his mind inevitably made it back to the Sorelli case.

Cursing to himself, he tried numerous other topics, including foreign policy, the yearly fun run, and the days he and his siblings spent working with their father and mother to build their house. It was all in vain. Somehow, his mind always segwayed back to the Sorellis and their possible involvement with the dead woman. Reilly had successfully curbed his obsession all these years because there hadn't been anything good enough to bring him anywhere close to the crime syndicate. Now, however, this could be it. This case could finally be the nail in their coffin. Reilly stopped pacing mid-stride and pondered that hope for a moment. He'd been after these people for so long and pushed Burrows down the same all-consuming path. What would it be like to finally have it put to rest? Reilly didn't have an answer.

Returning to his desk, he sat back down in his seat and picked up the paper sheets. The old man did his best to focus long enough to read them. It took him several minutes to finish one page. Another twenty passed before he finished the whole report. After flipping the final page, Rielly picked up a pen and signed off on the report before placing the papers back in the manilla folder from whence they came. He then set the folder in his stack of completed work. Having finally finished one report, he gathered up the next one on the stack and read through it. As he approached the end of the last page, the phone on his desk began to ring.

*　　*　　*　　*

The yellow sun was beginning to hang low in the sky. He looked at the watch on his wrist. It was a quaint thing, nothing too fancy. It had a silver body with two brown leather straps. The clock face read 4:15 P.M. The sun would be gone entirely beyond the horizon in a little over an hour. He'd sat here patiently all afternoon, sipping on his bottle of water, eating peanuts, and waiting. Nothing had occurred since the detectives had left the station several hours ago. Lifting his binoculars to his eyes, he peered down the street. Anthony's car was still parked in the same spot. Nothing had changed. The birds that had been serenading him left some time ago. There had also been no further disruptions from the trunk. Hopefully, Mr. Hunter realized escape was futile. He couldn't blame the man for trying, though. He'd have been disappointed if Mr. Hunter hadn't tried to free himself. The man was a brute, no doubt about that, strong as a mule too. Loading the large man into the trunk had been slightly more painstaking than he had first imagined. In retrospect, he should have had the trunk open and invited Mr. Hunter over for a question before knocking the man unconscious. Then, he would guide him into the cargo space while he fell. Maybe next time, he thought to himself.

With the sun setting soon, he needed to decide about tonight. When should he leave, and where should he take his hostage? With the cover of darkness, he was tempted to risk moving closer to the cop house, but it would be difficult to tell who was coming and going. No. Not the right play. Every minute the sun sank lower and lower, moving as fast as it could to the other side of the planet. He would leave and return in the morning, hoping to find clues of Anthony's whereabouts. If he could not place where Anthony was by 5 P.M. tomorrow, his plan would need to be altered. Anthony needed to be within the proper vicinity for Everything to go smoothly.

He inhaled a deep breath and savored the fresh pine scent that filled the sedan's interior. His vehicle was spotless on the inside. Not one piece of trash, or stray chunk of food, was anywhere to be found. He took pride in his car, just like he took pride in his plan. No one could have done it any better than he. Yesterday, today, and tomorrow, that's all there was. That's all there needed to be.

Softly, he whispered to himself, "But know this, if the master of the house had known in what hour of the night the thief was coming, he would have stayed awake and would not have let his house be broken into." Then, closing his eyes, he took in another deep breath. He'd come across this phrase in The Bible. He couldn't remember the passage, but he always felt it applied to him and his plans for Victor and Anthony Sorelli. But, of course, things would get extremely messy if anything were to last beyond tomorrow. That was part of the gamble, though.

Everything one does in life is a risk. But most of the time, it wasn't a very large risk. Most people live their lives 'risk averse', or so they tell themselves, but every time they step onto the sidewalk, drive a car, ride in a taxi, or turn on their oven, they risk their health, safety, life, or all three combined. But, of course, these risks usually pay off, and they go on to live their lives another day. But for some, that life isn't enough. They need the rush to live life on the edge. These are the people that run into burning buildings, jump out of airplanes, and commit murder.

All this considered, the man had done his best to mitigate the risks involved in this extreme plan. He'd studied all these people for years and was confident in the decisions they would make. He'd even studied the minor players, like the C.S.I. William Johnson, and Medical Examiner, Melinda Wright. He even knew approximately how long it would take them to find and finalize their results. If he managed to misjudge any of them, which so far he hadn't (other than Anthony's miraculous disappearance from the police station), Everything could come crashing down. He couldn't let that happen. He refused to let that happen. He repeated it over and over in his mind yesterday, today, and tomorrow.

Yesterday, today, and tomorrow.

Worry and doubt began to creep into his mind for the first time since he put his plan into motion. He hated doubting himself. It made him feel like one of the lessers. Lessers were nothing but cannon fodder. They possessed no real talent or brains. If any of them did happen to have a hint of either, they squandered it every time. Lessers deserved their unfulfilling lives. They were vermin to him. To show anything in himself that would be comparable to the lessers was abhorrent because he was anything but a lesser. Bile began to rise in his throat and into his mouth as his thoughts dwelled on his weakness. Slowly, he cracked his door and spat onto the pavement. Grabbing the bottle of water in the cup holder, he took a small sip and swished the liquid in his mouth. Leaning his head out the cracked door again, he spits once more. Finally, he closed the door and sat there, silently chiding himself and reassuring his mind. I've made contingency plans, he told himself. Everything will work out one way or another.

Again, he whispered just loud enough for himself to hear, "But know this, if the master of the house had known in what hour of the night the thief was coming, he would have stayed awake and would not have let his house be broken into."

CHAPTER 28

The three men sat silently in the car as they drove down the street. The setting sun emblazoned the sky with its farewell to their left. Luke looked out the window past Mason's head. It was about halfway behind the horizon. Soon it would be dark, and darkness is when the monsters come out to play.

When the detectives exited Wendy Grayson's house, they first noticed that the passenger side back door to the car was wide open. Both men froze on the front porch, staring at the sight. Their initial thoughts were that Mr. Sorelli had used his opportunity and taken to the wind. Slowly they walked to the car, Luke cursing himself with each step. Upon reaching the open door, they peered in to find that Anthony was still there, lying across the leather seats. Both men let out huge sighs of relief. They'd put a lot of faith and trust into the man and were pleased to see that he hadn't betrayed them. Luke and Mason made their way to the trunk and placed their equipment inside. The detectives looked at each other with eyes wide with disbelief. They knew they had dodged a bullet. Closing the trunk, they walked back to their respective sides of the black vehicle, Luke shutting the back door as he passed it and entered the car. Buckling his seat belt, Luke spoke to the prone figure in the back seat, "You gave us quite a scare."

Luke turned to see Anthony had sat up straight and was eager to respond.

"Yeah, sorry about that," Anthony replied. "It won't happen again." Luke gave him a slight nod and turned back to face the front, as Mason shifted the transmission into reverse and began backing out of the driveway. Mason pressed the accelerator, and the V8 roared to life as more gasoline entered the engine with the pressure Mason applied to the pedal.

"So, what did you find?" Anthony asked eagerly. "Anything good?"

The two detectives shared a glance before Mason responded.

"Nothing conclusive yet."

"Nothing conclusive?" Anthony's tone was full of disappointment and confusion. "What the hell does that mean?"

"It means we took several fingerprints and some physical evidence for analysis. There was no sign of anyone else besides you being in the house. There were also no obvious signs of any drug paraphernalia," Mason explained.

Anthony wrinkled his forehead. "Of course, there were no signs of drugs. Wendy didn't do drugs. I've already told both of you this." Agitation crept into Anthony's voice. He leaned back against the seat and crossed his arms over his chest.

Luke sat in silence, staring out the windshield, as Mason explained to Mr. Sorelli why they needed to be sure there were no illicit drugs in the house. The man was still shocked that the detectives didn't take him at his word. Luke's partner did his best to explain how even though they did believe him, they were still trained investigators and to be sure of a conviction (if they ever found who was responsible) they needed to do all the work, so there'd be no way the defense could poke holes in their case. Eventually, Anthony conceded and let the matter drop. Luke was glad of that. He needed the silence.

The next destination was the hospital where Wendy Grayson was employed. Hopefully someone there will be able to shed some more light on this thing, Luke thought. A small whiff of alcohol triggered Luke's mind. Putting his face to the old navy jacket, he breathed deeply. There it was his father's favorite drink: bourbon. No matter how many times Luke washed the thing, the odor remained. It was as if the fibers had been soaked in the liquor before they were sewn together.

Luke returned his attention to the window beside him. The world outside seemed to float like the old scenery wheels used in films almost a hundred years ago. The dead trees, the buildings, and even the pedestrians on the sidewalk became a blur of shapes and colors as Luke's mind drifted to thoughts of his childhood. Specifically, to one of his little league games. Luke cracked a thin smile as he thought about it.

The scent of the freshly cut grass mixed with his sweat. The sun was high in the clear sky. Finally, Luke was up to bat. Grabbing the aluminum baseball bat, he jogged onto the field, black helmet firmly on his head. He used to love baseball. From time to time, he still loved watching a game on tv or trying to get tickets to a Cardinals game when they were home. Hell, he remembered the thing that propelled him to want to take up the sport: the film The Sandlot. It was such an inspiring tale of chasing your dreams and friendship, and the connective tissue of the whole thing was baseball. In this particular game, however, it was the bottom of the ninth, and they lost by one. Luke's team had one man on second and two outs. It was up to eleven-year-old Luke to make sure the group stayed alive. Luke raised the bat and took up his stance over home plate. With a short glance at the benches, he could see his parents watching him with anticipation and hope. Returning his attention to the pitcher, Luke prepared himself for the throw. The first pitch was a curveball, Luke stepped but didn't swing. The umpire called 'strike one.'

Young Luke refocused himself and waited for the next pitch. Luke hit the second fastball, but it crossed the foul line. Sweat trickled down his face as he stared down the pitcher, waiting for the third throw. A splitter that ended up out of the strike zone, "Ball," called the umpire. Luke exhaled deeply and raised his bat for the next pitch. Luke swung and missed. Strike two.

The pressure now increased a hundredfold. Luke took his stance and concentrated. He was focused on nothing but the ball in the pitcher's hand. Nodding to the catcher, the pitcher reared back his arm, brought it forward with all his might, and threw the ball toward home plate. Luke saw it coming, and he tightened his grip on his bat. When the ball came within range, he swung with all his might, and, to his dismay, his ears filled with the sound of a THUD! Luke had missed.

The ball flew past him and into the catcher's mitt. The opposing team was cheering and celebrating as Luke made his walk of shame back to the dugout. In the distance, he could hear his father saying, 'It's alright, son, you did good,' but Luke knew what awaited him when they arrived home. Henry Burrows hated losing, hated it with everything he had. Even if it hadn't been Luke as the final batter, his father would still have been angry. However, Luke's father was never physically abusive. Rather, Henry was loud and would verbally berate Luke and his mother whenever they disappointed him. He threatened physical violence once or twice but never went through with it. Luke was always amazed at how his father could keep his composure in public while seething within. If Luke's team happened to win a game, or if Luke accomplished something, Henry would brag to the world about it. The man's public appearance and reputation meant more to him than anything else in his life, and to cope with the fact that it was all a facade, he drank.

Luke did have some good memories with his father. However, he could count those on the one hand. Luke didn't hate his father—he'd raised Luke the best he could, and Luke wouldn't be the man he was today without him—but after his mother passed away, Luke had not visited Henry more than once a year, up until the old man's death last winter. Luke's mother had been the one that could soothe him, even when he'd been hitting the bottle a touch too hard. Seeing the fermented liquid's effect on his father, Luke vowed never to touch a drop of the stuff. He was mocked and ridiculed in college for his decision, but Luke shrugged it off. He wouldn't classify his father as a bad man, but he also didn't want to become like his father.

Mason pulled the Charger into a parking spot in one of the middle tiers of Memorial Hospital's parking garage. The imposing structure housed five separate levels of parking spaces. The sound of exhaust from the muscle car echoed as they wound their way through each tier. This particular level was mostly empty. Mason had picked a spot far enough away from the elevator that if people did show up, they would park closer to it than his car. Mason shut off the engine of the motorized beast and looked at Luke.

"You ready?" he asked.

"Ready as I'll ever be," Luke replied. Turning to Anthony, he said, "You know the rule, don't leave the car."

Anthony nodded and said, "Can I at least step out and stretch before you two leave? I've been sitting in this back seat for hours."

Mason and Luke exchanged glances. Luke was initially against the idea, but what harm could it do? Besides, the man was taller than average and had cooperated thus far.

"Sure," Luke said, "you have five minutes."

"Thank you," Anthony said as he opened the back door on the driver's side and climbed out.

Luke watched him through the window. The large man stretched his arms over his head, bent at his waist multiple times, and began pacing the length of the car. Luke couldn't help but grin at the highwater sweatpants.

"So, do you think he'll stay again?" Luke asked, not removing his eyes from Mr. Sorelli.

"I hope so," Mason replied, "but if he doesn't, there's a surveillance camera aimed directly at our car, and cameras are scattered throughout the parking structure. So, we'll at least be able to track where he exits and in which direction he goes."

Luke nodded his approval. Anthony was still pacing, stretching different muscles as he did so. Luke wasn't sure how this case would play out, but he hoped it wouldn't come to a physical altercation. Anthony had the advantage in that arena.

"What're we going to do with him tonight?" Luke asked. "We can't leave him at the station."

The two men sat in silence, thinking about a possible solution. Then, after a bit, Mason finally answered.

"I can drop you both off at a safe house while I return the evidence to Will. I'll wait and help him if he needs it."

"Not a horrible idea," Luke conceded, his tone suggesting that he wasn't completely on board. Nevertheless, the thought of spending the entire night with Anthony Sorelli made him cringe.

"We can't hide him at the station," Mason explained. "We were lucky that Victor's spies didn't see him the second time. So, this is our best bet to keep him under our guard until we can release him."

"How come we can't switch roles?" Luke asked tenaciously, "Why don't you babysit, and I'll help Will."

"Because we need to keep up appearances," Mason justified. "It'll be late when I return, and, knowing you've been working late nights for the past few months, I'll take this one and take you home."

"But you're not taking me home. And I'll still be working," Luke retorted.

"Nobody else will know that" Mason answered, not budging an inch. Luke gave him a nod, and as he did, Anthony opened the driver-side rear door and entered the car. The tall man gave them each a thumbs up as he closed the door behind him.

"Thanks again. I appreciate it," Anthony said.

"Not a problem," Mason replied. Then, looking at Luke, he said, "Ready?"

In response, Luke grabbed the door handle and exited the vehicle. Mason and Luke shut their doors, Mason locked the car with his key fob, and they proceeded across the concreted ground toward the elevator.

*   *   *   *

Patients, family members, doctors, and nurses roamed the halls of St. Louis Memorial Hospital. The reflective tile flooring helped illuminate the walkways. Everything smelled sterile. Detectives Burrows and Mason had ridden the elevator to the main floor and were snaking their way through the maze of hallways and foyers, searching for the main desk. Inside every room they passed, someone was residing within, either dying, healing, or somewhere in between. Hospitals are a place of life. Hospitals are a place of death. Hospitals save lives. Hospitals lose lives. Hospitals were one of

Luke's least favorite places on the planet. He hadn't been in too many, but everyone smelled the same and had the same strange aura. The constant exchanging of souls created a tranquil yet disturbing feeling that seeped from every brick, stud, a sheet of plaster, tile, and piece of equipment in the building.

As Luke and Mason finally approached the desk they were searching for; Luke noted the young woman was sitting behind the circular workstation. She looked to be about the same age as the two detectives. Perhaps not conventionally attractive, but Luke also didn't think she was ugly. She had black hair, brown eyes, and a soft smile. She wore a white coat over a blue blouse and black pants. The name on her coat read: Ali Long.

"How can I help you, gentlemen?" Miss Long asked. Her voice was an average pitch for a woman. Her tone, upon first hearing it, could be mistaken for enthusiasm. However, Luke could detect a hint of sarcasm in her voice.

"You already have," Mason replied with a smirk. Ali Long's cheeks flushed red for a few seconds as she turned away and smiled a genuine smile. The man knew how to charm any of them, Luke thought. "But we wouldn't object to more," Mason finished.

Reaching into his pocket, Luke produced his badge. Showing it to the receptionist, he said, "I'm Detective Burrows with the St. Louis Police Department; this is my partner Detective Casanova."

Mason couldn't contain himself and let out a half chuckle at Luke's comment. The woman's smile faded slightly, unsure how to take the joke she'd just heard.

"Do you know a nurse by the name of Wendy Grayson?" Luke asked. It took a minute for the woman to register what Luke had asked her. She was still trying to determine if she should be offended by the joke or by its implications of it.

"I've heard the name," Ali finally answered, "but I don't know the woman. Is she in some trouble?"

Mason and Luke exchanged glances. The two of them agreed it would not be best to discuss any of this with someone who didn't know the victim. Instead, they needed to find some people who worked closely with Wendy and to see if they could give insight into who would want her dead.

"No, no trouble," Mason replied. "Is there anyone that you know that works closely with her?"

Ali shook her head and proceeded, "I can tell you she worked mostly in the ER."

"The ER. Thanks, sweetness," Mason said.

The two detectives turned to go. Luke glared at Mason and gave him an eye roll. They both silently laughed as they walked down another hallway to the Emergency Room wing of the hospital. Walking past many patient rooms, they could hear all sorts of different sounds coming from within them. From some came sobs and weeping. From others, there were sounds of laughter. The sound of television shows streamed from still others.

Some rooms were quiet, not a peep to be heard. The trek to the ER wasn't very long. Luke and Mason reached it within five minutes. Everything seemed relatively peaceful at the moment, which was good for them. They could ask questions and not worry about any staff assisting with some crazy injury. From their current position, Luke could see a female nurse standing in front of the reception desk, speaking with another nurse who sat behind it. The person in front of the tall, crescent-shaped table was a heavier-set woman with brown hair. She wore blue scrubs and tennis shoes. Behind the desk sat an older woman with graying hair and deep wrinkles.

"Evening, ladies," Luke said as they approached. The woman in the blue scrubs turned to face the interruption. She had a soft, round, attractive face with hazel eyes. Removing his badge again, he showed it to the women before continuing, "I'm Detective Burrows with the St. Louis Police Department. This is my partner, Detective Mason."

Confusion and curiosity played back and forth across the two women's faces. Then, before Luke could continue, the older woman asked in a frail voice, "What can we do for you, Detective?"

For a beat, nobody spoke. Neither Mason nor Luke wanted to ruin either of these women's days, but this was the job.

"Do either of you know a nurse by the name of Wendy Grayson?" Mason asked, breaking the silence. Both the women's eyes went wide, signaling to Luke and Mason that they did know her. The two females were lost for a minute, trying to figure out what two detectives could want with their friend.

"Yes, we both know Wendy," the younger woman answered. "Why? Is she in some trouble?"

Luke pursed his lips and was about to speak up when Mason beat him to it.

"Not anymore," Mason began. "She's dead."

The words were odd, even though Luke knew them to be true. Mason put as much empathy into his voice as one might expect from a man of his stature. The two women's eyes went wide, and their mouths fell open. The younger woman in the blue scrubs clasped her right hand over her mouth as she processed the information. Luke could see tears forming in their eyes.

"We're truly sorry for your loss," Luke said consolingly. "I know this may seem unsympathetic, but…."

"How?" The older woman cut him off. "Who did it?" Her voice was stern and determined.

"We're trying to figure everything out," Mason said.

"When?" The younger woman broke in. "On the news, there was mention of a woman's body found outside some hotel." Her voice was quaking as she spoke. "That's not…." She looked at the detectives, reading the confirmation written on their faces. "Oh, God!" Clasping her hand back over her mouth, she sank to her knees and began breathing rapidly. Bending down, Luke took her left hand in his and looked into her hazel eyes.

"I'm sorry for doing this," he began, "but I need you to breathe, okay?" She nodded her head slowly as the tears poured down her cheeks.

"Okay, follow me," Luke said. "In through your nose," Luke inhaled, exhaled out his mouth, "out through your mouth," Luke repeated the breathing exercise until she started mimicking him. "There ya go. In the nose, out the mouth."

The older woman had taken her seat behind the desk and was utterly silent. She looked as if she was on another planet. Completely spaced. Slowly, Luke rose to his feet, bringing the young nurse with him. Ushering her behind the desk, he guided her into another chair. The two detectives waited in silence as they let the news sink in. If this was how these two reacted, Luke believed Mason's story about Anthony's reaction to identifying the body.

"Now, I know this is a lot to take in. And we don't want to add any more stress or worry than we already have," Mason said, "but we need to ask the two of you some questions."

The two women nodded their understanding but remained silent. Mason looked to Luke for encouragement. Luke gave him a slight shrug as he brought out a small notepad and pen.

"When was the last time either of you saw Miss Grayson?" Mason asked gently. For a moment, neither woman said anything. Luke was beginning to wonder if they could handle the questions at this time when the younger woman spoke up.

"Monday night," she said shakily.

"Monday night," Mason repeated. "Do you happen to recall what time on Monday night?"

Inhaling deeply, the brown-haired nurse began to sob, "I don't know... um...maybe around ten-thirty or so." Her nose began to leak. Luke looked around the desk until he spotted a box of tissues. Grabbing it, he handed it to the crying woman. She accepted it, took two tissues from the cardboard box, and buried her nose into them, blowing loudly. Luke never really understood the science behind crying and runny noses. Why does your nose run when you cry? He asked himself. Mentally, he shook his head and returned to the task at hand.

"Okay, ten-thirty on Monday night," Mason started. "Did she seem like herself?"

The two women looked at each other, confused.

"What do you mean exactly?" the older lady asked.

"Well, was she preoccupied with something or anxious in any way? Was she acting out of character? Did she seem easily irritated or nervous?" Mason clarified.

"No, nothing like that," recounted the elderly woman. "She was the same old Wendy. Happy, always ready to jump in and do whatever is needed."

Luke was taking notes, and he smiled to himself as he wrote. Mason hated trying to read his notes. 'They may as well be in Chinese.' he had once said. Both women seemed to have controlled themselves for the time being. Luke prepared himself for another burst of tears and sobs.

"Do you know if she had any enemies?" Mason asked, beginning another round of questions. Each woman's face became distorted in its unique way. The younger woman scrunched up her nose, and her mouth was agape, but her bottom jaw hung slightly off center. The grayed-haired receptionist's eyes seemed to pop out of her head, and Luke swore he saw even more wrinkles appear on her already deeply lined face.

"Enemies?" stuttered the old woman in disbelief. "Wendy was the sweetest person in this hospital. I dare say in this whole city." She looked disgustedly at Mason for even suggesting such a thing.

Luke and Mason had grown used to it. Nobody enjoyed the persona of someone they admired being scrutinized or that person's integrity being questioned. More times than Luke could count. However, most people weren't who they appeared to be.

"Everybody liked Wendy," the young nurse put in. "Everybody, the staff, the doctors, the patients, the families."

Mason nodded, noting he understood. "Do you know if she was dating anybody?"

Now, this was a multilayered question that Luke had been waiting for. If they said yes, but didn't know who, they'd be most likely telling the truth. If they said yes and gave the name of someone besides Anthony, they were most likely covering for Miss Grayson. If they said no, they didn't know their precious Wendy as much as they thought they did. Both detectives waited with bated breath.

"No, not to my knowledge," said the younger woman. Luke didn't see any deceit in her face or body language.

"As far as I knew, she was single," the older woman concurred—still no sign of deception.

So, Miss Grayson either didn't discuss her personal life with her coworkers or willingly omitted that part of her life. The thought came to Luke's mind almost immediately.

"What do you know about Wendy other than her work here?" Luke asked, eyeing them intently.

Both women started talking over each other in a barrage of statements, making it hard for Luke and Mason to keep track.

"She's from Oklahoma." said the younger woman.

"Her mother's side is originally from France," added the older.

"She has two sisters, and her parents own three dogs," recounted the younger.

"When she was twelve, she broke her leg in a four-wheeler accident." offered the older.

And on and on they went. Luke noted that Wendy Grayson had decidedly not shared her relationship with Anthony Sorelli with these two women. Perhaps they could find someone here that she did confide that information, but he doubted it. Exhaling, Luke mentally prepared himself for more interviews resembling this one.

CHAPTER 29

Anthony hated waiting just as much as he hated feeling useless, which at this moment, is what he felt like the most. His girlfriend had been killed, and here he sat in the back seat of a Dodge Charger, waiting for Holmes and Poirot to return with the answers. Anthony had tried to take a nap, and he was tired. Finding a comfortable position in the back of this car for an average-sized man would be difficult, but it was more like impossible for a man of Anthony's stature. Every time he closed his eyes, all he could see was Wendy, either happy and living life loudly or still and dead on the silver slab in the morgue. Most of the time, it was an amalgamation of the two. The imagery was overwhelming. Anthony had no idea if he'd ever be able to sleep again.

Sitting up straight, Anthony peered out the window to his left. The sun had disappeared for the day. Blackness filled the multistory concrete structure, except for small orbs of yellowish light scattered throughout. He'd heard one car drive past a while ago. Since then, there had been no sign of any life close to his location.

Anthony had never visited Wendy at the hospital. It was something they'd argued about multiple times. She never understood Anthony's resistance to public dates that weren't at one of his family's establishments. The few other places, like the movie theater and the park, were reluctantly approved by Anthony as a compromise. He had also impressed her with the importance of keeping their relationship to themselves. But, again, Wendy needed help understanding this. They were happy. Why couldn't they share that with the world?

It took Anthony over a year to finally trust her enough to tell her about some of his family's illicit activities; the surprise meeting with his father had exacerbated the issue. Mostly, he told her of the gambling hall in The Cicero, the drug scene, and the bribing of public officials. He dared not try to explain the prostitution ring or the cold-blooded murder. She needed to know that publicly expressing their relationship could give certain people leverage to use against him, which they could then use against his family's empire.

Initially, she was in denial, but after a little more elaboration and some family history, she understood. It was the hardest discussion they'd ever had, and Anthony wasn't ready for the possibility of Wendy leaving him. Still, she'd threaten to leave if he didn't open up to her about his staunchness for the secrecy of their relationship. So, he'd rolled the dice in the hopes that they land true. Initially, she had asked for some time to think through everything. Anthony hadn't loved the thought of that and was worried it would be the prelude to their end. He'd argued about it but quickly realized his best chance was to trust her even more and give her space to work everything out for herself.

Nearly a month later, she'd called to set up a meeting with him. The look on her face that day was the look of finality. She had made her decision and was prepared to deal with the consequences. Anthony could see there would be no talking her into staying with him if she decided to leave. They sat across from each other at their usual table at Marco's, Wendy looking somewhat nervous but headstrong. Anthony appeared to be more of a nervous wreck than she was. His black hair was messy, and he'd thrown on a nice shirt, but it was coated with wrinkles from top to bottom. The black pants he'd worn were covered in lint. If he weren't Anthony Sorelli, he would not have been admitted to a table. Sitting there, all he could think was that she was leaving, and he would return to where he was a year ago: the opiate-addicted son of the most powerful man in the state.

The host had brought them their most requested bottle of red wine, and Wendy had finished her first glass before she told Anthony her decision. She'd decided to stay with him. Anthony nearly broke out into tears of joy when she'd said it. He didn't think he'd ever smiled so big before in his life.

Her decision did come with conditions that Anthony was eager to agree with. First, she wanted safety and nothing to do with illegal activities. She didn't want to be an unknowing accomplice. Anthony agreed. Secondly, Wendy required that he commit to getting clean and remaining sober. Anthony agreed sheepishly. She knew he'd been getting high behind her back, and she wasn't stupid. Last, she wanted Anthony to emancipate himself from his father's grip and the family business. Anthony paused, and his face went blank. He had not expected this.

Victor wasn't a good man but was still Anthony's father. She made it clear that this last requirement could happen after a period of time. Wendy understood that it would take time to make sure that when Anthony did finally free himself and the two could finally run off together, Victor wouldn't follow. If Anthony agreed to all three of her conditions, she committed to stay with him and to keep their relationship a secret until they were out from underneath the shroud of the Sorelli name and businesses. They discussed this final condition of hers for more than an hour. Eventually, Anthony conceded and vowed to free himself from his father and the family business by the end of the year. That was a little long, in Wendy's opinion, but she compromised since Anthony knew Victor and had a better understanding of what this request truly entailed.

Blinding white lights tore Anthony from the memory and brought him back to the backseat of the muscle car. Anthony blinked away the harsh light and waited for his eyes to readjust. When they did, the darkness of the parking garage filled them. Anthony let out a small sob and a sigh. He knew he'd failed Wendy. She was dead because he didn't have the gumption to stand up to his old man. When he had finally brought it up and his father pushed back, Anthony had laid the blame squarely on her.

*　　*　　*　　*

He'd waited two hours after the sun had set before driving off. There was nothing more to do tonight except keep his hostage alive for a little longer. With no sign of Anthony, his nerves were trying to get the better of him. However, he anxiously reassured himself that Anthony would appear on time tomorrow.

"Yesterday, today, and tomorrow." He whispered.

The sedan glided over the pavement like a stone sliding over a frozen pond. The beams of white light beaming from the front of the vehicle went ahead, piercing the thick blackness of the night. Driving at this time of the evening, numerous cars were still out on the roads. That didn't bother him since he was a studied societal chameleon. Glancing down at his speedometer, he confirmed his current speed at 37mph—just two miles per hour greater than the speed limit. Not fast enough to arouse suspicion but also not too slow either, as most people drive over the limit regularly. As he drove through the city streets, past buildings, cars, and some languishing people, he wondered if Mr. Hunter was still conscious. He didn't imagine much exhaust fumes entering the trunk, but he wasn't naive. He knew there'd be some leakage. Some might wonder what Mr. Hunter had done to deserve the fate in store for him. The answer was quite simple: he'd accepted Victor Sorellis's offer. If Mr. Hunter had rejected the employment opportunity, some other poor sap would have been tied up in his trunk. He cared nothing about Mr. Hunter specifically. The brute was more than a hinge on a door, an object to achieve an outcome. Besides, Mr. Hunter knew the risks of working for a man as vile as Victor Sorelli.

Victor Sorelli, some considered him to be an even better criminal mastermind than the great Al Capone. They were wrong, of course, not just because Victor Sorelli was merely a caretaker of what his forefathers had built but because there was nothing great about Capone in the first place. Capone, Luciano, Genovese, Sorelli... all are just peddlers of flesh. They offered nothing but fractured carnal desires, and in turn, they drained the caches of their dignity, wealth, and self-control and damned their souls to Hell. His hands tightened on his steering wheel, turning his knuckles white. At the same time, his right foot began to expound more pressure on the accelerator. In one sense, he admired them for taking advantage of the lessers.

On the other hand, they could be exploiting the lessers in a much more productive manner, but their greed blinded them and rotted them from the inside, causing them to turn into lessers themselves over time. Sooner or later, some lessers fight back, like Detective Burrows. The detective thought of himself as intelligent, but so do all human beings, no matter their station. Some lessers are smart enough to admit they know nothing, but most don't.

Flashes of red and blue lights and the sound of sirens abruptly streamed through the air behind him. His heart skipped a beat. Why would they need to pull me over? he thought. This morning, he had triple-checked the blinkers, tag lights, tail, head, and brake lights. Feeling the increase in his speed, he glanced down at his speedometer. Forty-one miles per hour. He cursed himself as he looked in the rearview mirror, the lights and blaring siren gaining on him. He looked out the windshield. He was at least two car lengths from the nearest vehicle. Rechecking the mirror, nothing had changed. The lights were growing brighter, and the sirens louder. Luckily he was already in the right-hand lane. As the flashing lights approached a car's length away, he pulled over to the curb and waited for the inevitable.

The heart in his chest was pumping rapidly. He braced for the encounter, remembering to keep calm and cooperate with the officer. He inhaled a deep breath and looked in the rearview mirror in time to see the police car drive past him and up the street. He let out a sigh and sat in that same spot for another fifteen seconds. He berated himself for letting his emotions take hold of his physical actions. It was a common problem among the lessers, and he loathed anything within himself that could misconstrue him as a lesser.

Putting on his left turn signal, he looked and waited for a car to pass before reentering traffic. He still had a decent way to go before he reached his destination for the night. He wondered if the sound of the approaching police unit was a beacon of hope for Mr. Hunter. Perhaps it was. Perhaps the man had hoped to try and make some noise to get the officer's attention. If he had done that the officer would have had to die, and Mr. Hunter's expiration date would have arrived sooner than initially planned. Reaching up with his right hand, he wiped the sweat from his brow. Gently, he pressed on the accelerator as he watched the needle creep upwards, eventually stopping it just above the 30. He looked down at the clock on the radio, 8:00 P.M.

He whispered, "This is going to be a long night."

*   *   *   *

The sudden roar from the muffler beneath him jolted Sam from sleep. His body jerked so sharply it caused him to wince as a sharp pain stabbed at his neck. His muscles cried out, begging to stretch and move freely. Lying there, it felt as though rigor mortis had prematurely taken root in every fiber of his body. Sam was unsure how long he'd been bound and gagged in the trunk. But it seemed like an eternity. As the vehicle returned to its forward momentum, Sam wondered if keeping him here this long was necessary for his capture or if it was a form of psychological and physical torture. The longest Sam had ever left somebody in a car trunk was a couple of hours. Usually, when you toss someone in the trunk of a vehicle, it's solely for discreet transportation. However, Sam decided that he would use it for torture when he made it out of this scenario. Even those not prone to claustrophobia would eventually crack after being confined in a small, dark, inescapable prison for hours.

Sam felt the car eased to a stop. After about a minute, it began moving again. Stoplight, Sam thought. He was still amazed at the sheer gall of his captor. Either the man didn't know who he was dealing with, or he knew exactly who he was dealing with. The former was the more probable of the two. Seeing as the entirety of St. Louis' criminal underworld knew Sam worked directly for Victor Sorelli, it would be suicide for any of them to attempt something like this. Maybe this was some up-and-comer that wanted street cred, thought Sam. But why wouldn't they kill me? That would send the message sooner than whatever this is. It boggled him.

There was no clear answer to it.

A hint of exhaust tickled Sam's nose hairs. He did his best to give a slight cough while still being gagged. If he rode in this trunk too long, he could die of carbon monoxide poisoning. Sam wasn't apprehensive about that scenario. If that were what his captor wanted to do, he could've easily run a hose into the trunk and left the car running for an hour. But, no, he was sure if that did end up being his demise, it would be a genuine accident. The man who'd kidnapped him wanted him for something else.

Sam felt the car's momentum slow again briefly before gaining speed. Someone must have slowed in front of the vehicle he was in to make a turn or to avoid something on the road. So far, the ride was smooth; if there were a silver lining to this scenario, that would have to be it. Again, the car slowed, and this time he could feel the centrifugal force pulling him to the left. They had made a right turn. Of course, not that any of it mattered. Sam had no idea where their point of origin had been. There was no way for him to tell which direction they were going nor what part of the city they were in. After a ways, they slowed to a stop, and Sam swore he could barely see a flashing red light through the black hood on his face.

The blinking light continued its rhythm for another minute; when the car began to move, he felt it turn left. Once the vehicle had straightened, the blinking light was extinguished.

The exhaust fumes were slowly becoming more frequent. Sam did his best to hold his breath when possible and tried to clear his lungs by coughing as well as he could manage with a rag in his mouth. The only thing Sam imagined that could be worse than this would be being bound with weights and gagged in a tank as it slowly filled with water, though this was a close second. The thought of drowning in that way sent a shiver down his back. His back muscles began to scream in pain as they quaked. He let out a small groan. Honestly, Sam wasn't sure how much more of this he could handle.

A sound from the outside tugged at Sam's eardrums. Trying to reposition himself, Sam focused on the noise. It was a siren. A SIREN! Sam's mind began to race, and his pulse began to quicken. This was his chance. As soon as he heard footsteps walking, he would make all the noise he could. He had to gain the officer's attention. What if it's not a cop? He thought. What if it's an ambulance or a firetruck? He craned his head, gritting through the pain, and listened again. It was a police siren. Hope soared through him. Sam had never been much for religion, but at that moment, he started praying like he'd been doing it his whole life.

In the midst of his prayers, he hoped his captor was nervous. He wished he could see the coward squirming behind the steering wheel. Finally, the sirens came closer, and he felt the car pull over and come to a stop. Thank God! He screamed to himself. He was finally going to be free from this tiny, confined hell. Even through the gag, he felt the corners of his mouth try on a smile. The sirens became louder, louder, and then…they passed him. NO! His eyes went wide. No! No! No! The police officer had left him in the hands of his kidnapper.

Sam was breathing short, fast breaths. He needed to calm himself. If he didn't, he could inhale too much of the exhaust. Sam took control of his breathing and quieted his mind. This was not what he'd hoped for, but he was in no worse shape than before. He could get out of this. He would have to wait a while longer. Sam said one more silent prayer that he would have the opportunity to kill whoever had taken him.

*   *   *   *

Wendy and Anthony were cruising down a country road, green grass on both sides. The sun was high in the clear blue sky. The V8 engine roared as Anthony hit the accelerator. He and Wendy were pulled against their seats. Wendy let out a short, excited squeal. Holding the steering wheel with his left hand, Anthony glanced at his girlfriend. He had never seen a more beautiful creature in all his life. Her fire-kissed hair was let down, draped just past her slender shoulders, and gave off the aroma of strawberries. She wore a teal tank top with cut-off denim shorts. Freckles were perfectly splattered across her ivory skin.

Taking her left hand in his right, he lifted and kissed the top of it. She gave him a wide smile. He looked deep into her eyes. They were as blue as the sky above them. She leaned over and kissed him on the cheek. His face flushed with blood, and he heard her giggle. Grinning, he thought nothing could be better than this. Then, looking back to the road, the silhouette of a person appeared in the middle of the street just twenty feet ahead of them. Releasing Wendy's hand, he gripped the steering wheel tight. The car slammed into the human form with a Thud! Anthony moved his right foot to the brake pedal and pressed it as far as possible. Rubber tires screamed against the asphalt in protest against the sudden change in momentum.

When the cherry red car finally halted, Anthony let out the breath he'd been holding. He hung his head for a few seconds, calming himself. More than anything, he hated that Wendy had to experience what had happened. Looking up he stared into the rearview mirror. Behind him, on the street, there was nothing but tread marks. Anthony furrowed his brow. He knew he saw someone on the road and heard and felt the car run into the person. He gently squeezed his left thumb and forefinger into the inner corners of his eyes. This needed to be clarified.

Without looking he reached with his right hand toward Wendy, searching for hers. When he felt it, he gripped it tight. Something was wrong. Her hand felt frigid. Anthony turned his head to look at his girlfriend. His eyes went wide, and his mouth hung open, letting out a gasp. Wendy was sitting in the passenger seat, her body limp. Anthony let her hand fall to the console. Her beautiful white skin had gone sickly pale. Wendy's blue eyes were open but there was nothing behind them. She seemed to be staring out the windshield. Suddenly, in the blink of an eye, Wendy's head straightened, and she stared directly at Anthony. His immediate reaction was to back against the door, which he did. Wendy held his gaze for another moment before she said it.

"Murderer."

Anthony's eyes shot open, and darkness filled his vision. He was breathing deeply through his nostrils. He was back in the rear seat of the detective's Charger. He had stretched his legs across the middle console and had dozed off. Anthony looked to his left and his right. Nothing out there but the faint yellow glow of sporadic lights spread through the garage. He had yet to determine how long he'd been out. For all he knew, it could've been ten minutes or two hours. All he did know was he didn't want to experience anything like that again. Pulling his legs off the console, Anthony bent at his waist, arms extended in front of him, as he leaned forward over the center console, trying to stretch his arms and back.

Anthony's patience was beginning to wear thin, waiting in the car like some dog. It was humiliating. Motion out of the corner of his eye caught his attention. It appeared the elevator had opened, and two male-looking figures exited. Finally, he thought.

*   *   *   *

Sam didn't know how long they'd been driving, and he lost count of the number of stops and turns they had made a while ago. He was beginning to become lightheaded from the fumes. They made his head spin, and with the added detriment of not being able to see while moving, he began to grow nauseous. The sound of the car had changed maybe ten or so minutes ago. It no longer sounded like they were on asphalt but possibly a dirt road. If that were the case, it was more and more likely Sam was soon to be removed from the cargo space. At this point, though, he wasn't sure if he would be able to put up much of a fight. Finally, he felt the car begin to slow and come to a stop. Sam waited for the inevitable acceleration, but instead, he heard the muffler die. This was it. This was where it all mattered. Sam perked up his ears and waited with bated breath.

*   *   *   *

Turning off the engine, he sat silently, staring at the cabin. He'd made it here without any more problems. The log-made, single-bedroom structure was tucked nicely away from prying eyes. No one other than he knew of its existence. At least, as far as he was aware, it was the perfect place to hold Mr. Hunter until tomorrow. Then, they wouldn't be disturbed. Reaching down, he grabbed the handle and pushed the driver's door open.

*   *   *   *

As they approached the vehicle's rear, Sam heard footsteps crunching on sticks and leaves. Still holding his breath, he prepared himself for anything. The sound of footfalls reached the back of the car and stopped. He heard a key being inserted into its slot. The sound of tumblers sliding filled his ears. With the creaking of hinges, he knew the lid was being raised. With all his might Sam tried to rise and lunge at his captor. However, the effects of laying in one position for multiple hours and breathing in carbon monoxide took their toll, and Sam could barely sit on his knees. He let out a muffled grunt as he rose. Something hard hit Sam's head. Pain shot through his right temple. Sam could feel himself falling as he slipped back into unconsciousness.

CHAPTER 30

"Here we are," Luke said as he flipped the plastic switch. "Home sweet home."

The sudden bright yellow light ignited within the glass bulbs temporarily blinded Luke and Anthony as they walked into the house. Luke shut and locked the door behind them. When he turned around, he couldn't believe what he saw. Looking around the small living room, Luke was appalled. Whoever had used this safehouse previously had left it in disarray. Half-eaten Chinese takeout sat across the living room's wooden coffee table. Wrappers of various colors and sizes were littered throughout the communal space like fallen leaves on the forest floor. The smell alone was horrendous. A mixture of rotting meats and fermented fruits assaulted both men's sense of smell. Luke scrunched up his nose, and his face became distorted in response to the pungent odor.

"Did you guys fire the cleaning crew?" Anthony asked as he covered his nose.

Luke threw him a sharp glare. Immediately he regretted it. He couldn't blame Anthony for the question; even though it was a jab at the department, it was well deserved. Luke had half a mind to call Chief Reilly and tell him he needed to light a fire under whoever had left this place in such a state of decay. But, instead of answering Mr. Sorelli, Luke decided to change the subject.

"Bedroom is the first door on your left." Then, raising a hand, he pointed down the small hallway behind Anthony. "Bathroom is the second door on your left."

Luke walked to the kitchen, and the rotten smell intensified as he did. He stepped to the trash can and saw that it was overflowing. Leaning down, he began lifting the bag out of the plastic container. The stench shot out of the garbage, hitting Luke like a laser beam directly in the face. Normally, Luke had an impervious gag reflex, but as he moved the black bag around, the garbage inside was awakened and released more toxic fumes into the air, causing him to heave. Turning his head to the side, Luke took a breath and held it as he finished tying off the garbage bag. Walking quickly, he went to the front door, unlocked it, stepped outside, and threw the horrid thing into the small rollable dumpster. Anthony had left the living room, probably headed to his room or the bathroom. All of the windows and back doors were locked, so there was no way he was getting out. Luke locked the front door, walked to the kitchen sink, opened the cabinet door beneath it, and grabbed a new trash bag. Finding the opening, he put the black bag out in front of him and started waving it up and down, letting the air force it open. Reluctantly he walked to the living room. While holding his breath, he began cleaning up the space. A small twinge of shame overcame him as he picked up the trash. His apartment suffered from a similar problem. It wasn't as rancid, but it wouldn't take much to get there.

This was the last place Luke wanted to be, even if it had been pristine. Babysitting a criminal while his partner was trying to find clues was not exactly his idea of a great time. Anthony was not just any criminal either; he was one of THE criminals. Of course, Luke had no proof of how much involvement Anthony had in his father's business dealings, but he was a purchaser and user of illegal opiates. Luke's heart and mind had been battling nonstop since Anthony Sorelli walked into the police station early this morning. He wanted to take down the Sorelli family and their empire so severely that he didn't care if Wendy Grayson's case was solved. Luke's heart just wanted to press Anthony until he admitted something about his father that Luke could use to secure a warrant for Victor's residence and any physical or digital documents therein.

Luke's emotions craved the takedown of the syndicate; however, his mind reasoned with the logic of Mason. The most likely outcome, if they pressed too hard at Victor and neglected Grayson's murder, was that Anthony would bottle up and call that piece of dirt David Quentin. Luke couldn't risk that happening.

Tying off the bag, he stepped to the front door, unlocked it, and threw the second bag of garbage away outside. Luke stood on the concrete porch for a brief second, enjoying the fresh air. The frigid temperature cooled his face. He returned to the house's interior with a sigh, locking the door behind him. Luke took off his overcoat and placed it over the back of a chair in the corner of the living room. Stepping back into the kitchen, Luke looked at the refrigerator and decided it was best not to open that cold Pandora's Box. Instead, he returned to the sink and searched beneath it until he found an aerosol can remove odors. Luke walked around the kitchen, dining area, and living room, releasing the scented spray.

When he felt he'd removed enough of the putrid stench, Luke sat on the gray couch behind the coffee table. As he stared into the black screen of the television set, an image of Emily's smiling face entered his mind. The corners of Luke's mouth tugged upwards, trying to create a smile. It was at that moment that an idea struck him. He could get Anthony to loosen up if he sympathized with him. Up until now. Mason had only shown empathy for the man, but Luke understood what Anthony was experiencing. Luke could open up about his journey, and that would give credence to his softer side. Especially with this being the first night since finding out Wendy was dead; it would be hard for Anthony to sleep. This could allow Anthony to start trusting Luke, and he might reveal something that Luke could use to take down Victor.

*　*　*　*

Water streamed out of the faucet, ricocheting on the white ceramic sink before rolling down the steep face and into the dark drain. Cupping his hands under the running liquid, Anthony let them fill up before splashing the cold water on his face. He stood for a second, staring at the streams flowing into the abyss. The bathroom's white walls felt as if they were inching closer and closer to him with each passing second. It seemed as though the plastered ceiling was starting to close in on the tile floor beneath his feet. The room was trying to swallow him whole. He placed his hands beneath the faucet and repeated his previous gesture twice more. Then, reaching his left, Anthony pulled down the small gray hand towel that straddled the wooden ring attached to the wall. Finally, the room adjusted itself back to normal. The walls and ceiling snapped into their proper places.

After dabbing his face with the rag, Anthony looked into the mirror. The man staring back at him was a pathetic pernicious persona of who he was supposed to be. His black hair was disheveled, stray strands falling over his face. Stubble had begun to sprout from his upper lip, spreading down to his chin and over his cheeks. Heavy bags sat under his hazel eyes like leather pouches on a saddle. The sound of the running water drummed in his ears.

Even after the nap he'd had earlier, and his body was still deprived of sleep and nutrients. The detectives had stopped at a fast-food burger joint after leaving the hospital. They'd ordered Anthony a cheeseburger and fries, but he barely ate them. They then stopped at a Walmart to gather a couple of deodorant sticks, toothbrushes, and toothpaste. They also asked Anthony to write down his sizes in t-shirts and pants and bought him a couple of pairs to choose from. He was not pleased with their plan. He didn't want or need to be hidden away at some safe house. Surprisingly, the detectives gave him their argument but said he could if he still wanted to leave. The illusion of free choice, and he'd fallen for it again. Of course, they were right, and he didn't have anywhere else he could go that the detectives would be able to inform him of any additional findings. Anthony's hands began to shake. The withdrawal was back, and with it came his inner fallen angel whispering to him.

What are we doing here? We need to go!

Anthony squeezed his eyelids tight together. This was the last thing he wanted to deal with right now. His inner voice became louder in his head. *Open the mirror. Maybe somebody left some Zantac or Benadryl.*

"You think that will do anything after we've been on high-grade opioids for the past couple of years?" Anthony whispered to his inner demon.

Listen, you piece of shit if you don't find something soon, we are all doomed! Do you hear me? We will all die.

Anthony gripped the edges of the counter hard, fighting the urges within him.

Just one more hit. That's all we need. One more hit, and you'll never have to do it again.

"I've heard that before," Anthony whispered through gritted teeth. "Now leave me alone!"

The voice stopped and retreated into the depths of Anthony's soul. Letting out a sigh, Anthony released his grip on the counter and opened his eyes.

Sitting on the counter was the plastic bag with the personal hygiene products. Anthony decided to go ahead and brush his teeth. It'd been a day or so since he'd done that, and the feeling of a clean mouth might give him a small boost in morale. After he finished, he reached out and turned off the water. Then, taking the small gray towel in hand, he dabbed his mouth. He did feel better now that he'd taken care of himself, even in that small way. Quietly, Anthony opened the door, shut the light, and entered the hallway.

The house was as silent as a crypt. Not wanting to disturb the stillness, he carefully stepped across the laminated floor, heading toward the living room. When he reached the end of the hall, Anthony peered in to see if Detective Burrows was in the room. He was. Anthony could see the back of the man's head sticking up past the left side of the back of a gray couch. The detective seemed to be focused on something across the room. Anthony leaned past the wall and looked. There was nothing except for a tv, but it wasn't on. The hardened man was probably just as tired as Anthony. He hadn't wanted to say anything, but Detective Burrows was not as put together as he led on. Turning his head, Anthony stared down the white hallway. He could go to the bedroom and try to sleep. His body cried for rest from its very depths. After the short nap, he'd taken in the back of the muscle car and that whole experience, Anthony was not eager for a repeat.

Reluctantly, he walked out into the living room. Stepping in front of the couch, he sat on the right side, leaving the center cushion as open space between him and the investigator. Anthony glanced at Burrows. The man didn't move. He didn't even acknowledge Anthony's presence. Surely he'd felt Anthony sit on the sofa. Was this some mind game the man was playing? Anthony wasn't sure. For another minute, he watched the detective curiously. He could barely make out the movement of the man's chest as he breathed. The expression on his face was that of disengagement.

The detective was lost in his thoughts, not caring, or wondering what Anthony was doing at this moment.

Burrows barely blinked as he sat staring off into space. It was bewildering. Eventually, Anthony turned away and also began staring at the wall. The questions and thoughts of what happened to Wendy started flooding his mind again. Anthony let out a sigh. Putting his head in his hands, he tried to think of something else— of anything else. The horrid thoughts just continued to nag at him. The detectives had said that they had not learned much at the hospital. Of course, there were still some people to interview because they weren't present during the detective's visit. Anthony wasn't sure what they would learn once they gathered those statements. As far as he knew, Wendy had kept her word and told no one that she and he were dating. He was about to get up and go to the bedroom when he heard the detective speak.

"I'm sorry."

Burrows' voice was soft and low. For a second, Anthony wasn't sure if the man was talking to him or himself. Then, the detective reiterated his statement.

"I'm sorry, Anthony," the detective said, a little louder this time. "I don't think I've told you that since you came to speak with me."

Anthony looked a little confused. He needed clarification on what the detective was referring to. Was it the loss of Wendy? Or for being a hardass? Was it about him trying to get Anthony to turn on his father?

"What do you have to be sorry for?" Anthony asked with a curious tone. Detective Burrows turned his head to face Anthony. The man's deep blue eyes were full of sympathy, and his face was stricken with grief. Anthony could see tears beginning to well up in Burrows' eyes.

"I'm sorry for your loss," the detective answered, thick with emotion. Anthony hung his head slightly. It was all anyone ever knew what to say in these situations. Even though the words didn't help, they made those who spoke to them feel like they'd made an effort. In reality, it would be all the better if they remained silent. But silence is terrifying. Nobody likes silence. Especially when they are immersed in a world of constant noise. From cars to phones to television, music, air conditioning units, and podcasts, there isn't a second when a cacophony of sounds doesn't surround one. Hell, people even sleep with music or nature sounds playing. A person will turn on a tv show while they perform other tasks for the sheer semblance of not being alone.

The rarity of silence is what gives it its power. The terrifying power of silence is that people are now forced to be alone with their thoughts, and people do not know how to work through their thoughts to reconcile with who they truly are. The incessant noise blots out this truth. People think they need to speak in times like these to help distract from the loss, but wouldn't it be better to let people work through the loss? To confront how they feel about it?

Anthony didn't respond to the detective. There's only one appropriate response, and Anthony doesn't feel any gratitude for Detective Burrows' sympathy. You expect sympathy at times like these, and Detective Burrows could very well be trying to use sympathy for his own game against Anthony's father. No, the best course is to stay silent and see the detective's next move.

"You know," Burrows began, still looking toward Anthony. "I lost my girlfriend two years ago."

Anthony looked up. Tears had begun rolling down the detective's cheeks. He was no longer looking in Anthony's direction. Instead, he had turned back to face the dead television. Burrows was leaning forward, his elbows on his thighs.

"I held her broken body in my arms," the detective continued.

Now Anthony was unsure of how to respond. The man's demeanor, actions, and voice sounded genuine. Anthony once again decided to remain quiet.

"She was beautiful," Burrows was saying. "She always knew how to make me laugh." A small smile broke across the detective's face, and a short chuckle escaped from his mouth.

"One time, she had this crazy idea," the detective continued, "to go out on a lake with a boat and water ski. Of course, she had never water skied before, so, um, we go and rent a boat and some skis. I showed her how to drive the boat so that I could ski first because I knew that once she started, it would be a while before I would get the chance. So, after I finish skiing, it's her turn. I try to be a good boyfriend and give her all the tips. She nods her head and goes, 'yea, okay. I got it.' I raised my hands in surrender and said, 'alright.' I go to the driver's seat and start pulling away, and what happens? She can't stay balanced." At this, Burrows started chuckling a little as he went on. "She falls over. I rope her in, and we try again, and again, and again. She couldn't stay upright if you paid her. Meanwhile, I'm back in the boat, cracking up, watching her face as she tumbles into the water. She never did get the hang of it."

Anthony smiled as the detective told his story. It was a sweet memory, and Anthony was glad he could hear it.

"She always got a little mad when I would laugh at her attempts that didn't go too well. One thing about her, though, she wasn't afraid to try anything." Burrows said.

"What was her name?" Anthony asked, genuinely curious.

"Emily," Detective Burrows answered. "Her name was Emily."

The two men sat in silence for another couple of minutes. Each pondered the love they had lost. Burrows' story struck a chord with Anthony. He too had many happy memories with his girlfriend. But, with her now gone, Sam working for his father, and his father being, well… his father, there wasn't anyone left to share those stories with. Anthony looked again at the hurting man beside him. He was waiting to see if the man would begin to pressure Anthony into revealing something. Instead, the detective just sat in a blue button-down shirt and black pants, his eyes, brimming with tears, boring into the blank, white wall. The detective hung his head and closed his eyes. Finally, Anthony decided to speak.

"Can I share a story with you?" He asked. The brown-haired detective looked over at him and nodded.

It took Anthony a minute to start. His hazel eyes filled with tears, and he started sobbing. Detective Burrows said nothing. He waited, allowing Anthony's emotions to run their course. Once he could get himself under control, Anthony began telling the man sitting next to him the story of his and Wendy's picnic that ended in them being covered in ants.

Luke sat and listened to Anthony tell his story. The blurry-eyed detective had surprised himself. He hadn't planned on becoming so emotional, but as he started, he realized that he hadn't opened up about Emily. He also hadn't shared his good memories with anyone, not even Mason. When Anthony opened up without any prodding from Luke, his conscience won out. He couldn't play dirty as he'd thought about. This was a healthy exercise for the both of them, and it would ruin his credibility with the man if he tried to prey on Anthony's emotional state. Reaching up, Luke wiped away tears from his cheeks. Anthony laughed when he arrived at certain parts, remembering details he probably thought he'd forgotten. That was the interesting thing about memories of those that have passed: facts one thinks aren't super important become some of the most important. Luke could see on Anthony's face that he was happy to be able to tell this story. Likewise, it made Luke happy to see Anthony finally smile. They both needed this.

When Anthony finished his story, he looked at Luke.

"Can I ask you something?"

"Sure," responded Luke. "Anything."

"How do you sleep knowing she's gone?"

Luke didn't respond right away. He'd expected this to come up but had not thought about it too much because Luke didn't have a great answer. Leaning back into the corner of the couch, Luke thought on this for a moment. Eventually, he decided to be honest.

"You won't get much sleep the first month or two," Luke said. "You'll spend your nights rolling around in your bed or sitting in a chair watching something mentally deteriorating on TV."

Anthony's eyes shifted from side to side. He wasn't enjoying Luke's answer.

"I'm sorry man, but it's the truth," he continued. "The little sleep you get will be interrupted by nightmares or dreams that turn into nightmares. You'll tell yourself it's a good thing. That it's because you loved them so much, that's why it hurts so badly— and you'd be right, but the night you do get your first full sleep, you'll think to yourself, 'I must not love her anymore' —which is most certainly a lie."

"I lost my mom when I was eight," Anthony interrupted. "I remember it hurt, but I don't think it hurt like this."

The two men stared at each other. Luke wasn't sure what Anthony wanted him to say…maybe nothing.

"As a child," Luke started. "You probably grieved differently and had more people to lean on."

Anthony gave him a slight nod.

"I'm no psychologist, so you can take what I say with a grain of salt. What I think helps is talking about her and your memories of her, good and bad. It doesn't have to be me," Luke interjected before he scared Anthony away. "But bottling it up gives your brain more ammunition to use while you sleep. That's not to say you won't have nightmares about her death, because you will. However, it may lessen the frequency of them." Anthony nodded slightly and remained silent. Luke was unsure how helpful he'd been, but he gave Anthony the only answer he knew to give.

Finally, after about a minute, the man sitting across from Luke spoke: "Did talking help you?"

Luke looked away. Anthony waited patiently for an answer but already guessed what it would be.

"It helped when I committed to it," Detective Burrows said.
A very honest answer, Anthony thought. He turned away to face the wall
where the tv sat dormant. He was unsure if he should share any more with
the detective. That one story would be good enough to allow him to sleep
for a few hours tonight. Anthony had felt authenticity from Detective
Burrows so far and decided to press his luck.

"Do you have a picture of Emily?" he asked.

"I do," the brown-haired man answered, his tone suggested that that
one had caught him off guard.

"May I see it?" Anthony asked kindly.

Reaching into his pants pocket, Detective Burrows pulled out his
cell phone. After opening it and finding the picture he thought best
represented her, he handed the phone to Anthony.

"Here she is," he said as Anthony took the multi-talented device.
Looking at the photo, Anthony felt his eyes go wide. Quickly he put on his
best poker face hoping the detective hadn't noticed. His breath had seized
as he stared into the phone. The face of the woman he hit with the car
filled his vision. The face of Luke's girlfriend, Emily.

"She's…" Anthony's words were stuck in his throat. He felt a bead
of sweat roll down his left temple. "She's beautiful." He finished, as he
handed back the phone to the detective. Anthony's heart began racing,
drumming loudly in his chest. He hoped the detective couldn't hear it. In
his head, he heard Wendy's voice repeat her earlier accusation: *"Murderer."*

CHAPTER 31

Consciousness slowly returned to Sam. He tried to remember where he was. The last thing he could recall was being tied up in the trunk of some car and having his chance to fight back but failing miserably. To be completely fair to himself, he had been confined in a cramped position for at least six hours and had been able to breathe in nothing but exhaust fumes. The whole experience felt surreal.

Sam opened his eyelids, and once again, he saw nothing but black. This time, though, it felt different. It felt like he was wearing a blindfold instead of a bag over his head. He felt nothing over his nose or on the back of his neck. He also noticed he was sitting upright, possibly in a chair. Sam's head was bowed, and he raised it slowly. His nerves immediately fired signals to his brain, letting him know this movement was excruciating.

Sam clenched his teeth and bore through the motion, lifting his head to its full height. Gently, Sam rolled his head around in an attempt to work out the stiffness in his neck. It was then that he realized he was once again tied up. He felt something around his abdomen and both of his arms. Silently, Sam cursed to himself. Of course, it shouldn't have surprised him when he thought about it. Why would his captor leave him untied? It would be stupid if he had. Sam smacked his lips together. He was no longer gagged. His mouth was parched—dryer than the forests of California in the summertime. Sam's saliva glands seemed to be completely drained as well. Sam tried to excrete moisture to lubricate the inside of his mouth. A deep grumble came from Sam's stomach. The man was hungry and thirsty. He had no idea how long it had been since he'd eaten or drunk anything, but it felt like an eternity. Sam was grateful not to be in the cramped car trunk anymore. However, his body was once again in a singular, unchangeable position. Gathering his strength, Sam tried to scoot the chair beneath him. Nothing happened. The seat didn't even budge. There were; however, small little chink sounds as he attempted to move. Chains. He'd been chained to a chair.

Channeling his anger and need for survival, Sam tried again. Nothing. Aggressively, Sam attempted a third, fourth, and fifth time. Every time the result was the same, with no sign of success. Finally, he let out a reluctant sigh and decided it was no use. He needed to save his strength. There was no telling what kind of torture this bastard had in store for him. Sam's mind had been pushed nearly to the limit in that trunk. He hadn't initially realized how far he'd come to breaking until the police sirens he had heard drove past him, shattering his hope. The psychological warfare that was being waged against him was formidable. Now that he was no longer in a confined space, Sam presumed he could handle whatever was thrown his way. But, as quickly as his confidence rose, the doubts began flooding in, threatening to tear it all down.

How can you be prepared? You're stuck to a chair that seems to be embedded in concrete.

Sam wasn't sure he had the answer, but he knew he couldn't give in to the fear that was knocking at his mental door. Once he did, that would be the end of the game. Sam shifted his focus to the world beyond his blindfold. Turning his head from side to side, he strained his ears to listen for the slightest sound. To his right, a small crackle and pop sang out to him. Quickly, he snapped his head in that direction. Another pop and crackle, along the same tune as the first, tugged at his hearing. Sam thought he felt a soft warmness filling the air from that same direction. A fire. There was a fire, and since Sam didn't feel any cold breeze on his face, it was safe to assume he was in a house or cabin. Since he'd been ungagged, Sam doubted he was anywhere close to civilization. With that, there was no point in trying to call out for someone to hear him. If there was one thing he was certain of, his captor wasn't stupid. A fool, maybe, but not dumb.

Sam began sniffing the air. The smells coming to him reminded him of the forest. Everything had an earthy, wooded scent—or maybe that was just the smell of the burning wood to his right. Taking a deep breath, Sam held it for a long while. He savored the fresh air after having inhaled so many toxic fumes. The thought of the exhaust made Sam cough, not a small, short cough. This was a coughing fit as his body tried to rid itself of any leftover toxins that could be residing in his lungs. The dryness of Sam's mouth and throat caused the coughs to be more painful than they should have been. The back of his throat began to itch and inflame, which threw him into more coughing fits. He leaned over as far as he could, coughing for nearly two minutes. Sam desperately needed water. If he suffered more prolonged episodes like these, his throat would begin to crack and bleed. Anger began to take root in Sam's mind. Thinking about everything he'd been through today fueled the rage boiling inside, from letting someone sneak up on him and kidnap him, to being bound and gagged in a car trunk to breathing in toxic air, to the police officer that had given him false hope, to being too weak to fight his way out when he had the chance resulting in again being bound and dehydrated. All for what? For some sick game, some moron decided to play? For some revenge on Victor Sorelli? Why was this happening to him? Sam had no answer, which only made him more enraged. His breathing began to quicken, and he felt his face turn sour. There was once again nothing he could do. He was at the complete mercy of his captor, no longer in control of his fate. That fact, more than anything else, was what made Sam angrier than anything.

"Why don't you come out and face me, you coward!" Sam yelled as best he could without incurring further damage to his throat. Pain saturated every syllable he uttered.

"Come on! Let's settle this like men!" Sam taunted his captor, trying to rile him up.

For a moment, there was no answer. Then, Sam's head turned violently to his right as a new sound entered the space. Footsteps. Slowly they came closer and closer to Sam's vulnerable body. With every other step, the floor creaked in protest at the weight it was forced to bear. Sam felt his heart increase its rhythm in his chest as each step became louder and louder. Finally, when the feet reached their destination in front of Sam, his heart threatened to burst through his chest and his restraints. Sam's breathing was short and rapid. He'd called out his kidnapper, and now he waited for their move.

Suddenly, Sam's jaw was gripped tight in the hand of his kidnapper. Sam went rigid and tried to free his face from the vise clenched around it. The feel and smell of the hand told Sam it was covered with a latex glove. This information only exacerbated his base survival instincts. Sam didn't think his heart could beat faster, but he was wrong. It was beating so loud and fast that Sam thought it would explode. The hand holding his jaw had the strength of a gorilla, forcing him to open his mouth and part his lips. Before Sam could blink, a cool, wet liquid hit his lips, pouring into his mouth and down his gullet. At first, Sam felt relief and took two huge gulps before his brain intervened. This could be poison.

Like a wild animal, Sam began thrashing his head with all the force he could muster until he'd freed himself from his kidnapper's grip and spit the remaining liquid out of his mouth. Everything had happened in the span of ten seconds, and Sam hadn't had enough time to react. His host had remained silent. Not a word, a grunt, or even a huff of frustration escaped him. Presumably, the man was still standing in front of him, though Sam hadn't heard him move. The dryness returned to Sam's mouth. It had soaked up all the liquid and was now begging for more. The more Sam thought about it, the more he felt like a fool. If his captor wanted him dead, he'd be dead already. Why keep him alive to force poison down his throat? Sam let out a short sigh. He would have to play this man's game if he wanted out of here, but it's hard to play a game when you don't know the rules.

"What was that?" Sam asked, his throat sore.
There was no reply—just the sound of wood sputtering and snapping from being licked by tongues of flame. Sam could feel his captor's presence looming before him. A dark aura suspended in the air.

"Was it water?" asked Sam. His body cried out for the life-sustaining liquid. "Or was it poison?"

Sam thought he sensed movement. He needed to figure out what the man was doing or if it even mattered. Then, a new sound emerged after a few seconds, and it startled him.

"Water," a robotic female voice said.

The man had used his cellphone to type out an answer and had the virtual assistant read it aloud. So, either his captor was mute or didn't want to risk giving away his identity with his voice. Interesting, Sam thought. He was about to ask for some more water when he stopped himself. What if he's lying? What if I didn't drink enough of the poison, and he needs me to take some more?

Sam battled with himself for two minutes before deciding that drinking the liquid was worth the risk. If he was right and it was water, he'd be helping himself heal. If he were wrong, he would die, but better to die from poison than dehydration.

"Could I have some more?" Sam asked quietly. "I'm sorry for earlier. Surely you can't blame me for reacting as I did."

For a moment, nothing happened. Then, Sam felt the rubber-clad fingers on his cheeks again. This time, Sam relaxed and opened his mouth of his own volition, ready to receive whatever liquid his captor possessed. The feeling of the water running over his tongue and down the back of his throat was ecstasy. Sam didn't slow down. He drank gulp after gulp, hoping against hope that his kidnapper was telling him the truth. Finally, after about thirty seconds, the ominous well ran dry. Sam breathed deeply, and his heart slowed to its original tempo. His mouth and throat were nice and moist. Sticking out his tongue, Sam licked his lips. This was a good first step in recovering his strength. That is, if he hadn't voluntarily poisoned himself, though Sam felt hopeful and refreshed at the moment.

The sound of footsteps caught his attention. His kidnapper had stepped back a few feet. Cautiously, Sam waited for something else to happen. After a couple of minutes, he decided nothing else would happen. Now Sam had to try to discuss it with his kidnapper. He needed to prod him and hopefully get the man to reveal his motive and, even more importantly, his identity.

*　*　*　*

He stood there, gazing at the pile of muscle in front of him. The room was dimly lit by an oil lamp and the fire in the fireplace. A warm yellow glow danced over the wooden slats that made up the structure's walls. Silently, he mouthed the words with his lips,
"But know that if the master of the house had known in what hour of the night the thief was coming, he would have stayed awake and would not

have let his house be broken into."

Mr. Hunter had awakened two hours after having been knocked unconscious. The man had struggled against the chains wrapped around his torso, as well as against the wooden chair that was bolted to the floor. He watched from the small kitchenette area as Samuel tried to gather information about his surroundings. The strong man had noticed the fire against the east wall. But he wasn't sure what all else Mr. Hunter had figured out besides that they were not near any other human beings. Simply because Mr. Hunter didn't initially cry out when he realized he was no longer gagged. Eventually, the goon went into a coughing fit, and he wasn't sure when it would stop.

Silently, he picked up the bottle of water beside him and unscrewed the lid. He was about to step out when Mr. Hunter issued his challenge. Pausing, he waited to see if Samuel would dare to taunt him again. Mr. Hunter did issue a second taunt. It was his turn to answer. Slowly, he walked into the living area, stopping directly in front of Mr. Hunter. Before the man could say a word, he grabbed him by the jaw, squeezing his cheeks and forcing the man's mouth open. Lifting the bottle, he began pouring the water down Mr. Hunter's gullet. After a couple of seconds, Mr. Hunter broke free of his grip and spat the water in his mouth to the ground.

Good, he thought. The chained man looked frightened. He had no idea what he had drunk, but the introduction of the liquid would cause his body to beg for it even more than it already had been. Now Samuel would show him some respect. A little time passed before Mr. Hunter asked what it was that he had been forced to ingest. At first, he wasn't sure if he should answer because it didn't matter. Then, after a small deliberation, he decided to satiate Samuel's curiosity and thirst. Bringing out his cell phone, he typed the answer into it and pressed the button, signaling the electronic device to read the word aloud. He knew this would throw Samuel into another conflict. What was to stop him from lying to the man? Nothing except his skewed integrity.

Soon, Mr. Hunter requested more water. The man obliged. After emptying the plastic bottle, he took a few steps away from his prisoner and gently placed the bottle on the ground next to his feet. Now he waited. He waited for the inevitable questions Mr. Hunter would ask. These were the questions the man's soul demanded answers to. Since he'd already given one response, it was only logical that he would give another. The real question was, could Mr. Hunter accept the answers?

"Who are you?" Mr. Hunter asked.

The chained man's voice had regained some of its original strength. Not moving an inch, the man remained silent. This was not a question Mr. Hunter would receive an answer to. So instead, he watched as Samuel's facial expression shifted from curiosity to impatience.

"Who are you?" Mr. Hunter asked again, this time with more force. Again, he did not respond. The question was one he had asked himself throughout his whole life. It was the question that all of humanity struggled with the most; who a person thinks they are could depend on many factors. A person's name that's who they are. Though what's in a name? Names are no longer what they used to be. Thousands of years ago, they had meanings. Jacob, in Hebrew, meant supplanter. David meant beloved. Ruth meant friend or companion. Today, names are nothing more than random syllables used to identify somebody without telling who that person is. Before, someone's name was all one needed to know everything about them. Now, who someone is wrapped up in their character, their actions, and their general demeanor. Over time, a person builds who they are and integrates it with their name.

"Who the hell are you?!" Samuel screamed, cracking his voice. He was angry, growing desperate for answers.

A thought struck the man, and he decided to give Samuel an answer. Unlocking his phone, he began typing. Once he had finished, he tapped the screen and let the device speak.

"The thief," said the electronic woman's voice.

He watched as anger gave way to confusion on Mr. Hunter's face. The man in chains had not been expecting that answer. A small satisfied smile crossed his lips as he stared at his prisoner's expression. It would drive the poor man's mind wild, trying to discern the meaning of that.

"The thief?" Samuel repeated. "What does that even mean? What is your name?"

Again, he tapped the rectangle in his hand.
"The thief."

Mr. Hunter let out a breath and rolled his head around, realizing he would not get any new information if he kept asking that question; Mr. Hunter was no doubt searching his mind for another. The man watched as Samuel's face changed from one irritated expression to another. He enjoyed seeing Mr. Hunter's brows furrow and then his nose crinkle. The man's lips went from compressed flat to a frown. His skin was red from anger.

Even though toying with Mr. Hunter wasn't the noblest thing to do, it sure was entertaining. The more he thought about it; it really didn't matter if Samuel knew his true identity. The man chained before him wouldn't be alive long enough to cause any harm with that information. However, he had a list of names that he wanted to know who he was, and Mr. Hunter was not on that list.

* * * *

"What are you stealing?" Sam asked, agitated.

He'd retrieved an answer from his captor, but it didn't make sense. The thief. Thief? What could he possibly be stealing? Was it some street name? If it was, Sam had never heard of the man before. The strange, covert answer made Sam feel like he was in some comic book. Of course, 'The Thief' could have been more creative compared to other villain names. Sam's muscles were beginning to get sore, and he tried to wiggle around in the chains. It was no use. The metal links were too tight. Sam wondered what his boss, Mr. Sorelli, was thinking. Undoubtedly, he thought Sam had run off and was probably bound to send someone after him to ensure he 'made it out of town. Perhaps, that's who this guy is… But, no. When people try to run from Victor Sorelli, he allows their bodies to be discovered by the rest of the underworld as a lesson. So, who was this damned fool that had kidnapped him? Sam's patience was thinner than a sheet of paper.

"What are you stealing?" Sam asked again. This time his tone was harsh and angry. For a beat, there was no response. Then Sam heard the high-pitched digital voice say, "You."

Sam felt his eyes go wide. Me? Why in hell would anyone steal me? After thinking about it for a second, he decided his question had been redundant. After all, he had been kidnapped. That's probably why his captor hadn't answered the first time. It was quite obvious what he was stealing. Sam leaned his head back and tried to think. This whole thing was absurd. Stealing him gained his captor nothing except being hunted by Victor Sorelli. Perhaps that's what this lunatic wanted. Maybe he had seen how valuable someone like Sam could be and wanted him to join him instead.

"Why me?" Sam asked. It was the obvious next question, and there was no way Sam could move on until this one was answered.

Another short pause, and then,

"It's not about you," said the mechanical voice.

Not about me? Thought Sam. Of course, it was. The coward just admitted he'd stolen Sam. Therefore, Sam must have something to do with this.

"Of course, it's about me," Sam stated. "You kidnapped ME, you dumb bastard."

"It's not about you," repeated the voice.

Sam's face flushed hot. So, this man had the audacity to tell Sam he'd stolen him, yet it didn't have anything to do with him?! The stupid, irritating electronic voice was beginning to get under Sam's skin. He was irritated all around.

"Then tell me what it's about," Sam said brusquely. ."Enlighten me on how your two statements make any sense." The rage was oozing out of him. It didn't help that he was, for all intents and purposes, blind. Gritting his teeth, he waited for a response. He could hear his breath going in and out of his nostrils as he tried to gain control of his emotions.

"It's not about you, Samuel."

*   *   *   *

After editing his answer and letting his digital assistant read the words, he watched as Sam fully committed to his rage. The man screamed in protest, jerking against his restraints, gaining no ground. Eventually, Mr. Hunter settled down and hung his head. Samuel couldn't understand the man's plans. He couldn't comprehend that he was taken, not for who he was, but for his position. Yes, Sam was who he had stolen, but he would've taken Joe Blow if that had been Victor's right-hand man instead of Sam. Looking around the room, he watched as the glow from the fire and the lamp intertwined themselves, casting shadows across the room. The yellowish-orange flames had kept the cabin warm against nature's frigid temperatures. This cabin was the perfect spot for things like this. It was the same spot he'd taken Miss Grayson two nights ago. Lifting his phone, he read the time. 10:46 P.M. Soon, it would be Mr. Hunter's turn.

Now that he thought about it, this could be his last time in this place. Nostalgia washed over him as he admired the small rocking chair in the corner, the mounted white-tail buck he bagged when he was young, the brown and white spotted Texas longhorn leather rug laying on the floor, and the photo on the mantle of him and his mom. It brought back many good memories; tonight, would be one more to add to the memory bank. In the back of his mind, he wondered what his mom might think about using their cabin like he was, but he soon decided it was best not to dwell on that.

"You will tell me why you took me." Samuel's low voice cut through the silence.

At first, he didn't respond. He just waited, knowing it would fester the anger once again. The psychological game had been fun, but it was now over. He would let Samuel dwell on their conversation for the remainder of his life. Then, he saw Mr. Hunter raise his head and point it in his direction.

"You WILL tell me why you have taken me," the broken man repeated, the anger boiling out of him.

Slowly, the man began walking towards Samuel. Each step was deliberately heavy. The sound echoed through the cabin. Thump. Thump. Thump. The wooden planks creaked underneath him with each step. His eyes never left Mr. Hunter's helpless form. He watched as his captive tensed with every step he took. Finally, he stopped less than a foot away from the trembling man and typed an answer on his phone. Bending down so he could look directly into the blindfold, where Sam's eyes should be, he held out the phone and tapped the screen next to Sam's ear.

"Or what?"

He heard his captive let out a growling breath. He stepped past Mr. Hunter and walked leisurely to the kitchenette.

CHAPTER 32

Anthony's eyelids fluttered open, the ceiling above him slowly becoming focused as his hazel eyes adjusted. The room was dark; the only light came from a small lamp in the living room, where Detective Burrows presumably still rested. Sitting up, Anthony leaned against the wall at the head of the bed he was sleeping on. This was now the fourth time he'd awoken from sleep. However, unlike the other three times, there was no nightmare this time. Instead, his mind and body had woken up on their own. Raising his arms above his head, Anthony stretched. As he did so, he let out a large yawn.

There was a small digital clock on the nightstand beside the bed. Red numbers indicated to Anthony that it was 3:49 A.M. He'd been able to sleep for an hour and a half since he had awoken. Reaching with his right arm, Anthony flicked on the small lamp on the nightstand. The filament in the glass bulb, filled with buzzing electricity, cast a warm yellow glow around him. The bed he sat in was a full-size mattress covered in charcoal gray sheets and a black comforter. Two pillows with covers to match the sheets sat at the head of the bed. There was no headboard or footboard, just a small metal frame that held the box spring and the mattress. The room was small, a 10x10 square. There was barely enough room to fit the bed, the nightstand, and the small drawers on the wall opposite the bed. Anthony had no idea how long people usually stayed in safe houses like this, but he didn't imagine it could be any longer than a couple of weeks at the most.

The walls of the bedroom were blank, painted white with no decorations, a sign that no one stayed here on a regular basis. This room belonged to whoever the police were trying to protect and/or hide at that given moment. Anthony raised his hands and rubbed his eyes. He really should try and go back to sleep, but something inside himself refused to let that happen. His mind raced back to the earlier conversation between himself and the detective. Anthony had opened up to Detective Burrows about his and Wendy's relationship. Nothing too personal, just a story about one of their dates. It didn't seem like much when he thought about it, but while telling the story, he realized that he had never shared any stories about his and Wendy's relationship with anyone. It felt good to have someone that could share his emotions about them. The detective had opened up about his experience with losing his girlfriend to the grim reaper. Anthony hadn't realized how much the two of them had in common. If only that were the end of the story. On top of everything else, the withdrawal, the loss of Wendy, and the guilt of murdering an innocent woman, now he knew who that woman was. Her name was Emily, and she had been Detective Burrows' girlfriend.

Pressing his fingers into his temples, Anthony let out a sigh. He had no idea how to proceed with this new information. A part of him wanted desperately to confess to the detective about his horrific crime, to finally get the weight of the secret off his shoulders. Still, there was no way of knowing how the detective would react to such a revelation. It had been almost two years since the horrendous murder, and Detective Burrows had surely come to terms with having the drunk as the scapegoat. A low hum suddenly filled the room. The heater had kicked on to warm the house to its set temperature.

Anthony remembered the day his father gave him his target. He wasn't given a name, just a picture, and a location, and told to make it look like an accident. Anthony took the picture with the name of the location written on the backside and went to prepare. He knew better than to ask any questions. It didn't matter who the woman was. His father never ordered a hit on anyone unless it was to protect the family. For all Anthony knew, she could've been a journalist or lawyer digging too deeply into the Sorelli family and looking to expose them. Only now did he realize her death was meant to send Detective Burrows into a self-destructive tailspin. Instead, it had backfired and sent Anthony spiraling out of control. How many others had his father ordered killed that were innocent? People were guilty by association and nothing more. Everything that has happened in his life these past two years can be directly linked to that night. It cracked Anthony's soul to the bone. To numb the pain, he'd turned to opiates. Anthony's head began to throb violently. He dug his fingers deeper into his temples, attempting to drill away the pain. It wasn't working. Glancing at the nightstand, he noticed it had a single drawer. There was most likely nothing inside, but curiosity, and the hope of possible pain relievers hiding away in the belly of the wooden beast, won out. Leaning over the side of the bed, he pulled open the drawer. The inside smelled musty, like it hadn't been opened in some time. A thin layer of dust had migrated through the small crack in the top of the drawer and settled across the contents inside. Sitting in one of the front corners was a small white bottle.

Anthony's heart skipped a beat. He gripped the bottle in his left hand and brought it out of the nightstand. Using his thumb, he wiped away the dust on the label revealing it to be a bottle of medicine used for indigestion. With disappointment and relief, he sat the bottle back inside the nightstand. There was nothing else that appeared to be drugs. There was, however, something else that caught his attention—a book. Anthony remained motionless for several heartbeats before reaching in and taking out the book. Even through the thin layer of dust, Anthony could read the title on the cover.

THE HOLY BIBLE.

Swinging his legs over the side of the bed, Anthony sat staring at the object in his hands under the warm glow of the lamp beside him. Gently he dusted off the cover. It was a rocky black landscape with golden craters in the shapes of the letters that spelled the title. Anthony had skimmed The Bible before. He knew some of the more popular stories it contained, Jonah and the whale, Noah's Ark, and David and Goliath, but he'd never really understood the fascination in such a thing. Anthony had never stepped foot in a church and had only prayed that one time to try and save his mother's life.

Bitterness and resentment began broiling inside him. He was furious at himself for even considering such a foolish notion. He was also mad at the fact that there was something that gave not only himself but others false hope. Closing his eyes, he took several deep breaths to calm himself. The book in his hands felt heavy, like it weighed three hundred pounds. He didn't know what to do. Part of him wanted to throw it into a fire, and another wanted to open it. Five minutes passed without so much as a twitch from Anthony. Finally, taking a deep breath, he had made up his mind. He opened the front cover of the Bible and came to an interesting page. It was a place to write about who had received the book and below who had given it. There he read:

Presented To:

_____

From:

_____*Charlie Wallace*_____

Anthony didn't recognize the name, but it was curious that the first line was blank. Perhaps Charlie forgot who he would give it to or decided they were unworthy of it and preferred to wait for someone else. Either way, it didn't matter. It was in Anthony's hands now. Not really knowing what to do or where to begin, he flipped the Bible open to a random page and began reading:

"And it came to pass after all thy wickedness, (woe, woe unto thee! saith the Lord GOD;) that thou hast also built unto thee a high place in every street. Thou hast built thy high place at the head of the way, made thy beauty abhorred, opened thy feet to everyone that passed by, and multiplied thy whoredoms."

None of that made any sense to Anthony, and honestly sounded pretty condemning for the so-called "loving God" everyone espoused. Flipping backward through the pages, he stopped again and began reading another section.

"The sons of Simeon were Nemuel, and Jamin, Jarib, Zerah, and Shaul: Shallum, Mibsam, his son. And the sons of Mishma; Hamuel, his son; Zacchur, his son; Shimei, his son. And Shimei had sixteen sons and six daughters; but his brethren had not many children, and neither did all their family multiply, like Judah's children."

This section was just a list of names. Anthony couldn't fathom any use the names would provide to anyone. Scanning the surrounding pages, he noticed that this part of the book was all names, long lists of families. This just reinforced his contempt for those that put a such worth on, what was in his mind, something so trivial. Deciding to give it one last chance, Anthony turned towards the end of the book and began reading a passage that had words written in red.

"Then Jesus said to those Jews who believed in him, 'If ye continue in my word, then are ye my disciples indeed; and ye shall know the truth, and the truth shall make you free.'"

Anthony paused there. That last part struck a chord in him. *"The truth shall make you free."* Perhaps this was what he was searching for, something to permit him to unload everything he had ever done. He reread that passage three more times. He was about to stand when his dark inner side began screaming at him.

You fool! You can't trust anything that comes out of that book. It's all a bunch of lies that idiots choose to follow so they feel secure about the prospect of death.

"No," Anthony whispered. "It can't all be lies. There have to be some nuggets of true wisdom in here."

Maybe there is, his fallen angel conceded, *but do you want to spill your guts to the detective in the other room? The man will come unhinged if you tell him what you did, and you think it ends with that? Hell no. If he doesn't beat you to death, he'll arrest you, and with a confession, there's nothing your lawyer can do! Then, they'll pressure you on your motive, and you'll have to rat out your father… if he doesn't sneak someone in to take care of you first!*

"My father wouldn't…." So, Anthony didn't get to finish.

He wouldn't kill you, would he? So, he needs you to take over the business? However true that might be, he's still young enough to remarry, make a new heir, and raise and train him for nineteen years before he keels over.

Anthony slammed the Bible closed and tightened his grip on the black leather-bound book, turning his knuckles white. Anthony began breathing heavily and closed his eyes.

We need to go now! The detective can no longer help us. He said it himself. They didn't learn anything new from the entire day. This has all been a ruse to get you to stay here. Go in there, kill him, and let's get out of here and find some pills!

In a flash, Anthony stood to his feet, grabbed the lamp beside him in his right hand, and yanked it free from the wall. Darkness swallowed the room. Slowly, he walked toward the door where light from the living room was creeping in beneath the frame. Quietly, he opened the door and stepped into the short hallway. For a long moment, he stood frozen. The light from the living room chased the shadows into the depths of the hall.

Bending at the knees, he reached down and picked up the cord to the lamp so it wouldn't drag across the floor. With one slow step at a time, he made his way to the living room. Within three steps, he had arrived and softly stepped behind the couch where Detective Burrows sat. The man's brown hair was a mess. Anthony compressed his lips together. This man had gone out of his way to open up and share something important with him. It was always a part of his plan. *It's his way to keep you here, in this cage.*

Looking down, Anthony stared at the lamp in his right hand. The metal base felt warm from the bulb burning atop it for quite some time. Then, feeling the object in his left hand, Anthony shifted his attention. The Bible. Anthony hadn't let it go. As he returned his attention to the man in front of him, Anthony felt anger and bitterness rising inside him. The beating of his heart increased, thumping faster and faster against his chest. He had intended to bash the detective in the head and make his escape from the safe house. Instead, he decided he would talk with the detective one more time to see if anything suspicious brought itself to the surface. Bending at his waist, he gently sat the lamp on the floor behind the sofa before rising, his heart beating rapidly. Walking to his right, he stepped around to the front of the couch and sat down. The detective's eyes shifted from the dormant television to Anthony's. He didn't appear surprised to see him.

"Expecting me?" Anthony asked curiously.

A slight grin crossed the man's lips. Anthony returned the smile.

"I figured you'd be back at some point," the detective said conspiratorially. "It's the first night after your loss. I've never known anyone to sleep the whole night."

Anthony tossed the Bible onto Detective Burrows' lap. Burrows flinched as the book hit his legs. Then, picking up the heavy tome, the blue-eyed detective chuckled.

"What's funny?" Anthony questioned, furrowing his brow.

"I'd forgotten about this," Luke replied as he opened up the front cover. Anthony wasn't too surprised that Detective Burrows knew about the Bible. He seemed to be overly familiar with this safe house. No one spoke for a couple of heartbeats. Burrows sat staring at the religious book. The sleeves of his blue shirt were rolled up to his elbows. Anthony watched him, trying to read his facial expression. A small light seemed to sparkle in his eyes as he stared into the dark-covered Bible as if it had unlocked some memory in the recesses of his mind.

"Do you know Charlie Wallace?" Anthony asked.

The detective nodded slightly. He closed the book and gripped it in his right hand before turning his head to face Anthony.

"I knew him," Burrows said. Sorrow began to seep into the man's voice as he continued. "Charlie was my previous partner before Mason."

"What's he doing now?" asked Anthony.

Burrows hung his head slightly before answering, "He died about... about a year ago."

"Oh, I'm sorry to hear that," Anthony said. "Was it from the job?" Burrows shook his head, "No, he was an older man, and he died in his sleep one night."

Anthony nodded his understanding. He had been very young when his grandfather passed away, and he didn't remember it. Unlike his mother, his grandfather had been elderly, and it made sense that his time was up. Growing old is fatal. The hum of the heater ended its long, single-note song, leaving the room quieter than it already was. Anthony wondered how Detective Burrows was still awake. He'd been up all day, running around trying to find clues to Wendy's murder and now he sat here, still awake, guarding the front door from anyone that may attempt to break in, or perhaps, to keep Anthony from breaking out.

"Charlie," Burrows began, "would leave a Bible at every safehouse." He was looking at the cover of the book. Gently, he rubbed his left forefinger across the cover, tracing the letters as he went.

"Why?" Anthony asked.

The detective shrugged his shoulders.

"He said he did it because every soul can be redeemed. No matter what they've done, blood was spilled so that everyone can live in paradise," Burrows replied.

"Did anyone ever take him up on the offer?"

"A few most didn't want to bother with it. Charlie never forced it down on anyone though. He just waited until he saw one of them reading it, or, if they asked about it, then he'd share with them."

A look of disgust formed on Anthony's face. The notion that some 'all-powerful God' existed and cared for everyone was absurd in his mind. Granted, there's no way to prove or disprove the existence of a god. But, even if Anthony conceded that there was a being that created the universe, he could not call that being caring. Apathetic was more accurate. Leaving his creation to suffer sickness, starvation, storms, and the numerous other atrocities that plague mankind. How could a 'loving, caring god allow such things to happen? How could this 'great being' sit back and watch, allowing cancer, rape, famine, hurricanes, and the like to persist? People that profess this god's name commit vile and malicious acts of sexual immorality, hatred, and theft, and he does nothing.

For someone to purposely leave the very book that confirmed these delusions lying around, to try to convince others to join in their insanity was —in the kindest sense— distasteful. Anthony didn't care to delve any further into the subject. Looking down, he noticed his right leg had started bouncing. His heart felt like a bass drum on a song, running one hundred and eighty beats per minute. A bead of sweat tore down the left side of his face.

Just hit him already!! Cried the voice inside his head. Anthony did his best to ignore it.

We need to go! Now!

Looking at Detective Burrows, he saw the policeman eyeing him studiously. Anthony wondered what he was thinking. Could he know what Anthony was planning? Did he equate it to the loss Anthony was experiencing? Perhaps he knew Anthony was once again going through withdrawal. Not wanting to cast the wrong idea, Anthony decided to speak.

"You're sure…" Anthony paused; he didn't realize how dry his throat had become. Swallowing some saliva, he continued, "…there wasn't anything useful from the interviews you did at the hospital?"

The searching, piercing expression faded from the detective's face. The man shook his head.

"No, however, I would like to know one thing," Burrows said.

"And what's that?" Anthony asked.

The detective paused for a moment and pursed his lips, trying to decide if he wanted to ask the question here or wait until they were back at the station. Then, finally, the man responded, "Why didn't Wendy's coworkers know you and her were together?"

Anthony didn't answer right away. Instead, he was a little surprised by the detective's question. He furrowed his brow and thought for a few seconds.

"Why does it matter whether they knew or not?" Anthony retorted. "It's none of their business anyway."

The blue-eyed detective cocked his head to one side and raised his eyebrows slightly.

"You're right, and it isn't any of their business. It's just unusual, that's all. I didn't expect everyone to know, but people, especially women, usually like to talk about the person they're in a romantic relationship with."

The two men stared at each other; eyes locked. Neither one wanted to fold. Anthony felt his blood begin to boil again.

He's baiting you! He wants you to explain that it's about your father. I told you this whole thing was a trap. Now come on! Let's get out of here!
Anthony gave Detective Burrows a slight smirk. Then, closing his eyes, he shook his head and sighed.

"I don't know what you want me to tell you, Detective," Anthony said as he opened his eyes.

Burrow's face hadn't changed. Instead, the man's blue eyes pierced the space between them and bored into Anthony. He wasn't buying Anthony's answer. The air in the room seemed to stiffen.

"The truth," Burrows responded.

The truth. Those words hung in front of Anthony like a fish on a hook. Then, finally, the phrase from the book in the detective's hand came back to Anthony.

The truth shall make you free.

The sentence repeated itself over and over in Anthony's mind. Part of him wanted to come clean and divulge the terrible things he and his family had done. The fact that he'd killed the woman on the road, Detective Burrows' girlfriend, and he'd pinned the blame on someone else. The image of her walking across the street filled his mind's eye. Blinking rapidly, he tried to erase the unwelcome recollection. The sound of the drunk's mumbles reverberated from the speakers in his head. The man's words had been so slurred, Anthony hadn't had the slightest clue what the intoxicated man had been trying to say. Anthony had ushered him roughly to the driver's seat before slamming the man's face into the steering wheel. Shutting his eyes tight, he shoved the memory away. He hadn't even confessed any of this to Wendy.

Why are you even contemplating this? He wants you to get emotional, so you'll slip and reveal something. This man doesn't deserve to know what happened to his girlfriend. He can't even figure out what happened to yours.

No, Anthony decided, he would keep silent. It was too much, too soon, and it likely wouldn't end well. Moreover, his father probably had secret documents that showed Anthony was mentally incompetent, so there was nothing he could say that would benefit the detective anyways.

Stop with all this nonsense! Let's get out of here and get some drugs. We'll feel so much better.

Anthony rose to his feet and stretched, hoping to signal to Burrows that he would try and go back to sleep. The man's hard expression faltered and turned into a look of disappointment. Anthony knew then that it was working. Walking around the side of the couch, he stood behind the sofa and stared into the dark kitchen. In the shadows, he could make out the shapes of cabinets and a countertop. After about a minute he turned around to face the living room's white walls. Bending to his knees, he picked up the metal lamp he had sat there earlier. It seemed to have gained tremendous weight since he'd previously held it. Silently, he rose to his full height and stared once more at the messy, brown hair on the back of the detective's head. Anthony could feel the blood pumping through his veins, each beat of his heart sending pulses to his temples.

Come on! The other cop could show up at any moment! Do it NOW!

"I've got to get out of here," Anthony whispered as he raised the lamp over his right shoulder and swung down, aiming the base of the object at the side of Burrows' head.

*   *   *   *

A small sound came from behind Luke, and it sounded like Anthony mumbled something. Turning his head to the right he caught a glimpse of an object coming toward him in his peripheral view. With reflexes, Luke didn't realize he had, and he fell to his left, nearly missing the hard object coming towards him; his head landed on the arm of the couch. Immediately he rolled off the gray sofa onto the floor and made three revolutions away from his attacker before bolting to his feet.

What the hell is Anthony thinking?! Luke wondered furiously. The dark-haired man was already on the other side of the couch, the weapon —which Luke now noticed was the bedroom lamp— gripped tightly in his hands, ready for another swing. Anthony was much larger than Luke and could easily overpower him in a hand-to-hand fight. Anthony was within striking range of Luke in two strides, hair wild, face red with anger, and dripping sweat. Luke dodged to his right, barely missing the lamp again. Anthony was moving so fast, and swinging so hard, he lost his balance and fell into the wall. Luke reached to his right hip and grabbed his firearm. Pulling it free from its holster, he began raising it at Anthony.

The angry man's height was an immense advantage; he reached Luke in a single stride, and before Luke could fully bring the gun to bear on him, Anthony swung the black lamp and struck Luke's hand. The gun went soaring across the house into the darkness of the kitchen. Pain shot up Luke's hand into his wrist. Clenching his teeth, Luke balled his right hand into a fist and slammed it into the left side of Anthony's face. The pain was excruciating. Luke made a short cry as he grabbed his right hand with his left. Anthony recovered from the punch like he never felt it to begin with. Coming in again with the lamp, Luke grabbed it with his left hand, blocking the blow. Anthony yanked on the lightning rod, pulling Luke toward him. Luke grabbed the metal lamp with both hands and used

Anthony's force against him. Instead of resisting being drawn into closer combat, Luke started running towards Anthony, throwing his larger opponent off balance, and forcing him to run backward. Anthony tripped over himself and went crashing into the carpet. Luke landed on top of him and managed to free the lamp from Anthony's grip.

Tossing the lamp across the room, Luke tried to gain control of his attacker's hands, but when he did, even with all the adrenaline pumping through him, Anthony was much stronger than he was. The stronger man twisted Luke off of him, grabbed Luke under his chin, and put him in a chokehold. Luke pushed at the man's arm, trying to free himself from the inhuman strength Anthony seemed to possess. It was no use. He could feel Anthony's hot breath on his head. The man seemed to be covered in sweat. Luke could feel the moist skin of Anthony's arm against his chin and throat.

"Anthony," Luke said in a weak, airy voice, "why are you doing this?"

There was no response. Luke wasn't sure if it was because Anthony couldn't hear him, or he didn't care to answer. Luke could feel unconsciousness claiming his mind. Panic began to set in. The thought that Anthony could end his life right here, right now. And for what? Luke was more confused by the man's recent actions than he was angry about them. It increasingly became harder and harder for Luke to focus as blackness overtook him.

*   *   *   *

Kill him! Kill him now!!

The voice boomed in Anthony's head. Staring at the top of the detective's head, Anthony could feel the rage inside him. Everything around him seemed to be in slow motion. Every breath he took echoed in his eardrums. Every pore in Anthony's body seemed to be open wide, sweat rushing out all over his body. Burrows struggled against Anthony's grip to no avail.

Kill him!

He could. Anthony could very easily end this man's life. More pressure for a longer period of time, and it would be done. Anthony felt his grip tighten ever so slightly. In a flash, the scene of Emily's death entered his mind, Wendy's voice overlaying it with one word,

Murderer.

Anthony blinked, and everything seemed to return to normal speed. He saw the detective cease his struggle to regain his freedom. Slowly, Anthony released his hold on the man. There was no resurgence of resistance, so Anthony let the man slump over onto the floor. Anthony's heart stopped for a second, afraid he'd murdered the detective. But after a moment, he saw the man's chest rise and fall slightly. A wave of relief washed over him. Then he realized the implications of what he'd just done. He'd attacked a member of the police force. Panic began to replace relief. Scrambling, his eyes darted all over the room, searching for something to help him figure out what he should do.

Let's go! Let's get some morphine or oxy and forget about all this for a while. Now!

Anthony's eyes went wide, and he ran to the front door. It was locked with padlocks, but it was still just a wooden door in a wooden frame. Backing up, Anthony raised his right leg, balanced on his left, and slammed his foot into the door. Nothing seemed to happen. Again, Anthony kicked the door. He heard the Thud! Nothing else happened. A third time he kicked the white, wooden door. This time he heard a Crack. That gave him some confidence. Taking a few steps back, he ran full speed at the door and turned, so his right shoulder took the impact. Another Crack! Anthony ran into the barrier again and again, over, and over. The solid wooden slats gave way a little more with each blow of force from the large man. The grains split and splintered until there was room enough for Anthony to make it out.

Wait!

Anthony paused as he started crawling out of the house.

Go find the gun. We don't have enough money; we may have to threaten Dylan.

Anthony backed up into the house and wandered through the dark kitchen on his hands and knees, feeling his way until he felt the cold metal touch his fingers. Grabbing it, he holstered it in the back of his waistband. Anthony returned to the broken door and crawled into the cold early morning air.

CHAPTER 33

He sat on one of the three chairs that surrounded the small table in the kitchenette, staring at the back of his captive. The man's dark hair was unkempt; he slumped in the seat he was chained to. Cracks and pops sang from the stone fireplace as the flames ate away at the logs. He had added more fuel to the fire three times since his psychological torture session with Mr. Hunter. The cabin's interior was nice and warm, filled with the orangish-yellow glow from the fire. Shadows danced across the wooden walls with each movement of the flames. Outside, the wind howled every so often, reminding him that the harsh, cold world was still there. Inhaling deeply, he loved the fragrance of the burning wood. The smokey smell of burnt oak brought a smile to his lips. He had dozed off periodically throughout the night. He needed rest for what was to come, and he wasn't worried about his captive breaking free.

Mr. Hunter had struggled against his restraints a couple more times throughout the night to no avail. The chained man had hurled insults, screamed, and asked multiple questions that were answered with silence. Nevertheless, the man was resilient, and he had to concede. That was fine. Breaking Mr. Hunter's spirit was not a priority. However, it would be beneficial, making him easier to move and control, but not a necessity for his plan.

Softly, he whispered to himself, just barely audible to himself, "But know this, if the master of the house had known in what hour of the night the thief was coming, he would have stayed awake and would not have let his house be broken into."

He'd given his captive a bottle of water every three hours. Mr. Hunter couldn't know that he was on such a routine schedule; all he knew was now, and then he was given hydration. However, the last bottle he'd given Mr. Hunter was different. He had crushed up several melatonin capsules and mixed them in the water bottle. He'd hoped it would be enough, as it was diluted with water. If he'd calculated correctly, Samuel should soon become groggy and eventually fall asleep. Reaching into his pants pocket, he took out his cell phone and checked the time. 4:38 A.M. It had been an hour since Mr. Hunter had drunk the drugged water. He wouldn't have much longer to wait.

CHAPTER 34

Tick. Tock. Tick. Tock. Tick. Tock.

Victor Sorelli sat on his king-sized bed, leaning against the headboard, listening to the sound of the clock on his nightstand. His mattress was draped with dark red sheets and a black comforter. The bed frame was made from oak, coated with a dark stain, and sat atop a plush carpet. The ends of the headboard rose six feet from the ground, the two carved columns reminiscent of ancient Roman structures. A large crown was carved in the center of the headboard. The footboard was a smaller replica of this same design. A small lamp on the nightstand beside his bed cast a yellow glow about the bedroom. The shadowy outlines on the walls seemed to be trying to escape the illumination of the glass bulb. Hanging on the wall opposite the bed was a sixty-five-inch flat-screen television. Along the east wall was the doorway leading to the master bathroom. Through the bathroom was the master closet.

Tick. Tock.

Victor glanced over at the clock. Its hands told him that the time was 4:54 A.M. Letting out a yawn, he reached up and rubbed his eyes. He'd tossed and turned all night, never sleeping for more than ninety minutes straight. A full day had passed without any news about Anthony or Sam. Yet, Victor's mind wouldn't shut itself down; different scenarios kept playing in his mind. One was that his son was dead, and no one knew. Another was that he was high somewhere, trying to decide if he should kill himself.

Sam was most likely on the run. He'd not stick around after causing so much trouble with Miss Grayson. Even though Victor had implied that the red-headed bitch would need to be taken care of eventually, he hadn't explicitly given the order. Sam should've known better than to go off and do something foolish. Victor needed Anthony solidly back in the fold before they got rid of Miss Grayson. Otherwise, they'd end up in what was now their current predicament.

Victor shook his head. Even so, no one else around the city had seen Sam yesterday. It was like he had vanished. There were no reports of him going to the airport or the bus station, and the tracker on his car showed that it was still in the city. Victor didn't think Sam had friends with those kinds of connections. The only other possible scenario was that Sam had entered into Witness Protection, but that process usually couldn't be done this fast. Besides, WitSec was a federal operation, and Victor hadn't broken any federal laws. So, there was no reason for federal agents to get involved in any of this. Although Victor countered his thoughts, Chief Reilly could have connections if Sam was stupid enough to go to the police.

Until this Houdini act, Sam seemed more loyal than Victor's son. Victor wondered if he had misjudged Sam's fealty after all this time. Swinging his legs over the side of the bed, Victor stood up and stretched. The carpet was nice and soft on his bare feet. His violet silk pajamas felt pleasant and smooth against his aged skin. Victor walked around the foot of his bed and began pacing the width of the room.

Tick. Tock. Tick. Tock.

There needed to be more conjecture and facts for him to formulate an excellent strategy for moving forward. He needed to know the whereabouts of both young men and, at the very least, his son. Everyone else that worked for him had their line of duties they were responsible for, and Victor couldn't allow any of them to be put on hold. Each business had a quota to meet, and interruptions could not occur. That signals potential weakness in Victor's kingdom and could stir up mutinous thoughts. No, there was only one person that could be trusted with this information and could also help. Victor stopped pacing and ran a hand through his thick black hair. His decision had been made, he would take a shower, get dressed, eat breakfast, and after breakfast, he would call Mr. Quentin.

*　　*　　*　　*

Anthony tore down the sidewalk as fast as he could. The cold wind was hitting him on the right side of his body, turning his sweat into ice. He ran twelve blocks at full speed before slowing down to a stop. He was curious to know if he was running in the right direction. He just needed to get as far away from that house as possible. Panting hard, Anthony put his hands on his knees and took several deep breaths. His throat was in pain from the cold air. Finally, looking around, Anthony figured out where exactly he was. Still a few miles from Dylan's house, but he at least knew which direction he needed to go from there.

Turning south down the cross street, Anthony began jogging. His adrenaline from the fight with Detective Burrows was still coursing through his veins. With each step, he could feel the gun he'd stolen hitting him in the small of his back. Anthony had no shoes on. The cold concrete smacked the bottoms of his feet as he made his way through the city in the twilight hours. He wasn't sure how it would go when he reached Dylan's house, but all that mattered was that he did.

Get a move on! We don't have time to waste.

He picked up his speed to a slow run. He also wasn't sure how long the adrenaline high would last, so he needed to push it as far as he could. As he passed a house on his right, a dog began to bark. He had no time to look back; he only hoped it was chained up.

With every step, he could feel the pain shooting up his feet. That meant his adrenaline was beginning to wear off. The sweat on his body felt frozen to his skin, a thin glaze of ice that crackled with each move he made. Anthony took deep breaths in through his nose and exhaled through his mouth. Just a little farther, he told himself. Just a little farther. The sound of the barking dog faded into the distance. He could make it. He would make it.

*   *   *   *

Mr. Hunter had succumbed to the melatonin around five o'clock. He walked over to his captive and nudged him hard, making sure the man was out cold. After untying the chains, he reinserted the cloth gag into Hunter's mouth and restrained his hands in front of him. Then, picking the large man out of the seat, he dragged him outside to the car and laid him down in the back seat before reentering the house. Now that he'd seen his victim, he grabbed the five-gallon jug of gasoline in the corner of the kitchenette.

Starting in the back bedroom, he began pouring gas onto the wooden floor going from room to room, and even up some of the walls. He soaked anything that could identify him as the cabin's owner if the fire department could get here too quickly, including the taxidermied buck and photos that hung on the walls. When he reached the living room, he made sure to keep a good distance from the fireplace. He didn't need this thing to start with him still in it. Once he'd completed drenching the cabin, with the fumes still filling his nostrils, he walked through the front door and stood on the porch. Taking out a box of matches from his jacket pocket, he picked one out of the box and dragged it across the striking strip. A small yellow flame burst to life on its tip. Gently, he tossed the match inside the door, aiming for the trail of gasoline. Instead, a large row of flames shot forth from its landing and spread throughout the wooden structure.

Taking out his phone, he checked the time. 5:10 A.M. It would take him a minimum of forty-three minutes to reach his destination without any delays. Then, the intense heat smacked him directly in the face. Looking up, he watched as flames swallowed the cabin. It was a place that held many great memories, but it was time to say goodbye. The windows on either side of the open doorway gave the impression that the cabin had grown a face. A face that stared back in horror as the flames grew higher and engulfed it.

It was a heart-wrenching experience, watching the destruction of a place he loved so much, but it was for the best. His eyes became watery as the smoke from the fire began to overwhelm him. He walked back to the sedan, opened the driver's door, and sat in the seat. Checking the back seat, he noted that Mr. Hunter was still unconscious as he had left him. Turning the key in the ignition, the engine roared to life. He put the vehicle in gear and began driving away. The rearview mirror was filled with yellow-orange flames waving through the air. Now it was time for him to set up the final piece of his game. He smiled to himself as he drove down the gravel road. Soon the Lessers would learn their lesson.

CHAPTER 35

Anthony's heart hadn't slowed since he'd fought with Detective Burrows. Now, as he ran down the sidewalk, passing beneath the goldish glow of the streetlights, his heart seemed to accelerate even more. Anthony could feel it thudding against his rib cage, trying to punch its way through. The inside of his throat burned with every breath of air he inhaled. The frozen sweat that clung to his body should have made him shiver, but instead, Anthony felt perfectly fine—not too hot or cold.

Dylan's neighborhood was quiet. No one else was out on the street. The cookie-cutter brick houses lined both sides of the pavement, each with a small front yard that was meticulously manicured. This was an upper-middle-class community. Unexpected visits were usually not tolerated, but Anthony would make sure Dylan understood the severity of this situation. Slowing down to a walk, he reached behind and tapped the pistol underneath his shirt. Dylan's house was the next one coming up. As he was walking, a car turned a corner onto Dylan's street and came cruising in Anthony's direction. For a split second, Anthony froze but quickly continued moving, trying to give the appearance that he belonged there. The sedan came and went, passing him without once slowing down. Anthony peered over his shoulder and watched the vehicle as it approached the end of the neighborhood and turned left down the main street. Anthony let out a sigh of relief.

Having reached Dylan's home, Anthony cut through the yard and onto the cement path that led from the driveway to the front door. When he arrived, he stared into the glass, seeing his warped, disheveled reflection staring back at him. Lifting a hand, he reached for the doorbell but couldn't bring himself to push the button. So instead, he lowered his hand to his side.

Come on, you wimp!!

The voice inside his head screamed at him. Looking at the distorted reflection, Anthony swore the voice was coming from the man staring back at him. Bowing his head, Anthony averted his gaze.

Kick the damn door down if you have to! We didn't come all the way here to back out now!

Anthony balled his hands into fists. Looking up, he stared back at the man staring at him from the glass. Anthony could feel his face going hot, and he thought he saw a devilish smile form on the lips of the reflection. The pounding in his head seemed to come back with a vengeance. Gritting his teeth, Anthony pushed the button that was the doorbell. He heard the distant ding-dong ring throughout the sleeping house.

There was no answer. After about a minute, Anthony rang the doorbell again, banging his right fist against the screen door several times. Finally, the metal of the door clanged loudly in protest. Silently, Anthony started pacing across the small entryway, opening, and closing his fists as he did so. Once again, there was still no answer. Returning to the doorbell, he rang it five times and smacked his fist against the screen door a multitude of times. Yelling would be his last resort. He didn't want to wake up any neighbors if he could possibly help it.

Frustration began to take hold of him. Dylan should have woken up by now. Why he wasn't coming to investigate, Anthony had no idea. He began pacing again. Anthony wasn't too worried about supply issues. He knew Dylan would have something, and it would be a particular price that they would have to negotiate. That is, if Dylan would answer the door. Anthony had no idea what time it was, but he was certain people would start waking up and leaving their homes soon; he wanted to be out of sight before that happened.

Anthony pressed the small white circle embedded in the brick for the fourth time and listened as the two-toned bell sang. He pressed it four more times in a row. Just as he raised his fist, preparing to assault the screen door once more, the main white door behind it swung wide. In the door frame stood Dylan Meyers. His curly brown hair was a mess, and a five o'clock shadow covered his lower jaw around his lips. His eyes went wide when he saw Anthony standing on his porch.

Dylan was wearing a black tank top and plaid boxer shorts. In his left hand, he held an aluminum baseball bat. Anthony didn't judge Dylan on his appearance, as his wardrobe needed to be better. The t-shirt and blue jeans he were wearing looked as if they were slept in, which they had been. His thick, black hair was an all-around catastrophe. His red, sweaty face didn't help matters either. Raising his arm slightly, he gave Dylan a small wave. Another moment passed before Dylan finally realized who he was looking at. Leaning the baseball bat against a wall, Dylan took a step towards the screen door and pushed it open slightly. Anthony took a step back, allowing the door more space to open.

"Tony?" Dylan said, his voice somewhat hoarse from being rudely awakened, full of surprise and confusion. "What in blazes are you doing here? It's nearly five-thirty in the morning."

"Hey, Dylan," Anthony greeted him as he scratched the back of his head with his right hand. "Sorry about this. I...I didn't want to bother you..."

"What the hell do you want Tony?" Dylan interrupted. "You know you're not supposed to be here without making an appointment!" He was whispering now, most likely in case his wife lurked somewhere near him. Shame wrapped itself around Anthony as he stood there on Dylan's porch. For a fraction of a second, the realization that he truly had become just another junkie gripped his soul. Then, as quickly as it came, Anthony shoved the thought aside.

"I need some meds, man," Anthony said, his voice low.

Dylan let out a sigh and hung his head. Anthony knew what Dylan was thinking. He thought he was right and was trying to figure out a way to get Anthony off his front porch without explaining anything to his wife.

"This is not a good time," Dylan said. "Come back tomorrow around..." he didn't get to finish before Anthony cut him off.

"No! Now! I need them now!" Anthony demanded. Reaching up Anthony stroked his mouth with his right hand. "I-I-I wouldn't be here now if I didn't need them."

"Tony," Dylan began, "we talked about the procedure when you first sought me out. You agreed that you would schedule a pick-up. No unannounced visits. It protects both of us."

Anthony shook his head and let out a little chuckle.

"Are you serious, Dylan?" Anthony asked. "I'm Anthony Sorelli. I don't need protection. You're the one that needs the protection."

Dylan's eyes went wide. Up until this point, Anthony had kept his true identity a secret from his supplier. However, it would be bad for business if it got around that Victor Sorelli's son was a druggie. A look of embarrassment crossed Dylan's face briefly. However, it was quickly replaced by an angry glare. Anthony could tell Dylan wasn't going to help him out willingly, but he decided to give him one more shot.

"Look, I'm not picky. I'll take whatever opiates you have on hand," Anthony said.

Dylan glanced over his shoulder. Taller than Dylan, Anthony also shifted his eyes to follow Dylan's gaze. He didn't see anything behind the man. Dylan let out a sigh.

"I'm sorry, man. Unfortunately, I can't take the risk," Dylan said as he closed the door backward.

Anthony reached out his left hand and grabbed the metal screen door, forcing it to remain open against Dylan's efforts. Anthony reached behind his back and under his shirt with his right hand. Tightly, he grabbed the grip of the 9mm in his waistband and swung it out into the open. He kept it pointed at the ground but wanted to ensure Dylan saw it. He did. Dylan's face went white the instant he saw what Anthony was now holding. Dylan swallowed before speaking again.

"Tony, there's no need for that," Dylan said while staring at the black pistol in Anthony's right hand. "We can work this out."

With a jerk, Anthony ripped the screen door out of Dylan's grip and swung it wide. Unfortunately, it hit the side of the brick entryway with a CLANG! The man in the tank top took two steps backward while Anthony stepped past the screen door and put out his left foot to stop Dylan from shutting the large white door.

"Your time being in charge of these negotiations is over," Anthony said. Dylan's left hand reached out in search of the baseball bat it was holding earlier. The tips of his fingers brushed the bottom of the bat handle, and Dylan tried to grab onto it. Noticing this, Anthony swung the pistol and aimed it directly at Dylan's face.

"I wouldn't do that," Anthony warned, his voice on a grittier edge.

Dylan released his grip on the aluminum bat and raised his hands to signify surrender. Anthony motioned for him to keep backing up. As he did, Anthony entered the man's home. From what Anthony could see, it was quaint. Tile entryway, hardwood floor in the living room. A couch and two recliners sat facing a flat-screen television mounted on the wall. Also along the walls were photos and those ridiculous boards with phrases like 'Live, Laugh, Love on them. But, of course, Dylan's wife was in charge of decorating. Once inside, Anthony shut the front door with his left foot.

"Take me to your stash," Anthony said, pointing the weapon at Dylan's head.

With a slight nod, Dylan turned and walked through the living room, around the bar that separated the kitchen and the living room. Anthony followed him through the kitchen, which housed a stainless-steel refrigerator and dishwasher, and into a small closet near the laundry room. With his right hand, Dylan flipped on the light. The closet walls were covered in wooden pallet planks. Each one was cut to different lengths and screwed into the wall. On the floor sat a basket of clothes and a small shelf that housed laundry supplies. Stepping into the closet, Dylan went to the wall to his left and pulled out a section of the plank. Behind the wood was a carve-out that housed a small Ziplock bag. Slowly, Dylan took the bag out of its hiding place and replaced the pallet plank. Unless one knew where to look, they'd never know it was there. Turning to Anthony, Dylan held out the small bag. Anthony snatched it out of Dylan's hand

and examined it. Inside were six white pills. Furrowing his brow, Anthony looked at Dylan.

"This is it? This is all you have?" Anthony pressed.

The man shrugged and gave a slight nod.

"I told you; you should have made an appoint.." Dylan never got to finish his sentence. Anthony smacked him in the throat with his left fist. Holding his throat, Dylan began to cough profusely.

"What is this?" Anthony asked.

"It's Oxy," Dylan choked out, barely audible through his bruised throat. Looking around the room, it dawned on Anthony that there hadn't been a peep from Mrs. Meyers this whole time.

"Where's your wife?" Anthony asked the puddle of a man in front of him.

With his left hand, Dylan pointed to his right. "She's in our bedroom."

Anthony shook his head before he spoke, "You're lying to me, Dylan."

Dylan's face was white as a ghost. He'd been caught.

"I don't blame you for trying to trick me into thinking she was here. It kept me from screaming at you, which, as it so happens, is good for me as well," Anthony reasoned.

Tears streamed down Dylan's face. Anthony was unsure if it was from the pain he was feeling in his throat, or the sheer emotional rollercoaster Anthony had just taken him on. Either way, it didn't matter. Shoving the plastic bag of meds into his pants pocket, Anthony shifted his eyes across the room. Dylan sank to his knees onto the hardwood floor beneath them. Nothing in Anthony's immediate peripherals showed another means to exit the house. Keeping the gun trained on Dylan, Anthony turned his body halfway around to look behind him. Looking across the kitchen, there was a wooden dining table at the far end, surrounded by three chairs. The table sat against an outer wall with two identical windows inset above it, covered in turquoise drapes. Presumably, the windows looked out into the backyard. That was it. He would go through the backyard, into the alley, and out of the neighborhood.

However, before he did anything else… Anthony turned back to the man kneeling in front of him. Dylan would likely call the cops and turn him in for burglary and assault. He'd, of course, tell them Anthony didn't get away with anything, but they'd still have probable cause to hold him and question him. But, no, the cops were already looking for him and he couldn't let Dylan aid in their efforts. Reaching down, Anthony grabbed Dylan by his shirt and hefted him to his feet. The man was reluctant but finally stood of his own volition. He put Dylan in front of him.

"Walk," Anthony demanded.

Slowly, Dylan began moving across the kitchen, hands again raised and open in a show of surrender. Passing the granite countertops and sink full of dishes. Dylan's wife had been gone for at least a few days. Anthony ushered Dylan into the living room. There, to his left, was the door to the backyard. Reaching out, Anthony gripped Dylan's left shoulder tight and pushed the man back down to his knees. Anthony could hear the man breathing, snot running in and out of his nostrils as he did so.

Glancing at the back door, I saw three rectangular panes of glass in the upper half of the wooden exit. Anthony could barely make out his reflection in the small panes, but he swore the man looking back at him was grinning ear to ear, pleased with what Anthony had done. Inside his head, he heard a roar of laughter, and he swore he saw his reflection laughing at him.

Ha ha ha!! Great job Tony! You see, I told you, you had it in you. Now do what needs to be done. Don't screw it up as you did with that pig.

Shoot this worthless welp.

Anthony felt the muscles in his face tighten. He turned back to Dylan.

The man was sobbing, praying he'd somehow make it out. Clenching his jaw, Anthony leaned down to speak to Dylan.

"Dylan, are you listening?" Anthony said in a calm tone. At first, there was no response. "Dylan!" Anthony shouted.

"Yes, yes. I'm listening," Dylan said through sobs.

What are you doing? Shoot him!

"I'm going to leave," Anthony began, "but before I can do that, I need assurances that you won't call the police."

Are you crazy? You can't trust him! Finish him off!

Anthony squeezed his eyes tight and tried to push the voice away.

"I-I-I promise. I-I-I won't c-c-call them," Dylan stammered.

"Can I believe you, Dylan?"

Dylan began nodding his head rapidly.

"Yes, you can. Absolutely," answered Dylan.

Shoot him!!

"Because if I find out that you ratted on me, I will end your life. Maybe not with a bullet to your head, but maybe to your wife's. Or maybe I'll have your spinal cord severed and paralyze you."

Anthony watched as Dylan shuddered at either of those scenarios coming to fruition. Anthony was confident Dylan had heard stories about those that crossed the Sorelli family. Of course, Anthony would need to find a new supplier after this, but that was another problem for another day.

You coward! You lousy chicken shit! Shoot this loser now!

236

"Shut up!" Anthony yelled.

As he did, he turned toward the back door and squeezed the gun's trigger. It let out a resounding Boom! as the muzzle flashed, and the 9mm, hollow point bullet rocketed across the air and hit smack dab in the middle of the center window in the door. The glass shattered; Dylan let out a yelp and fell flat to the floor on his face. Anthony was breathing heavily. Cool air drifted in from outside. Slowly he turned back to Dylan.

"Sorry about that," Anthony apologized. "Do I make myself clear? I have sources everywhere. Even if I'm not arrested, I will still know if you call this in."

"Yes. I understand completely," Dylan whimpered.

"Good. I don't want to send someone over here someday," Anthony threatened.

Anthony shoved the gun back into his waistband without another word and ran for the back door. Quickly, he unlocked it and ran into the cool morning air. The backyard was empty besides a propane grill on the concrete patio, covered up for the winter. Anthony trotted across the dead grass to the wooden fence, searching for the gate. It was in the far corner of the yard. Once there, he fumbled with the carabiner that locked the wooden gate from the inside. After finally getting it open, Anthony tore down the alley. Neighbors indeed heard that gunshot. He had to get as far away as he could.

He could feel the pills calling to him in his pocket, begging to be taken this very instant. Blinking furiously, Anthony pushed the temptation down. He needed to find a safer spot. Maybe if he made it a few blocks west, that would be far enough. There was an old, abandoned shop building that he could hole up in for a bit. With a destination in mind, Anthony picked up his pace. In the distance, he could have sworn he heard what sounded like another gunshot. The odds of that happening in this area of town, though, were inconceivable. Putting it out of his mind, Anthony ran.

CHAPTER 36

Other than the glow from lamp posts sporadically placed throughout the neighborhoods, the side streets of St. Louis were dark. Looking down, he checked his speedometer. 25mph. The exact speed limit. He had to be extra cautious now since his captive was in the back seat instead of the trunk. There was no longer any room for error.

He'd decided to take side roads through the city to stave off any possibility of being pulled over. Even though it took him longer than it would have, it was the best course of action. Zig-zagging through residential areas this early morning was also good because anyone up this early would likely head straight for the main roads since they would be more sparsely populated. Slowing down, he came to a halt at a STOP sign.

Looking both ways, he saw no other cars anywhere. He was about to pull ahead when he noticed the names of the cross streets. Birch Street, the street he was currently on, and Hammond Drive. He looked to his right. Hammond Drive was the street Dylan Meyers lived on. Knowing it was a long shot, he turned right and headed down the paved road. He was only about five blocks away from his destination now, anyway. He could go ahead and exit the neighborhoods and take Wilshire the rest of the way.

Accelerating the sedan to the twenty-five miles per hour speed limit, he gazed down the street. At first, he saw nothing, which was to be expected. Then, suddenly, he caught some movement up the road to his left. Someone was walking down the sidewalk. Quickly he shifted his eyes to the dash to check the time. 5:22 A.M. Glancing back up the road, he kept his eyes on the figure. As the two got closer, he could now see that this person was a male and a taller-than-average male. His heart skipped a beat in his chest. It was so immensely improbable that he dared not hope for it. Then, just before they passed each other, the man walked under a streetlight. There under the yellow glow, there could be no doubt. The dark hair, the shape of the face. That was Anthony Sorelli. A sudden wave of joy filled him. Knowing that Anthony would be this close to what would transpire was better than he could have hoped. His car windows were tinted, so he was sure Anthony couldn't see him, and it looked like

Anthony was trying to act as casually as possible, like someone out for an early morning stroll.

He watched Anthony in the rearview mirror. As he approached the intersection to Wilshire, he pressed on the brake to stop at the octagonal sign. He thought he saw Anthony turn towards him, but he couldn't be sure. He was too far away at this point. It didn't matter, though. All that mattered was he now knew Anthony's whereabouts. With a lever flick on the steering wheel's side, the turn signal sprang to life, indicating to whoever was out there that he intended to turn left. The rhythmic clicking filled the interior of the sedan as he pulled forward and made the turn. Once he straightened the car, the lever repositioned itself, and the clicking ceased.

Driving the next five blocks went without incident. Finally, he pulled the car into a strip mall parking lot. Four of the units were vacant, though two were occupied. One housed an off-brand cell phone company: the other, a local sandwich shop. At the edge of the parking lot, facing west down Wilshire, was Mr. Hunter's vehicle. He had moved it here yesterday before taking an Uber back to his car. Shutting off the engine, he watched as the headlights faded and the only light remaining was from the streetlights around them.

Opening his door, he stepped out into the crisp morning air. Walking to his trunk, he opened it and took out a pair of latex gloves. He put one on each hand, not wanting to leave any prints at the scene. Then, taking Mr. Hunter's key fob out of his pocket, he unlocked the other's car. He stepped to the backdoor of his sedan, shut the open trunk, and opened the driver's side backdoor before grabbing Mr. Hunter by his ankles. Forcibly, he pulled the man halfway out of the car and dropped the man's legs, his feet smacked against the pavement. Returning to the car, he grabbed Sam underneath his arm and hoisted him up over his shoulder. Slowly, he began walking the unconscious man to the other car, glancing about in the dark parking lot with each step. He wanted to make sure no one was watching. Even if there were, they'd assume it was someone helping out a drunk friend.

Once he'd made it to the car, he carefully reached down and opened the driver's door. The interior dome light came on, shining a yellow glow inside the black vehicle. Then, as easily as he could, he began maneuvering Sam into the driver's seat. As he did so, Sam suddenly woke up. The man began swinging his bound arms wildly, smacking his captor. Mr. Hunter was still groggy from the sleep medication. Sam must have felt the top of his head because suddenly, the man had gripped it tight and yanked hard. His head cooperated with the tug and went in towards Sam.

Taking Mr. Hunter's arms in his hands, he freed himself from the man's grasp. With a whack, he hit Mr. Hunter in the forehead with his fist. The drowsy man fell back against the seat and breathed shallowly. Sam's eyes had barely opened; he definitely was not fully conscious. Lifting Mr. Hunter's legs into the car, he reached behind and pulled a .45 revolver from his waistband. This was not something he had originally planned, but as he looked at the man before him, he couldn't resist the temptation. He grabbed Sam by the back of his head and shook him.

"Look at me, Samuel," he said in a low voice.

Sam moaned something in response.

"Open your eyes, and look at me," he said in a calm but authoritative tone.

Sam turned his head and did his best to raise his eyelids as far as he could. Then, after a few seconds, Sam focused on the face before him. And then there it was. A slight look of recognition and fear took hold of what little facial muscles Sam could control at the moment. Then, in a second, the fear turned to anger. Sam's face began to turn red, and he could see rage behind his eyes.

He grinned at his captive. He loved the grand feeling of power and control so much.

"Hi, Sam," he said in a cheerful voice.

Sam tried to say something, but it was unintelligible through the gag and his melatonin-induced drowsiness. Finally, he lifted the pistol and pointed it at Sam's throat. Mr. Hunter's face went white faster than anything he'd ever seen.

"Bye, Sam."

He took his index finger and pulled the trigger.

*   *   *   *

Anthony sat against the outer wall along the west side of the building. The abandoned place had been boarded up, and there were locks on both the front and rear doors. Anthony had contemplated shooting the locks off but decided against it. There'd been too many gunshots around this area already. A gust of wind sent frigid air against Anthony's exposed skin. It tore through the thin t-shirt he wore as well. The adrenaline he'd been running on was revived by the shooting of the pistol moments ago, and it still hadn't entirely abated. To his left, the sound of a cat squabble made its way into his ear drums. Anthony turned his head to see if he could make out any shapes that resembled feral felines.

The closest streetlight was broken, so it was difficult for his eyes to see that far away in the dark. He saw the outline of several dumpsters, but that was all. He was certain the dumpsters were oozing some putrid stench, but Anthony didn't notice. Sitting in the darkness, he stared at the brick building across from him, his heart throbbing away at his ribs. Anthony opened and closed his fists over and over again. His left pants pocket felt as if it were on fire. The urge to reach in and pull out the cause of the fire was excruciating. Anthony surprised himself. Everything he'd done these past couple of hours he had done for the contents in that pocket. Now, sitting here in this alley, Anthony was hesitating. All he could do was squeeze his fingers together in a fist, not reach into the pocket, and indulge himself in the sweet relief of the opiates.

Do it! Come on! We have what we need. Take some, and let's forget about all of this.

Anthony closed his eyes and leaned his head against the wooden building behind him. It was listening to that advice that landed him in this situation.

You can't blame me! I'm nothing more than your selfish desires.

Shaking his head, Anthony opened his eyes. To his right, he heard a vehicle passing by on the street. His mind flashed to the brief moments before he ran over Emily. Emily. Anthony didn't even remember her last name. He knew it was on the paper his father had given him when he'd assigned him to 'take care of her.' All he saw now was the look of shock and horror on the young woman's face before the grill of the car slammed into her.

Take the medicine. It will make you feel better.

Anthony let out a breath. Why was he hesitating? He couldn't think of a clear answer. Then out of nowhere, it struck him. Wendy. He was hesitating for Wendy. She would disapprove of this. She wasn't against proper medication if one required it, but she knew Anthony had become addicted. She would see this relapse and be more disappointed in him than she'd been in a long time. Flashes of memories started playing in his mind. A scene of him killing Emily, the look on Detective Burrows' face when Anthony attacked him, Dylan was kneeling before him sobbing, his father berating him.

Take your medicine!

The words screamed through his head. Every time he blinked; he saw an image from his past that he regretted. Things he had done that he needed to forget. Shoving his hand into his pocket, Anthony felt around until he found the plastic bag. Quickly, he pulled it out and held it before his hazel eyes. The six white capsules sat there like pieces of candy packed in a school lunch. Anthony wanted to toss them down the alley, throw them in one of the dumpsters and head back to find Detective Burrows and apologize for his behavior, but he couldn't. The bag was stuck in his grasp and would not be easily discarded.

Take them.

This time the words were a whisper. Anthony just sat staring at them. He needed to get rid of them, but he wanted to feel their magic again. Flashes of the crash flooded back to him. The headlights turned her silhouette into a human being. The smell of the drunk passed out in the back seat. The sound of her body hitting the car's hood and smashing into the windshield.

Without another thought, Anthony opened the bag and took out two capsules. Opening his mouth, he prepared to toss one in but stopped short. As he looked at the small object in his hand, Anthony briefly said a silent apology before tossing one pill into his mouth. After dry swallowing the first, he did the same with the second. He was unaware of the dosage, so he put the remainder of the meds back into his pants pocket. Sitting there in the dark, he waited for the numbing effects of the drugs to take over.

* * * *

Attorney David Quentin stepped out of his bathroom after having taken his morning shower to hear his cell phone ringing. Walking quickly across his bedroom, the souls of his feet trotting along the carpet, Quentin headed for his nightstand where his phone sat charging. He held the dark green towel wrapped around his waist as he moved. Water droplets flung themselves from his dark blonde hair onto the gray carpet beneath him. Quentin reached down and picked up the phone, but before he could answer, it stopped ringing. The pop-up on his screen displayed that he had three missed calls from Victor Sorelli. Quentin's eyes narrowed, wondering why Victor Sorelli would call him at six-thirty in the morning. Of course, there was nothing to do but call him back immediately, which is exactly what Quentin did. He redialed Mr. Sorelli and sat on the edge of his queen-sized mattress. The phone rang four times before there was an answer.

"Hello, David." Victor Sorelli's voice came through the phone speaker. It was dark and menacing. Quentin grimaced. Victor never used his first name unless he was irritated. He knew better than to keep Mr. Sorelli waiting, but surely he would understand.

"Good morning, Mr. Sorelli. I'm so sorry about missing your phone calls. I just now stepped out of the shower and noticed you had tried to reach me," Quentin responded in a tone that was a mixture of apologetic but firm. He would not give the impression of groveling. That would not serve him well. Sorelli respected strength and loyalty. Quentin possessed both.

For a moment, there was only silence. Neither man spoke. Quentin thought he could hear Victor breathing, but it was probably just static. "I need your help, Mr. Quentin," Victor finally said. Quentin let out a breath he hadn't realized he was holding.

"Absolutely, Sir. I can take care of whatever you need," Quentin answered, eager to find out about this new assignment.

"I received a call yesterday from my associate, Samuel Hunter," Victor began, "He informed me that he ran into you outside the police station, and you had intel that Anthony was inside."

"Yes, sir, Mr. Hunter and I spoke about Anthony yesterday."

"Sam said you told him you would stick around and wait to see if Anthony showed up again at the police station."

There was a pause, and Quentin confirmed Victor's statement.

"So," Victor continued, "I told Sam to come back to the estate and let you handle things there. But Sam never arrived here, nor did he inform me of any new developments that may have occurred to keep him away. I tried calling him multiple times, but he never answered."

"Okay," Quentin said slowly, acknowledging he heard Victor's statement.

Victor let out a sigh, not out of annoyance, but a sigh that signaled he was out of options.

"Quentin, I need you to try and find both of them. Anthony and Sam. They're both missing and need to be found sooner rather than later."

Quentin waited to answer. It was a daunting task, finding two men in a city the size of St. Louis, both having been missing for nearly twenty-four hours. Quentin didn't realize how much of a miracle worker Victor thought he was. Finally, after thinking it through for a few seconds, Quentin had his answer.

"I'll do my best to locate them, sir," the attorney said. He knew better than to make promises he could not deliver. "I have an idea where to start with Anthony, but is there anything you could tell me that would aid my search for Mr. Hunter?"

"I think Sam is running," Victor said, "I believe he did something that I suggested would have to be done at some point but did it without my go-ahead and is now on the lam."

Quentin nodded to himself as water dripped from his hair onto his face and fell onto the floor. Given the advantage Sam had of knowing Sorelli's network and the head start he had, there was little hope Quentin could find him, but he would try.

"I will reach out to all my contacts and start the search as soon as I'm dressed," Quentin said.

*　　*　　*　　*

"Luke. Luke."

The voice of Henry Burrows filled Luke's ears. Luke was in his childhood home. The tan walls and old red recliner gave it away. Luke didn't remember coming home, but he must have. Slowly, he walked up and down the hallway, opening every door and looking in every room. His bedroom was just as he'd left it years ago. Blue walls, with movie posters, taped to them, the twin bed in the far corner of the room with the navy comforter and sky-blue sheets. On the backside of his bedroom door was a poster of Pamela Anderson in her Baywatch lifeguard swimsuit.

He didn't know what his father wanted or even why his father was calling him. But, as hard as he tried, Luke could not find his father. Instead, the walls held photos of his family. His 'perfect' family. Luke shook his head. He never understood his father's obsession with holding on to the false perception.

"Luke. Luke."

The voice came again. He searched everywhere, finding nothing, yet his father's voice still called to him.

"Luke."

Every time, though, it sounded like it was coming from a new direction. Luke ran up and down his childhood home, but there was nobody there but himself.

"Luke. Luke, wake up."

That was puzzling. Luke was awake.

"Luke."

This time the voice had changed. It was no longer his father's, but he didn't recognize it either.

"Luke, come on, man. Wake up."

Mason's voice. Then it hit him. He wasn't in his childhood home. He was passed out on the living room floor in the safe house. Anthony had attacked him and…

With that, Luke's eyes snapped wide open, and he sat straight.

"Whoa. Easy there, tiger," Mason said, kneeling next to him.

Luke looked around the room. To his right was the lamp Anthony had tried to use to hit him in the head. He didn't see anything else out of the ordinary at this level. With an effort, Luke rose to his feet.

"Careful now, take it easy," Mason said, arms extended, ready to catch the disoriented detective if he lost his balance.

As Luke returned to full height, he noticed the front door. It had been repeatedly assaulted to the point of breaking apart. It must have been how Anthony escaped. Patting himself down, Luke made sure Anthony didn't take anything off his person. At first, he was relieved because he felt everything was where it was supposed to be. Then he checked his holster. It was empty. Panic took over Luke's mind in an instant. He began breathing rapidly, and his eyes darted around the room. It wasn't here.

Not good, not good, Luke thought to himself. Surely it had to be here. Luke closed his eyes and took long, deep breaths, calming himself. Once he removed the panic from his mind, he thought through the fight he'd had with Anthony. The dodge away from the swinging lamp, and the second dodge, there, Luke pulled his gun, but Anthony knocked it out of his hand. It flew into the kitchen. Quickly, Luke stepped into the kitchen and flicked on the light. The old linoleum floor was dull under the yellow light. Luke searched and searched, under the table, in the trash can, behind the trash can, and in the cupboards. Nothing. His weapon was not there. Mason was behind him, in his black coat, watching him with curiosity.

"My gun," Luke said, his voice hoarse and his throat sore. He winced at the pain and rubbed his throat gently with his hand. "It's missing."

"Do you have your backup?" Mason asked; his tone was neither angry nor displeased but neutral.

Luke checked the small ankle holster on his right leg and nodded when he saw the .38 Smith & Wesson revolver. That brought some relief, even if only a little. A look of concern was on Mason's face.

"Don't worry about this," Luke said, "I'll make sure you're clear of any shots fired our way."

"I'm not worried about this," Mason said, "Come on, we're needed elsewhere." With that, Mason turned and walked out of the house.

Luke was perplexed. Where else could they possibly be needed?

"What about the door?" Luke asked as he shut the damaged barrier behind him. Mason was already at the Charger. Luke's partner opened the driver's side door and stared at him.

"Get in. I'll explain on the way. And so will you." Mason said sternly. Luke entered the vehicle, and Mason pulled away from the curb and accelerated down the street. For a moment, neither spoke. They just stared out the windshield, watching houses and yards passing as they drove.

"Jim's coming to fix the door," Mason finally said, breaking the silence.

"Jim?" Luke said, confused, "Jim McAlaster?"

Mason nodded his confirmation. Luke was amazed. So, Reilly might not have to find out about this after all. That is if they find Anthony before he does something stupid.

"He owes me a few," Mason said by way of explanation. The interior of the car was decently warm. Mason mustn't have been at the safe house for very long before managing to wake Luke from unconsciousness.

"Where are we going?" Luke asked.

"Gunshots were reported around Wilshire and Grant about forty-fiveish minutes to an hour ago," Mason answered.

That didn't make much sense to Luke, and there was no reason to believe that report had anything to do with their current case.

"The responding officer found a lone car parked in a strip mall parking lot. When he examined it, he found a dead man in the driver's seat."

This raised Luke's curiosity. So, a dead man was interesting, but other detectives in the department could handle a call like that. So, Luke waited patiently for Mason to provide the clarity he was seeking.

"They called me when they couldn't reach you," Mason continued, "it turns out the car is registered to Victor Sorelli."

CHAPTER 37

The scene that Luke and Mason arrived at was somewhat reminiscent of two days ago when they found Miss Grayson. Multiple patrol cars surrounded the area, all of them flashing their reds and blues. Yellow police tape blocked off the car, and metal barriers blocked access to the paved parking lot. A crowd of onlookers had gathered, even in the cold temperature, to catch a glimpse of what was causing such a commotion. In the parking lot were the CSI van and the Medical Examiner van. Will and Dr. Wright were already on the scene, which was a good sign. However, Luke's patience was wearing extremely thin.

Mason flashed his credentials at the officer guarding the east entrance to the lot. The uniformed man removed the barrier and allowed Mason into the parking area. Carefully Mason pulled up beside the M.E. van and shifted the transmission into the park. The two detectives stepped out of the black muscle car and walked toward the crime scene. It was much more gruesome than Luke had previously imagined. The entire driver's side of the front of the vehicle was nearly completely covered in blood. The red, life-giving liquid had been sprayed across the windshield, steering wheel, gauges, dashboard, console, door panels, and passenger side window. This wasn't the first scene Luke had seen with so much blood, but it was the most contained in one area.

Luke glanced at Mason, who was studying the grisly mess intensely. Mason had listened to Luke's story about Anthony's escape with complete neutrality. He saw some relief come over his partner's face. Luke looked into the vehicle to try and see what had caused such a reaction. Even though the man was soaked in his blood, Luke and Mason could tell this was not Anthony Sorelli. This man's hair was the wrong color, and his body build was not nearly big enough to be Anthony. That was good, and it meant Anthony was hopefully still alive somewhere. A gust of wind sent shivers down Luke's body. He had forgotten his coat in a rush to leave the safe house.

Will Johnson was kneeling near the opened passenger-side front door, taking swabs, and collecting evidence. Will and Mason spent many hours reviewing the physical evidence from Wendy Grayson's home. Unfortunately, Mason had told Luke just before reaching this scene there was no indication of drugs in the house and no prints other than Miss Grayson's and Anthony's. So that whole ordeal had gained them nothing. Hopefully, they will learn something new here.

Dr. Wright was standing beside the victim, studying the situation. Her hair was in its usual ponytail, the streaks of gray flowing like a river throughout the brown strands. Her face expressed sorrow for the poor man before her.

"What do we know, Doc?" Luke asked, his throat still sore.
Dr. Wright turned to face him. For a moment, she didn't respond. Instead, she just stood and stared at Luke, presumably wondering why he would leave without a coat of some kind.

"According to his license, his name is Samuel Hunter. He's thirty years old, lives on Chesapeake Drive, and according to his liver temperature, he died at approximately five fifty-five this morning," Dr. Wright answered.

"Any idea on how he died?" Mason asked.

Dr. Wright threw a knowing look at Luke. The two of them exchanged a look, confirming Luke's fear. Mason noticed the two of them and asked to be let in on their secret.

"I won't be able to confirm anything until I get him back to the morgue, but" she paused, again looking at Luke. He gave her a nod, and she continued, "I'd say he was shot in the throat at close range, which resulted in him choking to death on his blood."

"And you two have seen this before," Mason said, referring to the shared looks between Luke and the Doc.

"Yes," Luke said. "And every time, someone has been connected with the Sorelli family."

Mason's eyes went wide. It was a detail only a handful knew about, including Chief Reilly and the late Detective Charles Wallace. The one similar M.O. in several of the cases linked with the Sorellis going back decades. It had been years since one had reared its ugly head, but the most recent victim sat before them.

Mason walked over to Luke and spoke in a hushed voice, "You think Anthony did this?"

Luke shrugged.

"From what I gather, every person this happens to be close to the family that disobeyed orders or betrayed them in some way," Luke said. "All the evidence is completely circumstantial as well. Maybe Anthony thought this Sam Hunter had something to do with his girlfriend's death and exacted revenge."

Mason's face was full of surprise with all the new information he'd been given in such a short span of time. This case took a whole new turn out of the left field.

"To answer your question," Luke continued, "we won't know anything until we find Anthony and test him for gunshot residue…"

"… and until Will finds the slug and runs a ballistic test on my weapon," Luke whispered this last part, more to himself than anyone else.

The two men looked out to the crowd of people across the street. It looked as if they were about to start overflowing into the street. Flashes from cell phone cameras blinked across the sea of people.

"We should have some officers disperse the crowd," Luke said.

"Good idea," Mason agreed.

Mason walked to the nearest officer and relayed the order. The officer nodded and repeated the order over the radio. Officers headed across the street and ushered everyone off to a symphony of moans and protests about hindering the freedom of the press. Mason returned to the bloodied car and stepped over to Will.

"Anything of interest, William?" Mason asked.

"There were some hairs in the victim's hand," Will responded. "At first glance, they don't look like they match the deceased, so I'm willing to bet they were the attackers."

Will was looking at the bullet hole in the passenger door panel with a flashlight. Mason opened his mouth to respond when a uniformed officer spoke up and pulled their attention elsewhere.

"Detectives," came an unfamiliar voice.

Both men turned around to find the officer running toward them. He was a wider man, about Luke's and Mason's age, with a black mustache and goatee surrounding his lips.

"Yes, officer?" Luke answered.

"We finished our ten-block radius search, and we found something the two of you should see," the officer said, breathless.

Mason and Luke exchanged a look of curiosity. Mason gestured for the policeman to lead the way. The man nodded, turned, and began walking to one of the patrol cars at the edge of the parking lot. The flashing red and blue lights danced throughout the twilight of the morning. Luke shivered slightly as the cold air wrapped around his exposed arms. They noticed a shape in the back seat as they approached the car.

"We found him nine blocks east of here." the officer said, "He was in an alley, alone and high as a kite."

Luke threw a glance at Mason, wondering if the other was thinking what he was thinking. Both men stared into the back window when they arrived at the patrol car. Sitting there, in a thin gray t-shirt and blue jeans, with his hands restrained behind his back, was Anthony Sorelli.

Victor Sorelli stood staring out the window in his bedroom. His dark red silk robe wrapped around him in a soft embrace. Black drapes stood guard on either side of the framed glass. From here, he could see the city skyline of St. Louis in the distance. Somewhere out there was his son and Sam. St. Louis was a relatively large metropolitan area, and he knew it would take time to locate the two men. His phone call with Quentin had gone well, he thought. The attorney had said he would do his best to locate the two missing men. He was still determining what all contacts the attorney had inherited from his predecessor, but he imagined they were quite extensive. It was easier than trying to hire a private investigator or trusting one of his other men to do the job as quietly as Quentin was sure to do.

At the window's edge, Victor saw that the sun was beginning to creep over the horizon. There was no way of knowing what this day would bring, but Victor hoped for the best. He hoped Anthony and Sam would be found and delivered to him by the day's end. Victor would deal with each of them in turn, and they would each deserve the punishments he had in mind. Anthony would be confined to his room under constant guard until he was sober and until he would move past the red-headed whore.

Sam, on the other hand, would not be so fortunate. Sam only thought he knew the many ways Victor made people suffer for betrayal. Unfortunately, Victor still had a few things up his sleeve that would make the traitor wish he were dead. He felt his face go hot and noticed he was clenching his fists tight. Victor let out a breath of regret. He didn't want to harm the boy. He'd been a good right hand, but it was time for it to be chopped off and replaced.

Turning from the window, Victor walked through his bathroom to his walk-in closet. He perused through his clothes, trying to find something he felt would personify today. In the end, he decided on a dark red button-down shirt, black slacks, and a white tie. He was sure this would make a statement to those two screw-ups once they were brought before him. Victor may be older, but he still reigned in his empire, and he would handle things the way they required to be done. Once fully dressed, he stepped into his bathroom, took his hair gel, and fixed his thick, black locks to perfection. They were tall and parted on the left side of his head. No gray hairs today. That was as good a sign as any. After fixing his hair, he headed downstairs for his breakfast.

* * * *

"You did what?!" Chief Reilly's voice boomed throughout his office as he stood from the chair behind his desk. Luke and Mason flinched slightly at the outburst.

The elderly man's face was flushed with blood, and the white hair on his head and face looked like flames bursting forth from his rage. It had been a while since they had seen this kind of reaction from Reilly. Shame began to grow in Luke. He looked away, not wanting to endure the daggers the Chief was staring into them.

Luke and Mason had left the gruesome murder scene shortly after discovering the inebriated Anthony Sorelli in the back of a patrol cruiser. They transferred Anthony to their vehicle, taking possession of the weapon—Luke's 9mm—and a plastic bag of drugs from the arresting officer, and had a GSR test run on the man. The initial results showed that Anthony had recently fired Luke's service weapon. When Luke unloaded the weapon, he confirmed that a bullet was missing from the magazine. Will had also found the spent slug, and Luke instructed him to quickly run the ballistics test on his service weapon to see if it matched the round in the car.

Stressing the urgency of these results, Luke reiterated the necessity for them multiple times to Will. Finally, Mason and Luke brought Anthony back to the station, bringing him in through the back, and put him in interrogation room two. Locking the door behind them, the detectives argued about their next steps. Mason wanted to inform Chief Reilly about the developments, but Luke did not. Luke wanted to wait until Anthony had sobered up so that they could interrogate him again and get answers before reporting to Reilly. Mason didn't like the look it would give if Reilly found out from other sources. Luke eventually conceded, so the two men told the Chief everything that had happened since they left the station yesterday afternoon.

Standing here now, with Reilly leaning over his desk, looking like he might take their heads off with one swipe, Luke was glad they had been the ones to inform him. Reilly's office was lit with white fluorescent lights that reflected off the pale gray walls. They were starting to give Luke a headache. Mason glanced quickly at Luke, saying, 'I hope you know how to get out of this.' The blinds on the office windows behind the detectives had been released to block any view from potential voyeurs.

"How in the hell am I going to explain any of this to the mayor?" Reilly asked, fuming.

The two detectives standing next to each other both looked at the ground. It was a valid question, and neither man had an answer that would suffice. Lifting his left hand, Reilly ran his fingers through his snow-white locks.

"You haven't read him his rights?" Reilly said, his voice somewhat calm.

"No sir," Luke answered. "He's too high to understand them, and it'd be thrown out the second it was discovered that he was inebriated when they were read to him."

Reilly nodded and turned to face the wall behind his desk, shoving his hands in his pockets as he did so. Luke wished he knew what the Chief was thinking. He could only imagine it was a way to save all their necks if any of this ever got out. The whole idea had been a mess. If he hadn't insisted on Anthony being a suspect and insisting they keep him around, they probably wouldn't be in this position. Luke knew Reilly would resign if he and Mason were allowed to remain on the force. It wasn't what any of them wanted. But dwelling on what could have been and what could be would not help their current predicament.

"Will you arrest him for murder?" Reilly asked, back still turned to them.

"It seems to be the logical thing. Even if it is circumstantial, we have enough to detain him on murder charges unless any evidence proves contrary," Mason offered.

"And if the ballistic test proves he didn't kill this man," Reilly began, turning back to face the detectives, "what then?" '

"We have him on possession of narcotics and assaulting a police officer," Luke said.

Mason and Reilly both shook their heads. Luke didn't understand the response. They had Anthony Sorelli dead to rights on both of those charges.

"If we charge him with possession, that snake of a lawyer will have him out on probation before you could sit in that chair," Reilly said, pointing with his right hand as he spoke.

"And you can't charge him with assaulting you because there's no record of him in that safe house, and it would be your word against his," Mason said.

Luke's shoulders sunk in defeat for a split second, but then a new thought hit him.

"The door. We have the door," Luke said with enthusiasm.

"Nope," Mason said. "Jim already replaced it."

"McAlester?" Reilly asked, throwing an inquisitive look at Mason. Mason nodded, and Reilly gave a slight look of surprise.

"Alright," Luke conceded. "If we don't have him on murder, we can't hold him, but he most likely knows Samuel Hunter, and he could give us insight into his murder."

Reilly and Mason looked at each other and then back at Luke. They both knew he was right, but they would have to get him to talk, and it already proved futile when they asked for Anthony's help to find his girlfriend's murderer. The man was either loyal, scared, or both. Luke and Mason would need to play this one as carefully as possible. There was also the risk of Sorelli's or the lawyer's informants stumbling upon the intoxicated man alone in the interrogation room. If that happened and David Quentin showed up, they would all be up a creek. There would be no way to pull that magic trick of keeping Anthony on the move and away from everyone again. They had even gotten lucky that the few men in the locker room either didn't recognize him or weren't on the Sorelli payroll. The odds of that happening again were slim to none.

"Go on," Reilly said, motioning them out of his office, "find answers."

*   *   *   *

Traffic was clogged as usual on David Quentin's route to his office. He'd spent the better part of his morning playing the conversation he had with Victor Sorelli over and over again in his head. It was not the phone call he expected to receive this morning. His mind was so distracted that he'd missed two exits that he needed to take and had to double back. He'd be later than usual, but no one would question it. They knew better when he was the one working directly with Victor Sorelli. That gave him free rein to be as tardy or absent as needed. And if they ever questioned, he needed to invoke the Sorelli name. Any doubts regarding his whereabouts would immediately cease. That brought a small smile to his lips. He enjoyed the power he had at the office. A little too much.

David's charcoal suit was finely starched. The creases in his jacket and pants were sharp and crisp, just as he liked them. He'd bought most of his suits from Men's Warehouse over the years, but he wanted to have a custom suit made that belonged only to him. Most likely, he would go with a shade of navy jacket with black slacks. Cufflinks were the most difficult pieces for him to pick out. He was still determining if he could get custom cufflinks. At any rate, the suit would be the most valuable thing he owned other than his house and car. Maybe I'll buy it for my birthday, he thought. Maybe not. No one would know except those he told. So, what would it matter? It wouldn't. But he still wanted one.

Traffic was starting to move again. Gently, he pressed the accelerator and felt the car move forward. Everyone proceeded ahead and came to a halt in what seemed like only a couple of feet. It was probably more like a good hundred feet, but the distinction was lost on the thousands of drivers sitting on the highway.

Mentally, Quentin began running through his checklist of informants he would need to contact about Anthony and Sam. The five people at the police station, eight at the hospitals, two at the train station, seven at the taxi companies, twelve at the airports, and all the Sorelli employees that run the day-to-day operations of the businesses. It was a long list, and it would take some time to go through them. But, with any luck, someone would know something about one or both of the missing men. And luck was all he had at this point. He dared not think what Victor might do if he failed to find at least one of them.

Behind him, a car horn blared. Returning to the moment, he noticed traffic had moved another few hundred feet. He proceeded to catch up with them. Inhaling deeply, he reveled in the smell of pine that permeated his vehicle's interior. Yup, he thought, today is going to be a long day.

CHAPTER 38

Anthony had no idea how long he'd been at the police station or how he ended up there. The last thing he remembered was taking the Oxy outside in the alley. As lucidity returned to him, he slowly noticed his surroundings had changed. Instead of being outside, he was now inside. Rather than being next to the abandoned wooden building, he was in a small room. It was dimly lit, more so than the alley, but not as bright as any other indoor area. He was sitting in a plastic chair with metal legs. The walls were a dull white. A metal table was before him, with nothing on it. On the wall in front of him was a large glass mirror, although it wasn't clear like most mirrors. The reflection was somewhat dulled.

His hands were behind his back, and he could not move them. They were restrained, probably by handcuffs. Anthony tried his hardest to push back the remaining effects of the drugs. He needed to hydrate. He was curious to know how that would happen with being handcuffed. The door to the small room opened as if on cue, and a man walked in. In his hand were three bottles of water, each with the lids removed and a straw put in place. The man was wearing a gray button-down shirt, black pants, and black shoes. He looked familiar to Anthony. The man had black hair, combed to the left side of his head, and green eyes. His jaw was firm and square. The man was tall, not taller than Anthony, but close to his height, he guessed. Then it struck him. Detective Mason. One at a time, the detective placed the bottles of water on the table in front of Anthony. When he finished, he looked Anthony directly in the eyes.

"Drink," Mason said, not harshly but not sympathetically either.

Without another word, he exited the room, leaving Anthony alone once again. Anthony watched him as he shut the door. Turning back, he stared at the dull reflection before him. Something had to have happened, he thought to himself. Even if the gunshot I fired was reported, I was well out of the search radius. It puzzled Anthony. He couldn't think of a single plausible explanation for his capture. Initially, he thought it was Dylan but quickly dismissed the idea. The way Dylan had been crying in his own puddle sealed his silence. No, it had to be something else. But what, Anthony did not know. Honestly, he wasn't sure it mattered. What mattered was that they had found him, and he had no idea how he'd get out of this one. I should call my lawyer, Anthony thought. Again, he dismissed the notion only when he figured out why they had him here. He would invoke if it turned out to be something he needed Quentin. Letting out a sigh, he leaned forward and began sipping water through the plastic straw in the first bottle.

*   *   *   *

Luke and Mason stood in the dark observation room, watching Anthony drink down the second bottle of water. The man hadn't initially reacted to seeing Mason, which meant the drugs still had an effect on his cognitive state. Luke didn't want Anthony to see him until he'd sobered up. Anthony had no idea the grilling he was in for. Again, Luke would have to restrain himself. He had let his guard down with Anthony once, and it hadn't ended well. Sure, one could argue the validity of the correlation between those events, but all that mattered to Luke was the end result. He and Mason had both noticed yesterday that Anthony talked to himself, which should have been a clear indicator to tread lightly. Of course, it didn't always mean one was mentally disillusioned, but most people talk things through with themselves in private.

Luke had begun to believe that Anthony couldn't have killed Wendy Grayson, but after the incident at the safe house, he was more than willing to believe in the possibility. Of course, the real test was to see if Anthony remembered their fight. If he claims not to, then they give him a polygraph. Anthony passes that, sees a psychiatrist, and he would have a case for insanity. Shaking his head, Luke couldn't let that happen. He would do whatever it took to prove Anthony Sorelli was mentally aware of the horrific murders he had committed.

"Good idea. Giving him the water," Mason said, snapping Luke from his thoughts.

"Thanks," Luke responded. "The more he hydrates, the sooner he'll be sobered up."

Anthony was halfway through the third and final bottle. The man was parched. Luke's black shirt was wrinkled from being stuffed in his desk drawer. After meeting with Chief Reilly, he and Mason showered and changed clothes. The hot water and clean smell helped Luke to feel refreshed.

"Any word from Doc or Will?" Mason asked.

Luke shook his head, his eyes still on the man behind the glass.

"Do you want me to bring him more?" asked Mason.

"No," Luke began, "when he asks to use the restroom you take him, and I will replace the bottles."

"Sounds like a plan," Mason said.

Both men stood in silence for a long moment. Then, finally, Mason walked over to the small table beside them and picked up the case file for Wendy Grayson. Luke let out a slight cough. His throat was still bothering him from his scuffle with Anthony.

"There was no brass at the scene, right?" Luke asked, not shifting his gaze.

"No, none was recovered, according to Will," Mason answered.

Luke nodded towards Anthony. "Do you honestly think he was competent enough to police his brass?"

Mason turned to look at the man before them. He was clearly in a better state of mind than when they had found him at the crime scene. Surely Mason knew what Luke was getting at.

"He could have taken the drugs after shooting Hunter," Mason answered.

Luke's lips turned into a frown. Crossing his arms across his chest,

Luke's line of sight never wavered from Anthony.

"Even so, you didn't see him when we fought. He was not in a clear state of mind. I think if he killed Hunter, we would have found the casing," Luke stated firmly.

"What are you saying?" Mason asked, curious.

Luke unfolded his arms and walked back to a chair sitting against the far wall. He knew it would get Mason thinking, and that's what he needed. He needed Mason to think like the defense.

"Just throwing out points his lawyer will most likely bring up," Luke parried.

Mason turned to face Luke, a look of understanding coming across his face.

"You want me to play defender," Mason returned, finally joining Luke in this exercise of wit.

Luke nodded. Mason tilted his head and turned back to peer at their guest. There had been too many times when detectives were on the same side of a case, and no one thought through any of the potential holes a good attorney could poke in their case. Because of that, criminal people went free on reasonable doubt. Luke would not let that happen this time. Every single avenue would be examined and re-examined until he was satisfied with the answers. Luke let out another couple of coughs.

Glancing at his watch, he noted the time. 7:23 A.M. With any luck, Anthony would sober up in the next couple of hours. Most of the cops should be out on patrol by then. Leaning back in the chair, Luke waited.

*　　*　　*　　*

Victor's breakfast had been excellent. There was coffee, sausages, biscuits, and eggs. Quite the typical breakfast in Victor's house, but exquisite, nonetheless. After eating, he went to the library for a while and read. The red walls of the library accented the ivory shelves that wrapped around the room. It had been a good long while since he'd taken the time to read anything that needed to be more work-related. He decided on A Tale of Two Cities. It was quite an enjoyable experience, and oh, how he missed it. Yet another reason why he needed to have Anthony on board. Retirement beckoned to him like a long-lost love.

In his youth, he never thought he would want to retire. All he ever wanted was to be in charge of the empire and run it the way he saw fit. But, of course, with the passage of time comes experience and wisdom. He'd done what he set out to do, and now it was Anthony's turn to keep what their forefathers had built and build on to it. As society and laws change, so must businesses. They must be ready for anything, and Anthony must learn how to charm and persuade the lawmakers into working for the benefit of the empire. But first, Anthony must be found. There still needed to be an update from Quentin. Victor had thought about calling him, but he knew it would do no good. The lawyer was busy looking for the missing men. Quentin would call as soon as he found anything regarding Anthony or Sam.

After his leisurely reading, Victor returned to his office. The eyes of his animals watched every move he made. Then, sitting in the large leather chair, he began working, calling the gentleman's club, the hotel, and the restaurant, and receiving updates on their revenue and any potential problems that would need to be dealt with. To his surprise, there were no problems. It had been a while since there hadn't been even a single issue with one of his many establishments. The news just reinforced his hopeful attitude for the day.

Looking at the watch on his left wrist, he read the time. 10:36 A.M. It had been a successful morning so far, and Victor wanted it to stay that way. But then, a knock came on his office door.

"Come in," Victor said.

The door opened, and in stepped Jonathon. The butler wore his usual white shirt, black jacket, bowtie, pants, and black shoes. Victor stared and waited for the man to speak.

"Sir, am I to assume that the staff will still have an early day today?" Jonathan asked.

Victor was surprised. The staff always left at 3:00 in the afternoon every Thursday. So why on earth would he require them to stay on this one?

"Of course, Jonathon," Victor replied with a smile.

"Thank you, sir," Jonathan said with a slight bow as he exited the room and shut the door.

Shaking his head, Victor returned to his work. He was looking at the candidates for this year's midterm elections. There had to be at least one he could lure into his web. He was a third through the list when his cell phone rang. Quickly, Victor grabbed it off the top of his maple desk and noticed the caller I.D. said it was David Quentin. Victor's heart skipped a beat. It was unusual for him to experience nervousness. It had been years since he'd ever felt the emotion. His stomach started to churn, and his heart rate started to increase. Closing his eyes, he took three deep breaths and calmed himself. With his right index finger, Victor tapped the answer icon. Raising the phone to his ear, he spoke with authority.

"Quentin. I hope you have some good news for me."

The attorney's voice was clear, "I found him."

*   *   *   *

For the third time, Anthony returned from the restroom to the interrogation room to find three new water bottles with straws sitting on the metal table. Anthony let out a sigh. He turned to talk to Detective Mason, but the man had already left. He walked leisurely to the chair and sat down. This was becoming torturous. He knew what they were doing— detoxing him. More than ninety percent of the drugs had worn off by this point. He honestly didn't know if he could drink another sixty ounces of water. Anthony leaned back in the chair and stared past the bottled liquid into his reflection. He knew they were back there, or at least Detective Mason was, watching him.

Anthony's curiosity had started to get the better of him over these past several hours. He wanted to know how they found him, whether or not it was good detective work or pure luck. He also wondered if Detective Mason was alone behind the glass. Perhaps Burrows was still incapacitated. That thought turned his stomach six ways from Sunday. He'd restrained himself and knew that Detective Burrows was alive when he left that house. Knowing his luck, they were probably going to try and convince him he'd killed Burrows and would try and guilt him into giving up his father. It was a foolish plan. But Holmes and Watson, hiding behind the glass, couldn't know that Anthony had stopped and checked on his victim. Shaking his head, Anthony was ready to move to the next phase.

"I'm not drinking another drop," he said loudly. Nothing happened. "I am perfectly lucid," he continued. He waited for several minutes, but there was yet to be a response. Maybe they were no longer there? Anthony tried again.

"I will not voluntarily water-log myself. You hear me?" Anthony raised the volume of his voice. "Come on, Detective. Come play your game, and let's get this over with." Again, nothing. Now Anthony was becoming frustrated. He did not want to spend another couple of hours drinking and pissing his time away.

"You come in here and tell me whether or not I'm under arrest or I want my lawyer." Anthony's voice was louder. "You hear me? I will scream my head off until someone in the hallway gets curious and finds out you have me here without cause."

Just then, Anthony heard a door open and close. Finally, he thought. The door to the interrogation room swung wide, and Anthony turned, ready to welcome Detective Mason back. Anthony opened his mouth to speak, but he froze. The man that entered the interrogation room was not Detective Mason but Detective Burrows. Anthony had guessed wrong. Now he had yet to learn what their strategy might be. Burrows shut the door and slowly walked to the chair opposite Anthony. Pulling it from under the table, he sat down and stared at Anthony.

For several minutes neither man spoke. Anthony tried to gauge what the cop was thinking but couldn't get a read. He didn't look angry or resentful. Instead, the detective looked conflicted, like he was trying to work out a deep philosophical question. Remembering their fight, Anthony noted the look of confusion the man wore. Perhaps he wanted to know why Anthony had done such a drastic thing. With complete honesty, Anthony wondered the same thing. Burrows' black button-down shirt was covered in wrinkles like it had been shoved in a backpack and left for months. Anthony shifted in his seat. With each passing heartbeat, Burrows' gaze penetrated deeper and deeper into Anthony's soul. Anthony couldn't match the man's persistence. Looking away, Anthony rolled his neck around, trying to loosen the stiff muscles. The metal chains around his wrists were beginning to chafe his skin.

"You think you could remove these bracelets?" Anthony asked, giving them a good shake.

"No," the detective answered.

Anthony let out a sigh and waited. He wanted Burrows to start grilling him, but the man just sat there in silence. Closing his eyes, Anthony leaned back and tried to wait him out. The blackness behind his eyelids suddenly filled with Emily's face of horror before he ran her down. With a gasp, Anthony sat leaned forward and opened his eyes. He looked at the detective, and his expression hadn't changed. The temperature in the room seemed to rise dramatically. Anthony felt beads of sweat running down the sides of his head. Anthony couldn't take much more of this. Burrows was toying with him, and Anthony had questions of his own.

"How did you find me?" Anthony asked a little aggressively.

"Doesn't matter," Burrows answered calmly.

"The hell it doesn't," Anthony retorted, raising his voice. "I was far and away from your safe house. There's no way you knew exactly where I'd be."

The detective shrugged but said nothing. Anthony had to give him credit. The man was getting under his skin. He'd thought through and expected so many other scenarios based on their last meeting, and the fact that Burrows had yet to reveal his strategy was not something he had seen coming. Anthony let out a little chuckle.

"Am I under arrest?" Anthony asked.

"Not yet," Burrows said. The man's brown hair was semi-fixed up. Burrows lifted a hand and scratched at the right side of his head.

"Then I want to leave. Now." Anthony said.
"Don't you want to know what happened to Wendy?" Burrows asked.

There it is. There's the play. So predictable it was pathetic.

"You don't know what happened to her, and don't you dare try and use her against me again," Anthony said warningly. "Taking me around on your little wild goose chase. I'm not falling for that nonsense again."

"I can arrest you for possession or assaulting a police officer at any time," Burrows said confidently.

"Then why don't you?" Anthony asked.

"Because I'd rather arrest you for murder," Burrows said.
Anthony froze but maintained his current expression. There's no way he could know Anthony killed his girl. So, this had to be another ploy.

"I already told you, I didn't kill Wendy," Anthony said, trying to get ahead of the cop.

"I believe you."

Anthony was now more confused than ever. There was only one other person he could be arrested for killing: Burrows' girl Emily. Still, there was no way he had any evidence of that unless Anthony had said something in his inebriated state. But, of course, that wouldn't hold up in any court anywhere.

"Who was it I supposedly whacked?" Anthony asked incredulously.

"Samuel Hunter," Burrows answered.

Anthony's eyes went wide.

"Sam's dead?"

CHAPTER 39

"Sam's dead?"

Anthony's voice went from impatient to utter surprise. Luke watched as the man's facial expression also changed from agitated to shocked. The widening of his eyes, the slightly agape mouth, and the decreased tension in his body posture all pointed to Anthony's ignorance of the fact. It was not, of course, proof of the man's innocence. He could have very well been under the influence of the opiates, however unlikely. The drugs usually made one groggy and incapable of such calculated homicide. So, not the drugs, but it could be argued that Anthony had suffered a mental break at the news of Wendy Grayson's death. His attorney could try to prove multiple personality disorders or other physically dangerous mental illnesses. Luke, on the other hand, didn't buy that scenario either. He believed that Anthony was fully aware of what he was doing when he'd attacked the detective.

People make stupid decisions all the time, for some reason or another, and instead of fessing up to them, they try to blame something or someone else. Every day, each person is faced with choices to make. Choices have consequences, and sometimes those consequences are beneficial. Other times they are detrimental. Sometimes the choices one makes to achieve a goal are to the extreme.

When Anthony first arrived at the police station, Luke could see mild signs of withdrawal. He had no idea how long it had been since Anthony had had his last fix, but his body was in need of another. Throughout the remainder of the day, there were other minor instances of the same kind. Luke had made the false deduction that Anthony could fight through his addiction withdrawal. He had been wrong. But there was no way to prove it without Anthony testifying about the reason for his attack on Luke—so he could get high, especially since the threat of charges being brought to bear on the assault was a bluff. Luke had no idea why Anthony started stealing opiates, and he didn't care. All Luke knew was that he had seen similar situations with his alcoholic father from childhood.

Looking at the man sitting before him, the three water bottles sitting like a barrier between them, it was unclear to Luke what Anthony's role in these murders was—if he'd had any role. Luke honestly believed the black-haired man hadn't killed his girlfriend, but two murders within days of each other that were connected to the Sorelli family were no mere coincidence. Keeping his expression unreadable, Luke spoke.

"So, you knew Mr. Hunter?"

Anthony sat in stunned silence for a few seconds. His eyes were staring at the floor on his right side. Finally, Anthony's lips began to move, and short stutters were spawning from his vocal cords. Then, stopping to swallow and clear his throat, Anthony tried again to reply.

"Sam and I were best friends when we were in school," Anthony's tone was filled with sorrow, but his face was still a mask of disbelief.

Creases began forming on the man's forehead. He was most likely about to become defensive and combative. Most likely, he was thinking that they were saying this to try and pry information out of him. This meant that Luke needed to take extra care in asking his questions. Before he'd entered the room, Luke had sent Mason to print out the crime scene photos and bring them to him when he signaled him. However, it was not yet time to play that card. For now, he would see what he could get out of Anthony based on trust alone.

"So, you knew him rather well," Luke stated.

The handcuffed man shifted his eyes and leaned his head back. Then, after a moment, he shook his head slightly. Luke furrowed his brow briefly.

"Not really," Anthony said, irritated.
"You just said the two of you were best friends." Luke pointed out.

"In school," Anthony clarified. "After we graduated, we went our separate ways for a while, and things were different when we reentered each other's lives."

"People tend to change over time," Luke said, agreeing with Anthony's story.

"Not always for the better," Anthony said softly.
So softly that Luke barely understood the words. Holding his poker face in place, Luke kept his eyes on Anthony's face. There was a subtle shift in the man's expression. For a brief moment, Anthony looked like he was staring into space but was back before most people would have noticed. Luke couldn't be sure, but he thought Anthony saw some distant memory related to his statement. Possibly about how Samuel Hunter had returned home a changed man. Lifting his hands off his lap, Anthony leaned forward and placed them on the metal table.

"Would you be able to tell me why we found Sam in a vehicle registered to your father?" Luke asked.

Anthony arched an eyebrow. Anytime Victor was brought into the conversation, the man clamped up. For a moment, Anthony sat studying Luke. Luke remained silent and waited patiently for an answer.

"My father employed him," Anthony finally said, suspicion edging into his tone.

Luke gave a slight nod and made a mental note of the information. Now was a crucial moment. He was deciding whether or not to press the specifics of Hunter's job could keep Anthony talking or could shut him down permanently. Luke held Anthony's gaze for another couple of seconds.

"Did that seem to help repair or strain your relationship?" Luke finally asked.

A puzzled look crossed Anthony's weary face. The man was exhausted. Luke wasn't sure how much sleep the larger man had gotten before he went on the attack, but it couldn't have been much. Whatever sleep he received while inebriated was also of little use to the man's health. Luke could see the dark circles under Anthony's eyes. Anthony had regained some energy when becoming defensive earlier, but the sudden news of Sam Hunter's death seemed to have taken that from him.

"With whom, my father or Sam?" Anthony responded,

Luke shrugged, "Both," he spoke.

Anthony let out a sigh.

"It was a strain on both of those relationships," Anthony said, looking away from Luke.

Giving a slight nod, Luke crossed his right leg over his left. A sudden whiff of nasty body odor hit Luke in the face. Trying his best not to make it obvious, Luke scrunched his nose to defend against the putrid smell.

"Did Sam know about you and Wendy?" Luke asked curiously.

This was something that could be important. If, for some reason, Anthony thought Sam had any part of doing with Wendy's death, he could have sought revenge. Luke knew firsthand how overwhelming thoughts like those were. Nevertheless, he had been able finally to push his vengeful thoughts against the Sorellis away for the most part.

"Sam knew we were together," Anthony said coldly.

The sudden shift in Anthony's tone perked Luke's attention. Obviously, there was something there, and Luke would need to try and find out. How he went about it would be the tricky part. So far, Luke has done a decent job of establishing connections without pushing too deep into anything. Luke thought through multiple options for several minutes, which could have been better.

"Was there any jealousy on Sam's part?" Luke asked cautiously. Anthony looked at the detective with a twisted, confused look. The man was trying to figure out why Luke had asked such a question. Which meant the answer was no. Mentally Luke braced himself for the verbal barrage Anthony was most likely going to fire at him.

"Of course not," Anthony said, his forehead still wrinkled. "Sam had his women. He had no reason to be jealous of Wendy and me."

"Noted," Luke said. Then, opening his mouth, Luke tried to move on, but Anthony spoke up first.

"Why would you even ask such a question?"

Luke didn't respond; he merely stared at Anthony, letting the handcuffed man work through it alone.

"Is that why you think I killed him?" Anthony continued, "Because he made a move on Wendy? That's absurd."

Cocking his head to the side, Luke shrugged.

"I thought Sam killed Wendy because he couldn't have her. But then, after realizing that you sought revenge and murdered him," Luke said. Anthony's face went rigid, and his hazel eyes were full of ice. The two men once again faced off, staring each other down. Neither one broke eye contact for a solid three minutes.

"Am I wrong?" Luke finally asked.

"Very," Anthony answered, his tone was dark and his voice low.

Placing his right hand on the metal table between them, Luke let out a small sigh. Now there was no way around pressing the man for more information about his father. Unless, of course, Luke wanted to change the subject completely but now was not the time for that. He had two murder victims on his hands that were tied to Anthony. It was now or never.

"Then please, correct me," Luke said, gesturing with his right hand toward the man across from him.

Anthony gave a small snort.

"I did. Sam wasn't interested in having Wendy. That's everything you need to know," Anthony said.

"I can't just take your word for it," Luke responded, "Give me the names of the women Sam dated. That would be a good start."

"I don't know their names," Anthony scoffed. "I told you we had drifted apart."

"Then how did he know you and Wendy were together?" Luke asked, raising an eyebrow.

Anthony didn't answer right away. The large, olive-skinned man was probably wondering how to answer this or if he should even answer the question. Luke sat quietly and waited.

"My father told him," Anthony said through clenched teeth.

Luke was finally getting somewhere. It wasn't much, but it was a small admission that Anthony hadn't previously given. Scratching at an itch on his left cheek, Luke uncrossed his legs and sat up straighter.

"Why would your father have any need to tell something about your private life to one of his employees?" Luke asked, eyeing Anthony carefully. Anthony shifted in his seat and stared down at the floor. For a second, Luke thought he heard the man mutter something, but he wasn't sure. The rotten stench of body odor began its second assault on Luke's nasal cavity. Shutting his eyes briefly, Luke wrinkled his nose to try and defend against the ghastly smell.

"I'm not privy to my father's business," Anthony said.

"Surely you questioned your father about it, though? Right?" Luke said, "I know I would have let my father know he'd crossed a line."

"We talked about it."

"And he didn't ever tell you why he told one of his many employees?"

"Sam wasn't just any employee. He worked directly with my father, like an assistant."

"Still, why did his 'assistant' have to know about your private dealings? Does your father not trust you?"

Anthony opened his mouth to respond but stopped himself. The man must have realized he was about to divulge something important about his father's operations. Silently, Luke swore at himself. He was so close. Granted, he did learn one new piece of information—Samuel Hunter's role in the Sorelli crime empire. Luke still didn't know precisely what Mr. Hunter did, but it was a good guess that he jumped whenever Victor said to.

The dark-haired Anthony's face hardened as he looked back at Luke. Luke kept his face clear of emotion. He didn't want Anthony to perceive any enjoyment from any answers he gave or irritation in the man's indirect or nonanswers. Luke had to put on the best poker face he'd ever worn. He was certain Anthony didn't trust him, which was understandable, but Luke had more reason to distrust Anthony than vice versa. The large, distraught man had turned on him and forced him unconscious. For what? To get high? To murder his former best friend? These were the questions, and Luke needed the answers. The urge to press the man on his father's businesses was overwhelming, but without Mason in here to play 'good cop,' it would most certainly backfire. Of course, it would probably backfire with Mason in here, but there was less of a chance, no matter how slight it might be.

A new sound caught Luke's ears. It wasn't deafening, and it was a rapidly repetitive rhythm. A soft thud, over and over and over again. Glancing under the table, he noticed Anthony's right leg bouncing up and down. The heel of his foot hits the floor repeatedly. That was another thing Luke had seen when they transferred the inebriated man from the patrol car to their Charger. He wasn't wearing any shoes. The arresting officer said they had searched but didn't find any near his position. The man's adrenaline must have been so high not to feel the constant tearing from the terrain or the frigid temperature. After taking the pills, those had surely numbed him from any such pain. Shifting his gaze back to Anthony's face, Luke would bet a month's pay that the man could withstand a substantial amount of pain. Luke had no idea what techniques Victor would have even used, but he was sure Anthony had a higher pain tolerance than most.

I'll take that as a no. Luke finally said, again keeping his face neutral. Anthony didn't look at the detective. Instead, he turned his head to the right and stared blankly at the light beige wall. Luke leaned forward and put both hands on the table, clasping them together. For a moment, Luke thought about bringing up Wendy again but decided against it. Samuel Hunter's death was the key to finding out who was behind both murders. He was sure of it. Luke was even more convinced that Victor Sorelli was involved in at least one of the murders, most likely Wendy's. He probably wanted Miss Grayson out of his son's life and ordered her killed. If Sam were the one who did kill Miss Grayson, then that would give even more credence to Anthony's guilt regarding Hunter's death. The two most significant pieces of evidence (the bullet and hairs) would convict or clear Anthony of Hunter's murder. Waiting on them, and keeping Anthony here while they waited, was the hardest part.

These theories made more sense than the ones he and Mason had conjured up when only discussing Miss Grayson's murder. Luke's desire to see the Sorelli family behind bars grew with every heartbeat. Even though most evidence in the first case was circumstantial, they had ample evidence in the second. If only Luke could get Will's forensic analysis before Anthony's slimy attorney showed his face, it would be much easier to have the judge deny bail.

"Anthony," Luke said.

Nothing happened. The man just continued staring into the recesses of the wall.

"Anthony," Luke said again.

Once again, nothing. Luke caught himself before his facial expression changed. It was close, of course. A puzzled look wasn't the worst way his face could be seen. Still, neutrality was the name of the game he was playing.

"Anthony, look at me," Luke said, softening his tone slightly. Anthony stared at the wall, his black hair in a mess. Luke wondered if he was lost in thought or perhaps Anthony was ignoring him to make a point. Either scenario was plausible. The wretched stench emitting from Anthony tried climbing its way up Luke's nostrils again. Reaching up with his right hand, Luke rubbed the bottom of his nose. The attempt to stifle his sense of smell barely worked. Luke would have to push past the putrid smell for the rest of the interview, however long that would take.

"Why doesn't your father trust you, Anthony?" Luke asked.

No response. Luke's patience was beginning to thin. He still had plenty, but this was working at it faster than he imagined.

"Why doesn't your father trust you?" Luke asked again. This time his tone hardened just a bit, letting Anthony know this was a serious matter.

"Why should I believe you?" Anthony finally spoke, his tone telling Luke he was in denial.

"Believe me about what?" Luke responded, truly curious.

"That Sam is dead?" Anthony said, turning back to face the wrinkled shirt detective. "How do I know he's dead?"

Damn it, Mason, where are you? Luke asked himself. The other detective was sure taking his sweet time to obtain the crime scene photos. Other than that, Luke had no proof. Even though he was telling the truth, any doubt in Anthony's mind could shut him up. Seeing photographic evidence of his former friend's death was no guarantee that he'd start singing like a canary, but it would gain him some ground in the trust arena.

"Have I given you reason not to trust me?" Luke asked contemptuously.

"You mean besides dragging me around the city all day on your wild goose chase?" Anthony retorted.

"It was not a wild goose chase. We must collect all that evidence and do those interviews regardless." Luke said.

"Yea, but I didn't need to be there. You implied that I would find out more about Wendy's death when you knew I wouldn't. Not until the evidence had been processed."

"Not true. We would have told you right then if we had learned anything that we thought would jog your memory into helping us find her killer."

"Bullshit!" Anthony shouted.

Luke blinked in surprise at the outburst. This could have gone better. But, first, he needed Mason to show up. Then, like an answer to a prayer, Luke heard the door handle of the interrogation room turn.

About time, Luke thought.

Turning to greet his partner, Luke froze. Standing in the doorway was not Detective Mason but Attorney David Quentin. Quentin's face was red hot, and Luke felt his stomach drop thirty stories. The attorney spoke loudly to both of them,

"What the hell is going on here?"

CHAPTER 40

The door slammed shut as David Quentin strutted over to stand beside Anthony. Anthony looked the man up and down. The attorney wore a crisply starched charcoal suit with a white shirt and a tie that matched his jacket. His darkening blonde hair was neatly combed, and his face fumed red. In his right hand, he carried a black leather briefcase. The lawyer's sudden appearance shocked both Anthony and Detective Burrows. Up until Quentin walked in, Burrows had done well at keeping his emotions hidden. Now, Anthony could see confusion and disgust on the detective's face. Anthony should have known that Quentin would learn of his presence here. Now that he had, there wouldn't be much the detectives could do. Quentin would make sure of that.

"I asked you a question, detective," Quentin said impatiently. Anthony threw a glance at Burrows. The detective's face was once again under control. Silently, Anthony wondered how long it would take for Quentin to get him out of there.

"I'm trying to solve two murders, and Anthony here is trying to help me," Burrows said, motioning toward Anthony with his left hand. Quentin let out a snort.

"Really? You expect me to believe Anthony just waltzed here of his own volition," the attorney replied.

Anthony winced. That was what he had done yesterday. He wasn't sure how he'd ended up here today.

"Ask him yourself?" Burrows said, a hint of pride in his voice. Anthony slanted his eyes and gave Burrows a cold glare. Quentin turned his head and looked down at his client. Anthony could feel the man's eyes staring at him.

"Tony? Did you voluntarily come to the police?" the lawyer asked. Anthony sighed. There was no way around it, and he would have to confess that he freely came to the police. If he were speaking to anyone else, he wouldn't have a problem, but Quentin worked for his father. And like Sam—even though there was supposed to be an attorney-client privilege—Anthony knew the lawyer would relay this news to his father. Because, after all, his father was the one paying the man.

"I voluntarily came to the police station to speak with Detective Burrows yesterday," Anthony admitted. But, as he said the words, he could hear the shame in his voice.

Quentin looked back at Burrows. A wave of new anger heated his face. "So, you lied to me," Quentin said accusingly.

"No, I did not," Burrows started, "I told you he wasn't here, and I didn't know where he was, which both were true. He wasn't here, and you searched the building yourself. And I had no idea where exactly he was at that moment."

"Semantics," Quentin scoffed. "You knew where he had gone."

"That wasn't what you asked," Burrows replied, keeping his tone calm.

Quentin rolled his eyes and let out a sigh, "So," he began, "who died and what makes you think my client has any information about them?"

"Wendy Grayson, your client's girlfriend, and Samuel Hunter, your client's former friend and an employee of Victor Sorelli, who is your client's father," Burrows said, a hint of pride seeping into his voice.

The sharp-dressed attorney stared at the detective for a long moment. Burrows never took his eyes off Anthony. Anthony wanted to figure out who killed Wendy and get out of there, not necessarily in that order. For the most part, Anthony's head was clear of the drugs. He still wasn't sold on the line about Sam's death. It was odd, though. As far as Anthony knew, Sam was clean and clear of the police radar. So how could they have known that Anthony and Sam knew each other? Anthony searched his memory banks, trying to see if Burrows had told him, and he wasn't paying attention. There it was they supposedly found Sam in a car registered to his father, Victor.

"And you're not looking to charge Mr. Sorelli for either of these deaths?" Quentin asked suspiciously.

"Not for Miss Grayson's, no. We do not believe he was involved." Burrows said.

"So, you are hoping to charge him for Mr. Hunter's murder?"

"Hoping is a strange word to use," Burrows began. "I wouldn't say hoping. I'd say…"

He was cut off by the attorney, who had a devilish grin on his face. "If you're involved, Detective Burrows, with my clients, the Sorellis, then I would very much use the word 'hoping' in regard to past experiences," Quentin said matter-of-factly.

Burrows gave a smirk and tapped his fingers on the metal table. The man's emotional control was being put through the grinder now, and Anthony could see it starting to crack.

"As I was saying," the detective started again, "I would say we have evidence that points to your client potentially being guilty in the case of Mr. Hunter." Burrows' tone had hardened slightly.

"What evidence?" Quentin demanded.

"After your client was released from our custody yesterday…" Burrows began, "he was found blocks from the scene of the crime with the potential murder weapon on his person, as well as having ingested illegally obtained opiates."

Anthony looked away in disgust and shame. Released from our custody. That was such a load of bull, but Anthony didn't want to go into any details of his escapades after leaving the safe house. So, he sat there in silence and once again felt both sets of eyes boring into him.
We need to get out of here! He screamed at himself.

"So why haven't you charged him yet?" asked the attorney.

"We were hoping he'd admit to what he had done. Especially after he stated he used to be close with the victim," Burrows said, his tone returning to its neutral position.

"I want to see this evidence," Quentin said.

"My partner should be back anytime with the crime scene photos," Burrows replied.

The interrogation room door opened as if on cue, and Detective Mason entered with a manilla folder in hand. The other detective was wearing an olive button-down shirt with blue jeans. Mason stood frozen in the doorway, contemplating a drastically different situation than what he was expecting to walk in on.

"Speak of the devil," Quentin said.

Both detectives looked at him for a quick second before Mason entered the room and handed the folder to his partner. Letting the folder fall through the air, it hit the table with a thin slap. Anthony stared at the rectangular mouth that held photographic evidence of Sam's death. Anthony felt his stomach start to turn. He'd asked for this before Quentin barged in and took over the meeting. The sound of his blood pumping through his veins suddenly became deafening in his ears. Anthony swallowed and waited for Burrows to open the folder.

"Not here," Quentin said, "Not yet."

The attorney motioned for the detectives to follow him into the hall. Burrows let out a sigh as he picked up the folder and stepped into the hallway with Mason and Quentin. The large gray door was closed, and Anthony was left alone. He didn't understand why Quentin would want to look through the photos without him. There was a part of Anthony that was relieved. He wasn't sure he was ready to see Sam dead. Granted, he didn't know how Sam was killed, and he could look normal like Wendy. Or he could be a gorey mess. Anthony didn't know. And the not knowing was the part of him that begged to find out.

Anthony noticed his right leg was bouncing up and down, quite rapidly. He needed to figure out when he'd started doing that. Standing to his feet, Anthony began walking around the room. He was tired of sitting. Rolling his neck around, he tried to stretch out the muscles.

You're pathetic.

Anthony turned to face the one-way mirror. In it, he saw his reflection, but it wasn't exact. This version had a look of pure contempt written on his face.

First, you wouldn't stand up to daddy about your girlfriend. Now she's dead. The reflection said.

Anthony turned away, not wanting to hear any of this.

Don't turn your back on me, you miserable piece of filth.

Whirling around, Anthony faced himself. This other version of himself. Good doggy. Now, where were we? Oh yes. Now, Sam is dead, and you can't handle the fact that you may have done it, is that it? Come on, Tony. You've done it before. There's no reason to suspect you couldn't have done this.

Emily's frightened face filled Anthony's mind. The sound of her body slamming into the drunkard's car echoed in his eardrums. Anthony closed his eyes to try and shut out the memory.

There's only one way of escape, and you know what that is.

"The drugs don't last long enough," Anthony whispered. He stepped behind the chair he was previously seated in.

So, we'll just take more. His reflection said, throwing his arms wide. The problem will be getting away from the lawyer.

"No," Anthony whispered.

No? No, what?

"Taking more drugs will not fix the problem," Anthony said, his head hanging low.

Without them, all you have is pain, misery, and the memories of the horrendous things you've done to innocent people. All you'll ever be able to see is their faces pleading with you as you destroy them.

"No!" Anthony shouted as he swept his arms across the table, sending the three water bottles flying into the wall opposite the door. Water flew all around, drops falling everywhere. Two plastic bottles hit the wall before bouncing off and falling to the floor, where they ejected more of their contents. The third bottle fell to the floor just before it reached the wall. There was a small shiny stream on the metal table. Anthony looked up and saw that his reflection had shifted back to normal. Was he right? Was there no other way to escape the constant guilt and torment he felt? Anthony sat back in his seat, placed his elbows on the table, and set his head in his cuffed hands. Anthony gritted his teeth.

There has to be another way, he thought to himself.

Just then the door to the interrogation room opened and the three men reentered the beige room. Everybody stopped and stared for a second at Anthony's mess, but no other comment about it was made.

"Tony," Quentin began. "I don't want you to say anything, ok?"

Anthony looked at him with a puzzled look. Why wouldn't Quentin want him to say anything?

"The detectives are going to show you some photos and potentially ask some questions. So, I don't want you answering without speaking with me first," Quentin continued.

The attorney unbuttoned his suit jacket and sat down next to his client. Both detectives were already seated, and Mason was wiping away the water that was pooled up on the table in several spots. After he had gotten the majority of the table dry enough, Burrows placed the manilla folder on the table and opened it. One by one, he pulled a picture out of its cream-colored jaws and placed them before Anthony. Each photo was a different angle of the same scene. A well-dressed man was sitting in the driver's seat of a car, drenched in blood. Leaning forward to examine the photos closely, Anthony immediately recognized the dead man. Sam. Anthony's heart seemed to be caught in his throat. Red liquid covered the car's interior, along with Sam's throat and part of his upper torso. In one of the photos, he saw a small hole in Sam's throat. Anthony caught his breath.

"He was shot in the throat," Detective Burrows was saying, "Blood poured out from the two wounds while simultaneously filling his lungs." Anthony's eyes didn't move. Instead, they were fixated on the photographs. Then, out of nowhere, Anthony's throat felt like it was the Sahara Desert, dry for hundreds of years. How he wished he wouldn't have wasted the bottles of water.

"Your former friend suffocated in his blood," Detective Burrows said, empathy filling his voice.

"Anthony," Detective Mason started, "do you know who did this?" Out of the corner of his eye, Anthony saw Quentin turn to watch his response. Anthony remained motionless, still looking over the gorey images before him. So, it was true. Sam was dead. The methodology was so distinct, the answer was right there in front of his face, but he didn't want to believe it.

"Anthony. We've seen several murders over the past four decades with the same M.O. Do you know what else they all have in common?" Burrows asked.

Anthony heard the man but was still lost in the details of the photos. This can't be right, thought Anthony. He wouldn't do this.

Oh yes, he would retort an angrier voice inside Anthony.

"Every person who has died in this horrendous fashion was either a close associate or rival of your father's," Burrows answered his question.

Anthony's head suddenly felt light and fuzzy. The fluorescent lights seemed to brighten out of nowhere. Closing his eyes, Anthony tried to calm himself. Finally, after several moments, Anthony opened his mouth to speak.

"I.."

"Tony," Quentin interrupted loudly. "What did I say? Don't say anything."

Anthony didn't acknowledge he'd heard the man. He instead went right back into his statement.

"I didn't do this," Anthony said; his words were heavy as if he had trouble getting them out.

"Tony, don't say another word," Quentin warned.

"If you didn't do this, then tell us who would benefit from Sam's death," Mason said.

The three men surrounding Anthony watched him closely. They each waited for him to do or say something they could use for their gain. Then, reaching up with his left hand, Anthony picked up one of the photos. He held it in his fingers, staring at it. Anthony could feel his eyes welling up. The picture he'd picked was one where he could see Sam's face: the whiteness of it from the loss of blood draining from his veins, Sam's wide eyes, open mouth, and throat dyed red.

"I'm so sorry, Sam," Anthony said, tears streaming down his cheeks.

"Detectives, can I speak with you outside?" Quentin said, rising to his feet and buttoning his suit jacket as he did so. Burrows and Mason looked at each other, Burrows rolled his eyes, but they followed the attorney out of the room. Leaving Anthony there alone, crying at the loss of his former frie nd.

*   *   *   *

Luke couldn't believe this. The damn lawyer was ushering them out of the interrogation again. This is why he hated lawyers. They slowed everything down. Of course, he understood why everyone had the right to a defense, but why couldn't a lawyer acknowledge when his client was guilty, and everyone could move on?

"My client is clearly under duress from finding out someone he cared about is now gone. Two people, might I correct myself. He is in no condition to answer cognitively." The attorney said once they were ways down the hall.

"That's why you're here, counselor," Mason said. "To help him think through things before he answers."

The snake of a man gave a slight smirk. His charcoal gray suit was very lovely, Luke had noted earlier. He wondered if the man spent as much time caring for his clients as he did his wardrobe.

"Either charge my client, or we're walking out of here," Quentin said his facial expression stiffening.

"We can hold him for forty-eight hours without charging him," Luke said, crossing his arms across his chest.

Quentin gave out a small chuckle. "Don't be ridiculous. You've already had him over twenty-four."

Looking at his watch, the attorney shook his head. Luke wondered what scheme the slithering suited serpent was cooking up this time.

"I'm going to go talk to Chief Reilly about this," Quentin said as he started down the long hall, "Don't talk to my client without me."

After the man had rounded the corner, Luke looked at his watch. 12:35 P.M. He was sure Reilly would help them out, but he needed to figure out how much time that would end up taking.

"Have you heard anything from Will or Doc?" Luke asked Mason.

"Nope," Mason said, shaking his head.

"Alright," Luke began, "You call Will. I'll call the Doc. We have to get answers, and we have to get them fast."

*   *   *   *

He smiled to himself as his plan began to reach its conclusion. Sure, there were a few more bumps, but they would be dealt with. Nothing would be sweeter than watching all of their faces once it was over.

Softly, he whispered to himself, "But know this, if the master of the house had known in what hour of the night the thief was coming, he would have stayed awake and would not have let his house be broken into."

*   *   *   *

Standing before St. Louis Metropolitan Police Chief Gregory Reilly were three men: two of his best detectives and one finely dressed attorney. Looking at the three of them next to each other, Reilly couldn't figure out if the lawyer was overdressed or if his detectives were underdressed. Reilly's snowy white facial hair was combed and formed neatly, just as he liked it. The ends of his mustache were curved upwards in the handlebar fashion, and his goatee was still and straight. The patch of snow on top of his head was likewise manicured, combed over to the right side of his head. Reilly's office was dimly lit. Only three incandescent lamps shone dull yellow glows throughout the room. What he was about to do wasn't something he wanted to do, but one of the hats he wore was a political one, and that's the hat he had to protect at the moment.

David Quentin, the well-dressed attorney, had stormed into his office demanding the release of his client, Anthony Sorelli. Reilly initially refused, but Quentin kept pushing. Finally, he'd threatened to call the mayor and tell him about Reilly's approval of Mason and Burrows' field trip with Anthony Sorelli. How in the hell the slimy bastard had even found out about that, Reilly could only guess. Nevertheless, he had to try and compromise with the man. So, the two of them had eventually come to an agreement, one that only Quentin would see as a win. Reilly knew he'd lost this battle and was about to admit defeat to his soldiers. Letting out a small sigh, Reilly tugged at the sleeve of his dark red shirt.

"Detectives," Reilly began, "Mr. Quentin and I have discussed the complicated situation before us and have come to a solution that neither side is happy about, but one that will benefit everyone."

Reilly watched as the detectives' eyes shifted between each other, the lawyer, and their Chief. He could see their wheels turning, trying to figure out how long they would have. This wasn't right, and he knew it, but they had already bent the rules and would now pay the price for that.

"It is now," Reilly looked at his watch. "12:58 in the afternoon. You have until seven o'clock this evening to bring charges against Mr. Sorelli. If you do not, he will be released."

Both of the detectives' mouths dropped open. The lawyer gave a thin smile. Reilly felt like a cheap puppet. He hated having to answer to the mayor.

"Chief, that's only six hours," Burrows said.

"Then you best get to work," Reilly said, a hardness creeping into his voice.

He didn't want to be the bad guy, but he knew he couldn't be seen playing favorites. Not to mention, the attorney would be watching the three of them very closely. They also knew the man had informants on the force, so they could only trust themselves. Quentin would make sure they were each watched as often as possible.

"But Chief," Mason started.

"No buts, detectives. You have six hours. And with each passing second, your time frame shrinks. I suggest you get out there and find your answers instead of standing here arguing with me," Reilly interrupted. Pulling out his leather chair, he sat down and tapped the space bar on his computer. "You're dismissed."

The three men shuffled out of his office one after the other. The attorney gave him a curt nod as he shut the door. Reilly scoffed. How could anyone has known about their plan? The question ate at him with every tick of the clock. Maybe Anthony had told him, but his phone had been here the whole time, and Quentin hadn't had one second alone with Sorelli since he arrived. The glow from Reilly's computer screen burned his aging eyes. He'd thought about investing in the blue light lenses several times but never put much stock in them. It always sounded like some traveling conman pitched to him.

Leaning back, he rubbed his eyes. All he could do now was hope and pray the boys could find something to hold Anthony Sorelli here. If they didn't, both of these cases would go in the "Unsolved Sorelli" folder, which was the last thing Reilly wanted. He'd let those murderous fiends get away with too much over the years, and it was time to put an end to it.

* * * *

The clock read 3:26 P.M. Luke was about ready to chunk David Quentin in a cell for obstruction of justice. How did Reilly expect them to find anything in the short time they had been given? It was impossible. He had called Dr. Wright, and all he had learned was that Mr. Hunter's hands had been bound when he was killed. Not insignificant, but not enough. She had also said he had burns on the inside of his esophagus. Most likely from breathing in chemical fumes. Where the man would have been recently exposed to so much of it to cause the kind of inflammation she was seeing, Dr. Wright couldn't say. Mason had called Will, but he didn't have anything new to offer either. So now, he was going through Mr. Hunter's online accounts and banking statements. Luke was trying to find any known associates or family that would be willing to come in for an interview this afternoon. Not surprisingly, no one could make it.

All of a sudden, Mason's phone began ringing. Shifting from his computer, Mason answered. Luke perked his ears up to listen for anything that could be good news.

"Hold on, Will, hold on. I'll put you on speaker," Mason said.

Luke ceased his typing and rolled his chair over beside Mason's phone.

"Okay, Will, you have both Luke and me here," Mason stated.

"Alright, guys, I have news for you." Will's distorted electronic voice came through the speaker.

"Please tell me it's good news," Luke said.

"I'll leave that distinction to the two of you," Will replied. "Now, the ballistic test does not match the 9mm found on the suspect."

Luke leaned back, a look of defeat on his face. This was not good news.

"However, it does match a Colt.45," Will continued.

Luke leaned forward again, new hope surging through his body.

"Also, we have hair samples from Victor and Anthony Sorelli from past subpoenas. I ran the hairs we found against them, and they did not match either of the men. Sadly, that's all I know for now. I hope it helps."

"It does, Will, thanks," Mason said as he ended the call.

Both detectives looked at each other. Now they had no reason to believe Anthony killed Samuel Hunter. Luke's mind was racing with all the possibilities. All they could do now was run gun registrations and saw if any viable suspect owned a Colt .45.

"Do you want to tell him, or should I?" Mason asked.

"We don't have to tell anyone anything," Luke answered. "We still have three and a half hours."

CHAPTER 41

David Quentin couldn't help but smile as the next several hours ticked. He stood back and watched as the two detectives scrambled to come up with some evidence that they could use to keep his client detained. They had spent a decent amount of time on their computers going through records and accounts. They both made several phone calls to potential witnesses and their forensic team, William Johnson, and Dr. Melinda Wright. Quentin stood in the shadow of the hall that led to the interrogation rooms, watching them panic. They had gone in a couple of times to ask more questions to Tony, but Quentin was always there to keep him from spilling anything that could potentially jeopardize the situation.

Keeping his eyes on the detectives, Quentin let his mind drift back to his confrontation with Chief Reilly. The look on the old man's face when he had mentioned the illegal ride-along he'd approved for Mason and Burrows. It was a mixture of shock and hatred. Quentin had to smile at that. Of course, he had no idea the extent of where Burrows and Mason had taken Tony, nor did he know how long they'd had him, but one of his informants had called him and explained that Sorelli was rumored to be riding around town with the two detectives. Quentin didn't know that Reilly had sanctioned it, but he knew the man's relationship with Burrows. Reilly would have taken the man's badge if he hadn't at least run it by the old policeman first. Once Reilly had let his poker mask slip, Quentin knew he had him. All there was to do then was hammer out the details.

Having caught the police chief by the short and curlies, Quentin could have walked out of the police station with his client then and there. Instead, he knew it would play better with everyone if he compromised and gave them some time. It wouldn't equal the full forty-eight hours, but it was damn near thirty-six, and they would have to deal with it. Luckily, Victor Sorelli had secured the election for Mayor Tyler, and the Mayor wanted this whole thing to go away so that his gambling addiction would not be made public. Having the mayor on their side helped persuade Reilly into cooperating sooner rather than digging his heels in and giving credence to the stubborn jackass everyone knew he was. Glancing at his watch, Quentin noted that it was 5:55 P.M. The detectives' time was just about up.

*   *   *   *

Holding his hair tightly in his hands, Luke stared at his computer screen in defeat. They were in their final hour and had come up with nothing. Mentally, Luke shook his head. He couldn't believe that after everything they'd done in the past twenty-four hours, their best lead would be ushered away, never heard from again. Anthony was holding back. They could see it; Anthony knew who was responsible for Sam's death. That information could, in turn, help them find out who murdered Wendy Grayson. He and Mason would have probably been able to coax it out of him by now if it weren't for the sound barrier that was David Quentin.

Luke was positive it was all crashing down on the poor man. The loss of his girlfriend and his childhood best friend in a couple of days. Luke also didn't know how much Anthony knew of his father's dealings, but something in the back of his mind wanted him to ask about Emily. He wanted Anthony to turn his father in for her death more than the other two.

"What do you want to do, Luke?"

Mason's voice snapped Luke from his thoughts. Letting go of his hair, he sat up straight and looked at his partner. Mason was just as distraught as he was, but he seemed better at hiding it.

"Well, unless we get a break in the next…" Luke checked the time, "twenty-eight minutes. After that, I'm not sure there's much we can do."

Mason frowned. He knew as well as Luke did that they'd never be able to get to the Sorellis regarding these two murders after today. Mason had been trying to check registries of Colt .45 owners in the state of Missouri, but it was taking longer than he anticipated. Neither Victor nor Anthony registered any weapons, which wasn't a surprise. Luke was sure they had some weapons, but none they'd be willing to be caught with.

"There's no point in talking to Anthony again. The attorney won't let him answer anything," Mason said.

Luke looked toward the hallway that led to the interrogation rooms. David Quentin stood just past the frame, smirking. The damn attorney knew he'd won and was celebrating to himself. Granted, getting his clients off as free and straightforward as possible was his job, but it still filled Luke with hatred. Standing to his feet, Luke never let his gaze drop from the attorney.

"Let's go chat with Mr. Quentin," Luke said as he began walking toward the man.

Mason stood and followed Luke across the room. Walking past several desks home to other detectives and section leads, Luke could see the smirk on the lawyer's face growing as they approached. Luke felt his face warm. Then, taking a deep breath, he tried to get a hold of his anger. Exploding on the attorney would do nothing but make sure Luke would never be involved in anything that even looked in the direction of the Sorelli family. "Would you like to speak to my client again, Detectives?" Quentin said as they closed the distance between them.

"No," Luke said. "I want to talk to you."

"Me?"

The man was taken off guard, which was exactly what Luke wanted. He may be ready to help keep his client quiet, but Luke wanted to see what would happen if they started pressing him.

"Yes, you," Luke began. "I want to know why you're being such a hard ass about this?"

Mason remained silent but kept his eyes focused on the attorney. The two detectives had put the man in a corner and were hoping to get lucky in this last-ditch effort.

"I'm just doing my job, Detective. Just as you are doing yours."

Quentin's face still held his smirking grin, but Luke thought he saw a hint of annoyance cross the man's eyes. If Luke was completely honest with himself, he didn't think Quentin would give them anything, but he wanted to see the man take some heat.

"If you believed that, then you'd let us keep Anthony for the remainder of the forty-eight hours," Luke said.

"You have already crossed the line of your authority, both of you." Quentin raised a finger and waved at the detectives.

"Damn it, Quentin!" Luke raised his voice, "Two people are dead, and both have ties to Anthony Sorelli!"

"That's circumstantial, as is finding him near the strip mall parking lot at Wilshire and Hamilton," Quentin said, his tone going hard.

Out of the corner of his eye, Luke noticed Mason's eyes narrow for a few seconds. Quentin had looked over at the other detective, and both men held

"Now," Quentin said, looking at his watch. "You have less than twenty minutes. I'm going to begin prepping my client for his release. I suggest the two of you get everything on your end in order."

Without another word, the attorney turned and strode down the off-white hallway. Luke and Mason looked at each other before turning to go back to their desks. There was still a look of suspicion on Mason's face.

"What is it?" Luke wondered.

"I'm not sure. I'm going to check on a few things. Then, I'll be back," Mason said.

Luke's partner walked past their desks and out of sight. Shaking his head, Luke sat down at his desk and put his head in his hands. This was it.

This is where it all ended.

*   *   *   *

Anthony Sorelli sat staring at himself in the two-way mirror. The detectives had come in multiple times trying to convince him to give up his father, but Quentin kept him on the straight and narrow. The sorrow he felt for Sam was still there, but it had begun to dwindle, replaced by hatred for his father. He couldn't believe it, but it was all right there in the photographs, his father's preferred way to deal with rats or competition: the signature bullet to the throat. It was a slow and painful death, and it helped to send a message of what awaited you if you dared cross Victor Sorelli. First, Wendy, and now Sam was gone. Why would his father have put a hit out on Sam? As far as Anthony knew, Sam was a loyal sheepdog. For some reason, he couldn't figure it out.

To his left, the sound of the door opening caught Anthony's attention. Turning, he saw his lawyer walk into the room and close the door behind him. No detectives. Anthony eyed Quentin curiously.

"They're not coming this time," his attorney answered his unspoken question. "The camera and microphones have also been disabled. So, it's just us."

Grabbing a chair, Quentin sat across the table from the young man. The attorney looked somewhat uncomfortable like he needed to talk about something painful. Anthony remained silent and waited for the lawyer to speak.

"Tony," Quentin placed his interlocked hands on the table between them, "in a few minutes, you will be released from the custody of the police. They have been unable to produce sufficient evidence to bring any charges against you—none that would stick. But before they let you leave, I wanted to talk to you about Sam."

Anthony sat up a little straighter. This was unexpected. Anthony had thought about asking the attorney if he knew anything, but this was the first time they'd been alone, and it had slipped his mind.

"You have seen your father's message in Sam's murder. I do not know who he assigned to do the hit, just so we can avoid that question."

"Why would dad even want Sam dead? He's more loyal to the old man than I am," Anthony pressed.

"From what I understand," Quentin said, "Sam proceeded ahead of schedule regarding Miss Grayson. When your father found out, he was furious. Sam had vanished shortly after being sent to locate you. Your father called me to try and find him."

Anthony sat in stunned silence. Sam had killed Wendy. Anthony's father had ordered Wendy murdered? After going round and round with himself over that possibility, he couldn't believe he had ever stood up for his father. Victor Sorelli was nothing more than a cold-blooded monster. Finally, rage began boiling inside Anthony. There was now only one thought on his mind. Vengeance.

CHAPTER 42

Anthony didn't see the pedestrians, buildings, trees, or landscapes under the streetlights as he sat in the passenger seat of David Quentin's sedan. Even though he was staring directly out the side window, everything was a blur of colors and motion. Anthony and his attorney had vacated the police station not too long after Quentin had informed him of his father's treachery. Anthony didn't see, hear, or care about further conversations with the detectives. His focus was trained solely on his father. He had mindlessly made his way from the station to Quentin's vehicle without uttering a sound. Climbing into the car, he'd buckled his seatbelt and turned his head to stare out the window. Quentin was driving him home. In his current mental state, it was not safe for Anthony to drive himself. His expression was that of stone; no emotion showed on the outside. Inside though, Anthony was seething. All he wanted was revenge for Wendy's death.

I told you he was guilty.

Anthony ignored his voice bouncing around his head. Not only was he angry at his father, but he was also angry with himself. He had gone back and forth over the whole thing and had recognized this possibility. The sting of betrayal was brutal.

I should have known better. Anthony told himself.

You're damn right, his angrier side responded. Too bad the detectives took the drugs. We could be flying high, forgetting about all of this.

Anthony shook his head. He knew how ridiculous that was. Eventually, he'd come crashing down, and everything would flood back ten times worse. He knew better, but he couldn't help himself for some reason.

Covering the pain was more accessible than dealing with it.

For a brief moment, Wendy's smiling face filled his mind. Her red hair was curled and draped over her shoulders, and dimples made themselves home in her cheeks. As fast as the image entered Anthony's mind, it was replaced with the memory of her lying dead on the stainless-steel tray in the morgue. Anthony closed his eyes and felt a single tear roll down the right side of his face. Turning the memory into a swirling mess, his mind was filled with what he imagined the scene was between his father and Sam. In his father's office —the stuffed animals watching everything from their silent perch on the walls—his father stood behind his desk, with Sam standing opposite. There were no words he could hear, but he knew they were discussing terminating Wendy. Anthony felt his stomach tighten at the mere thought. Opening his eyes, he forced the scene from his mind. The glow of streetlights seemed to be gone. Only the light from the crescent moon aided the headlights of the sedan. They had left the city and were now on the outskirts of St. Louis, getting closer to the mansion with each passing second. From his left, it sounded like Quentin was speaking to him, but Anthony sat in silence, giving no acknowledgment to the attorney. Staring into the darkness, he imagined watching the life leave his father's eyes. Anthony's heart began to increase its rhythm.

Yes, he must die. You mustn't chicken out this time.

A sudden change in the ambient sound broke Anthony from his trance. It was the sound of gravel underneath the moving wheels of the car. Their momentum had also slowed as they approached the black gate to the grounds. Quentin stopped the car and swiped his passkey. The mechanical sound of the gate lock disengaging rang through the evening air, and the metal bars rolled away to their right. Quentin drove his sedan to the side of the mansion, shifted to park, and turned off the engine. Both men sat in silence.

"Are you sure you're going to be okay?" Quentin asked.

Without speaking, Anthony gave his answer. He gripped the door handle, opened the door, stepped onto the gravel drive, shut the door, and proceeded to the side entrance of the monster's lair.

*   *   *   *

Detective Luke Burrows sat at his desk in utter defeat. His one and only witness/suspect had been given another free pass. Partly due to Luke's hubris, to make matters worse. That's what he got for thinking he could bend the rules and get away with it. Mason had been absent when he'd released Anthony to David Quentin, and he was still missing. Luke had no idea where he'd gone, but if it was meant to help their case, he was too late. From behind him, a roar of laughter filled the room. Luke didn't even need to turn around to see who it was. Bill Watts. The fat smokestack was shooting the bull, ignoring the stacks of paperwork on his desk. For a brief moment, Luke thought about throwing something at the lard of a man but decided against it.

Luke had stayed at his desk since watching Quentin and Anthony walk out of the station. He knew he should update Chief Reilly, but he couldn't bring himself to share his failure. Letting out a sigh, Luke leaned forward and tapped the space bar on his keyboard. Out of the corner of his eye, he saw a blur pass him, and then it sat across from him at Mason's desk. Looking past his computer, he saw it was Mason.

"Where the hell have you been?" Luke asked.

"Sorry, I had to check on something. Its case related." Mason said. He looked around the room and then rolled his chair around to the side of Luke's desk.

"Well, it doesn't matter now. They've left, and we aren't likely to see either Sorelli male for the foreseeable future," Luke said contemptuously.

"It does matter," Mason began. "Remember before I left, we had just spoken to Quentin?"

Luke nodded.

"And he was very specific about where Sam Hunter's body was found. Too specific."

Luke swiveled his seat to face his partner. He wasn't sure what Mason was getting at, but he did his best to follow.

"We told the press to keep the location details confidential. So, I checked all the news reports, blogs, YouTube videos, and even local newspapers. None mention the strip mall parking lot or the street intersection."

"Surely we must have told Anthony where Sam was found." Luke challenged.

Mason shook his head, "Nope. I watched all the footage. We never mentioned it. So how could Quentin have known where it was?"

Luke felt a new surge of energy filling his body. A spring of hope lifted his spirits. Quickly he tried to stomp it out. He couldn't rely on hope here. They needed something more.

"We're going to need more than that to bring him in," Luke said.

"I know. I rechecked Colt .45 gun registers, and guess who owns one?"

Luke raised an eyebrow.
Mason nodded, confirming his suspicions.

"Okay, give me the keys to the car," Luke said, standing to his feet. He grabbed his father's coat off the back of his chair. Mason pulled the keys from his pocket and tossed them to Luke.

"Where are you going?" Mason asked.

"To cut Quentin off at the Sorelli property. You call a judge and get a warrant. Meet me there with a couple of patrollers. I'll do my best to keep the situation under control."

With that, Luke took off down the hall, out the back door, and hopped into the black Dodge Charger. Putting the key in the ignition, he turned it over, and the engine came to life. Luke threw it in gear and stepped on the gas. The muscle car roared as Luke charged from the parking lot. Unfortunately, he didn't have any lights or sirens installed. Hopefully, he could make it to the Sorelli property without incident.

Victor Sorelli walked down the long red hallway from the parlor to his office. He had yet to receive an update from Quentin since the attorney had informed him that he had located Anthony. His son was back at the police station. This time he was certainly in custody. It was uncalled for. Victor had let loose on the phone, saying he was going to call Mayor Tyler and have Chief Reilly and his two pet detectives crucified. Quentin had reassured him that he could handle it and would have Anthony home by 9:00 P.M. Ceding the territory to his lawyer, Victor ended the call and put his trust in the man. David Quentin was a brilliant attorney and would be able to secure his son's release without drawing any unwanted suspicion.

Victor had retired to his parlor with one of the many books from his library, Dante's Inferno. After finishing his favorite Dickens novel earlier, he realized how much he had missed it with the turning of each page.

Inferno was one that always seemed to stick with him. He was never sure why. Victor wasn't religious and wasn't sure if he believed in heaven or hell. However, the mere idea of a place that was home to the scourge of the earth for all eternity had haunted him since he'd first picked up the novel all those years ago. A place where murderers, traitors, rapists, drug dealers, adulterers, and others' souls were tormented forever. It was hard to imagine such a place. Mostly because it was hard to fathom eternity. It's a concept the human mind cannot comprehend while living within the confines of time.

With the progression of age, the thought of what lies beyond the door of death occupied his mind more frequently than it once had. Victor always thought he'd live forever with the legacy of the Sorelli name. What it had accomplished over the last century, and what it would accomplish over the next. His son, Anthony, had taken a sledgehammer to that idea, sending cracks to its very foundation. Victor understood why it was imperative only to have one heir. His father had told him stories of how his great-uncles had tried to tear apart his grandfather's fragile kingdom. It seemed logical, but the wild card had always been living.

Life was never predictable. People were predictable to a degree, but life enjoyed making a mockery of those that thought they could outsmart it. It would lob financial trouble, health crises, natural disasters, and whatever else it could to knock you off balance. Victor had thought they'd been lucky until his wife couldn't conceive, and then seven years after she gave birth, she was diagnosed with cancer. Even with all the money, influence, and power, one could wield, life would not bow to Victor Sorelli. It was a hard lesson but one he thought he'd finally learned. Checking his watch, he noted it was 8:15 pm. He stopped at the door to his office. Soon, he would have the unpleasant task of walking his son through a similar lesson. Opening the door, Victor turned on a lamp and walked behind his desk. The small, yellow light sent shadows scurrying to the corners of the room.

Glancing around his desk, he noticed the piece of paper he had come in to check. Reaching out to pick it up, he saw something move out of the corner of his eye. In the far corner of the room was a large shadowy figure. The figure wasn't in the room's light, so Victor had no idea who it could be. Freezing where he was, he straightened and looked directly at the corner. Now that he was staring at the phantasmic shape, he knew at least two people were back there.

"Who are you?" Victor demanded, his voice menacing.

One of the figures stepped forward and into the light. A pistol was in the person's right hand. It was aimed directly at Victor. That didn't bother Victor. There had been many occasions where he'd been threatened with a firearm. What stopped Victor cold was the person holding the gun.

"Hi, dad," Anthony said.

"Anthony, I wasn't expecting you so soon," Victor said, trying to put enthusiasm into his voice. Victor looked his son in the eye while making sure he kept watch on the other figure still in the shadows. His son's face held the look of a man who had been betrayed. There was hurt, anger, and sorrow all mixed.

"How could you?" Anthony asked.

"How could I...what?" Victor asked, genuinely confused. His son's voice was composed and calm but barely so. Victor could sense he'd start losing control of himself soon.

"Don't act like I'm some moron. You know what you did."

"I've done a great many things, Anthony. You're going to need to be more specific."

"Wendy!" Anthony shouted, spit flying from his mouth. "You had Sam murder her. Why?"

Anthony's face turned red, and the anger took over the other emotions fighting for control. Victor's eyes shifted to the silhouette behind his son. The figure had not moved. Looking again at Anthony, he noticed something familiar about the weapon in his hand. Taking his hidden key, he opened up the locked drawer and saw precisely what he expected. His gun was missing.

"Answer me!" Anthony barked. "Why would you have Sam kill the woman I loved?"

Victor remained silent, staring past Anthony to the figure behind him. Part of him couldn't help but wonder if Quentin had failed and if this was some ploy by the police. Then, shutting the drawer, Victor stood up straight. His aging back protested, sending sharp pains through his muscles.

"Why don't you have your friend join us? It's not polite for a host to not know who he is entertaining." Victor said.

With that, the figure moved. It took only two strides for the man to enter the yellow glow of the lamp. Standing behind Anthony in a finely starched charcoal suit was David Quentin. Victor raised an eyebrow at the attorney. Quentin finally greeted the man.

"Hello, father."

CHAPTER 43

The V8 engine roared as Luke slammed his foot on the accelerator. He had finally made it out of the city and was now barrelling down the county roads. Luckily he had weaved his way through the metro without incident, though many angry drivers had honked, cursed, and given him the finger as he zig-zagged in and out of traffic. Running three red lights had been one of his more dangerous choices, but he needed to reach the Sorelli property as quickly as possible. The half-crescent moon could have helped more with adding light to the countryside road. Flicking the lever on the left side of his steering wheel, the high beam lights ignited before him. They would help make this portion of the drive somewhat safer.

Since he'd left the station, his mind had been on David Quentin. Why would the lawyer murder Sorelli's right hand? It didn't make sense—unless Sorelli had ordered him to—but doing so would put Sorelli's best attorney at risk. Luke shook his head, trying to put the pieces together. Granted, all they had was that Quentin owned a Colt .45, and he seemed to have knowledge that he shouldn't have. Finally, Luke said a silent prayer that Mason would obtain the warrant for Quentin's arrest. They could then take a hair sample and try to match it to the ones found on Mr. Hunter.

Luke's gut told him they were right. What he hoped for more than anything was getting a confession that Victor had ordered the attorney to murder Mr. Hunter. Luke couldn't foresee an any better opportunity to take down the crime boss. If Quentin stayed silent and took the fall, Luke would have to wait to try another way. He felt his stomach turn into knots. No, he thought, Sorelli has to fall now. Luke could find a way. The mere thought of fabricating a narrative, or evidence, sent ice through his veins. It wasn't right, and it was the same mentality that had allowed Sorelli to own many other officers in the Metro PD.

Shame suddenly fell on Luke like a stone falling from a cliff. He would do his duty, no matter how much it made him sick. Luke believed in the system. Even though he saw time and time again how people like Quentin aided evil men like Sorelli through the holes. The holes needed to be plugged in, but the system still worked for the most part. Vigilante justice was a road best untraveled. Once that door was opened, there was no telling how or why it should be used, and closing it again was another struggle on its own. Looking at his speedometer, it read 88mph. Pressing down on the pedal, he hoped he wasn't too late. He prayed Quentin would still be at the Sorelli mansion.

*   *   *   *

"Hello, father," Quentin said.

He watched as Victor's face contorted itself. Anthony turned and stared at him with the same look of confusion. Quentin smiled in satisfaction. He had been waiting for this moment for the majority of his life. Working daily to be near his family had taken up much of his time growing up. It was so much more than what he'd hoped for.

The sacrifices he had made in his personal life had been worth it. Quentin had had a few friends as a child, but they'd drifted apart fairly quickly in the final years of high school. Once he was in pre-law, there had no time for a social life. He'd dedicated every waking minute to studying and eating on occasion. As he worked his way through law school, a plan had begun to formulate in his mind of how to take, as his own, what his father cared for most in this world: his empire. The key to that was through his half-brother.

"Father?" Anthony said, still staring at the lawyer.

"Yes," Quentin replied, "he is my father." He motioned to Victor. "And you are my brother."

"Liar!" Victor said, his voice low and menacing.

Anthony turned back to look at Victor. Quentin still held his victorious grin. There was a look of disbelief on Victor's face. The crime lord knew who Quentin belonged to, but he didn't want to admit it. Anthony noticed it as well.

"Dad?" Anthony said, curiosity taking hold of him. The gun was still being pointed at Victor.

"It's impossible!" Victor said defiantly.

His father was becoming angry, and Quentin understood why. He had long ago forgotten about this part of his life and never imagined it would come back to haunt him. But now, it was, standing before him in flesh and blood. So, Quentin decided to enlighten Anthony and bring light to their father's secret.

"Nearly thirty years ago, you had a young woman who was a housemaid. Her name was Mary Baker. She was a fantastic housekeeper. Everything was always clean and made presentable for you and your precious family. She had long brown hair and brown eyes. One day she noticed how you began to flirt with her whenever your wife wasn't in the room.

"After a few weeks, you had confessed to her that your wife could not get pregnant. You seduced her and promised you would leave your wife for her if she were to conceive your child. She kept her end of the bargain: taking your seed and creating a child."

Quentin watched as Victor turned his face from him. The shame started to make its way through the man's blackened soul. Quentin had taken several steps forward. He now stood on Anthony's right side. Glancing at his half-brother, he noticed Anthony's grip on the pistol had loosened slightly. Turning his attention back to Victor, he continued.

"But the unthinkable happened. Your wife, Isabella, became pregnant shortly after Mary. You were thrown a curveball and handled it in normal Sorelli fashion. Divorce would be much nastier with a child involved, and you are obsessed with pure bloodlines. So, there was only one thing to do. The bastard must not be born. You fought with Mary about it, and she finally gave in. She would go the next morning to the clinic and have the child killed. Then, she would take the remainder of your money and start a new life.

"You had one of your goons drive her to the appointment. However, you underestimated my mother. She convinced him to remain in the car.

Entering the clinic, she waited her turn, and when called, she went to the doctor. Becoming hysterical, she told him she had changed her mind but needed something to show the 'abusive father' so he would leave her alone. "The doctor wasn't sure about the ethics of the situation, but doctors that murder the unborn have little to no ground when speaking about morality or ethics. So, he gave her a packet that explained any symptoms she might experience. Walking out in tears, she hopped in the car and was driven to her apartment. Your man would report that everything went as planned. Mary packed up and moved to Tennessee. Giving birth to me there and giving me her mother's maiden name."

Victor was staring at Quentin now, ice in his eyes. He hated being made a fool of, and his mother had done it. Not only had she done it, but Quentin had also tricked his old man.

"I've seen you stare at me sometimes." Quentin said, "You could see her or yourself in me. I'm not sure which, but you have recognized it before." For a long moment, there wasn't a sound. The three men stood in the red office, eyes shifting between each other. Quentin could see small shakes in Anthony's hands. His brother was struggling to keep it together on top of the withdrawal he was undoubtedly battling.

"Is this true?" Anthony asked, looking at Victor.

Their father kept silent but stared directly at Quentin, giving no indication he heard Anthony's question. Quentin could see the anger building in Anthony and the hatred seething in Victor. It was everything he'd hoped it would be. Anthony suddenly blurted out,

"Answer me, you son of a bitch!"

*   *   *   *

Luke was almost to the Sorelli property when his cell phone rang. Not bothering to check the caller i.d., he answered it.

"Luke," Mason's voice said through the speaker. "Have you made it there yet?"

"Almost," Luke answered, "I'm a couple of miles away. Have you secured the warrant?"

"Not quite but get this. A cabin northwest of the city was set on fire early this morning. Crews got there and managed to put it out before it spread. Anyway, the owner of the cabin is a woman named Mary Baker."

"Get to the point," Luke said, irritated.

"Mary Baker is David Quentin's mother."

"And?" Luke asked, still trying to figure out what importance this played.

"When they collected evidence, they found an old glass perfume bottle. It was mostly empty and scorched pretty badly, but I had Will test the chemical makeup of what was left in it to see if it matched the chemical makeup of the perfume found on Wendy Grayson. There's an eighty-three percent match, which Will is certain was contaminated by the fire's smoke and heat."

"So, our new theory is Quentin killed Wendy and Sam?" Luke asked.

"Why?"

"I don't know, but I also looked into Mary Baker. Unfortunately, she died in 2016, but she seems to have been employed by the Sorreli's in her 20's. She worked as a maid for years and then suddenly packed up and moved to a small town in Tennessee."

"Can you get to the point already, Mason?" Luke said, with impatience growing in his voice.

"I'm getting there. It turns out her bank statements show a large influx of cash weeks before she moved to Tennessee. She could have been paid off for some reason or another."

"By Sorelli?" Luke asked.

"Sorelli or his wife. She was still alive back then." Mason answered.

"There are still some holes, but I think we could make it all stick together with the right confession."

"Get that warrant and get here fast," Luke said before hanging up. The turn for the Sorelli's driveway was approaching. Luke let off the accelerator to keep his car from spinning out of control. Luke spun the steering wheel hard to his right when he reached the drive. The nose of the charger turned in the indicated direction while the rear swung around to the left before straightening. Luke hit the gas and tore down the gravel drive, throwing the small rocks in the air as he went. The black, iron gate up ahead was shut. The charger roared and hit the gate head-on, giving his iron steed more fuel. Luke aimed for the end of the barrier, knowing that was its weakest point. The metal bars screamed against the vehicle's exterior. The gate gave way and came off its track, allowing Luke to continue towards the looming mansion ahead of him.

*   *   *   *

Anthony couldn't believe what he was hearing. David Quentin had turned his entire life on end and kicked down the field. He had a half-brother and didn't even know it—this whole time. Anger was boiling over in Anthony. There was so much happening and not enough time to process everything.

Shoot him! He's done nothing but lies to you your entire life.

His father had still not answered his questions. Anthony's hands were beginning to shake. The thought of Wendy and Sam's death brought more hurt to his heart. He needed to hear his father admit to it. He needed to hear the words. Without thinking, Anthony pulled the trigger of the gun. The sound echoed through the room, and his ears were ringing. The bullet slammed into the crimson wall behind his father. Jerking to his left, Victor looked stunned. Anthony wasn't paying any attention to Quentin. His full focus was on his backstabbing father.

"Is it true?" Anthony asked again, yelling above the ringing in his ears.

"Is what true?" Victor asked contemptuously. The shock was now gone. His father's face was angry. Anthony wasn't sure if it was at him, Quentin, or both.

"All of it! The affair, the coerced abortion, talking to Sam about killing Wendy and having Sam killed for acting without approval. All of it." He watched as his father's eyes shifted between him and the lawyer to his right. Anthony knew his father liked to think through every decision. He would only answer once he figured out the most probable outcome. End him now!

Anthony wanted so badly for this all to be over. He wanted revenge for Wendy. Sam had gotten his just desserts. Now it was his father's turn.

"It's true." His father finally said. Victor's head remained held high. There was no shame or remorse in his voice.

*　*　*　*

It had worked. Quentin couldn't hide the smile that began to spread across his face. After years of planning and replanning, theorizing, and studying. Quentin had played his cards perfectly, and the two Lessers before him hadn't the slightest idea. Quentin could see Victor was still confused about Sam's death, but Quentin knew how the man thought. He knew that when confronted with no one else in the room, Victor would confess to crimes he didn't commit. His father so stupidly thought that he could still convince Anthony it was in his best interest. No one else in the world knew how to help him except Victor. If only Victor knew the extent of the damage done to his son, he would have recalculated his answer. Instead, Quentin remained silent and watched the scene he had orchestrated play out.

*　*　*　*

"Why?" Anthony asked, sorrow mixing with the anger in his voice.

"Why what?" Victor asked.

"Why did you have Sam kill Wendy? I loved her."

"Because she was poisoning you!" Victor shouted. It was the first time he'd raised his voice. Anthony was taken aback by the outburst. "She seduced you, and once she had you between her legs, she wouldn't let you go. You may call it to love, but it was nothing more than lust with a dash of empathic counseling sprinkled throughout."

"You have no idea what you're talking about." Anthony retorted, steadying his hands, and pointing the gun directly at Victor's chest.

"Don't I? Months after finishing your assignment, you suddenly have a drug problem. I try to help, but you push me away…"

"You told me to grow a pair and to shape up." Anthony interrupted, "You call that helping?"

"You weren't a child. The time for coddling had long passed. So, you needed to get through it because that was only the first. And if you couldn't handle that, you wouldn't be able to handle everything else."

"Killing innocent people is wrong, dad. So no, I probably couldn't run the business like I thought I could."

"Wrong," Victor scoffed, "Who defines right and wrong? Who defines innocent or guilty? I'll tell ya who, me. I do! If I say kill the bitch that means she's guilty. If I say bury that bastard in the ground before he stops breathing, that means it's right. And when you grow up and take charge, you get to decide!" Victor aimed his right index finger at Anthony, jabbing towards him as if he could physically press his words into Anthony's skull. Anthony closed his eyes and shook his head. He looked at his father, his eyes filled with tears.

"She was the best thing that ever happened to me. She believed in me and wanted me to improve myself," Anthony said mournfully.

"Did you tell her what you did?" Victor asked.

Anthony didn't answer.

"No, of course not!" Victor said, "You were afraid that if she found out why you were really on drugs, she wouldn't want anything to do with you."

An image of Wendy's beautiful face filled Anthony's mind, her gaze shifting from adoration to disgust. "Murderer," she whispered.

Kill him.

It's not right, Anthony told himself.

He's guiltier than sin itself! Kill him!

"Murderer," Wendy's voice whispered again.

The memory of Emily being run over flashed in his mind.

Do it!

Anthony's finger pressed ever so slightly against the trigger. Tears streamed down his face.

The words from the Bible echoed through his mind, "the truth shall make you free."

Kill him now!

Sam's bloody body stood beside Wendy in his mind. Together they both said, "*Murderer.*"

"The truth shall make you free."

Kill him!

All of this happened in mere seconds. Anthony's hand began to shake again. This was another decision he would not be able to come back from. Finally, Anthony let the gun slip from his grasp and fall to the floor.

*   *   *   *

Quentin watched in disbelief as the pistol left Anthony's hand and clattered onto the floor. The revolver luckily didn't fire with the impact. What was Anthony doing? He was supposed to kill their father. This wasn't part of the plan. The plan didn't work unless Anthony killed Victor. Quentin's mind was scrambling. He had to salvage this, but how? Quickly he played through all the possible outcomes. There was only one solution. Quentin grabbed the gun off the floor, pointed it at Victor, and pulled the trigger.

*   *   *   *

Anthony had nearly forgotten about the lawyer standing to his right until the man picked up the pistol and fired it off before he could blink. Anthony watched in shock as his father gave a gasp and staggered backwards to the wall. Victor gripped at the new hole in his body as he fell to the floor. Turning, Anthony faced his half-brother with a new wariness.

"You pathetic piece of filth," Quentin said as he aimed the gun at Anthony. "You had one job and couldn't even do that."

Anthony was confused. Quentin wanted him to kill their father.

"Yes, that's right," Quentin said as if reading Anthony's mind. "I needed you to kill our father."

"Why?" Anthony asked. It made no sense to him. If Quentin wanted him dead, why not do it himself?

"Because if you kill him, get arrested—again—I won't be there to help you. With you behind bars, I become the executor of the estate. Everything would belong to me, as it rightly should. I would burn the Sorelli name's memory from the earth's face. No one would remember you, your father, or anyone else. This empire would become the Quentin's from now until eternity. But I'm not stupid like our forefathers. I'm not going to paint my name on everything. It will be made to look like the empire dissolved to the lower tier members, but in reality, I will be pulling the strings."

"Why not kill dad and frame me later?" Anthony asked.

Quentin let out a sigh. He seemed annoyed that he needed to explain himself. Maybe to a psychopath like Quentin, it was clear, but not to Anthony.

"Because the cops need to have a motive. You killing your father randomly wouldn't add up, but if you kill him out of revenge for murdering your girlfriend…" Quentin let the sentence hang in the air.

Anthony just stared at the man. It was insane. The amount of time put into something like that was unfathomable.

You wimp. Now, look what you've done.

"Now, since I put too much faith in a Lesser like you, I have to improvise," Quentin said angrily.

Just then, the door to the office flew open with a WHACK! Entering the room with his gun drawn was Detective Luke Burrows.

*   *   *   *

The first thing Luke saw when he kicked in the door was David Quentin pointing a gun at Anthony Sorelli. It had taken him longer than anticipated to find anyone. The mansion was huge and clearing the rooms by himself took time. He had begun to lose hope until he kicked open this last door. The room smelled of gunpowder. Doing a quick scan, Luke saw a hole in the wall behind an oak desk. Anthony's face looked as if he'd been crying. Quentin's face looked angry and annoyed.

"Drop the gun Quentin," Luke said. "You're under arrest for the murders of Wendy Grayson and Samuel Hunter."

Luke saw Anthony's eyes go wide from the corner of his eye. This was news to him. Quentin smirked but kept the gun pointed at Anthony.

"You have no evidence," the smug attorney said. "If you did, you'd be here with a warrant and backup."

"They're on their way, don't you worry," Luke said. "And I have plenty of evidence. We have your hair found on Sam's hands. The perfume bottle from your mother's cabin. The fire was a nice attempt, but it didn't quite get the job done."

Luke watched as Quentin's eyes narrowed. There was no fear on the man's face. Cautiously, Luke wondered if he could ease in closer. Then, lifting one foot off the ground, he prepared to step forward.

"Don't move," the attorney said, pressing the gun against Anthony's chest.

Slowly, Luke put his foot back down on the floor. Watching the two men, Luke wondered what had transpired before he'd come charging through the door.

"What if we make a trade instead?" Quentin finally said.

"You have nothing I want," Luke said. The sheer arrogance of the attorney was baffling.

"You sure?" Quentin asked. "What about the man that killed your precious Emily?"

Luke's heart stopped. Everything seemed to slow down around him. He tried to speak but couldn't find his voice.

"I already know who it was. He's in jail as we speak." Luke said, not believing the words as they left his lips.

The attorney looked at him with a raised eyebrow. "You don't believe that, and you shouldn't believe that."

"Why should I believe anything you say?" Luke asked, anger seeping into his voice.

"Maybe you shouldn't, but you should at least hear me out and then decide for yourself. Better hurry, though. This offer ends in two minutes."

No one moved for a few heartbeats, and no sound was uttered. Luke's suspicions about Victor Sorelli having a hand in Emily's murder flooded his mind like an overflowing river. No one else was here yet…he needed to know what Quentin knew. Even if it turned out to be b.s., he'd never live with himself if he let the possibility slip away.

"Alright, tell me. Who do you think killed Emily?" Luke finally said.

"Oh, I don't think I know," Quentin said as he grabbed Anthony by the shoulder, whirled the large man around, and shoved him toward the detective. "Here he is."

*　　*　　*　　*

The detective couldn't believe what he'd just been told. Anthony? Any other day he'd have believed it in a heartbeat, but Luke had shared that personal loss with the man, and he had said nothing. A look of betrayal crossed Detective Burrows' face. Then, it was replaced by anger in a blink of an eye. Burrows grabbed Anthony by his shirt and pulled the larger man to his knees. Anthony didn't fight him; he stared up at the detective, trying to keep his face neutral.

"Is it true?" Burrows asked.

Anthony said nothing but looked away. He knew this was one of Quentin's traps: using the truth to his advantage. Anthony didn't want to go to jail, and he didn't want to admit to the horrid crime he'd committed.

Take his gun! Kill them both, and let's get out of here!

"*Murderer*," Wendy whispered in his mind.

"The truth shall make you free."

Take his gun!

"The truth shall make you free."

"*Murderer.*"

"Hey, asshole!" Burrows' voice screamed, "Did you kill Emily?"

The gun!

"The truth."

"*Murderer.*"

Gun!

"*Murderer.*"

"Truth."

"Yes!" Anthony said, tears once again flowing down his cheeks. "I did. And I'm so…"

Anthony didn't get to finish. Burrows' right fist came crashing against his left cheek. Anthony spits blood out onto the carpet. He stared back up at the detective. He could see the hurt in his eyes, the pain that Anthony had caused, not once but twice. Burrows struck him again. Anthony didn't groan, protest, or fight back. This is the bare minimum of what he deserved, and he was so thankful to finally have the weight off his shoulders. His secret was out, and there was no need to hide it any longer.

Even in the midst of the detective's anger, he hadn't felt this much relief even when on drugs.

* * * *

Luke stared at the man before him, and blood dripped from his lip. Luke felt tears of his own on his cheeks. After all this time, he'd been right. The Sorellis had been behind Emily's death. Rage broiled inside him. Again, Luke slammed his fist into Anthony's face, a third time, then a fourth. Luke took in short raspy breaths through his mouth. The anguish had shot up like a geyser. Luke pointed his gun directly between Anthony's eyes. This was it, and justice would be done. Emily's murderer would be dead and gone. Anthony looked up and into Luke's eyes. The larger man knew what was coming and was prepared to take his punishment. With the squeeze of his finger, it would all be over. That thought froze him cold. It would indeed all be over. He ran through the chain of events again, plugging Quentin into the necessary spaces. This is what the lawyer wanted. He knew if Luke killed Anthony, he could trade his testimony against Luke and the entire Sorelli crime syndicate for a reduced sentence. Luke's life would be over, and Quentin knew how to manipulate the legal system better than anyone else. Raising his arm, Luke pointed the gun at Quentin.

"Put down the weapon and get on your knees," Luke said.

* * * *

Quentin couldn't believe it. The damn detective was defying him too. After studying all of these people for years and planning this out to the last detail, in the last few minutes, it had fallen apart, been put back together, and was once again falling apart. They had all made the proper choices within the parameters the past few days, and now they all of a sudden had grown a brain. No, it couldn't end like this.

"I have a better idea," Quentin began, "Anthony and you get in a gunfight and end up killing each other."

As soon as the words left his lips, Quentin smiled at Burrows and pulled the trigger.

* * * *

The gun boomed through the mansion. In the blink of an eye, Anthony

323

rose to his feet, shielding Luke from the bullet. It slammed into the larger man's back. Anthony let out a yell and staggered forward and to his right.

Luke was so stunned. It was a wonder he didn't shoot Anthony in his torso. As Anthony staggered out of the way, Luke returned fire. Quentin fired off the remaining three rounds from the revolver. One bullet hit Luke in his left shoulder before two of Luke's bullets sunk into Quentin's chest. The lawyer gasped for breath. Luke probably hit him in a lung. As he fell to the floor, a dark red puddle emerged beneath the lawyer's shirt.

CHAPTER 44

SIX MONTHS LATER

The cold air from the air conditioner bit at the neck of Detective Luke Burrows as he sat waiting for the person he was meeting. Looking up, he noticed his seat was placed directly underneath the air vent. This summer afternoon, he wore blue collared shirt and black slacks. Luke let out a sigh as he let the seconds tick away. This was the sixth time he had been here; each time was a little easier than the last.

As he waited, he reflected on the past several months since the encounter at the Sorelli mansion. His partner, Detective Brandon Mason, had arrived shortly after the conflict had been resolved by gunfire. Luke had called for an ambulance, seeing as he and Anthony had both been hit. After dealing with the EMTs and answering questions from Mason about the whole thing, Luke watched with mixed emotions as the ambulance drove off with Anthony strapped to a gurney. They rushed to the hospital as fast as they could, not knowing if the slug had caused any internal damage.

After writing up his report, Reilly suspended him until the Internal Affairs investigation concluded. For a couple of months, it didn't look promising for Luke. The I.G. questioned him for weeks, trying to ensure everything that had happened was legal. Luke had admitted to assaulting Anthony even before the investigation. He knew trying to hide that piece of information would only hurt the outcome.

Mason and Reilly had kept him updated on their progress in rounding up the remnants of Sorelli's empire. Within the first month, they shut down the marijuana dispensary. In the second month, they had taken many dealers off the street. Four months in, they had taken down the prostitution ring that was being run through Crystal's Gentlemen Club.

Last month, Mason shut down the gambling hall in The Cicero, and finally, just three days ago, Mayor Robert Tyler was arrested for embezzlement.

All in all, there were many successes to boast of. Several players had left the city, some leaving the state, after hearing Victor and Anthony Sorelli were dead. A few had tried to fight for control, but it was so massive and compartmentalized that no one besides the Sorellis could know how everything was connected, which is why he was back here today. He needed new information on a man by the name of Creed Harding. Luke hadn't much on him except he had formerly worked for Victor Sorelli and was presumed dead. Rumors had been circulating that Harding would try his version of a criminal empire. Luke wasn't about to let that happen. Behind him, the door opened, and a man in an orange jumpsuit, escorted by a guard, walked past Luke, and sat down across from him. Only a metal table sat between them.

"You can remove those," Luke said to the guard.

Bending down, the guard removed the handcuffs from the prisoner's wrists and exited the room. The man in the orange jumpsuit rubbed his wrists and smiled at the detective. Luke couldn't help but smile back at him. Sitting before him was a man he'd grown to respect, Anthony Sorelli. Anthony had survived his bullet wound and confessed to everything he'd ever done for his father, including murdering Emily. Luke had listened to him tell that story multiple times, and it felt good to finally have closure. The drunk that Anthony framed was released with the utmost apologies from the department and Anthony himself.

Anthony agreed to help the St. Louis police department if they promised to protect him. Being in prison with fellow criminals he had ratted on was not a good recipe for a long life. Chief Reilly concurred, and Anthony Sorelli was declared dead on the operating table. Anthony grew a beard as full and black as the hair on his head. He was also given a new name, Evan West.

Most people would question why Luke would respect the man that killed the love of his life. It wasn't easy by any means; it was very complicated. Luke had resented and hated Anthony for nearly three months. He despised coming here and talking to the man. However, after many hours of listening to Anthony, Luke could tell he had shaped up. There was no more drug use, and he had even started attending a prison Bible study. Listening to the guards, Luke learned that Anthony was a model prisoner. He never got into trouble and helped get a few others out of some scrapes. Luke went to church a couple of times a month, partly because it was what Emily would have wanted. Anthony still professed not to be a Christian, but he said the night at the safehouse (when he found the Bible) helped push him to come clean to Luke. He was still skeptical but wanted to learn more about what the Bible said from someone who understood it.

"If this is true, God will show himself to me," he always said. Luke was impressed with how much the man had changed and how he seemed to be helping others. That's why he respected him: for bettering himself and those around him.

"How are you doing, Evan?" Luke asked.

"Can't complain," Evan replied. "How can I help the St. Louis PD today?"

*   *   *   *

Anthony, now Evan, looked at the detective sitting across from him. Detective Burrows had slowly warmed up to him, and he was glad. He was doing his penance for his sins. Being sent to prison seemed the best thing to happen to him. He'd gotten clean and found a group of men that could relate to his inner struggles and temptations. The devil on his shoulder was still whispering, screaming, doing whatever he could to get Anthony to fall. So far, Anthony had resisted. He knew from talking to the others that he would eventually give in and not let it define him. The best thing to do when it happened would be to come clean as soon as possible. Hiding it would only make it worse.

Scratching at his new beard, he thought about the night he admitted to the detective what he had done. Burrows could have killed him there but didn't. When he'd questioned him about it, Burrows had said he realized it was what Quentin needed him to do. The honesty was hard to hear. Anthony had hoped it was because Burrows saw the humanity in him. Sadly, that wasn't the case, at least not at that moment. But, over the past few months, Anthony could sense that Burrows was finally seeing who

Anthony truly was.

* * * *

Luke slid a file across the table to him. Reaching out, Evan picked it up and opened it. There was no change in his facial expression. No hint that he was surprised by what he was seeing.

"Do you know that man?" Luke asked.

Shutting the file, Evan looked Luke straight in the eye,

"Creed Harding," he answered. "Thought he was dead."

"You don't seem surprised to see that he's not," Luke noted.

"There were always rumors. Dad tried his best to find him. Wanted to make sure, ya know? But after never finding anything for months, he put it to rest."

"What should I expect from him?" Luke asked.

The bearded man leaned his head back and thought about it for a few minutes. Luke wasn't sure if that meant not much or too much. Then, settling into his seat, he patiently waited for Evan to answer.

"Mind games," Evan finally said.

"Mind games?" Luke repeated.

"Yeah. Creed is very good at deception. Dad always said he was an ex-spy. Not sure I'd go that far, but the man thinks fifteen moves ahead. Dad was always adamant about not leaving clues. Keep your hands out of it as much as possible. Creed likes to play with the police. He'd leave false clues or actual clues that were very vague. Once, he purposefully left his fingerprint at the scene."

"Like Quentin?" Luke asked.

"No. Quentin was careful to leave no clues and manipulated all of us to get what he wanted. Harding liked to screw with dad and the cops. He knew it was only circumstantial. It was a public place, and nothing else pointed to him. Harding enjoyed being brought in for questioning. Dad hated it, though. That's why he marked him for termination. He was becoming more of a potential liability than an asset."

Standing to his feet, Luke grabbed the file from the table. Looking at the man before him, he could still see remorse in those hazel eyes.

"Thanks, Evan. I'll see you later."

Turning to the door, he heard Evan call to him.

"Detective."

Luke paused, turned, and faced the man.

"I'm sorry."

Tears were welling up in the man's eyes. Luke looked at him with sorrow and sympathy. The man had apologized every time they met. At first, Luke was sure he was doing it to ease his conscience, but now, he knew Anthony was genuinely sorry and sincerely wanted, no, needed Luke's forgiveness. To this point, Luke had always just said, 'I know.' For a few seconds, neither man spoke. They just stared at each other, an understanding passing between them.

Something Charlie Wallace used to say suddenly popped into Luke's mind, 'Living in unforgiveness and bitterness is like drinking poison and waiting for the other person to die.' Luke wasn't sure Charlie was the original author of that phrase, but now he understood more than ever.

"I forgive you, Anthony," Luke finally said as he turned around and walked down the hall.

As he walked, his steps echoed through the prison hallway. Luke's shoes clacked on the tile with each stride. Suddenly, Luke felt like a weight had been lifted off his shoulders. Anthony and Luke would never be close friends, but they could move forward from the horrific event that connected them. His cell phone rang when Luke was near the middle of the hallway. Grabbing it from his pocket, he answered it.

"Hello."

"Luke, meet me at Memorial Hospital."

It was Mason's voice. He sounded distraught.

"Why? What happened?"

"Doc's been shot."

Made in the USA
Columbia, SC
14 December 2022

73899708R00198